An
English
Christmas

Books by Paula Tanner Girard

LORD WAKEFORD'S GOLD WATCH

CHARADE OF HEARTS

A FATHER FOR CHRISTMAS

A HUSBAND FOR CHRISTMAS

THE SISTER SEASON

THE RELUCTANT GROOM

THE SEVENTH SISTER

Published by Kensington Publishing Corp.

PAULA TANNER GIRARD

KENSINGTON BOOKS
http://www.kensingtonbooks.com

KENSINGTON BOOKS are published by

Kensington Publishing Corp.
850 Third Avenue
New York, NY 10022



All Kensington titles, imprints and distributed lines are available at special quantity discounts for bulk purchases for sales promotion, premiums, fund raising, educational or institutional use.

Special book excerpts or customized printings can also be created to fit specific needs. For details, write or phone the office of the Kensington Special Sales Manager: Kensington Publishing Corp., 850 Third Avenue, New York, NY 10022. Attn. Special Sales Department. Phone: 1-800-221-2647.



ISBN 0-7582-0046-3

First Kensington Trade Paperback Printing: October 2001
10 9 8 7 6 5 4 3 2 1

Printed in the United States of America

# Contents

# A Father for Christmas

# One

Millicent Copley raced toward the rear of the country manor just a pace in back of her exuberant son. Like a kite, her bonnet flew behind, held only by the ribbon tied beneath her chin.

With all the enthusiasm of a six-year-old, Master Rupert threw open the heavy oak door and burst into the warm kitchen. "I won! I won!"

An elderly, pumpkin-shaped woman turned from stirring a pot on the stove and eyed the muddy prints following him. "Well, ye certainly have now, haven't ye? And brought in half the outdoors while ye were doing it."

Millicent, her cheeks pink from the crisp December air, stood in the doorway and looked down at her mud-splattered clothing. "Oh, my! Mrs. Woodstock will think us unredeemable, I am afraid."

Of course, Mrs. Woodstock, quite used to the young mistress' lighthearted ways, thought no such thing. All who knew her considered Mrs. Copley to be kind, pretty, and self-effacing. However, as was expected of her, the cook placed her hands firmly on her hips and clicked her tongue, "Tch! Tch! Well, ye better take off yir wet wraps before ye catch yir death. There's hot chocolate in the pot and scones fresh from the oven on the table."

Rupert had already pulled off his scarf and mittens and was climbing onto a stool alongside the wide working surface. He grabbed a scone and smeared it with raspberry jam. "You may have won, Momma, if you had not fallen in the mud puddle," Rupert said solicitously.

Laughing, Millicent removed her soiled pelisse. "Yes, I just may have done."

From the look of condescension on Rupert's face, it was plain to see that he really didn't think that possible. But not one to give in to such arrogance, even in an adored son, Millicent challenged him back. "I dare say, young man, I can still give you a run for your money any day."

"But not for long, Momma. Soon I shall be a man and then you will not be able to keep up with me."

For a moment a twinge of anxiety struck Millicent, but the tug at her heart was quickly dispensed as the inner door opened and a plump freckle-faced girl looked into the kitchen.

"What is it, Sukie?"

"A letter came for you in the post half an hour ago, ma'am."

Millicent quickly pulled off her soggy half-boots and padded into the main house. "It must be a letter from your grandmama," she called back to Rupert. "Mayhaps your Aunt Cissy has had her baby."

It was a letter from her mother, all right, but it wasn't the news she'd expected.

*Jedburgh Border*

*Dear Millie,*

*The doctor says he does not know how he miscalculated. He now thinks the baby will not arrive for another three weeks, so your father and I cannot possibly be back before Christmas. Since this is Cissy's first lying-in, she begs us to stay on until end of Twelfth Night. Your father said that because we took our traveling coach, it would be impossible for you to come all the way to the Scottish border by yourselves. It distressed me to think that you and Rupert would have to spend the holidays alone, but do not despair, dear, for as I was writing this I had the most inspired idea. I shall write to your brother-in-law, Lord*

*Copley, in London, and ask if he can arrange to fetch you to the city to spend the holidays with them.*

Mrs. Huxley wrote more about Cissy's home in Jedburgh and about their new son-in-law, and ended saying how pleased she was that she was able to think of something that would keep Millicent and Rupert happily occupied during the holidays. They would exchange presents when they returned in January.

Millicent had been a widow now some five years since Captain Bertram Copley had been killed in the Peninsula. Her only solace was that before his death, her sweet husband saw their baby christened, and knew his son showed no signs of the disfiguring facial birthmark which had marred Bertie's short life. Rupert was perfect, eyes the color of chestnuts like his grandfather Huxley's, and the blond curls of the Copley men which wreathed his cherubic face. An angel and the joy of her life, or so his mother viewed him. In fact, it was the way Millicent saw most everyone—as warmhearted as herself.

The next two weeks passed without a word from Baron Copley, and Millicent despaired that she and her son were faced with the dismal prospect of being alone in the large house on Christmas. Rupert had always had his grandparents and his Aunt Cissy around until Cissy's marriage the year before. Millicent, her spirits never for long on the down side, determined to do everything in her power to give her son a special present to make him happy. Rupert was a practical lad and had never been one to ask for expensive or useless gifts, so Millicent had no fear that he would overstep the boundaries of sensibility and wish for something she couldn't acquire in the village.

They had gone outside to make tracks in the first light snow when she asked, "Rupert, what would you like more than anything else for Christmas?"

Delight filled the boys eyes. "Oh, Momma, do you really mean I can have anything I want?"

With a smile and a nod of her head, Millicent assured him that she did.

"I want a father."

That wasn't the sort of thing Millicent had had in mind, and she was at a complete loss as to how to reply.

"Robert has a father, and Pokie and Beenie. All four Dowser boys share one, but they don't mind. Why can I not have a father, Momma?"

Unexpectedly, Millicent felt her cheeks burn. "I would have to get married."

"How does someone get married?"

Millicent bit her lip. She'd try to explain it simply. "Well, when two people like each other well enough, they go to a clergyman and tell him they want to live together for the rest of their lives. Then, he has them sign a piece of paper which says it is all right."

"Is it hard?"

"Not if you love someone."

"I am a little young to get married, am I not?"

"Yes, I believe you are. It is better to wait until you grow up."

"Oh," said Rupert, losing interest in the subject the minute a rabbit bolted from the hedge and ran across the yard. Off he scampered after it.

Letting out a sigh of relief, Millicent watched him go. Dedicated to educating and raising her son, she'd accepted none of the proposals which had come her way over the last five years. Besides, how could any man really be of interest to her after her gallant and humorous Bertie? She would have to think carefully how she could sway her imaginative son to make a more realistic choice, but then it was still four weeks before Christmas. Surely by then she'd persuade him to think of something more feasible.

* * *

Some twenty miles north of Cross-in-Hand at his country estate in Kent, Ernest Lance, Marquis of Wetherby, oldest son and heir of the Duke of Loude, called his valet. "Jespers, prepare my things. We shall be going to London."

Used to his master's quixotic decisions, Jespers asked patiently. "Is it to be a long stay, your lordship?"

To tell the truth, Wetherby hadn't thought of why he was even making the trip. His spirits were not much for doing the pretty of late, and now that all four of his happy cohorts—the Merry Five, they'd called themselves—had betrayed him by tying the knot, life had lost much of its flavor. None of his new acquaintances had half the imagination for derring-do escapades as he and his friends had hatched.

Wetherby was quite aware that the *ton* considered him to be a handsome devil. He was brown-haired, brown-eyed, medium-tall, of athletic proportion, carefree, and good-tempered. He prided himself on being a sportsman, a bruising rider. However, all these attributes did nothing to assuage his growing boredom.

Upon the death of his mother, the marquis inherited her Orchid Hill estate near Tunbridge Wells, and a small income. Although it wasn't a great deal of money, he didn't need his father's largess anymore to meet his bills. The house had fallen into disrepair over the last three years, but Wetherby had kept on a small staff in case he wished to use it during the hunting season. Now it seemed he stayed longer and longer.

"No, I don't suppose I'll spend more than a few days, Jespers. Just long enough to catch me up on the latest news."

Sir Jonathan Bridges told him on passing through that he'd heard that his last paramour, Mrs. Hawthorne, had taken up with Lord Hazelton's second son. Wetherby couldn't blame the widow. He hadn't been to town for several weeks and he couldn't expect so affectionate a lady to wait for him to call. Perhaps Genevieve was still available for a few evenings of fun. Dancing girls from Drury Lane were more easily entertained and not in the least demanding. A bauble or two satisfied them.

Wetherby called for his groom. "George, have the coach readied." His mother's old traveling carriage was small and compact. It suited him well enough to transport Jespers and himself back and forth from the city, enabling him to leave his more fashionable coach at the mewes in London. In good weather or foul, he preferred to handle the ribbons himself and usually rode up with the coachman. So his lordship set off for London with very little direction of what he should do with himself once he got there.

Upon arrival at Loude's Hall in Grosvenor Square, he found a letter awaiting him.

*Roxwealde Castle, Devonshire*

*My dear Wetherby,*

*I hope this finds you well. Sarah wished to spend our son's first Christmas in the same place she and I met and married. Her parents are coming from Elmsdale to be with us. Since you are the only one of the Merry Five who is yet footloose and fancy free, perhaps you will be able to come for the holidays. Unless of course you have far more exciting escapades on your calendar.*

*Your friend,*
*Andersen Copley*

*P.S. I am sure you will be pleased to know that I have not asked Lord Favor or his daughter Lady Caroline to join us.*

Wetherby snorted and thought back to the party the baron had invited him to nearly two years ago at his ancestral castle in Devon. The five merrymakers had planned on taking their pretty lightskirts for a week of fun. Aspiring actresses, they'd called themselves. Instead of the out and out frolic they had all anticipated, it had ended up being a matrimonial pit for four of his best friends. Only he and Lady Caroline remained unattached. Once she'd been the most sought-after debutante of the *ton*—and the target of Wetherby's own pursuit for two years as well—but his interest diminished substantially when she humiliated him by openly snubbing him in favor of the baron.

Lord Copley, however, had surprised them all by marrying his hostess Sarah Greenwood, the daughter of a country squire. Caroline had returned to London, and instead of licking her wounds from her failure to capture the baron, renewed her flirtation with Wetherby. He thought he'd expressed his feelings quite fully when he'd said he wished to have nothing further to do with her, but Wetherby found that Caroline could be a very determined woman when she wanted something badly enough.

Now as he again ran down the letter, a positive thought struck him. A few weeks in Devonshire could very well provide an escape from Caroline's unwanted attentions. It would also give him a good excuse not to have to spend the holidays at his sister Evelyn's house in Warwickshire with her placid husband and their tribe of children. Where, no doubt, he'd also have to take another raking over the coals by his father. "Find a woman of good bloodlines, settle down and produce an heir. That's an order, you do-for-nothing!"

Wetherby began to feel much more the thing. "I say, Jespers, how does Christmas at Roxwealde sound to you?"

The valet maintained his usual noncommittal mask, but the good servant remembered with a definite acceleration of his heart the beautiful old castle which had been the center of a colorful party not two years ago. Of course there was the baron's lion, Dog, who caused Jespers some apprehension, but that was a mere trifle compared to the draw of good food, lively spirits, and a certain pretty little maid belowstairs who had caught the servant's eye. "Whatever suits you, my lord."

The marquis hit the palm of his hand with his fist. "That is it then, by God! We shall go."

Wetherby grabbed some paper and penned off a quick acceptance to Baron Copley. Then with his father's wiggings ringing in his head, the marquis set out for White's, whistling.

The club proved rather quiet that afternoon. A light rain had been falling all day. Wetherby handed over his hat and damp coat to one of the footmen and accepted a brandy from a passing waiter.

Two gentlemen sat in the bow window, Lord Alvanley and Poodle Byng. The former called to the marquis. "Come sit down, Wetherby. Deuced dull day if I do say so myself. Nobody has slipped on the pavement and I had a bet with Poodle here that someone was bound to take a spill in the next ten minutes. Half an hour has gone by and not one soul has taken a tumble. No fun in that."

Wetherby glanced out the window in time to observe two young women of obviously questionable reputation—because they wouldn't have otherwise been on St. James Street—pull up their skirts to avoid dampening their hems in a puddle. The sight sent the blood surging through the marquis's veins. What a pity, he thought, that they weren't allowed to entertain women in their clubs. Liven things up a bit.

"I say, Wetherby, do sit down," Byng rasped. It was considered a privilege to be asked to share the seats in the front window at White's where Beau Brummel himself held sway. Whereas not long ago he would have been amused by their banter, the marquis now found the men's shallow remarks only annoyed him. He made the appropriate excuses to leave their company and wandered into the gentlemen's gaming room. Three men dozed before the fire, while a foursome sat at a table playing whist. From their intense expressions and rumpled clothes, he took it they'd been at it for some time. He stood wondering whether he could find enough men to get up a game, or whether he should amble over to another club. Before he could make such a momentous decision, he was greeted from behind.

"Your lordship, what brings you to London?"

Wetherby turned to face the Honorable John Teagardner, his jovial face and several chins snuggled into his high collar like a red hen on its nest.

"Teagardner," the marquis said, delighted he'd found at least one affable face. "Actually, I was contemplating going over to Waitier's for a good meal."

"Why don't you join Filmore and me at Grillon's. I promised Mrs. Teagardner we'd meet her for lunch." John stepped aside to reveal a slightly-built, nattily-dressed man standing behind him, smiling, not in the least offended by being dwarfed by the young giant. But then John dwarfed everyone.

Teagardner had been another of the eligibles who had succumbed to the edict of his parents to get married and start his nursery. He always did everything in as generous a manner as he was oversized, and started off by having twin sons. The bets that his wife was again increasing were circulating in the clubs, but no one could tell for sure because Mrs. Teagardner was as big around as he.

Filmore stepped forward and extended his hand, his deep voice belying his small stature. "Are you here for the holidays, your lordship?"

"Not really. I've just accepted an invitation to join the Copley family in Devonshire."

"Zounds, Wetherby! In those godforsaken moors?" Teagardner expounded. "Ain't that dangerous? I hear his lordship has wild beasts wandering all over the place."

Wetherby's good humor took a turn for the better. Knowing he wouldn't find anyone with better dispositions than the two men in front of him, he readily agreed to have lunch at the famous hotel. Still, he couldn't resist one backward glance at the card players.

"You won't be able to join them," Filmore said, shaking his head. "Raggett says they've been at it for over thirty-six hours, and Kendale seems to be cleaning up as usual. He took me for two thousand pounds last week. I was lucky. Most of the members think it's dashed unfair that he be permitted to play. They don't consider him *ton,* y'know, but he still manages to get himself invited. They say if it weren't for Lord Blackmere's patronage, the man wouldn't be allowed to set foot in any of the clubs."

Wetherby looked over at the expressionless face of the hawkeyed player who was accepting a note from the Earl of Markham. "I see nothing wrong with the fellow, only that he seems to win every contest he enters. I would like to have a go at him myself sometime." A good confrontation with a worthy opponent, Wetherby thought, might be just the antidote he needed to restore his spirits. However, if the man had been playing for a day and a half now, there would be no challenge in it.

By the time they arrived at Grillon's, their party had swelled to six, because Mrs. Teagardner had invited Lord Boswick and Mr. Elroy Bennington. "I found them languishing at Hatchard's Bookstore," she claimed. "They looked like they needed a good meal."

Wetherby was only slightly acquainted with Boswick's family, but he felt he knew Mr. Bennington quite well. It was at the infamous party at Roxwealde Castle where his sister Anne Bennington had eloped with Henry Smith, one of the original Merry Five. It was at the same soiree, Wetherby remembered with a bit of male pride, that he'd introduced young Bennington to the delights of his first *affaire de coeur* with one of the little doxies.

The meal proceeded in a most pleasant manner, the food excellent and the conversation friendly. The afternoon would have been a complete success had not Wetherby spotted Lady Caroline sitting with friends at a nearby table. She waved, but he acted as though he didn't see her. She was proving to be a real thorn in his side, but the more he ignored her, the more she did to gain his notice. This time she fluttered her handkerchief high above her head. Only Caroline could make such a gesture look charming instead of ill-mannered. Wetherby made a great show of brushing an imaginary spot from his sleeve. Finally, with a certain sense of satisfaction, he caught a sideways glimpse of her raising her nose, and with a sniff, she turned back to her partner.

Mr. Teagardner rapped the marquis on the arm. "I say, Wetherby, you're not listening. M'wife asked you a question."

"Oh, I am sorry, ma'am," the marquis apologized.

Mrs. Teagardner, with a glance toward Lady Caroline, laughed. "I only asked if you are having Christmas with your family, my lord."

Reprimanding himself for letting the termagant make him forget his manners, Wetherby gave Mrs. Teagardner his full attention. "As I told your husband, I am going to Devonshire. However, I do plan to be in town for a few days. I hope we can get together again. The day has been most pleasant."

Teagardner scraped the last spoonful of pudding from his plate. "Wish we could, but we leave for our house near Haslemere tomorrow. Plan to be there for the holidays, y'know. Expect the whole family down from Cambridgeshire."

Wetherby turned to the viscount. "Surely you will be in town a bit longer, Filmore."

The young lord ran his finger around his collar. "To tell the truth, my family wants me home before the week is out. The Bandit King, y'know."

Wetherby frowned and looked at the other two men. "How about you?"

Boswick shook his head. "My father says the same. I'm not to go out at night unless I am accompanied by the four men he has hired."

Only Elroy Bennington answered with a cocky grin.

Wetherby raised his eyebrows. "You don't seem to be afraid of the notorious bandit," he said facetiously.

The young man sat back and folded his arms across his chest. "Why should I be?"

Mrs. Teagardner gasped. "Elroy, how can you ask that? Your father is one of the richest merchants in England."

"Don't make no difference. The Bandit King only kidnaps sons of noblemen."

Eyes wide, Teagardner looked at the marquis as if the horror of it all had just dawned on him. "I say, Wetherby. You ain't thinking of making that long journey to the Devonshire moors all by yourself, are you? Never know where that jackanapes is going to strike. If you remember, the first Christmas he snatched Lord Brett's son in Yorkshire. The year after, it was two kidnappings, one in Cheshire, the other in Norfolk. Last December he grabbed Baron Duffmire's son right off a street here in London. No telling where he'll choose to do his mischief this year."

The marquis laughed. The chance of meeting up with the Bandit King held little terror for him. He felt confident that he could hold his own with any vagabond. All the victims had been foolish young men from wealthy, titled families. Fearing harm to their sons, their parents had paid the ransoms before notifying the authorities, and the victims had returned telling tales of the polite, masked man whom they had named the Bandit King.

"He always wears a black hood and no one can identify him," Filmore said. "He prints his ransom notes and his only signature is the black pearl he sends to his victims' homes."

"Well, I am not taking any chances with my sons," Teagardner exclaimed. "We'll be at home for the holidays."

Seeing the startled look on Mrs. Teagardner's face, Wetherby said reassuringly, "He doesn't kidnap babies, John."

"One never knows with scoundrels, does one?" the big man said defensively. "I'd be careful if I were you, Wetherby. Why don't you leave a few days early and stop off at our house on your way? Should be much safer than staying at a public place."

"Kind of you. I may just do that."

So arrangements were made and dates set, and although he laughed about it, the marquis was encouraged by friends he ran into to accept their hospitality at their country estates on his journey to Devonshire. Knowing that all the inns along the way would be crowded this time of year, Wetherby humbly acquiesced. Especially when he was assured that several of the households included charming young daughters.

The next few days proved so busy with visits to the bootery and his tailor and the purchasing of Christmas presents that Wetherby found little time to socialize, let alone visit Drury Lane. Genevieve would have to wait. He sent her a small bottle of perfume with his regrets and returned to Orchid Hill. Early Boxer gifts of money went to his staff, and Jespers packed his new wardrobe. With a sense of accomplishment, Wetherby realized he had four days before he was due at the Teagardners'. The trip to Haslemere would only take one full day, which left him three days to relax at Orchid Hill.

Meanwhile in the Huxley manor outside Cross-in-Hand, Millicent had all but given up hearing from Lord Copley when a special messenger arrived bearing a letter. She quickly tore open the seal.

*Roxwealde Castle, Devonshire*

*My dear sister-in-law,*

*Forgive the long delay in writing to you. Your mother's letter was sent to our London address long after we had removed to Roxwealde. I have just now received it.*

*She explained your circumstances, and though we will not be in London, we insist that you join us for Christmas. However, I would not think of letting you travel over two hundred miles alone with a child when the weather is so unpredictable and bands of thieves lie in wait ready to rob unsuspecting holiday travelers.*

*Therefore, I am making arrangements for you to be escorted by my good friend, Ernest Lance, the Marquis of Wetherby—a most honorable gentleman—whom I would trust with my own life. I have every confidence that he will see you safely to our door. I have sent a missive to him by special messenger also, so you should be hearing from him shortly. You met his lordship in London when Sarah and I came to town after our marriage a year and a half ago. I am certain you remember him.*

*Truly yours,*
*Andersen*

Millicent dropped the letter and clasped her hands to her burning cheeks. Did she remember the marquis? How could she forget the handsome rogue and the passionate kiss they had shared outside in the darkened garden at Lord Copley's ball?

"Oh, my goodness! How can I face him?"

# Two

Millicent took a deep breath and closed her eyes. While the humiliating remembrance of that evening flooded her memory, she tried valiantly to persuade herself that it had been a terrible case of mistaken identity. Or was it? After all, she was the one who had run straight into the circle of Lord Wetherby's arms. From the tales that Millicent had heard of the marquis's character, he was quite used to having women throw themselves at him. It probably had not bothered him one tittle to kiss another woman until his real ladylove turned up.

Millicent picked up Lord Copley's letter and stared blankly at his words, envisioning the large mansion on the River Thames.

The large crush that night at the ball had proven to nearly suffocate Millicent, and she'd sought a moment of solitude in the vast park that ran down to the water. In the daytime the gardens had seemed inviting, but at night, even with the gaslights set at intervals, the twisting paths and maze of high shrubs proved quite confusing. Blackness had engulfed her. She'd found herself impossibly lost and had turned to retrace her steps when she ran head-on into the solid form of a man. Their impact knocked the breath from her. Then, without a by-your-leave, the rogue caught her up in his arms and kissed her.

He broke the embrace and whispered in her ear, "Where have you been, my enchantress?"

Although they'd met only briefly in the receiving line, Millicent had recognized his voice instantly. Ernest Lance, the Marquis of Wetherby. Before she could speak, he'd pulled her full against him and kissed her once more with such intensity that Millicent thought she'd never catch her breath again. She'd not been held by a man like that for over three years, since Bertie. She'd responded and kissed him back. Oh, the shame of her wanton actions would stay with her the rest of her life.

Her lips were still shamelessly pressed to his when a desperate voice—a very feminine one—came from the other side of the hedge. "Your lordship?"

The marquis raised his head slightly and with a voice, husky with passion, whispered in her ear, "Who are you?"

Before Millicent could do more than gasp, the other woman repeated, "Your lordship? You know who I am, but I cannot find my way through the hedge."

With her heart pounding wildly, Millicent had taken advantage of Wetherby's distraction to break loose. She rushed toward the house, but her path led her under the yellow arc of the gaslight, and she thought he might have recognized her. She was sure her fears were well-founded, for when the marquis returned to the ballroom half an hour later his gaze fell upon her. Instantly he made his way toward her. She'd tried to get away, but to no avail. He'd cornered her, and with more charm than it was fair for any man to possess, asked, "My dear Mrs. Copley, may I have the pleasure of this dance?"

What a loose woman he must have thought her to be, to have succumbed to his wiles so readily. She had darted away and sought the refuge of her room. For the remainder of her stay in London, Millicent had done her best to avoid the marquis.

Then and there, Millicent had decided that the hustle and bustle of the big city was not for her, and with a great deal of relief, she returned at the end of the Season to the tranquility of her father's home in Sussex.

Yet as remote as the little village was, gossip about the Quality filtered down to Cross-in-Hand, and Millicent heard that the marquis hadn't married. The rumors had it that he continued to pursue—or was pursued by—half the great beauties of the *ton.* Now here it was a year and a half later, and heaven help her, his lordship was coming into her life again.

Wetherby was taking a turn about his mother's small conservatory. The pale winter light filtering in through the unwashed glass covered the statues and leafless plants in a shroud of fog. The orchids were gone now, the baskets hanging empty. A few potted palms drooped sadly, and ivy vines climbed most everywhere.

He was lost in contemplating how it had once looked when Jespers hurried in. "A messenger from Devonshire just arrived with this missive for you, my lord."

It was another letter from Lord Copley, and began as the other had done; but as the marquis read on, a growing sense of uneasiness settled over him.

> *My dear Wetherby,*
>
> *You remember making the acquaintance of my sister-in-law Millicent in London. I told her you would be happy to escort her and her son Rupert to Roxwealde Castle when you come. It should not pose any undue inconvenience, since they live but a mere twelve or so miles south of Orchid Hill. I have written to her to expect to hear from you in the near future.*

Wetherby stared at the letter. "Good God, Jespers! How can he do this to me?"

"Do what, my lord?"

"Lord Copley has asked me to escort his sister-in-law and her son to Devonshire."

"Is that a problem?"

"She lives in Cross-in-Hand. That is south of here by far more than twelve miles, I'm afraid. Also the roads will be muddy ruts this time of year. Haslemere is due west and a day's ride. If we are to be at Teagardner's on time, we shall have to leave a day earlier than I had planned. That will mean Mrs. Copley will have to be ready in two days."

"Can you not inform her of that, my lord?"

Wetherby looked at his valet in utter amazement. "Notify a lady to be ready to leave on a two-hundred-mile journey in two days when she thinks she has two weeks to prepare? You must be mad, Jespers."

Jespers looked suitably corrected. "Yes, my lord, I see your meaning."

The marquis came back into the main house and headed for his study. It was outside of enough that he was being asked to play nursemaid to a country matron and her child.

"Blast! If I'd known this ahead of time, I would have had my family coach sent down from London. 'Tis too late now, I left orders for it to be repainted while I was gone. No telling how many trunks she will have. Just think what that will mean for you, Jespers."

The valet, who had just begun to regain some of his composure, asked apprehensively, "Me, my lord?"

Wetherby seated himself at his desk and pulled out a piece of paper. "You will be crowded inside the carriage with a woman, her child, a maid, and most likely a nurse for the boy."

Jespers's eyes enlarged alarmingly.

In the meantime, while Wetherby was hunting a decent pen, he tried desperately to conjure up a picture of Mrs. Copley. For the life of him he couldn't recall what she looked like. He believed her hair was brown. When he'd been introduced to her, she kept gazing at the floor, and when large groups formed, she would disappear. In deference to his friend, the baron, he'd promised to seek her out at the ball and ask her to dance.

He'd had a devil of a time all evening trying to find her. It was as though she had been deliberately trying to avoid being seen, but when he finally approached her and asked her to stand up with him, she'd bolted like a cornered animal. He wondered what could have attracted a lively fellow like Captain Bertram Copley to such a mouse.

If Wetherby remembered correctly, that was the evening he'd begun his affair with the willing Mrs. Hawthorne, a pretty widow of good *ton* but of little means. She'd agreed to meet him in the maze, and he thought he'd found her when a surprisingly enticing morsel came flying into his arms. At first he had believed the mysterious woman to be Mrs. Hawthorne, and when he'd received such a heated response to his kiss, he'd congratulated himself. Several men had courted Mrs. Hawthorne, but only a few were fortunate enough to be the recipient of her charms. Then to his shock he discovered that it wasn't his paramour he held in his arms—but another. A strange, warm fairy creature who then vanished as quickly as she appeared. Many times he'd wished he could find her again, but he never did. He began to think perhaps she'd not been real at all. She had to be Venus sent to give him her blessing, because in those few stolen moments, she'd so inflamed his blood that he'd found himself quite easily persuaded to Mrs. Hawthorne's wishes to form a liaison.

Wetherby remembered more vividly Master Rupert. Lord Copley had insisted, "Come Wetherby, you must meet Bertie's beautiful son."

They had gone to the third floor nursery, where Andersen introduced him to his blond, curly-headed nephew. Rupert was the baron's spitting image, except that the child's eyes were brown instead of blue. Wetherby had remembered staring into those dark eyes much the same color as his own, regarding him gravely.

After the baron had taken his leave, Wetherby stayed on to play a game of swords with the boy. He remembered letting the lad win the duel, much to the child's merriment. In fact, finding a willing audience for his wild tales of adventure of knights and their fair ladies—which the marquis had loved to make up since childhood—he had spent, much to his own surprise, the entire afternoon engaged in nonsensical games abovestairs with a four-year-old. Afterward, Wetherby remembered feeling that the time in the nursery was far more satisfying to him than the social chitchat going on in the salons below.

However, he had no illusions that a few hours in a playroom with a child were anything like spending several days with one in a coach. For the first time since he'd received Copley's letter, the corners of his mouth turned upward. Heaven help Jespers.

Now having found all he needed to write a note, Wetherby smoothed out the paper on his desk. "Children are perpetual motion machines, Jespers. Master Rupert will be all over you. You know I always take over the ribbons and will be riding up with John Coachman."

His valet's voice had taken on a decided tone of anxiety. "Perhaps I can sit behind in the rumble seat with the groom."

The marquis dipped his pen in the inkwell and began to write. "What, and have you sick with pneumonia by the time we arrive in Devonshire? You will stay inside. There is nothing for us but to make do. I shall send the baron's rider back immediately to Cross-in-Hand with a note for the widow Copley telling her to be ready in two days."

Master Rupert straddled one of the brick pillars which flanked either side of the entrance gate leading to the Huxley manor. His gaze did not leave the road. He'd been there since dawn, swathed in his winter coat, his woolen muffler wrapped several times around his neck to ward off the damp air. A long, wooden sword painted a silver-gray to look like metal fit snugly in the sheath attached to his belt.

His mother had only told him this morning that they would be making a journey to Devonshire to have Christmas with the

Copley family. "We will be escorted by a friend of your Uncle Andy's, the Marquis of Wetherby. I expect his lordship at any time, so you must rise and be ready."

Rupert could not believe his good fortune. Ever since that day in London when the marquis had come to the nursery and played with him, Rupert had thought him quite splendid. Now he would have the chance to be with his lordship every day and learn how to be like him. Rupert had dressed quickly and gone outside to await Lord Wetherby.

Millicent stood below. "Rupert, you must come down now and have some breakfast."

"I cannot, Momma. His lordship may arrive any minute."

"But you only had—" Millicent shrugged and pulled a cherry tart from inside her cape. "Here, take this at least."

"Thank you," Rupert said, reaching for the confection. "Do you think he will be riding a big white charger, Momma?"

"I should hope not," Millicent said. "It would be very difficult for a horse, no matter how big, to carry our trunks on his back."

Rupert snorted. "You know I did not mean that. I am certain he will bring a grand carriage for you. That is one of the rules," he said, stuffing the tart into his mouth and staring back down the road.

Millicent sighed. "Your head seems to be filled exorbitantly with rules and codes this morning, young man." Taking one more anxious look toward the village, she turned back to the house.

She had just reached for the door when Rupert let out a yell. "Momma, he's coming!"

Millicent's hand froze in the air. The temptation to look overcame her and she turned to see a black speck on the horizon growing larger and larger as it sped through the village toward them. Mesmerized, she watched as the maniac holding the ribbons turned the four berserk beasts just in time to skim neatly between the two brick pillars. "It's Lord Wetherby," she gasped. "The man is mad!"

From his precarious perch, Rupert waved his sword above his head and urged them onward.

Millicent covered her mouth to keep from crying out, and rushed into the house.

Rupert leaped from his perch and ran after the carriage. Before the groom could descend from the rumble seat, the gentleman dressed in fine boots, several capes, and a tall beaver hat had already thrown the reins to the coachman and jumped down from the high seat. Rupert recognized him immediately. No nobler a man had he ever seen, and in that instant he knew that his dream was about to come true. Lord Wetherby was the man he wanted for a father. Convincing his mother might take a little longer. He was compelled to rush forward, but now that he was a sophisticated six-year-old, he drew himself up as tall as he could and refrained from throwing himself in an unmanly fashion into the marquis's arms.

Wetherby looked with amusement at the boy sporting a red mustache. "Master Rupert, is it not?"

Rupert made a sweeping bow, nearly clipping Wetherby's knees with his sword. "Yes, my lord. Master Rupert Copley at your service."

Wetherby watched half the crimson mustache disappear with a quick lick of the tongue. "What is that?" asked the marquis, trying to keep his attention on the stick in Rupert's hand.

"My sword. A good warrior must always be prepared."

"Ah, true, true. That is a magnificent weapon."

Rupert bent forward and whispered, "It is not really steel."

"Well, it had me fooled," Wetherby said.

Rupert beamed. "Really, your lordship? Our stablehand Devlin made it for me. See, he even carved a design and my initials in the handle."

" 'Pon my word," Wetherby said warmly. "That is indeed a remarkable feat." Then inexplicably, his tone changed, and he said almost sternly, "But, I am here for another reason—to take you to your uncle's. When do you think your mother can be ready?"

"Oh, Momma had everything packed last night."

A look of disbelief spread over Wetherby's face.

"She has been wondering what was taking *you* so long," Rupert said smugly, giving the marquis a sideways glance.

As soon as Millicent was inside the house, she pulled off her coat and handed it to the maid. "Hurry, Sukie! His lordship is coming. Find Beetles and tell him I shall receive the marquis in the parlor."

No matter how one looked at it—from the gray skies above to the gray of her thoughts—the day didn't look promising. Sidestepping the two trunks set in the middle of the hallway, Millicent entered the small sitting room off the entrance hall. A tremor shot through her and she reminded herself for the tenth time that morning of her resolve to remain calm when the marquis arrived. Pulling her shawl up over her head and shoulders, she seated herself in a shadowy corner away from the fireplace, and waited for Lord Wetherby.

The marquis was ushered into the entrance hall by a shaft of wheat in a dark suit. "I am Beetles, my lord. Mrs. Copley says to show you into the parlor."

After the brisk air of the out-of-doors, the heat of the room threatened to smother him. Wetherby squinted. It was so blasted dark, he could barely make out the woman who rose to greet him. Nonetheless, he smiled broadly and put forth his best manners. "Mrs. Copley?"

A shawl covered most of her head and he had to strain to hear her.

"Lord Wetherby?"

He detected a slight movement away from him. She seemed much shyer than he remembered. "Thank you for being so punctual, madam. If we are to stick to schedule, 'tis imperative that we leave as soon as possible." It was all he could think of to say.

"I did not know you had a set agenda, my lord. You should have said," Millicent spoke louder than she meant. "Surely there is time for you to take a little refreshment—coffee, perhaps? Mrs. Woodstock has made some of her delicious cherry tarts and scones with whipped cream."

She looked up at him, and for a second he caught a glimpse of her eyes—gray—plain gray. " 'Twill not be necessary . . ." he started to say more, but got no further before a serving girl clothed in a rich aroma of bakery goods and spices carried in a heavy tray. She placed it on the table in front of the fireplace, and without being told, poured two cups of steaming coffee.

Wetherby had not eaten much that morning, and his mouth began to water as he succumbed to the tempting smell. "Well, perhaps . . . while your luggage is being loaded." As she came out of the shadows, he thought he detected a smile. However, it was hard to tell, for she pulled her shawl tighter around her face. The skies forecast a bitter day, and he hoped she wasn't of such a delicate nature that the long journey ahead would prove to be too hard for her—or a burden to him.

In truth, Millicent was roasting. She could never persuade Beetles that it was not necessary to keep the rooms so hot when her mother wasn't there. She pulled out a handkerchief and patted her forehead. "Please be seated, my lord."

Wetherby took the chair on the other side of the table, farthest from the fireplace, and helped himself to a scone. "If you will have your butler tell my men where you have your things, they can help get the carriage loaded."

"That is considerate of you, my lord. Beetles is getting too old to do any heavy lifting." Millicent turned and spoke to Sukie. "Tell him to show Lord Wetherby's men the two trunks in the front hall."

Wetherby reached for a biscuit. "Where are your other bags?"

"Those are all we have, my lord."

Surely he'd heard incorrectly. None of the women of his acquaintance could possibly take a trip without half a dozen pieces. Niggled by a bit of conscience, Wetherby thought of his own three trunks that he'd had Jespers reduce to two jam-packed ones when he found he'd have more passengers. In addition, there were his three servants' valises and several boxes of gifts he'd purchased for his various hosts. "Certainly that is not all you plan to take—?"

"The quickness of our journey was unexpected, Lord Wetherby. I did not even have time to purchase Christmas gifts for my brother-in-law's family." She hesitated a minute. "I had hoped that perhaps we would have time to do some shopping in the towns we pass through."

The anxiety in her voice prompted him to reply, "Oh, yes . . . yes, we can do that. I do apologize for the abruptness of my note, but what I meant was where are your other wardrobe trunks?"

"There are no others—unless you mean Rupert's and my portmanteaux. But they are small enough to fit under our seats. You did say that we will be staying a few nights at inns, did you not?"

On the pretext of hearing her better, Wetherby leaned closer to try to gain a better look at Mrs. Copley. "What about your lady's maid? Does she not have a valise?" It was obvious to him that she dipped her head purposely to avoid his scrutiny.

"I would not think of taking Sukie away from her family during the holidays. After midday feast, all our servants are allowed the rest of the day with their kin."

Wetherby couldn't think of a less pleasant way to spend a holiday.

"Christmas is a time to celebrate with family, is it not, my lord?"

It had not been so for the marquis for more years than he could remember. His mother had died four years before, but she'd been in ill health for a long time before that. She'd spent a great deal of time in the solitude of Orchid Hill or taking the waters at Tunbridge Wells, seeking relief. Wetherby had been quite fond of his mother really, but he was away at school most of those years and seldom saw her.

Wetherby felt it better that he change the subject. "You do not plan on taking a maid?"

He thought he heard Mrs. Copley chuckle—a delightful sound that rose from deep inside her. "I am used to doing for myself, my lord."

Wetherby couldn't imagine getting along without the ministrations of Jespers. "The boy does have a nurse—or a governess."

"No, I saw no reason to employ one," she replied.

Wetherby frowned. He'd been led to believe that Copley provided generously for the boy's care and talked often of sending his nephew to Eton. Surely the baron would want to be made aware if his nephew was being allowed to run unsupervised without any instruction. If the baron's sister-in-law was neglecting the boy's education and spending his allowance frivolously, wasn't it Wetherby's duty to his friend to look into the matter? She wished to go shopping. He'd watch her closely and observe how she spent her money.

Millicent rose. "Now if you will excuse me, my lord, as soon as I get my wraps I shall be ready to leave."

"Oh, yes, of course." Wetherby sprang to his feet, showering his legs with crumbs, but Millicent was already out the door.

Wetherby brushed off his buckskins and helped himself to another cherry tart. Now that he knew where Master Rupert's mustache came from, he carefully wiped his mouth with his napkin to avoid suffering the same sort of adornment on his chin. Assured that his face was clean, he left the room.

When he next saw Millicent, she clutched an embroidered bag much larger than an ordinary reticule. She wore a brown wool pelisse and a bonnet with a thick veil which covered most of her face. He offered his hand to help her up the coach step, but the instant she placed her gloved hand in his, she withdrew it and entered the coach under her own power.

Wetherby wondered what it was he'd said or done to get him started on the wrong foot with the shy widow. Perhaps he'd stared a little too long, trying to see through the veil. He raised his hand and spoke in an aside to Rupert. "I'm afraid I offended your mother in some way. I did not mean to embarrass her."

Rupert's eyes twinkled. "Sometimes I get confused too, your lordship. The Code does say that ladies are frail creatures, but Momma keeps insisting she is not helpless."

"No, I can see that," said Wetherby, a bit puzzled by what the boy meant by *The Code.* "But we men never know for sure about women, do we?" he finished with a wink.

"No, sir. We do not." Rupert giggled and tried to reciprocate, but he'd never winked before and he feared he did a very poor job of it.

Jespers, coming close behind, took one look at the sword dangling from Master Rupert's belt, and insisted on climbing into the rumble seat with George.

Inside the coach, Millicent kept her head down until she heard the carriage door click. "Is he gone?" she whispered.

Rupert removed his sword and carefully placed it beside him on the seat. "Yes, Momma."

"Good," Millicent said, with a deep sigh of relief, leaning back against the squabs.

Rupert glanced over at his mother. "What were you searching for on the floor?"

Millicent felt the heat rise to her face. "One never knows when one will find a lucky penny," she prevaricated.

"That is a capital idea," Rupert said, looking at the floor of the carriage, then back up at his mother. "Oh, you are bamming me, aren't you Momma?"

Millicent's ready laughter turned to alarm as she saw her son press a finger to his left lid and contort his face. "Whatever are you doing, Rupert? Did you get something in your eye?"

"I'm winking."

"For heaven's sake! Wherever did you learn such a thing?" Millicent held up her hand to silence him. "No, don't tell me. I have a very good idea." She would not allow Rupert to be led astray by that vagabond. Whether or not her brother-in-law thought he could trust his own life to Lord Wetherby was his own business, but she knew that when it came to the safety of her son, the rogue would bear watching.

# Three

As Lord Wetherby prepared to mount the driver's box, he heard a burst of laughter. What an extraordinary woman. One moment she acted like a frightened rabbit, the next her gaiety hinted of an altogether different nature.

In one fluid motion, he leaped up to the high seat. "I shall handle the ribbons, John," he said. As the coachman relinquished the reins, the marquis called down for the tall, gangly Devlin to release the bridle of the lead horse, and at the same time, he glanced back to make sure all was clear. Beetles, three women and two other men stood in front of the pleasant country manor, waving. He never remembered his father's servants seeing his family off when any of them left their various estates. Although all the Huxleys weren't going to be home for Christmas, the front door was framed with pine boughs and sprigs of holly. It looked very much like a part of a holiday pageant, and for some reason, instead of producing a smile, the thought made him sad—and he didn't know why.

Wetherby cracked his whip. The bays sprang forward, catapulting the carriage down the driveway.

They rode for three hours before stopping at a small country inn to eat lunch and to rest the horses. Millicent and Rupert climbed back into the coach, and instead of closing the door behind them, Lord Wetherby asked, "May I join you? We will be traveling together for the next two weeks, and as yet, we have had little time to get to know one another."

Rupert let out a chirp and quickly pointed to the seat next to his mother. "My sword takes up so much room I wouldn't want you to be uncomfortable, my lord," he said innocently.

Wetherby removed his hat and stood humbly awaiting Millicent's invitation. To his amazement and with some annoyance, the woman hadn't uttered one word since they'd left Cross-in-Hand. Now, she merely nodded and edged over as far as she could away from him. He settled himself on the seat and motioned for George to close the door. With a wink at Rupert, the marquis faced Millicent; but that puzzling lady seemed to have found something of greater interest to view out the small window. He wondered what there could be about him that prompted her to turn to the window every time he addressed her. Wetherby was used to women encouraging his interest, and now he found himself at a loss as to how to address a female who gave him the back of her head. He chose to ignore her snub altogether. "While we ride, I can acquaint you with our itinerary," he said, with utmost smoothness.

However, regardless of his mother's cold reception, Rupert couldn't hide his enthusiasm at having the marquis join them. "We thought you got lost this morning," he said, inching as far forward as he could without falling into the marquis's lap.

Wetherby was not accustomed to being in such tight quarters with children. He sat back and folded his arms across his chest. "I *did not* get lost," he said defensively.

"That is all quite all right, my lord," Rupert said. "Most people watch for the windmill." Then making a careful study of the marquis's posture, he inched back against the squabs and crossed his arms.

Wetherby caught the mimicry. Eyes twinkling, he relaxed. "Yes, I saw it. 'Tis a good landmark."

"Well, next time you come to visit us, you will know what to look for."

Mrs. Copley suddenly gained her tongue. "Rupert! You must not talk to his lordship in such a straightforward manner."

Wetherby jumped, but it seemed that her tone startled him more than it did her son. However, Rupert looked over at him so apologetically that Wetherby felt obliged to rescue the boy from further tongue-lashing. "I realize there was little time to explain at the manor—to tell you that I received an invitation to the Teagardners' in Haslemere. You may have met them at your brother-in-law's in London." He was glad to see that that diverted her attention.

Millicent clasped her hands together and faced him. "Oh, dear. Were the Teagardners expecting you tonight? Andersen . . . that is, Lord Copley, led me to believe that you would be taking a straight route to Devonshire, and it would not be out of your way to fetch us. If I'd known it would be an inconvenience, I would not have . . ." She didn't finish.

Once Rupert saw that his mother was now off on another tack, he settled back and stretched his legs the length of the seat, knocking his sword into Wetherby's knees and stopping his mother's apology in midsentence.

Wetherby heard the quick intake of breath from behind the veil. Without losing his smile or taking his eyes away from Millicent, he quickly handed Rupert his weapon. "My dear lady, let us hear no more on the subject," he said smoothly. "Believe me when I say that it has not been an inconvenience, but my pleasure, to serve you."

Rupert's eyes gleamed their approval. "That is Number Five of the Code, is it not?"

Feeling at a complete loss as to the codes the boy kept referring to, Wetherby didn't know how to react, so he simply nodded. Presently, Rupert became absorbed in watching the snowflakes that began falling outside, and soon had his nose pressed to the window.

Wetherby tried to maneuver in such a way as not to crowd Mrs. Copley, but he couldn't escape his leg pressing against hers in the tightly packed coach. Even with the thick robe covering her, he felt her quiver at his touch—as if any contact with him could prove dangerous. The poor little mouse wouldn't even be a mouthful for his appetite. He gave her what he hoped was his most reassuring smile, but how could he guess her reaction behind that demmed silly piece of gauze? "Have no fear, madam. I sent a message ahead from Orchid Hill informing the Teagardners that you and your son will be accompanying me. In fact, I received several other invitations to stop over at friends' on my way to Devonshire."

He had to lean toward her to make out her soft reply. "Oh, I am sorry if we have caused you to miss out on anything."

"But you have not. I sent word to them also. All the houses have adequate facilities and are used to entertaining many guests. We will be stopping at the Maudlins' in Hampshire. They have two daughters who have already been presented at court. Lady Maudlin has arranged a holiday ball. I also received an invitation further on in Somerset from my friend Sir Jonathan Bridges, a congenial old bachelor who loves company. His sister lives year round at their ancestral home, and he is spending the holidays with her there. Everyone has promised parties aplenty. Fear not, you will not have a dull moment."

Again Wetherby was met with silence, yet he sensed she was watching him, so he doubled his effort to bring her out. "Tonight, however, since we cannot reach Haslemere before dark, we will probably stay over near Horsham. It is a pleasant market town with a variety of stores."

Originally the marquis had planned to go directly from Orchid Hill to the post road at Guildford, which would have taken him south to Haslemere. Now, because of this unexpected and inconvenient detour to Cross-in-Hand, he'd have to cut across Sussex through tiny hamlets and narrow country lanes, most of them muddy traps at this time of year.

Not a word came from behind the veil.

Wetherby's smile froze on his face. What did she have to be so prickly about? It was he who'd been thrown a whole day off schedule, not the other way around. Yet he was the one trying his damnedest to be pleasant about the situation. "You mentioned wanting to purchase some Christmas presents, and I thought since we do not have to make such an early start tomorrow as we did this morning, perchance you would like to take a look in some of the shops before we continue."

She clapped her hands so quickly, she nearly startled him off the seat. "Oh, that will be delightful!"

Wetherby was just congratulating himself for having finally seduced some positive reaction from his reluctant traveling companion when the coach lurched, tilted dangerously to one side, and came to an abrupt stop, throwing all three passengers into a tangle of arms and legs on the floor.

Rupert quickly clambered back up on the seat and started jumping up and down on his knees. "Oh, that was a jolly good spill, was it not, my lord?"

Wetherby clasped Millicent's shoulders and raised her gently to a sitting position. Her bonnet sat sadly askew, and as one might do for a child, Wetherby reached over and put it straight again. The veil hung tattered and torn down one side of her face. It was a pleasant face, he thought: young, gray eyes wide, lips half parted. More like that of a girl fresh out of the schoolroom who had never been kissed. Wetherby removed his hands. What was he thinking of? The woman was mother to a six-year-old boy.

"Are you all right?" he asked her, just as Jespers opened the door.

Millicent nodded. She made a few futile attempts to drag the veil back over her face, before she shifted her gaze to her hands in her lap.

"I'm glad," he said, watching with a surge of male pride as the color crept into her cheeks. She would be such an easy conquest, he thought. What a pity Lord Copley had appointed him her protector. If their circumstances had been different and she were more adventurous, their journey could have proved most interesting. With a shrug, Wetherby turned to answer his valet's anxious enquiries. "We are all fine, Jespers. Is anyone hurt?"

"It does not seem so, my lord. The coachman says we hit a pothole. He's checking the wheels. The groom says the horses are all right."

"Thank God for that," Wetherby exclaimed. Stepping from the vehicle, he took a closer look at his servant. "Jespers, your face is blue and your nose as red as a beacon. When we get under way again, I want you inside."

The valet looked apprehensively at the boy, who was climbing out of the coach with sword in hand.

By now they had attracted a number of fellow travelers: farmers, a tinker, and one of the local gentry on horseback, all asking if they could help.

While Wetherby was assuring the crowd that nothing was seriously wrong, he glanced sideways to see Rupert, his sword withdrawn and at the ready, walking stoically beside him.

The coachman approached him. "There seems to be no damage to the vehicle, yir lordship."

"But you have a bad bruise on your face, John."

"Nothing worse than I've had b'fore."

"Nonetheless, it looks a nasty blow. You climb back up with George. Jespers will be riding inside. I can handle the ribbons alone."

The coachman chuckled. "Seems ye have a partner a'ready."

Wetherby looked up to see Rupert sitting in the driver's box, then back at the unmoving Jespers, whose eyes were riveted on the interior of the carriage.

Wetherby walked back to where he knew Mrs. Copley could see him, and called over his shoulder, "Master Rupert, perhaps your mother will permit you to help me drive the coach."

Rupert shrieked, "Oh, Momma! May I?"

Wetherby gave Millicent one of his most trustworthy smiles, and raised his eyebrows. From the disapproving look she gave him, she obviously did not share the same opinion of his abilities to tend to her son. However, she had finally nodded her assent. Jespers quickly climbed in. With one last glance at Millicent, Wetherby closed the door. He hoped she wasn't going to be so missish the entire trip.

Wetherby swung himself up and took his seat beside the wide-eyed boy. A snowflake settled gently on the end of Rupert's turned-up nose, melting almost instantly. "What did she say?"

"She gave her permission."

"Oh, jolly good!"

Wetherby reached over and wrapped Rupert's muffler one more time around his neck. "It might be a good idea to sheath your sword."

Rupert eyed the long stick. "But what if we are attacked?"

"I don't believe we need to worry about that in broad daylight. Besides, I don't see how you can possibly hold such a formidable weapon and handle the ribbons at the same time."

Rupert looked at the reins in the marquis's gloved hands. "Me?" he said, then quickly plunged his sword into its sheath. "You are right, my lord."

Wetherby signaled for his groom to release the horses.

"You are going to teach me how to drive neck or nothing?"

The marquis chuckled. "That I am," he said good-naturedly, placing his hands over Rupert's. Now that he had the loquacious child out from under the wing of his protective mother, he'd surely be able to glean some helpful information from him. A sliver of guilt ate at Wetherby. He wasn't used to the feeling, but he was determined that it was his duty to find out what the widow was doing with all the blunt Lord Copley was sending her.

Rupert wriggled as close to the marquis as their thick clothes and his sword permitted.

Wetherby grinned down at him. "I'll have you tooling along with the best of them in no time at all."

"Just like you, my lord?"

Wetherby threw back his head and laughed. "Of course, just like me."

As the horses sprang into action, Rupert reveled in the feel of the strong, hard body next to his. The marquis's hands, completely encompassing his, were both strong and gentle. Rupert savored the brisk wind, the clippity-clop-clop of the horses' hooves, and the closeness of Lord Wetherby. He wanted very much to lean his head against the great coat and savor the moment, but that of course wouldn't be in keeping with his new grown-up situation, and he sat boldly upright once again.

The only thing he truly wished for was that his mother could be with them. He wondered why she'd been so quiet since they'd left Cross-in-Hand. She didn't seem to take too well to Lord Wetherby. It wasn't at all like her. She liked everyone. Maybe she was just bored, all shut up in the coach. Momma loved excitement. She was very good really with the ribbons, and had even won a race driving their donkey cart against Mr. Brussels's old cob and wagon. Next time they stopped he would mention it to the marquis, and maybe he'd ask her to sit in the box with them.

The snow fell faster. Rupert opened his mouth and let the moist flakes tickle his outstretched tongue. He heard a deep chuckle from above and, embarrassed, snapped his mouth shut.

"I haven't done that in a long time," Lord Wetherby said.

Embarrassed to think the marquis would think his game a childish one, Rupert looked up, not quite knowing how to respond.

The marquis was letting the snowflakes fall on his own tongue, then, eyes sparkling, asked. "Did you ever get your tongue stuck on an icicle?" He didn't wait for an answer before going on, "I did once. Learned my lesson fast."

Rupert laughed. "Me, too." Oh, he had to make his mother see how much fun his lordship was!

Inside the coach, Millicent raised her hands to her bonnet. *Your brains must have gone begging for you to let Rupert go off with that madman,* she chastised herself. Her veil hung in shreds. It didn't much matter. Lord Wetherby hadn't recognized her nor did he remember kissing her in the garden in London. She would have seen it in his eyes if he had. She should have been relieved, but she wasn't. Disappointment was more what she felt.

A shiver of apprehension ran through Millicent, and she clasped her hands in her lap to keep them from shaking. When Lord Wetherby had asked her if she were all right, she had only nodded, because she'd not been able to say anything with him being so close. He'd studied her with those dark, shadowed eyes and said, "I'm glad," as if he really meant it. Oh, she could see that the marquis was a dangerous and wicked man.

Millicent looked up as if she could see right through the roof of the carriage. Rupert was right when he told her, "Soon I shall be a man and then you will not be able to keep up with me." He needed a father, a just and honorable gentleman who could watch out for him. She must stop being selfish and begin to consider marrying again.

As Millicent thought of the men who had courted her, a cloud of dismay settled around her. There was Mr. Peebles the shopkeeper, who had a squint and couldn't put two sentences together; Devinian, Squire James's son, who would inherit his family house and two hundred acres of fine farmland when his papa died but spent all his time, and much of his father's money, gambling; and Mr. Ketchup, a widower with three grown children. who was old enough to be her father. The other two men who'd asked for her hand had married long ago. She sighed. There had to be someone out there who would be up to the mark, but until she could attract such a paragon, she'd have to protect her son from scalawags like Lord Wetherby. Rupert winking! The very thought of it brought a blush to her face.

A stifled cough startled Millicent. Lord Wetherby's valet sat observing her with great interest from the opposite seat. Wrapped in her own thoughts, she'd forgotten all about him. Although his muffler was wrapped to his bulbous nose and his hat was pulled down to his ears, he still shivered uncontrollably.

"Goodness," she cried, all concern for herself evaporating, "you must take this robe." But as she gave him her fur coach rug, she noticed he favored his left hand. "Oh, my, you have hurt yourself," she said sympathetically. "Why did you not say?"

"It is only a slight twist, madam," Jespers mumbled through the thick layers of wool. He watched her warily as she leaned over and tucked the rug in and around his legs.

Millicent gave him a sympathetic look. "Nonsense. Nothing is just *slight* if it hurts. Let me see it," she said firmly.

The servant obeyed, holding out his arm like a child to his mother.

Millicent peeled back the edge of his glove and pressed the flesh gently.

Screwing up his face, Jespers made quite a pitiful sight.

"You have sprained your wrist." Millicent reached into the space between her and the side of the seat, pulling out a large linen bag. She extracted a piece of cloth and tore it into strips. "I shall bind it up." As soon as she'd wrapped his wrist, Millicent pulled his glove over the bandage and placed his hand carefully on the coach rug with a little pat.

"There now," she said, "doesn't that feel much better?"

Adoration shown in the valet's eyes. "Yes, madam," he said, relaxing with a sigh. Five minutes later, Jespers was snoring.

Millicent melted back into the squabs and once more looked

out the window, seeing nothing. What a pickle! She didn't even know how to attract a man. That was her failing. She didn't know how to flirt. There had been no one to teach her, least of all her mother. Her parents were all that were kind and giving, but they'd grown up as neighbors and melded into marriage as if it were the most natural thing in the world. False pretense was foreign to their nature.

She had just celebrated her sixteenth birthday when she'd met the humorous, outgoing Captain Bertram Copley at a seaside picnic. Their courtship was short, and with the war hanging over them like a dark cloud, her parents had permitted them to marry. A year later, Rupert was born, and Bertie dead, killed in battle.

Four years later, Millicent had embarked with the greatest of expectations on her first trip to London to meet her new sister-in-law's family. Bertie's brother, Andersen, Lord Copley, had married the daughter of a country squire like herself. Not only was Sarah Greenwood friendly and generous, but Millicent's and Sarah's fathers found that they were both related through the dowager Countess of Dankleish, who had been a Huxley. It was at the countess's mansion near Kingston-on-Thames that Millicent had stumbled into the arms of Lord Wetherby. Oh, the humiliation of it. It only emphasized the fact that she didn't know how to go about in polite society. The strain had been more than she could bear, and it was with a great deal of relief that she had returned to her father's house in Cross-in-Hand with her son.

Atop the carriage, Wetherby found that Rupert didn't need much prompting to divulge his life history the way he saw it. "My grandfather is mayor of Cross-in-Hand," Rupert said proudly. "Momma says that is a very important job—nearly as important as fighting in the war. Momma said you are a marquis and will be a duke someday and could not go to war because you are an only son."

*So she had been discussing him with Rupert.* Wetherby remained silent and let the boy run on.

Rupert nodded knowingly. "I suppose you have been studying awfully hard to be a duke."

Wetherby circumvented what he considered a sticky subject by digging for more of the information he wanted. "My school days are long behind me and of little import. But tell me about your lessons. Your mother said she does not feel it necessary to hire a governess for you?"

"Hah! I am too old for a governess. I am six years old, and being tutored to go to Eton. Momma pays Mr. Tipple to teach us. He fought in the war like Papa, only he didn't die—he just lost his legs."

"She hired a crippled soldier to instruct you?"

"Momma says he isn't crippled in his head and that is what is important."

"I stand corrected," Wetherby said, hoping he'd not said something to disrupt the boy's discourse. "I did not mean that he was not capable." But it sounded to Wetherby as though she'd just brought the man in off the streets. Why hadn't she engaged a tutor from one of the fine preparatory institutions?

Rupert didn't seem to notice the marquis's reticence. "Grandpapa had a schoolroom made in the back of the stables, so that Mr. Tipple doesn't have to go up and down stairs. He has a chair with wheels on it. We take turns pushing him."

"Who are *we?*"

"Momma and me . . . and the others."

"Ah, children of the local gentry?"

"No, Sir Alden's sons live in the big manor on the hill and have their own tutor. Jason Hibbit already goes to Harrow. Then there are the Collings. They have only daughters and their own governess until they go away to some school for girls in London. But there is the curate's son Robert and his sister Penny." Rupert stopped a minute, obviously running the names over in his mind. "Billie Bee is the blacksmith's son and Momma thinks she just about persuaded his father to let his daughter come, too. Then there are Christina and Angie Strawberry who come on their days off from working in the big house on the hill, and the four Dowser boys when their father can spare them from the farm. Pokie and Beenie are our stableboys. Momma says they have no excuse for missing school." Rupert laughed at that. "Of course there is Sukie . . . Momma insisted she at least had to learn to write her name."

Wetherby was not quite sure he'd heard right. "But that is unheard of—servants being taught to read and write?"

"Momma says it is just as important for girls to be educated, too."

"I mean . . . how can a farmer pay for four sons? How can serving girls afford tuition?"

"Momma pays Mr. Tipple. She says that Uncle Andy gives her lots and lots of money. More than we can ever use, and when we can do good for others, it is selfish of us to keep it all for ourselves."

*Good God!* Wetherby thought. He'd wondered why her wardrobe was meager enough to go into one trunk. Copley would be fit to be tied to find out that the monies he was sending for his nephew's comfort were going to servants and a crofter's sons. Wetherby felt little relief in finding out that she was not using her allowance selfishly, but rather irresponsibly. Foolish woman. Her naivete wouldn't be appreciated by the local gentry either when they found their servants demanding better wages and fewer work hours.

Wetherby could see that Mrs. Copley needed someone who could manage her affairs and keep her from squandering her son's allowance on ill-conceived schemes and misdirected charities. That was what Wetherby decided he would tell the baron as soon as he saw him. And he would also urge Lord Copley to find his sister-in-law a husband as soon as possible.

# Four

That same afternoon in London, Lady Caroline Cavendish, beautiful beyond reason and quite accustomed to having her own way, was just rising from her bed. "How dare Wetherby treat me that way? I could not sleep another minute for thinking about it."

Suzette looked at her employer and shook her head. "It is no wonder, *mademoiselle,* after the way you rebuffed his lordship. But I do not see why you persist to let it bother you after your father ordered you not to see him."

Throwing her arms wide, Caroline flounced back onto her pillows, spreading her golden curls in an arc around her head. "That is because Papa needs a son-in-law who is deep in the pockets to pay his bills. He says the marquis does not have the ready, yet I do not see that it stops him from acquiring anything that pleases him."

Caroline curled a lock of her long hair around her finger. The only child of the Earl of Favor, she was quite aware that she couldn't go on forever unmarried. Although her father had told her that he didn't consider the Marquis of Wetherby eligible for her hand on his small allowance, she couldn't keep from being on the lookout for the jackanapes.

The effect of the earl's edict only served to make the marquis appear more attractive. Yet all her attempts to entice the stubborn man were getting nowhere. When she hinted that she'd be staying in London over the holidays, Lord Wetherby had had gall to tell her, "I'm sorry, my dear, you will have to find someone else to entertain you. I shan't be here."

Caroline jumped off the bed and began to pace the room. "I overheard him accept an invitation to the Teagardners' while I was dining at Grillon's. Then at Lady Sefton's I heard Lady Maudlin say that Wetherby was going to spend a couple of days at their country house in Hampshire on his way to Lord Copley's. They have two daughters they wish to marry off, but the eldest, Prethoria, is quite certain that he is coming especially because of her. Silly girl! Knowing Wetherby, he will dally there a few days and be off. I heard he'd received enough invitations to set him up for a month, but I know he has to be at Roxwealde Castle by Christmas. It is for certain that with all his charm he will not have to stay at many inns along the way." She turned to Suzette. "Have you found out if he has left London yet?"

The petite woman held out her mistress's robe and waited for her to shrug into it. "*Oui.* He has gone back to his estate in Kent."

Caroline tapped her chin with her finger. "Then he must be leaving from there. Have you found out any more information on what his itinerary will be for the trip?"

Suzette tied the sash around her mistress's slender waist. "I have, *mademoiselle.* Your chambermaid Jesse has a sister in Lord Wetherby's residence here in town, and she has told her of all the invitations his lordship has received for the holidays. Your coachman likes the cook's daughter, and he told her that the marquis's men spoke in the mews of their route. I can find out exactly where his lordship plans to stay."

Caroline looked at her companion with a new appreciation. "You are a great asset, Suzette."

Suzette held her head proudly. "Your father was kind to me. He gave me employment when I had no means."

Caroline gave a very unladylike snort. She knew her father had hired the girl because she was cheap. But for a fraction of a second, Caroline wondered about the war in France which had caused those like Suzette to lose all their wealth and position—but it was only a passing thought. The little dark-haired woman was French, and such an occurrence would never happen to someone like herself. After all, Caroline was British. Besides, there were more important matters that concerned her now, such as the exciting game of recapturing the attention of the Marquis of Wetherby. A little shiver of anticipation ran through her.

"Suzette, make me a list of all the homes Lord Wetherby will be visiting during the holidays."

"*Oui, mademoiselle.*"

"And I want my trunks brought down from the attic."

"*Oui, mademoiselle.* Is there anything more?"

Caroline sat down at her dainty escritoire. "I went to boarding school with Prethoria Maudlin. She came to Cavendish Hall in Gloucester last year; now it is her turn to entertain me." Caroline riffled through her supply of stationery, selected a few sheets, crumpled most and threw them to the floor. "As soon as you make up the list, fetch me some fresh paper. I have several letters to write."

While she waited, Lady Caroline began to devise her plan. The marquis could not escape her forever.

Half an hour before sunset, Wetherby turned over the reins to his coachman and spoke to Rupert. "I don't want your mother blaming me if you catch your death."

Rupert snorted.

Wetherby was not used to small boys, so it took awhile before he finally realized that more than a suggestion was needed to get Rupert back in the carriage. However, he had a feeling that an outright order might start a rebellion.

Rupert looked at him slyly. "I should not wish you to catch your death either, my lord. If you promise to come with me, I shall ride inside."

"Checkmate!"

Rubert grinned smugly.

Wetherby, glad that he'd been able to resolve the situation without bloodshed, boarded the coach.

Now they approached the outskirts of the market town of Horsham. "It is not large by any means, Mrs. Copley, but I think you will find the Pig and Goose a quite exceptional inn," Wetherby said as they pulled into the courtyard. He had still not managed to further engage the widow in any meaningful conversation; yet that didn't stop him from maintaining an amiable facade. "I have stayed here often and found the accommodations comfortable and the food excellent."

Anticipation of things to come made Wetherby smile as he looked out the carriage window at the familiar two-story stone building. He always received a warm reception at the Pig and Goose, and unless the proprietor Ben Feverfew had managed to marry off his obliging redheaded daughter since his last visit, Wetherby would expect as much tonight. The detour may have been well worth the inconvenience.

Wetherby was not disappointed. Just as their party entered the common room, Clara Feverfew came from one of the private parlors with a tray full of dishes. Her flaming hair couldn't stay hidden under the mobcap, nor could her well-rounded charms be disguised by any number of aprons. He sent her a message with his eyes, but he was sorry to see she missed it, because she was glaring at Mrs. Copley.

"Oh, I say, she *is* very pretty, is she not, my lord?" a voice piped from somewhere under his left elbow.

Guiltily, Wetherby jerked his gaze away from Clara and looked down at the boy standing beside him. He was beginning to feel as though he was growing a second skin.

"Rupert, where are your manners?" Millicent spoke sternly.

Rupert tried to look repentant.

Caught off guard, the marquis winced. The woman's eyes

were like a hawk's. She stood, lips pursed, looking at her son—but somehow Wetherby felt that her censure was meant for him.

A beefy man with long sideburns hustled toward them. "Lord Wetherby. How good to see you, milord."

"Feverfew." Wetherby inclined his head, and without missing a beat, orchestrated a well-ordered arrival. "George, have the lads set the night bags down at the foot of the stairs until I register. Jespers, see that they are directed to the proper rooms." Only then did he turn to the big man bobbing his head up and down in front of him. "I would like a room for my charges, Mrs. Copley and Master Rupert. I am seeing them safely to her brother-in-law's, Lord Copley, in Devonshire, for the holidays." He said this louder than was necessary, but unfortunately he saw that Clara had already disappeared into the kitchen. He was sure he could straighten out any misconceptions the hoyden had about his and the widow's relationship later. Aloud, he said, "I will have my usual."

The proprietor rubbed his knobby hands together. "Anything your lordship wishes. A room for the lady and the boy is available now, but there will be a little delay while your accommodations are made ready." Which meant someone was already in the rooms and would be told to move.

Wetherby could have easily said that he'd take other facilities, but the rear apartment was much more to his liking—and—convenient to the back stairwell which he liked to use to come and go as he pleased. There were decided advantages in having a title. "We will want a private dining room and one of your wife's delicious meals as soon as possible. We are quite famished."

"Oh, yes indeed, I am quite famished, too," Rupert echoed.

Wetherby quickly remembered his manners. "Mrs. Copley, forgive me. You surely want to refresh yourself after the long journey." He gestured toward the stairs, where a serving girl stood waiting to take them up to their room.

He thought the widow was about to say something to him, but instead, she addressed her son, "Come, Rupert."

Wetherby watched them go, then handed his hat and coat to Jespers and entered the parlor. "Have wine sent in. I can wait in here while my room is being readied." Wetherby settled onto a chair in front of the hearth and stretched his legs toward the fire, letting his mind drift off pleasantly to the evening's entertainment he anticipated for himself after he'd done his duty and seen mother and son off to their room after supper. Let no one ever say that the Marquis of Wetherby lacked *savoir faire.* He chuckled. Mrs. Copley would surely disapprove of what he planned for the evening. Strangely, her pursed lips came to mind instead of Clara's full red ones, and he wondered what it would be like to kiss them.

Millicent entered the bedroom behind the serving girl. The marquis had no scruples whatsoever. He couldn't even stop his rakish ways when he was among strangers. She'd much rather have been running about the countryside with Rupert, instead of being cooped up in that coach all day. He probably thought no one saw the unconscionable way he'd looked at that innocent young girl belowstairs. What a racket. Was no one safe from the Marquis of Wetherby? Apparently not.

As soon as their portmanteaux were placed on a stand and Millicent was shown the trundle under the high bed, the serving girl curtsied and prepared to leave.

Millicent threw her a smile. "Thank you, dear. I shall speak to Mr. Feverfew about how kind you have been. The bed looks lovely—not a wrinkle—and you arranged the towels in such a pretty pattern on the rack."

The girl looked at her, unbelieving "Oh, ma'am, no one ever notices the little things I do."

Millicent glanced around the small and pleasant room. "Well, they should. 'Tis plain you took great effort to make things tidy for your guests."

"If you wish for anything else, ma'am, you just ask for Sally," the girl said breathlessly. Then bobbing a deep curtsy, she closed the door behind her.

Rupert had already pulled off his hat and scarf and shrugged out of his coat. "Can we hurry, Momma? Lord Wetherby will be waiting for us. I am going to ask if he will play a game of chess with me after we have eaten."

If she'd had her choice, she would have had supper sent up to their room. Well, one more hour with his lordship couldn't be that bad, and she was starving. The aroma of roasting meat and freshly baked bread wafted up from below. Millicent removed her bonnet and tugged her mobcap into place in front of the mirror. Since the knave obviously had no recollection of their encounter in London—an encounter which had haunted her for a year and a half—she had no further reason to hide her face from him. "I think we shall eat supper and come right back to our room," she said a little peevishly.

Rupert's pleading eyes held no sway over his mother.

"Don't you want to find a present for your Uncle Andy?"

"Oh, yes, Momma. And something for Aunt Sarah and Percy, too."

Millicent smiled lovingly at her son. That seemed to give him another train of thought to pursue. "So if we want to be up early to go shopping tomorrow morning, we shall get to bed as soon as possible."

Which is what they did. But Rupert had never been in an inn overnight before, and after they had said their prayers and his mother had fallen asleep, he lay on the trundle listening to the somewhat raucous voices echoing up from below, mostly male, he noticed. How did men act and what did they talk about when they were away from the ladies? How was he ever to find out if he didn't have a father to tell him? He would keep a close watch on the marquis to find out how to go about it.

Unhappily, Rupert's plans for his mother and Lord Wetherby were not going as well as he wished. They had barely spoken to each other at supper. The marquis was too formal when he was around her—his manner quite different than it had been when the two of them had been tooling across the countryside atop the carriage—and his mother wasn't any fun at all. Then after they'd eaten, Momma had whisked him upstairs before he'd had a chance to ask the marquis to play a game of chess. His lordship was doomed to spend a lonely evening speaking to strangers. It wasn't fair.

Rupert tossed restlessly, running all sorts of schemes around in his mind. Sleep had totally flown out the window. Curiosity, restlessness, and temptation had taken their place. He must see if he could find the marquis.

Wide awake now, Rupert slipped out of bed and dressed. He thrust his sword into its sheath and opened the door as quietly as he could. Stealthily, he crossed to the end of the corridor and pressed his nose through the bannisters. Most of the ruckus was coming from the taproom at the end of the commons area. Rupert quivered. He knew he dared not descend those stairs, for he'd surely be sent packing right back up again. He had to find another way down where he could watch the goings-on and still remain unobserved.

Rupert heard a door open and close nearby. He held his breath and flattened himself against the wall. The sound of footsteps led away from him and soon faded. Cautiously, he followed the sounds to a back stairwell. He had forgotten there would be servants' stairs which would lead to the kitchen and rear courtyard.

He crept down the steps to a black hallway. The rattle of pots and pans and muffled voices came from the right. Not quite sure which doors led to what, he opened one. A lantern hung on the wall bathing shelves stacked full of sacks and containers with a pale yellow light. He had just concluded that he'd have to go to the length of the hallway to find the taproom, when he heard a squeal—high-pitched and excited—a woman in distress! Rupert swallowed hard. He'd never rescued a woman before, and he was sadly in doubt as to how one went about it. However, he'd read enough daring tales about chivalrous knights to know that the faint of heart never won fair maidens. There was no one that he could see to call to for help. Rupert was on his own.

Again the cry came, louder this time, and very near. Rupert ran to a heavy wooden door that was slightly ajar, and pressed his ear to the crack. He heard shuffling noises and knew there was a struggle within, but now the lady's cries were muffled and he feared for her life. A shiver ran down Rupert's spine and sweat dampened his brow, but he was a stout lad. Drawing out his sword, he bravely threw his shoulder against the door and heaved it open. "On guard!" he called out into the shadows.

To his astonishment, the marquis rose up before him, a maiden swooning in his arms. "My lord!" Rupert cried in relief. "Thank goodness you are here. I see you have saved the fair lady already."

"What the deuce!" If Wetherby could have disappeared through the floor, he would have. Clara raised herself quickly from where she lay back in the marquis's arms, and stared mesmerized at the small person who stood before them waving a wooden stick in the air.

"Are you all right, my lady?" his voice piped. "Did you see who her assailant was, my lord?"

Wetherby shook his head in disbelief.

Rupert turned concerned eyes back to Clara, who now stood stuffing her hair back under her mobcap. "I hope you were not frightened too badly, my lady. Do you know who the knave was? He must be punished."

Wetherby, striving to regain his composure, said, "I think he has been punished enough, Master Rupert. Now, what are you doing belowstairs?" He looked uneasily over the boy's shoulder, as if looking for someone. "Where is your mother?"

Rupert shifted from foot to foot. "She is asleep, my lord."

"And you sneaked out. That was naughty, was it not?"

"Yes, my lord. But just think what would have happened to the pretty maiden if we had not come along when we did." Rupert cast a shy glance up at Clara, then bowed. "May I escort you back to the kitchen, my lady?"

Clara, her eyes still glistening, her lips full and pouting, brushed down her skirt. "I think I hear my father calling me," she said, and with a toss of her head, marched out the door.

Wetherby sighed. "I think it is time you returned to your room, also."

Rupert watched Clara go, then sheathing his sword, turned bright eyes on Wetherby. "I think I shall have to tell Momma about your brave exploit, my lord."

Wetherby took the boy's free hand and led him out into the corridor. "I don't think that a wise idea at all, Master Rupert."

"But tonight you combined both Codes Four and Five. That is quite remarkable, my lord."

Wetherby frowned. Whatever the devil this code business was, he wasn't about to ask the boy now, or he'd never get him to bed. "A deed bragged about loses its value. Besides, if you tell your mother about me, she will know that you disobeyed her."

Rupert hung his head. "I broke Number Three, didn't I? I shall have to put an *X* in my journal, and I have not had to put a bad mark in for ever so long. Mr. Tipple said it was quite remarkable that I had done so well for four straight weeks." He blinked back the moisture welling up in his eyes. "I'm sorry if I am a disappointment to you, my lord."

As a tear spilled over and ran down Rupert's cheek, an unfamiliar surge of tenderness tugged at the marquis's heart, and he grabbed wildly for an antidote. "If I combined Four and Five, as you said I did, then you must have done also. Surely that means something." Wetherby crossed his fingers that it worked.

"Oh, do you think so, my lord?" Rupert perked up hopefully. "Yes, I must have done."

"Ah," said Wetherby, more in relief for himself than for Rupert. "So I should think that Four and Five combined would cancel out your one minor infraction of Three." He had no idea of what they were talking about, but he prayed it worked.

The frown on Rupert's forehead disappeared instantly. "Oh, you must know if it is so, my lord."

On the contrary, Wetherby was beginning to think that he knew nothing—especially about little boys. The fact that he'd been one himself at one time didn't help him at all. However, they were now at Rupert's bedroom. He saw the boy inside, and quietly closed the door behind him.

God! How could one small boy wreak such havoc in so short a time? Wetherby decided he had two choices: he could go downstairs to join those in the taproom, or he could go to his own room. He chose the latter. The evening was already in shambles, and for some reason his desire to go after Clara had left him.

The next morning, a light sprinkling of snow powdered the ground. After a warm meal in the private dining room, the three set out to explore the shops. Wetherby called for his carriage, but Mrs. Copley, with a surprising show of willfulness, stuffed her hands inside her muff and insisted she wanted to walk into town. "It is such a short distance, my lord."

Finally, they reached a compromise. They would go into town by foot, but the coach would drive in later to carry them back to the inn.

The marquis took his fine walking stick, and Rupert his sword. Wetherby was beginning to think that the child would look undressed without it.

Holiday decorations appeared everywhere. Wreaths decorated the shop doors and evergreens framed the shop windows. Bells tinkled when the shop doors opened, much to Rupert's delight. Confectioners' shops were especially set up to tempt small boys, and Wetherby insisted on stopping in nearly every one to buy some sort of goodie or another.

Rupert discovered a little tea shop where a nativity scene made of bakery goods and confection was featured in the middle of the shop window—they specialized in Christmas biscuits shaped like camels and stars. Wetherby insisted they buy a box to take to the Teagardners, and of course bought a sack for Rupert.

Millicent finally protested. "You will spoil him, your lordship."

He saw her nose wrinkle, and he suspected she was trying not to smile. "I doubt that," Wetherby laughed. "He seems a sensible boy." In truth, Wetherby hadn't had so much fun in a long time. His sister's children were so rotten that they merely asked what else he had for them once they'd opened all their gifts. Before he thought, he found himself calling, "Happy Holidays" to the proprietor as they left the shop.

But it was the young widow who captured Wetherby's attention. He heard her laughter and turned to see the two of them running from window to window, pointing at some gimcrack or another. Wetherby had a hard time keeping up with them. It was as though they had forgotten he was with them, and a sense of being left out unsettled him.

At one time when Wetherby had caught up with Millicent, Rupert had completely disappeared from view. They found him peering down an alleyway at a passel of urchins who were rummaging through a trash barrel. He collected Rupert and was about to give the boy a scold for running off, when Millicent disappeared. After a few minutes of frantic searching, Wetherby found her coming out of the same alleyway, closing up her reticule.

"The children said their mother is ill and they had no food," she said, as if that explained the matter.

"Good God, Mrs. Copley! You must not go about without an escort," Wetherby scolded.

She looked at him as if he belonged in Bedlam. "In Cross-in-Hand I go everywhere by myself."

He wasn't sure his meaning was getting to her. "But you must not do so where you are a stranger in a strange town. You never know who means to do you harm."

"Who in the world would want to harm *me?*"

Wetherby looked at her upturned face and couldn't answer that either.

His lordship's scrutiny unsettled Millicent, and she quickly changed the subject. "We only have a little time and I must buy gifts for the Teagardners. You say they have twin sons, my lord? How old are they?"

Wetherby looked blank. Her eyes twinkled. Why had he thought her eyes plain? They were like soft gray clouds with flecks of gold in them.

"When were they married?"

"The twins? They are only infants."

Millicent put her hand over her mouth and for a second he suspected she was trying not to laugh. "I mean . . . when were Mr. and Mrs. Teagardner married."

Wetherby gave a crooked grin and concentrated on the answer. "Just before pheasant-hunting, if I remember correctly . . . two seasons back."

Her laughter came softly from inside her. "That sounds just like a man. I calculate then that the children must be under two years of age."

Wetherby had the uneasy feeling that she was making fun of him. He had thought his to be a very logical answer.

Millicent selected two rubber balls, one red, and one blue.

Later, she purchased a pair of gloves for Mrs. Teagardner and a silk scarf for the woman's husband.

Wetherby didn't know why he bought Mrs. Copley the expensive cashmere shawl. Perhaps it was because it reminded him of the purplish-pink fragrant orchids his mother used to raise at Orchid Hill, their clove-scented fragrance filling the air each June and July. Perhaps it was because he saw her admiring it and he wanted her to have something prettier than that plain brown coat she wore. When she was attracted to a display of ribbons, he quickly paid the clerk and tucked it under his arm, handing it to her when they arrived on the street.

"Oh, my lord, you should not have." She held it to her face and looked at him for just a second, questioning. The color, he noted, brought out the pink in her cheeks.

Wetherby realized it was the first time he'd bought a gift for a lady without expecting anything in return—unless it was to have one more of those few and fleeting smiles. She didn't disappoint him.

He coughed. " 'Tis time we get back to the inn for a bite to eat before we go." Wetherby said. "It should not take us more than two or three hours to reach Haslemere."

Rupert frowned. Wetherby put it to the child's reluctance to leave the shops, but by the time they returned to the inn, he knew something was definitely bothering the boy, but he couldn't figure out what it could be. Perhaps his mother had been right, and he'd eaten too many sweets. Yet the boy ate a hearty lunch without complaint.

But now there was no time to find out, since John had the coach ready. For some unexplainable reason, Wetherby found himself selecting to ride inside, as did Jespers, who was showing a great deal of attentiveness to Mrs. Wetherby, and beat the marquis in assisting her up the step. So all four crowded in together and set off for the Teagardners'.

One look at her son's Friday face, and Millicent didn't beat around the bush. "Is something wrong, Rupert?"

The boy wriggled on the seat and gave the marquis a pleading look. "No, nothing, Momma."

"It is not like you to be tired. We went to bed so early last night you should have had a good night's sleep. Well then, it will be off to bed early for us both tonight. We have had a busy day."

Wetherby was still concerned about Rupert, but glad that at least Mrs. Copley had seemed more kindly disposed toward him since he had given her the shawl. She sat now with it draped across her shoulders. For a moment when she turned to the window, he saw her hold the soft fabric to her cheek. While she was absorbed in the sights outside the coach, Wetherby leaned toward Rupert and said confidentially, "I want you to know that if there is anything that you need talk to me about—man to man—I shall always be glad to hear you out."

Rupert forced a smile as his gaze flicked to his mother. He told himself that he must set aside his own concerns for the moment and rejoice in the new developments between her and his lordship. The look Momma had cast in the marquis's direction when he had presented her with the colorful shawl gave Rupert hope that his lordship was gaining some favor in her eyes. To Rupert's way of thinking, if the marquis was too modest to brag about his feats of honor, it was up to him to make his mother realize how brave his lordship was. That thought renewed his spirits completely, and Rupert decided then and there that he must reveal to her what he'd seen with his own eyes. Then she would realize how brave his lordship was and what a perfect father he would be.

"Momma, I must tell you how Lord Wetherby rescued the pretty, red-haired maid at the inn last night."

# Five

Millicent's eyebrows shot up to her hairline.

Rupert was happy he'd gained his mother's attention so quickly. Before he lost it again, he breathlessly recounted the entire tale from the attack on Miss Clara by an unknown assailant to finding Lord Wetherby with the swooning girl in his arms. Oh, he could see that his mother was impressed by the way her eyes widened and her mouth popped open without a word coming out. Thus encouraged, Rupert proceeded to describe in greater detail everything he had seen the marquis do the night before. If he embellished the story a bit, he felt himself justified, for he wanted to paint his lordship in the most dazzling light possible. "Don't you think Lord Wetherby is a very bold and daring man, Momma?"

Rupert hadn't meant to embarrass his lordship, whose face was now a brilliant shade of red, but it was well worth the effort to see his mother absolutely speechless. Even Jespers seemed moved by the tale, for he was shaking all over.

Rupert sat back quite satisfied. His plan to make his mother take notice of his lordship's many outstanding attributes was working perfectly. If he received a scolding for having left their bedroom without Momma's permission, then so be it.

Millicent didn't know what to think. Rupert had been with her in their room all night. He must have had a terrible dream. Oh, she hoped so. What other explanation was there for it? The marquis had been so kind to them all morning. Then there was the unexpected gift of the shawl. Or was it all a ploy to cover up his tryst? She'd found out firsthand in London that he had a penchant for kissing the ladies. But how could Rupert become privy to the rogue's assignation? Millicent chewed on her lower lip. No matter how much she wanted to laugh at her son's silly story, deep down she feared there could be some truth in it.

As Rupert's tale turned exceptionally graphic, Lord Wetherby's presence became all the more evident to Millicent. His maleness filled the small coach, triggering feelings she'd long forgotten. Pictures flashed across her memory. She saw a young couple running through the meadow hand in hand, falling into the high grasses, lying in each other's arms. Heaven help her! Her thoughts were becoming those of a wanton woman, and she was too ashamed to look at him for fear he could read her thoughts.

For the next three hours, an uneasy silence engulfed three of the four occupants in the coach—until late in the afternoon, when they entered the great woods of Haslemere. Wetherby supposed it to be not more than four o'clock; yet under the dense umbrella of ancient pollards, it was already night.

Rupert, with his face to the window and his sword in his hand, seemed oblivious to any strain. "Oh, Momma, do you suppose we shall see any dragons?"

"I imagine they are out there, dear, but I doubt if they will let themselves be known to us."

Wetherby was glad to see a smile finally grace Mrs. Copley's face as she and her son became caught up in the make-believe world of their own. She seemed to have accepted her son's story of Clara's rescue as nothing more than a figment of a child's overactive imagination. At least, he hoped so.

The Teagardners' large manor house stood in a clearing on the lower slope of the high Black Down. It was impressive more in its size than for its architectural splendor. There were deer prints in the thin dusting of snow along the carriageway, and though it was winter, there seemed no evidence that formal gardens existed even in summertime.

They were greeted at the front door by John Teagardner himself. "Welcome, welcome," he shouted, as if they were a mile away instead of only a few feet. "So this is Mrs. Copley. Glad to see you again, ma'am—Wetherby. Bangs, take their wraps." A short, stout fellow in livery stepped forward, followed by a sliver of impeccability dressed in black who detached himself from the shadows and came to stand beside Teagardner. "Popper here will see you to the library—Mrs. Teagardner doesn't want to mess up the sitting room." He didn't explain that statement any further, but fell into step beside Rupert. "You must be young Master Copley. My, my, how you've grown. This way, everyone. Mrs. Teagardner is waiting."

Millicent, Wetherby, and Rupert dutifully paraded behind Popper and their host down the hallway and through the double doors off to the left. A shambles greeted them. The floor was strewn with torn papers and toys. A huge log blazed invitingly in the deep fireplace. Plump Mrs. Teagardner struggled up from where she sat on the floor, stepped over one crawling baby, then another, and greeted her guests. "My, oh, my, you must be Millie," she said, holding out her arms to Millicent.

"Mrs. Teagardner," Millicent said, the corners of her mouth turning up.

"Jane. Just plain Jane, dear. Wetherby," she said, "do come in. Just be careful you don't trip over anything. And this must be Master Rupert. Go over and play with the children, dear. Oh, I didn't mean you, Rupert. I meant Mr. Teagardner. Now let us all sit down here somewhere—" She bustled around putting pillows back on the sofas and sweeping a cloth rabbit off onto the floor. "John insists on having the children with us as often as we can. He says they are more fun to watch than a kennelful of puppies. Of course, we knew you'd want to see them right off."

The two roly-poly babies crawled over to the marquis, clutched the tops of his boots with sticky hands, and proceeded to pull themselves up.

"Ain't they something?" Teagardner crowed. "Only nine months old and already trying to walk."

No matter how ambivalent her feelings were toward Lord Wetherby, Millicent's sense of compassion came to the fore. Taking pity on his plight, she extricated one pair of sticky hands from the marquis's formerly spotless trousers. The instant she picked up one infant, the other plopped down and howled. Rupert dug out one of the rubber balls from his mother's satchel and rolled it to the child. The crying stopped.

Considerably relieved, Wetherby dragged a chair as far away from the hazard area as possible, and was about to sit down when a commotion erupted outside in the hall.

The doors flew open and a whirlwind in deep blue velvet sailed into the room. Her blond mane, curled and coifed, and her trim-waisted figure, bespoke the daughter of a peer. "Ernest, darling," she said, extending both gloved hands to Lord Wetherby, "what an unexpected surprise!" Before he could react, she stood on tiptoe and kissed his cheek.

Millicent rose quickly, the baby still in her arms.

Teagardner laughed heartily. "Oh, forgot to tell you, Lady Caroline arrived only this afternoon, too. Ain't that a coincidence?"

Rupert jumped to his feet, eyes wide with wonder. In that instant, he knew he had fallen in love.

Wetherby eyed Caroline warily. He didn't miss her familiarity with his first name, and he could see that the Teagardners and Mrs. Copley didn't miss it either. Disentangling himself from her arms, he bowed formally. "It is indeed a surprise to find you here, Lady Caroline. May I present Mrs. Copley. You may have met in London some time ago."

Rupert rounded to Wetherby's side, and studied his lordship's every move with great intensity.

Caroline narrowed her eyes and assessed Millicent. "I'm

afraid I didn't have the pleasure," she said, casting a look of suspicion at the marquis.

Wetherby didn't think Caroline would acknowledge a country girl like Millicent even if she *had* met her. "I have been asked to escort Mrs. Copley and her son to Roxwealde Castle for the holidays."

"Andersen's sister-in-law?" Caroline looked in horror at the child chewing on the corner of Millicent's shawl and pulled her scarf tighter about her shoulders, as if to save her own clothes from a similar fate. "I didn't think she was your type, Wetherby," she said only loud enough for the marquis to hear.

Millicent thought Lady Caroline one of the loveliest women she'd ever seen. She couldn't blame Lord Wetherby for being enchanted by her. She tried her best to curtsy, but soon found it an impossible feat while holding a wiggly child in her arms. "My lady," she said breathlessly.

"Charmed," Caroline said, never once lowering her chin from its exalted state. "What a lovely shawl, my dear—"

Millicent placed the baby on the floor. "You are most gracious to mention it, Lady Caroline. Lord Wetherby gave it to me."

Caroline stepped back and studied Millicent. "Really? I hate to tell you, but it is all wrong—totally inappropriate for that drab-colored suit."

Millicent looked longingly at Caroline's fine attire. "I agree with you wholeheartedly, my lady."

The chit's concurrence threw Caroline off balance and completely cancelled the clever barb she'd had on the tip of her tongue.

Millicent leaned closer and said confidentially, "I am afraid from the dark looks he is casting my way that Lord Wetherby thinks the same as you. He probably feels his stature lowered considerably, having to escort such a country goose as I."

A sudden surge of feminine rage ran through Caroline.

"How dare he?" she found herself saying. "No matter how high in the instep Wetherby considers himself, he has no right to insult a woman."

"Oh, please do not mistake what I meant," Millicent said. "I am quite aware that I never acquired the high state of polish such as you possess. In Cross-in-Hand, I am afraid I never thought beyond dressing modestly."

"Good heavens! You come from Sussex." Caroline said it in such a way, that it seemed a statement that explained everything.

Millicent became thoughtful. "But now that I think of it, his lordship did buy me the shawl yesterday and asked me to wear it right away. I had not thought until now that he may have been embarrassed to be seen with me."

Caroline huffed. "What business has that bounder to be passing judgment on what a woman should wear? Men meddle too much in affairs they have no business meddling in." She looked harder at Millicent. "However, the fact that I am a woman makes it perfectly proper for me to give you a few suggestions along those lines, my dear."

"Oh, my lady, you are too kind."

Caroline was about to agree when Teagardner called for her attention. "Here, here, Lady Caroline, you haven't met Master Rupert yet."

Rupert tried desperately to imitate the marquis's graceful bow, but he was unable to move.

"Rupert!" Millicent said. "Remember your manners!"

His mother's words broke the spell. Rupert fell to his knees at Caroline's satin-slippered feet, and bowed his head. He wanted to tell the lovely lady that he would be her servant forever, but his tongue remained glued to the roof of his mouth.

Caroline stared down at the curly blond head, and for once in her life, she couldn't think of a word to say, either. She never cared for children nor particularly wanted to be near them, and here was one paying her the homage she expected of all men. She could think of nothing else to do but pat him on the head.

Lightning from heaven had struck Rupert twice in as many minutes: once when his vision of the perfect woman glided into the room; and now when she had given him her blessing, anointing his head with her touch.

"How sweet," Caroline cooed, looking smugly at Wetherby. "Some gentlemen know how to treat a lady."

Rupert scrambled to his feet and ran to stand by the marquis. "She is an angel, is she not, my lord?"

Wetherby put his hand on the boy's shoulder and gave it a squeeze. He didn't want to disillusion one so young. The lad would soon learn the truth about women like Caroline—probably the hard way—as was the wont of most of her suitors.

"Well, now," Mrs. Teagardner said, "here is Nurse Picking and Nina to fetch the boys." A friendly-faced, angular woman and a young serving girl stood in the doorway. "Rupert, dear, go with Miss Picking. Your things have already been taken to the nursery."

The exaltation that had lit Rupert's face for the last few minutes was extinguished with those few words. No one except Wetherby noted the change, the drooping shoulders and downcast eyes, as the boy obediently followed the two women and the twins out of the room.

Mrs. Teagardner had already turned to Millicent. "I have given you a room in the west wing next to Lady Caroline's apartment, dear. I do hope you don't mind that yours is smaller, but she had her companion with her and quite a number of trunks to accommodate. Lord Wetherby said you were not able to bring your abigail with you, so I have assigned Mercy to help you in any way that you wish. She is a cheery girl and most obliging."

"I am sure she will do just fine," Millicent said.

"The girl should be in your room now unpacking your

things," Mrs. Teagardner said. "Popper is in the hall and will point you in the right direction. I am sure Lady Caroline will not mind showing you your room when she goes up. Wetherby," she said, turning to the marquis, "your valet has already had your things taken into the east wing. That is to the right. Now, if everyone will excuse me, I must see the cook about the pudding. Dinner will be at seven o'clock."

Caroline sniffed and walked off ahead of Millicent, up two flights of stairs to the landing of the second floor. Two large potted plants stood sentinel at the corners of the stairway that led to the third floor. The two women continued down the hallway to the left, and when they reached the third door, Caroline pointed elegantly with a wave of her hand, then proceeded on, still not saying a word.

"Thank you," Millicent called after her.

After the abrupt dismissal, it was with some surprise when two hours later Millicent opened to a knock to find Lady Caroline standing outside her room, dressed to the eyes in silvery-gray silk and lace, her hair trimmed with green ribbons that matched her emerald necklace. "May I come in?" she asked, sweeping in without waiting to be invited. Her gaze took in the pile of clothes on the bed. "You are not ready yet?"

Millicent patted the bun at the back of her head and looked sadly at the two frocks, a dark green with a bluish tint, and a brown that was lighter than her traveling costume. "I sent Mercy down to iron my blue muslin. I could not make up my mind which one to wear."

Caroline threw up her hands. She'd never seen anyone of supposedly good breeding who knew less about fashion. "These are terrible," she said, picking up the dresses, then dropping them into a jumble on the bed.

"I know," Millicent said, in desperation. "I would give anything to be as modish as you, but I am afraid I am a hopeless case."

Caroline agreed, of course, and could not pass up the temptation to show the little country chit how right she was in her assessment. She opened the clothes press and looked inside. "You must have something with more possibilities."

Millicent peered over Caroline's shoulder as if she hoped to see a miracle happen, and a beautiful frock of magnificent hue would appear which Caroline had somehow overlooked.

At that moment, Mercy entered the room carrying the blue gown.

Caroline snapped it out of the maid's hands and viewed it from every angle. "It will have to do," she sighed with resignation.

As soon as Mercy had buttoned up the back of her frock, Millicent began to cover her hair with her mobcap.

"Oh, for heaven's sake!" Caroline cried, throwing her hands into the air. "You do not plan to wear that dustmop on your head."

"I don't have anything other," Millicent sighed.

"Where is that shawl Wetherby bought you?"

Millicent hurried to get it, and handed it to Caroline.

"Stand still while I figure out what I should do with you." Now caught up in the opportunity to show her superior expertise as a lady of high fashion, Caroline draped the soft cloth over Millicent's head, then drew the corner up and over one shoulder. "Do you have a pin of some sort?"

Millicent pointed to a small box atop the dressing table.

Caroline opened it and rummaged through the modest collection of necklaces and eardrops. "These are useless. You, gel," she said to Mercy, "go next door and tell Mademoiselle Suzette to fetch my jewelry box."

"Oh, my lady, I cannot possibly expect you to lend me any of your fine jewels," Millicent lamented.

"Nonsense, I can do as I please," Caroline said, opening the door for Suzette and telling her to place the chest on the table. She withdrew several pieces before making her selection, a delicate gold and multi-jeweled clasp that she used to pin the shawl on Millicent's shoulder. "There. that will have to do. It gives you a little color, and since we will be sitting down, the lower part of your frock will be of little import. Now show me the fan you plan to take."

"I left it at home," Millicent said. "I did not think I would need it visiting my brother-in-law."

"*It?* Surely you have more than one."

Millicent blushed. "A fan is only needed in the country to keep cool in the summer or to swat flies."

"Heaven forbid!" Caroline expounded impatiently. The young widow presented her with a challenge she'd never contemplated—and Caroline was ready for a fresh challenge—one which would give her an excuse to be near Wetherby. "You are nothing but a lump of clay ready for molding," she said, starting for the door. "But . . . a bit of advice before I go. Don't look straight into people's eyes—it confuses them."

"It does?"

"It does—especially if it is a man. Flutter your lids and glance up through your lashes—like this." Caroline illustrated.

Millicent tried.

"You look like someone who has a speck of dust in her eyes. Don't you know how to flirt?"

Millicent sighed and confessed, "No. I fear it is one of several of my shortcomings. The marquis said that we will be attending a party at the Maudlins' Hampshire estate in a few days, and I would give anything to learn how to go about it. I watched you at the Countess of Dankleish's in London—just the way you twirled your fan was magnificent. It seemed almost as if it spoke a language all its own."

Caroline bathed in Millicent's adulation. "It does." she said solicitously. "Tonight before we retire, we shall have a little coze and I can show you some movements. Perhaps I can find a fan to loan you. I always bring one for every ensemble."

"You are so kind, Lady Caroline."

Caroline shook her head. The gel had no idea how to play the game, but she seemed biddable enough, and it might prove amusing to teach her some of the tricks of *le beau monde.* Caroline preened in front of the cheval mirror. "I see that helping you has unraveled a couple of my curls. I must go back to my room to have Suzette recomb them. I shall see you at dinner, Mrs. Copley."

"But it is nearly seven o'clock now," Millicent said.

"A lady is never prompt," Caroline said, sweeping out the door.

Nonetheless, Millicent proceeded toward the head of the stairs and had just reached the end of the corridor when a small figure jumped out at her from behind a potted plant. "Rupert!" She no sooner got the words out of her mouth than she saw Lord Wetherby approaching them from the east wing. She lowered her voice to speak to her son. "Whatever are you doing here? And why are you dressed in your Sunday clothes?"

"Momma, I don't want to eat in a nursery with babies."

"Where do you plan to eat, then?"

The marquis was now upon them. "What is this I hear? You are expected to eat in the nursery? A fine young man of your education and maturity? Unthinkable!"

Rupert threw him a grateful look.

By now Caroline had joined the party. She raised her eyebrows at the sight of the child.

Millicent saw no alternative but to tell the truth. "The blame must be laid at my feet, I am afraid, my lord. Rupert is allowed to eat with his grandparents and me at home. He has done so since he was four years old."

"Oh, I say," came the jolly voice of their host from the floor below. "Is everyone hungry?"

Wetherby saw the stricken look in the boy's eyes. "We shall see what we can do," he whispered, placing his hand on Rupert's shoulder and guiding him down the stairs toward their host.

"I say, Teagardner, don't you think that Master Rupert here is a fine young lad—on the brink of manhood?"

The big man took out his quizzing glass and bent over to observe Rupert better. "By Jove! Indeed he is."

Lady Caroline followed close behind. She fluttered her fan, then snapped it shut. "Really, Wetherby, I never knew you to take to children."

Millicent watched carefully, and even though she held no fan, she tried to move her hand in rhythm with Caroline's. She sadly concluded that she did a poor job of it.

Wetherby caught the strange movements out of the corner of his eye, but kept his downward path until they stood on the next landing. "Don't you think a lad of his stature should eat with the adults?"

Rupert glanced hopefully back and forth at the two men.

Teagardner bounced his several chins up and down. "I can think of no reason why he should not. Popper, see that another place is set at the table. That will please Mrs. Teagardner, y'know. She was just saying 'twas a pity we were short one man to make an even number. Much obliged to you, Master Rupert, if you would join us."

They had all now reached the hall below, and Popper announced that dinner was ready to be served.

Wetherby bowed to Mrs. Teagardner and as he offered her his arm, spoke again. "Teagardner, you cannot expect a guest to take his own mother into dinner, now can you? I am sure that Master Rupert would make an excellent escort for her ladyship."

"Oh, right, your lordship," the big man boomed, extending his arm to Millicent. "D'you mind, Lady Caroline?"

Caroline did not miss the comradery in Wetherby's eyes as he winked at Rupert. She'd been told that there comes a time when a man begins to think about starting his own nursery. The thought of getting into bed with the marquis did not bother Caroline one bit. If being sweet to the boy was what it took to bring Wetherby to heel, she would play the game. She bathed Rupert in a brilliant smile and curtsied. "Master Rupert, I shall be honored to have you escort me to dinner."

Rupert held out his arm the way he'd seen Lord Wetherby do. The moment Lady Caroline placed her hand on his, he was sure he'd evaporate into thin air, but when he saw that he hadn't, he raised his head high and proudly walked his princess into the dining room.

# Six

Dinner went quite well, considering. The Teagardners were excellent hosts. Mrs. Teagardner never let the conversation lag, and Mr. Teagardner made sure the footmen kept the plates full and the wine flowing. Rupert was even allowed a small amount of watered-down claret.

Millicent tried to engrave on her mind every inflection of Lady Caroline's voice and every graceful movement of her hands, so that she could repeat them later.

Rupert, seated to the left of Mrs. Teagardner and beside Lady Caroline, did his best to keep his nose above the table and not spill any food onto his lap. Occasionally, when he cast a glance in the direction of his mother, a shadow came over his eyes, but he quickly recovered and basked in the glory of the lovely lady beside him.

Lord Wetherby was alternately amused by his hostess's chatter, suspicious of Caroline's overzealous interest in the boy, and fascinated by the strange twists and turns of Mrs. Copley's wrists. Rupert's odd mood swings confused him, but he put it down to the child's excitement at being permitted to eat with the adults.

Finally satisfied that all their guests were thoroughly stuffed, Mrs. Teagardner led the ladies into the drawing room. When the gentlemen joined them after their port and cigars, they declared it a delightful but exhausting day and all said their good-nights. John Teagardner, however, begged the marquis to come see his collection of butterflies in the library before retiring.

Rupert delayed as long as possible after Lady Caroline had

left, hoping to be included, but when he saw that he wasn't, he reluctantly followed his mother.

Millicent was not fooled by Rupert's attempts to prolong the journey to the second-floor landing. The pale yellow light of the candles cast flickering shadows up and down the hallways. "There is nothing for it," his mother said. "You must return to the nursery for the night."

"Why can I not stay with you, Momma?"

His request presented a quandary for Millicent. If Lady Caroline came to her room for a coze, she couldn't have a six-year-old listening in on her lessons in flirting.

"I don't want to sleep with babies, Momma."

"Of course, you don't," came a deep voice behind them. "No man wants to sleep with babies."

Millicent jumped. She hadn't heard the marquis come up the stairs behind them, but she was too much out of countenance with her problem to be startled. "And where do you propose for him to sleep, my lord? In the corridor? My room is too small," she prevaricated.

"Hmm," Wetherby stalled. The wine had mellowed his brain and loosened his tongue more than he had thought. Now he was in the pot. "Meant to tell you how lovely you looked tonight, ma'am." He did think the shawl wrapped around her face gave her something of an ethereal look—like the Virgin Mary in the nativity scene at St. Vincent's. No, that really was not what he was thinking. He managed a weak smile. "There is a spare room across from mine. I don't think the Teagardners will mind if he stays there."

"Oh, Momma, please?"

Millicent had an uneasy feeling that whatever she decided was going to lead to trouble somehow, but she knew Rupert would be very unhappy if he had to go to the nursery. Besides, she was certain that one night near Lord Wetherby couldn't erase all that she had taught her son over the last six years.

"Well . . ."

Rupert gave a whoop. "Oh, thank you, Momma." Then, remembering his manners, he bowed to the marquis. "Thank you, my lord."

"But, Rupert," Millicent said, "you don't have your nightclothes. I would hate for you to upset Miss Picking. Do you think you can get your clothes without waking the babies?"

"Oh, yes, Momma," Rupert cried, running to the corner of the stairway. He pulled out his portmanteau and his sword from behind the potted plant where he'd hidden them, and hurried back, smiling smugly.

Millicent fisted him on the arm. "You," she said, giving him a kiss on the cheek. "You knew just what I would say."

Rupert popped her back. "Fooled you that time," he chortled, turning and running toward the east-wing corridor. "Good night, Momma."

"Just for one night, Rupert," she called after him.

"Yes, Momma," his voice echoed back from somewhere far away.

Wetherby saw the byplay and grinned. "The little devil!"

Her laughter caught him off guard. "Yes, he is sometimes." The smile was still on her face as she turned to look up at him. "Good night, my lord."

Wetherby raised one eyebrow. "I believe you forgot something, Mrs. Copley," he said. And without so much as a by-your-leave, he cupped her face in his hands and kissed her on the cheek. "Good night," he said.

He smelled of wine and slightly of tobacco, and Millicent heard him chuckling as he walked away from her. Her hands went to her face. My goodness, whatever had he meant by that? Lord Wetherby's inclination to kiss came at the oddest and most unexpected times, she thought, as she scurried to her room.

* * *

Wetherby caught up to Rupert halfway down the corridor. God! Fine escort he was turning out to be. He'd wanted to take Mrs. Copley in his arms and kiss her thoroughly. He was totally reprehensible, he thought with a grin. It had to be the candle-light and the wine.

"My chambers are here," he said to Rupert, opening the door and calling inside. "Jespers, Master Rupert will be staying in the room across the hall tonight. Would you fetch him a pitcher of water and some towels." That done, the marquis walked into the room opposite and lit the candle on the table beside the bed. It was a pleasant room with a sizeable bed, a single window, and the usual table, chair, and chest of drawers—but it was very cold. Wetherby changed his mind. "Come back to my room, and while you are getting ready for bed, I shall have Jespers start a fire for you."

That seemed like a good idea to Rupert, and he picked up his portmanteau and sword and followed Lord Wetherby back across the hallway. The marquis's room was much bigger—and warm. Jespers came out of a connecting door, carrying a towel. "The housekeeper will have gone to bed by now, your lordship. I shall give Master Rupert one of your linens and go down to the kitchen to get the water."

Wetherby gave him instructions to set a fire, and sent him on his way.

It didn't take long for Rupert to divest himself of his clothes and pull on his nightshirt. Meanwhile, Wetherby had shrugged out of his coat and vest and donned a dressing robe. He was standing in front of the blazing grate when Rupert came out from behind the screen washed and pink-cheeked from his efforts. For the first time, Wetherby saw the resemblance to his mother. The boy stood politely, waiting.

"Would you like to sit by the hearth until Jespers has a fire going in your room?" Wetherby asked, indicating one of the chairs that were placed opposite each other.

Rupert climbed into one of the highbacks, clasped his hands in his lap and turned an expectant smile on the marquis.

Wetherby cleared his throat. What did one say to a six-year-old when one wasn't trying to pry for information? "I thought your mother looked quite lovely in her new shawl tonight at dinner." The frown that had bothered Wetherby in the coach and at dinner reappeared, and he was at a loss as to the reason. "Does it bother you that I bought your mother a gift?"

"Oh, no, my lord," Rupert said, wriggling uncomfortably. "It is just that . . . It is just that when you bought the pretty shawl, I was reminded that I had no Christmas present for Momma. I saved my pennies all year, but we had to leave so quickly there was no time for me to buy her a present. Then in Horsham this morning, I was going to give some money to the poor children in the alleyway, until I realized that if I did I would not have enough left to buy Momma something. Was that selfish of me, my lord?"

So that was what had been bothering the lad. Wetherby thought back to the incident. He remembered ringing a peal over Rupert's head for going into an alley full of beggars, but until now he'd not put any significance on seeing Mrs. Copley coming out of that same alley, closing her reticule. The impossible woman had given the ragamuffins some of her own blunt. This Wetherby couldn't understand. "No, I do not think it at all selfish," he said to Rupert. "You say you have not bought your mother a present yet. Do you have something in mind?"

"I was thinking of buying her a bow and arrows—she bought me a nice set last year—but when I saw how much she liked your gift, I began to think that perhaps she would like something different."

Wetherby had a hard time trying to conceal his smile. "When we leave here day after tomorrow, we will be going through a rather large town with many fine shops. Would you like for me to help you select something more . . . more appropriate for your mother?"

"Oh, would you, my lord?" A glimmer of hope shined in the boy's eyes. "I think you get a good mark for that." Rupert turned thoughtful for a moment. "Does that come under Code Number Three or Five, do you think?"

"What is this *code* you keep speaking of?"

Rupert turned a knowing look at Wetherby. "You know, the Code of Chivalry—like the stories you told me in London."

Wetherby looked at him with amazement. "You remembered those?"

"Oh, yes, and Mr. Tipple read to us a lot about knights of old and how brave and noble they were. Wait!" he said, jumping down from the chair and going to the table where he'd placed his portmanteau. He opened it and pulled out an oblong, leather-bound journal. He returned to the hearth and placed the open book on the marquis's knees. "Mr. Tipple said that each night I should review what I have done during the day. He told me to put a star for the good things and an *X* for the bad."

Wetherby ran down the list: One, Faithfulness. Two, Loyalty. Three, Respect. Four, Valor. Five, Ladies. Before he could query further, Rupert had turned several pages.

"See, my lord, I have even started a column for *you.*"

Wetherby's gaze became riveted on the first mark. "What is this star for?"

"That is when you insisted John Coachman ride up back because he banged his head."

Wetherby didn't know that the boy had noticed.

Rupert continued, "This one is for when you picked Momma up off the floor of the coach." He pointed to two stars beside *Number Five.* "This, of course, is when you rescued Miss Clara. I thought that deserved two stars, don't you?"

Wetherby winced. His life had been on stage and he hadn't been aware of it. What else had the boy seen? He supposed he'd be sorry for his next question, but he asked anyway. "What are these *X*'s for?"

Rupert blushed. "That is when you took the Lord's name in vain. I'm not quite sure if that belongs on *One* or *Two.* You have quite a few of those, my lord," he said apologetically.

An uneasiness ran through Wetherby's conscience, and he flipped back to Rupert's page. "I see you put similar marks beside the same numbers, Faithfulness and Loyalty."

Rupert sighed. "I said *the word,* too. I thought if you said it, it must be a way of praying, but . . ."

"But, your mother did not take it that way," Wetherby finished.

Rupert looked sheepish. "Momma said it was swearing, and I was not to do it again."

Wetherby raked his fingers through his hair. "My God! That is my . . . goodness," he changed quickly. *'Tis more than enough that I must chaperone the unpredictable Mrs. Copley and her eagle-eyed son, but am I to be monitored for everything I say or do for the entire next two weeks, as well?* "Those sound like your mother's rules, not a warrior's."

"Oh, Momma would be a splendid knight, my lord—if she were not a woman. Women are frail creatures to be protected, are they not? That is rule Number Five." Rupert paused a moment to reflect. "Momma says that my father was the bravest of soldiers. She said he looked so handsome in his uniform. Did you know my father?"

"I did—and your mother was right. I never met a more valiant officer."

Rupert smiled proudly, and Wetherby wondered what it must be like to be so worshiped by wife and son. Captain Copley had been a fortunate man.

Wetherby closed the book and attempted to change the subject. "I wonder where Jespers is? You should be able to go back to your room as soon as he has a fire going." Saying this,

Wetherby looked expectantly at the door, but when his usually prompt valet did not appear, he sighed and said, "Is there anything else you would like to do?"

"I haven't said my prayers yet. Momma always listens to them."

"Oh, yes—of course," Wetherby answered. He couldn't remember the last time he'd done any praying—unless it was at the gaming wheel.

Rupert looked across the room. "My bed at home is not as high as yours."

Wetherby didn't know what was expected of him, so he remained sitting where he was.

"If it is all right with you, I will kneel here," Rupert said.

"Oh, yes. I suppose that will do."

Rupert knelt down in front of the marquis and steepled his hands against his legs. His prayers were lengthy, and included all of his family and seemingly everyone in the entire town of Cross-in-Hand. Wetherby even found himself included. "I am sorry if his lordship forgets *Your* rules now and then, God, but Momma says he will be a duke someday, and I suppose that is a great burden to undertake—so if *You* want, I shall be most happy to remind him when they occasionally slip his mind." Finally winding down, he said, "I will hear your prayers now if you wish, my lord." Truthfully, Rupert wanted very badly to hear what a man prayed about.

Wetherby was obliged to say something, so he mumbled a few unintelligible words, adding some *"Bless my's,"* and hoped his attempts passed muster.

"A man does not use as many words as a woman, does he, my lord?"

Jespers appeared at that moment and saved his master's supplications from further scrutiny. "I have fetched a pitcher of water and built a fire in Master Rupert's room, your lordship."

Wetherby felt Rupert's hands tremble against his legs. He

didn't know why he did so, but he reached down and took one of the boy's hands in his. Rising, he walked Rupert to the adjoining dressing room. "Would you like to sleep in here tonight?" he asked.

"But isn't this where Jespers sleeps?"

"I do not think Jespers will mind staying in the room across the hall."

The subject of their conversation raised his eyebrows but said nothing. Quietly collecting his nightshirt and a few other articles, the servant started toward the door.

On seeing the embarrassed look in Rupert's eyes, Wetherby leaned over and made an aside behind his hand. "Besides, Jespers snores abysmally. I hope you do not snore."

"Oh, no, your lordship. Not so as anyone has complained," he whispered back.

"Good, good, then we shall make good sleeping companions, you and I."

While Rupert and Lord Wetherby contemplated the heavy burdens of chivalrous behavior, Millicent was in her room receiving lessons in the importance of artifice and deception.

In a chair across from her, Lady Caroline studied her protégée. "You say that you have been invited to a country party at Sir Gifford Maudlin's in Hampshire?"

Millicent nodded.

Caroline made a grand sweep of the room with her arm. "Then let us imagine that a gentleman of the first stare has arrived at the ball. His piercing eyes take in every woman in the room. They settle on you for just a second. Now keep your fan in your left hand—that means you have some desire to make his address . . ."

Millicent giggled. "Why don't I just ask a friend to introduce us?"

Caroline raised her gaze to the ceiling. "No, no, no!" she

scolded. "He must come to you, you ninny. Intrigue. Mystery. That is what attracts a man to a woman. Though I truthfully can say I doubt that you will ever be able to attract anybody of any consequence."

Millicent sighed. "I am afraid I am not too intriguing."

"Listen to me. Take your fan and let it rest on your right cheek."

Millicent did.

"That means, *Yes.*"

"*Yes*, what?"

Caroline sighed in resignation. She knew full well that her charity toward the young widow was doomed to failure. "That is what you want the gentleman to ask. He will seek you out just to satisfy his curiosity." She sat back a moment and laughed.

"What is so funny?"

"I was just thinking about a party two years ago where three young bucks all started in my direction at the same time from three different places in the ballroom. They collided in the middle of the floor and knocked each other over."

"Oh, you must have some fascinating stories to recount," Millicent said, laying her fan in her lap.

Caroline leaned forward and spoke confidently. "Well, I have had my share of admirers."

"Do tell me all about them."

The genuine interest in Millicent's eyes was an impelling temptation for Caroline to set aside her original plans of making a flirt of the young widow—especially now that she'd admitted to herself that it was a lost cause anyway. So for the next two hours she regaled Millicent with stories of all the broken hearts she'd left behind over the last three years. However, the one thing Caroline didn't tell her was that she was readying the final battle plans for her one last conquest, the Marquis of Wetherby. "It is too bad that I must leave tomorrow, or I would have given you more instructions," she said, preparing to exit the room. "Just remember to be mysterious."

"I shall try," Millicent said, realizing for the first time why she'd only attracted such dull fellows of late. "Thank you for the fan."

"Think nothing of it," Caroline said. "I did not like it anyway. The lace is unraveling and the colors are too dull."

Wetherby went riding the next morning. To his surprise and some annoyance, he found Lady Caroline up and ready to accompany him.

"Good morning, Ernest."

"You are looking lovely as usual," Wetherby said. He had to admit that Caroline was the picture of pulchritude, the pink of the *ton.* She wore a scarlet riding outfit with a black velvet bonnet, its sweeping brim and scarlet plumes an appropriate setting for her yellow hair. But the whole picture didn't attract him as it once had.

"We might as well go together, since we seem to be the only ones of a sporting nature."

Caroline was right on that account. John Teagardner, with his expanding girth, had told the marquis that he himself found carriages much more to his liking; but he admonished Wetherby to select from his stables any mount that he wished.

Although Rupert had been reluctant to sleep in the nursery the night before, he'd been agreeable to Wetherby's suggestion that he go entertain the twins after breakfast.

"Just like you did for me in London when I was little," Rupert said, remembering.

"Exactly. Except that I think amusing two children instead of one will earn you another star, Master Rupert," Wetherby called out, watching the boy skip up the stairs.

Wetherby was now without companionship for a morning ride, for he supposed Mrs. Copley would stay abed late. He rather missed seeing her this morning. He'd wanted to explore a path through the dense forest, but Caroline had had other ideas, and had set her horse on a tamer trail, skirting much of the medieval part of the woods. It made little difference to him, so he followed. He looked back and saw her groom riding behind at a discrete distance.

"Knowing how particular you are about what is under you, I am surprised you did not bring one of your own horses, my lord."

Wetherby studied Caroline through heavy lids. "I shall ignore your barb, Caro. There was no way of knowing what weather we would encounter this time of year on a cross-country trek. I wasn't going to take the chance of one of my fine racers stepping into a mud hole and breaking a leg. Besides, most of the estates I am visiting have plenty of cattle, and Lord Copley has assured me that now that he has regained his fortune, his stables are well stocked also."

"I have other invitations, too."

"Then you will be off after breakfast?" he asked hopefully.

"Actually, I plan to leave after we have our noon meal."

They were now on an open road, and without having to say anything, they let their horses break into a gallop. Wetherby had to admit, Caroline was an excellent horsewoman. "Don't you think we should turn around now?" he asked.

"Oh, they don't expect us back 'til later," she said, nonchalantly taking the next path.

Suspicion made Wetherby turn in his saddle. He hadn't really been paying attention to the road behind them, and now he saw that they were being followed by a donkey cart, as well as the groom.

Caroline smiled. "Mrs. Teagardner gave me the direction to their hunting lodge. She said they pay an old forester to keep a fire going all winter in case anyone wants to use it. I asked Cook to pack us a picnic basket. I hope you don't mind."

"You know I don't like your maneuvering, Caro."

She threw a pretty pout. "You have to be hungry, darling. Surely you will not say *no* to Bolognese sausages, chicken pie, and slices of lamb . . ." her voice trailed off. "I do believe that besides some of her finest breads, Cook has included some cheeses, fruits, and nuts, and of course wine."

Wetherby could hear his stomach rumbling. "Stop! I beg for mercy."

"I knew you would not be difficult."

He held up his hands in surrender. "Does a starving man have much choice?"

Caroline reined up in front of a wooden structure, more cottage than lodge. Smoke curled from the chimney. "It looks as if we were expected."

By the time they arrived back at the manor later that afternoon, Caroline's coach was at the front entrance awaiting her. She didn't bother to change her clothes, but after making her *adieus* to the Teagardners, she boarded with her companion and set off. John remained outside to see them off.

The picnic lunch hadn't been as unpleasant as Wetherby had anticipated. Lady Caroline was in fine fettle: charming, witty, very beautiful, and not at all pushy. The two servants sat at a discreet distance in another corner of the room, eating. If Wetherby didn't know her better, he'd have thought Caroline to be an unselfish and caring person. The cottage had been warm and comfortable and they'd stayed much longer than he'd planned. However, now that they were back at the manor house and Caroline was gone, he looked for his charges. "Where is Mrs. Copley?"

"Why I have no idea, my lord," Mrs. Teagardner said. "Lady Caroline asked that a picnic lunch be packed, and I gave her directions to our hunting lodge. She mentioned that Mrs. Copley said something about going into the forest. I took for granted that she was with you."

Apprehension filled Wetherby. "Call Master Rupert. He went up to the nursery to play with the twins."

"He was there early this morning, but Nurse Picking said his mother came to fetch him soon after. The maid told me that Master Rupert was talking nonstop about dragons the whole time."

"Good God!" Wetherby said. "It will be dark in a couple of hours."

"What is the matter?" Teagardner asked, coming into the room.

"Oh, my dear," said his wife, "Millicent and Rupert have come up missing."

# Seven

"Surely she must be close about," Mrs. Teagardner said, as she instructed Bangs to assemble all the servants. "We shall ask everyone if they have seen them."

Since Miss Picking's midmorning sighting, no one had.

The stablemaster reported as soon as he came in, "All the cattle taken by his lordship's party are back in the stables, including the donkey cart."

"Then that means they are on foot," Wetherby said.

"Oh, my goodness, no one would go far afoot in this weather." Mrs. Teagardner protested.

Wetherby found himself becoming more and more ill-at-ease. "It is better we spread out in different directions. I know they did not go the west road or we would have seen them."

"Yes, yes, right you are," Teagardner blustered, waving his arms about in great circles. The serving maids flew to search the kitchen gardens and around the manor house. The stableboys said they'd check the outbuildings, and the older men fanned out into the woods surrounding the park.

Mr. Teagardner called to Popper to bring his coat and hat. "I shall take the phaeton and cover the lanes in and about the immediate area. Surely Mrs. Copley and Master Rupert are on one of the paths and have just wandered farther than they realized."

"There is always the forest," Wetherby said, not wanting to think that a possibility. But Miss Picking's mention of dragons was Wetherby's only clue. Rupert had been so positive that he'd find a dragon in the forest. Therefore, Wetherby reasoned, that is exactly where Rupert and his easily persuaded mother would have gone.

The denseness of the ancient monarchs was so forbidding that even Wetherby would hesitate under normal conditions to go in alone. However, he had no choice. So while Teagardner was having a team of bays hitched to his family carriage, Wetherby singled out a broad-backed farm horse, much like the medieval destriers ridden by armored knights. Such a mount could better traverse the rugged hillsides, and, God forbid—carry an injured or unconscious person out.

"If we don't find them by dark," Teagardner said, "I'll have word sent to the authorities in Haslemere first thing tomorrow and request a search party."

Half an hour later, Wetherby came upon them by chance in a glen. All traces of snow had disappeared, leaving a musty ground cover of mud and rotting leaves. First, he heard a voice—a very loud voice. The violent pounding and cracking sounds that followed brought to mind a wild beast crashing through the forest. Hurriedly, he dismounted. Leaving his horse tied to a tree, he crouched low and ran toward the ruckus. From where he hid, he could see only Mrs. Copley teetering atop an outcropping of rock, her hand clutched to her breast, obviously in great distress. Wetherby was about to spring into action to save her from a nasty fall when from the foot of the rock he heard Rupert's voice, calling out encouragement. "Fear not, fair damsel, I shall slay the dragon and set thee free."

Not quite believing what he heard, Wetherby parted the branches of the bush and leaned closer. He heard the *whack* and saw a dead branch thud to the ground. He glimpsed an incensed Rupert, arms uplifted, sword in hand. The boy was shouting his words as if he were reciting verse.

*"The valiant knight's sword cut a wide arc in the air. The blade came down, hitting its mark, Crack! The demon beast fell to the ground. Triumphantly, the warrior looked up at the pretty damsel*

*quivering precariously on the tall rock, trying to keep her footing. Thee need fear no more, my lady, he cried. I have saved thee!"*

Rupert bowed.

Millicent splayed her hands across her chest. "That you have, my brave knight. Surely I would have been devoured by the beast if you had not rescued me."

Wetherby, caught up in the fanciful sights and sounds unfolding before him, nearly became oblivious to the danger of his being discovered.

Rupert placed his foot solidly on the dead branch he'd whacked from the tree. " 'Tis a pity, Momma, that there are no more dragons to slay."

Millicent laughed heartily. "Thank goodness for that!"

"Well, I do not feel that way," Rupert complained. He wiped the leaves and bark from his sword. "*Women are frail things to be protected,*" he said. "*They are cherished and honored, to be watched from afar and never handled roughly.*"

"Ahah," Wetherby said, under his breath. "Number Five of the Code, if I remember correctly."

"Oh, posh!" Millicent said. "At the moment I don't want to be watched from afar, young man. Give me your hand; this rock is slippery."

"Of course, fair lady," Rupert said, sheathing his sword and clambering up the short slope to help his mother.

Wetherby was tempted to step forward, but if he did, Mrs. Copley would know he'd been spying on them. He didn't want to add eavesdropping to her list of his failings. Besides, Rupert seemed to have things firmly in control.

Millicent accepted her son's hand and stepped carefully off the rock.

"I think it vastly unfair that the knights of old did not leave at least a few dragons to slay, don't you, Momma?"

Millicent set her bonnet straight and brushed off the few leaves that had clung to her pelisse. "I believe we have enough dragons to face in this life without adding to the lot." Suddenly, she looked up through the canopy of trees. "My goodness! Wherever did the time go? If we do not hurry, dear, we shall be caught in the dark."

Wetherby had already backed off to where he had the horse tethered. He mounted and waited until he heard them approaching before making himself known. He hoped it would appear that he'd run into them accidently. "What a surprise, Mrs. Copley. I was myself just on my way back to the manor." He thought he saw relief in her eyes.

"May I offer you a ride? I am sure you are exhausted after being out all day," he said.

She eyed him warily. "I don't believe so, my lord."

"The animal is nothing to be afraid of—"

"Oh, I did not mean—" She got no further.

The marquis leaned down and in one movement, slipped his arm around her waist and swooped her up onto his lap.

Millicent gasped.

He put his face down close to hers and spoke for her ears only. "Madam, I do not have time for missish vapors. The horse is perfectly safe."

Millicent snorted.

Rupert stood with his head straining back, eyes transfixed, staring up at the marquis.

Wetherby reached down his hand to him. "Well, Master Rupert, what say you?"

Rupert grabbed the gloved hand. "Oh, I should like that above anything, your lordship."

"Well, at least one of you is agreeable," Wetherby quipped, swinging the boy up behind him.

Millicent wanted to glare at him, but the rim of her bonnet, already smashed beyond repair, wouldn't permit her to do so. Besides, any movement was nigh impossible, the way his arm held her prisoner against his body.

"We had best hurry. 'Twill soon be dark as Hades, and I do not particularly look forward to spending the night with you in this medieval jungle. The temperatures will most likely plunge to freezing."

Millicent attempted to thrust an elbow into his stomach, not that it did much good, taking into consideration their thick apparel.

Wetherby chortled, picturing her standing on top of the rock. Actually, it might be quite enjoyable holding Mrs. Copley all night. Yes, the little widow was showing far more pluck than he had first thought her capable of. "I believe the Teagardners will be waiting for us."

Millicent held onto her hat. "Lady Caroline bid me good-bye last night. She said she was leaving early today, and I need not get up to see her off. Did she?"

So Caroline had schemed to keep Mrs. Copley from attending their picnic. "Yes, she has gone."

"I shall miss her," Millicent said.

Wetherby felt that the woman *missed* the point altogether. "Yes, Lady Caroline has a way of leaving an empty void whenever she departs," he said.

"She is so gracious—and generous. And I think she likes you, my lord."

Wetherby smiled in amusement. "You don't say. I had not noticed."

"Men of your ilk probably wouldn't."

Wetherby wasn't quite sure what she meant by that, but under the circumstances, he felt it might be too dangerous to ask. Instead he pulled her even closer. That shut her up.

Rupert squeezed his arms tighter around the marquis. "Oh, this is jolly, your lordship. Can't we go faster?"

"Hang on," Wetherby warned, and with a shout of laughter, he urged the horse into a gallop.

The moment they burst out of the forest, the wind whipped

their faces and the rain fell, but they arrived back at the manor house just before dark. Rupert heralded it all as a great adventure, but what surprised the marquis the most was that not once did Mrs. Copley scream or cry. In fact, if his ears hadn't been filled with the capricious howling of wind and rain, he'd have said that he'd heard her laughing.

They stayed another day with the Teagardners. Wetherby wrestled with his conscience. He was trying his best to take on the responsibilities delegated to him by the baron, but he was beginning to question his abilities—and his patience—at being guardian to two free spirits such as Mrs. Copley and her six-year-old boy. His experience with widows had been much differently directed, and as for children, the only ones he knew were his nieces and nephews. He gave them presents, and then they were hustled off to the nursery.

That evening when the men joined the ladies after dinner in the library, Mrs. Teagardner excused herself to go check on the twins, and her husband hauled Rupert over to a particular shelf of books. Wetherby grabbed the opportunity to approach Millicent. She sat by herself in a corner of the room making those crazy gyrations with her wrists that he'd seen before. "Mrs. Copley . . ." he began.

The minute she saw him, her face turned red, and she quickly clasped her hands in her lap.

Her reaction momentarily threw him off balance, but he recovered himself nicely and continued, "Andersen, Lord Copley, has entrusted you to my care. You don't seem to realize the start you gave us when you disappeared for hours. In the future, you are not to go anywhere unless you are accompanied by me or one of my men." He thought his request a reasonable one, but Mrs. Copley obviously didn't agree.

"That is ridiculous!" she quipped. "Why, in Cross-in-Hand . . ."

Wetherby gave her his best scowl. "While you are under my care, madam, you will obey me. Is that understood?"

He was afraid she was going to come back with another argument when he discovered Rupert dancing up and down at his elbow.

"Oh, your lordship," he said breathlessly, "you must come see the book about King William's knights that Mr. Teagardner has found. Perhaps we can read it before we go to bed. Momma, may I stay with Lord Wetherby tonight? Please?"

Wetherby kept his gaze on the boy. "That is a splendid idea, Rupert. I should like that." Then, grasping at straws, he bowed to Millicent. "Excuse me. I believe Teagardner is signaling me." With a grin, Wetherby made his escape before Mrs. Copley could ring a peal over his head.

Millicent pursed her lips, but Rupert paid no heed. "It is only one more night. Please, Momma. Let me stay with Lord Wetherby."

She shrugged. The man was impossible. but her son was even more persistent. "Oh, all right. But just tonight."

"Thank you, Momma," he cried, running back across the room toward where the two men stood talking.

Millicent wrung her hands. What was she thinking of? Her problem was that she could never say *no* to Rupert. She watched her son become engaged in a deep discussion with Lord Wetherby. Curiosity engulfed her. Of course, she certainly wasn't interested in the marquis, but as a mother, she just wanted to know what he talked about to her son when they were alone. She'd questioned Rupert to find out. Rupert told her about Jespers letting him have his room and how he and Lord Wetherby had said their prayers together. She couldn't picture the marquis talking to God. Well, after tonight, she would be the one to hear her son's prayers and tuck him into bed.

* * *

"Momma is ever so much fun," Rupert said, later that night as he got into his nightshirt.

Wetherby tried to hide his amusement. Although he'd witnessed the whole episode, he encouraged Rupert to recollect the entire dragon fight.

"But it would be so much more jolly if we had someone to play the dragon. Grandpapa says his lumbago hurts too much to hop around—and what good is a dragon that cannot huff and puff and rear up on his hind feet?" He looked at Wetherby hopefully. Rupert sighed. Lord Wetherby didn't seem overly eager to volunteer for that part, so he brought out his journal and they contemplated which marks they deserved.

Wetherby put his arm around Rupert's shoulders. "Indeed you displayed *Valor* and *Respect,* however . . ." Wetherby said, looking into the two big brown eyes and clearing his throat. "There is one matter—of *Loyalty.*"

"I didn't swear," Rupert said.

"No, no, I didn't mean that. There is also a matter of loyalty to your country, your king, and your liege lord. Your uncle has appointed me your guardian. You and your mother went out without my permission. I have spoken to her about this omission already. But I am afraid we shall have to put an *X* down in your journal." The destitute look in Rupert's eyes made Wetherby melt a bit, but he knew that if he was to have any peace during the remainder of their journey, he had to be adamant. "Just a small *x,*" he said, marking an almost invisible letter on the page. "Have I made myself clear?"

Rupert nodded solemnly.

"Well then," Wetherby said, with a bit more joviality, "I do believe it has been an exceptionally good day, and that we both deserve several stars."

"Except for one thing, my lord," Rupert said.

Wetherby raised his eyebrows. "And what is that?"

"I think Momma would like you a bit better if you did not tell her what to do."

"I disagree," Wetherby said. "Consider Number Five. Aren't women frail things to be protected?"

Rupert chewed on his lip. That part of the Code still puzzled him. However, the marquis was an older man and knew all about ladies, so he must be right.

"Now, it is time to say good night," the marquis said.

Rupert knelt at the marquis's feet and listened, then mumbled his own prayers the way his lordship did.

Wetherby winced. He'd have to do better next time, or Rupert's mother would have his hide.

The following day, the weather became Wetherby's ally in that it was so disagreeable that no one was able to go outside, and Millicent couldn't have disobeyed his order even if she'd wanted to.

They spent their time engaging in games of cards, playing with the twins, or just making pleasant conversation. Although it was a far cry from what he'd pictured his holiday to be, Wetherby was surprised to find that he was enjoying himself. Millicent and Mrs. Teagardner played with the twins, and though he couldn't bring himself to play the part of the dragon, he afforded he saw nothing unmanly about John Teagardner down on the floor with the children, roaring about in a most ferocious way.

"To Basingstoke," Wetherby called up to John Coachman just before entering his carriage the next morning. Settling himself beside Jespers, he explained to Millicent, "Not only is it on the wide mail-coach road going west toward Sir Gifford Maudlin's Hampshire country seat, but it is a growing town that should afford you a larger range in shops. As the cloth industry is increasing, it is spilling over into the rural towns surrounding greater London."

It had not escaped Wetherby's notice that Mrs. Copley was wearing the purple-pink shawl that he'd given her. Although it gave her some color, it unfortunately still had to cover the same homely brown suit she'd worn each day of their travels. He found himself wanting to buy her something prettier. Perhaps a deep purple traveling suit with gold trimming. Or something in a silver-gray to match her eyes. After all, Wetherby did consider himself somewhat of a connoisseur of women's frocks. He'd paid enough to clothe his ladybirds over the years—and he always insisted on getting his money's worth from the modistes he engaged.

As soon as Wetherby had obtained rooms at the Hantsworthy Arms outside Basingstoke, he had John Coachman carry them into town.

The holiday spirit was evident everywhere. Sprigs of holly decorated market stalls, bells jingled on horses' harnesses, and happy moods brightened the faces of shoppers carrying armloads of packages tied with red ribbons. Fashionably bonneted ladies getting out of coaches to enter the milliners or drapers called "Happy Holidays" to each other, and men in high beavers tipped their hats as they entered the coffee or tobacco shops.

When they reached the center of town, Wetherby had his coachman drop them off near an apothecary's shop. "Pick us up around half six, John." They could explore to their hearts' content, and still have time enough to return to the inn for supper.

Wetherby found that there were two separate areas of shops they wished to see, and as soon as they had browsed through the bookstalls and market area, they had to proceed past a poorer section of old brick residences that had turned into rentals for the spreading population of factory workers. They also found a greater number of beggars on the streets than they'd seen previously on their journey: homeless soldiers in worn army uniforms, legs or arms missing, eyes bandaged;

ragged adults and hungry-eyed children huddled around fire-pots in garbage-strewn alleys.

Millicent, eyes wide, pulled her shawl tighter around her shoulders. "How terrible," she said.

Wetherby took her arm to hurry her on. "I am sorry you have to see this, but it is just a little farther to the shops I wish to show you."

"I did not mean . . ." she started.

Just then three little urchins, wrapped to their frostbitten noses in rags, spilled out of an alleyway. "Please mister," said a tiny, brown-haired snippet, "can you spare a ha'penny for some bread?" Behind them stood a woman with a baby in her arms, shivering in her thin tattered coat.

Millicent started to open her reticule. "What is your name, darling?"

"Betsy Collins, m'lady."

Wetherby didn't hesitate to step in front of Millicent and dig into his pocket. "Here, buy a whole loaf," he said, placing a coin in the small hand.

The child chirped, "Thankee!" and handed the money to her mother.

"God bless ye, sir," the woman said.

"That was kind of you, your lordship," Rupert said, gazing up with admiration.

Thankfully, it was only a short time until they burst onto a street lined with brightly decorated shops. Wetherby glanced at Millicent. He wished he could bring back a smile to her face as readily as he had to her son's, and he spent several minutes pointing to the holiday windows, a man with a monkey that held a cup, and a group of children singing carols on a street corner. Wetherby was glad to see Millicent's eyes brighten. He said in an aside to Rupert. "I shall keep a sharp lookout for a trinket for your mother."

"What are you two whispering about?" Millicent asked.

Rupert, his eyes dancing, put his finger to his lips.

Wetherby looked sheepish.

"His lordship was just asking me if we would like some hot chocolate and a jelly roll, Momma." Rupert said smugly.

Wetherby innocently glanced up and down the street. "Why, yes, that is exactly what I was saying."

Millicent tried unsuccessfully to hide her smile. "That would be very welcome. It is turning quite chilly."

"We just passed a very nice tea and confection shop called Grandmother Willowby's," Rupert said helpfully.

"Then Grandmother Willowby's it is," Wetherby said.

They spent the rest of the afternoon shopping, but no matter how diligently he searched, Rupert couldn't make a decision on a present for his mother. They had now made a complete circle of the town and were almost back to their starting point, when Lord Wetherby leaned over and spoke to Rupert. "Do you want to go back to the little jewelry store and look at the eardrops we were shown when we were in before? I think your mother would like them."

Rupert nodded.

Wetherby had noted that the proprietor's wife had the connecting shop, one that sold fabrics and laces made by the local women. He turned to Millicent.

"Would you like to revisit the little sundry shop on the corner? I saw you looking at some of the lace earlier."

While Millicent was occupied in looking at handkerchiefs, Wetherby and Rupert stole into the jewelers. They viewed the small display, but Rupert couldn't make up his mind.

"You aren't sure," Wetherby said.

For a few minutes, Rupert seemed preoccupied with watching something outside in the street. Then, looking once more at the eardrops, shook his head. "They aren't special enough."

Wetherby put his arm around the boy's shoulders. "Then we shan't take them. Never fear, we will be stopping in other villages. Now let us collect your mother and go back to the inn for a good supper." But when he looked for Millicent, she was nowhere to be seen. "Damnation!" he spouted. "Where the devil did she go?"

"I saw her go back in the direction of where all those poor people were huddled around the fire in the alley."

"Good God! That foolish woman!" Wetherby bellowed, grabbing Rupert and heading into the crowds billowing from the factories. He was too angry—and frightened—to worry about all the *X*'s he would be getting in Rupert's journal that night. "That is too rough an area for a lady to be walking alone. She could be . . ." He stopped midsentence. He didn't want to frighten Rupert with his own unsettling thoughts.

# Eight

Millicent was coming toward them when he saw her. Unhurt. She smiled when she spied him, and he wanted to run up and take her in his arms. But all he could say was, "Hell, woman! I ordered you not to go off alone."

Her eyes widened and her smile disappeared. It was then that he noticed she wasn't wearing the shawl he'd given her. "They stole your wrap. You are fortunate nothing worse happened. As soon as I get you away from here, I shall notify the authorities."

She grabbed his arm. "Oh, don't! It wasn't stolen. I gave it away."

Wetherby stared at her. "You did what?"

"I gave it to Mrs. Collins. I could not bear to think of her having such a threadbare coat. She told me her husband was injured in a factory accident, and they have been put out on the street."

Wetherby looked over her shoulder at the wretched woman bending over the open fire, wearing a cashmere shawl worth a king's ransom. He gritted his teeth and said, "I suppose you gave her some money, too?"

"I didn't have much, only enough to feed the children for a few days."

Wetherby shook his head in disbelief as he watched Rupert pull out his little drawstring bag. "Wait," he said, reaching into his own pocket. "Put your purse away and take this to the woman. It should be enough to get them lodgings for a while." He watched Rupert trot off, smiling. Wetherby knew good and well the blunt he was giving them should find the family a room and food for at least three months. Perhaps by then her husband would be well enough to go back to work.

They didn't speak again until they were in the coach going back to the Hantsworthy Arms. He should have been pleased that Millicent was once again looking on him with favor, but his own disposition was in a hole. Why the shawl? Did she think so little of him that she could so easily throw away the present he'd given her?

Rupert seemed to hold the same question in his mind, but he wasn't as reticent in seeking the answer.

"Why did you give away your pretty shawl, Momma?"

Wetherby folded his arms across his chest and waited to hear what Millicent had to say to that. Of course, she couldn't know how much the shawl was worth. But he thought she could give him some credit for his generosity.

"What sacrifice is it to give something you can well afford to give, my lord?" Millicent said. "Remember, Rupert. A gift has more value if you give something you hold dear to your heart."

*Something you hold dear to your heart.* Wetherby pondered that for a moment. She'd meant his shawl; but then if it meant so much to her, how could she have given it away? He didn't understand at all.

Tomorrow they'd be at Maudlin's estate. Three days of parties. That should keep Mrs. Copley well enough occupied so he could enjoy himself.

The next day they arrived at Maudlin Manor. It was a grand house. Sir Gifford was only a baronet, but his was an old and distinguished family of great worth, and he'd married wealth as well. They were ushered into the drawing room to meet Lady Maudlin and her two smiling and rather good-looking daughters, Miss Prethoria Maudlin and Miss Angelina. Their eyes were all for the marquis.

"I am sorry Sir Gifford is not here to greet you, my lord,"

Lady Maudlin simpered, all the while watching Wetherby's reaction to her daughters. "We expect him and young Harry back from London by tomorrow."

Millicent had just curtsied to her hostess when Rupert squealed, "Momma! Momma! Lady Caroline is here. Isn't that stupendous?"

"What a pleasant surprise," Millicent exclaimed sincerely as she turned to see Caroline entering the room.

"My, oh, my!" Caroline gushed, acknowledging Millicent only slightly. She curtsied, and held out a gloved hand to Wetherby. "We do seem to turn up at the same places, don't we, my lord? It must be fate."

Wetherby took her fingers and gave her a crooked smile. "If you say so, Lady Caroline. You seem to have more inside information on those matters than I do."

Caroline looked with annoyance at the child dancing attendance in front of her. Then catching Wetherby's solicitous demeanor toward the boy, she extended her hand to him. "Master Rupert."

Rupert tucked his sword out of the way and took her hand in his, bowing exactly as he'd seen Lord Wetherby do—only deeper and longer. Her fingers smelled of dark flowers and exciting adventures, and he was reluctant to let them slip from his grasp. Once more, Rupert entered the gates of heaven.

Wetherby watched him and chuckled.

Caroline narrowed her eyes. Perhaps being nice to the boy would serve a purpose after all. She honored Rupert with a brilliant smile.

Guests continued to arrive. All of Maudlin Manor was in preparation for the Christmas Ball, to be held the following evening. Millicent got up to the nursery only briefly to see that Rupert was settled.

"Lord Wetherby has forgotten me altogether," Rupert commiserated.

"Now, darling, you know that his lordship did not expect to have to take us on his holiday, so we must try not to be a nuisance to him—or he may drop us by the wayside altogether," Millicent said, with a twinkle in her eye.

"Oh, Momma, do you think so?"

Millicent laughed. "Of course not, silly. A true gentleman always carries out his obligations."

Rupert glanced sideways at his mother, grinning. "You are bamming me again, Momma."

Millicent knew Rupert was unhappy. There were no children at Maudlin House, and he had been installed in the old nursery on the third floor with only the housekeeper's elderly sister, Mrs. Peesbody, to watch after him. "Think on the bright side, dear. We will only be here two more days, then off again to your Uncle Andy's."

"Then I shall pretend I am being held prisoner by a wicked sorcerer and he has appointed a wicked witch to guard me."

Millicent looked over at the old woman in black bombazine who was sitting in a rocking chair by the window, knitting. "Rupert, that is not kind of you. Mrs. Peesbody is probably just as uncomfortable having to stay up here with you as you are with her."

Rupert shuffled his feet.

"Perhaps if you try, you can find something you have in common."

Rupert looked doubtful.

"You be pleasant, now," she said, before she shut the door behind her.

That evening, Sir Gifford returned in time for dinner with his one and only heir. Mr. Harry Maudlin, a well-proportioned young man of three and twenty years, soft-spoken, with quick blue eyes.

There were twenty-four guests at the dinner table. Ascot

Delphinny, a bright young man dressed in the latest of fashion, accompanied the Maudlins back from London. Sir Richard, another Oxford man, had driven over with his mother. It was obvious to all that Lady Maudlin was making certain that there would be no shortage of dancing partners for the ladies at her ball.

Millicent soon realized that most of the guests were already acquainted and the conversation flowed freely among them. She wore her dark blue gown with a single strand of pearls, her hair pulled back and simply tied with a matching ribbon. She found herself seated far from both Lady Caroline and Lord Wetherby, the only two people she really knew. Therefore, she mainly listened, smiled, and observed the elegant crowd, admiring their fashionable clothes and their unabashed ability to flirt so freely.

Strangely, Wetherby noted that Caroline's attention was directed more toward Millicent than toward him, and he wondered at her motive. Her pursuit of him was obvious, and it was no secret that Lady Maudlin's purpose in inviting him to the party was to meet her daughters. Yet Caroline seemed to show no great concern over having Prethoria or Angelina throw themselves at him. Caroline's interest in anyone of her own sex was usually to size up her competition—however, that was not the half-lidded study she directed at the little widow. Wetherby found his suspicions growing.

It was to Millicent's great surprise, also, when she answered a knock later that night to find Lady Caroline standing for the second time in only a few days outside her bedroom door.

"May I come in?" she asked, sailing past Millicent and seating herself elegantly in a dainty chair.

Millicent didn't hesitate to welcome her visitor. "With all those people, I have not had a chance to tell you how happy I was to see you."

Caroline rearranged the folds of her gown over her knees.

"That is not why I am here. Why did you wear that terrible blue dress again?"

Millicent seated herself across from Caroline. "You said it looked better on me than my green or brown ones."

"But that evening I draped it with that lovely shawl that you said Wetherby had given you. Why did you not wear that?"

Millicent looked down at her hands. "I don't have it anymore."

"You cannot mean that he took it away from you? Wetherby may be a scoundrel, but he'd never take back a gift."

"Oh, he did not. I gave it away to a poor woman who had no warm wrap." When Millicent had finished telling Caroline the whole story, she was met with silence for one whole minute.

Then Caroline jumped up and pulled Millicent out of her chair. "Mrs. Copley," she said, "I can see that someone needs to take you in hand. What pray tell do you plan to wear to the ball tomorrow night?"

Millicent hunted for an answer, for it was a question she'd asked herself several times. "I did not think that I would be going to any fashionable parties. It was just to be a family affair at my brother-in-law's. Perhaps it would be better if I did not attend. Lady Maudlin really did not expect me."

Caroline walked around Millicent, studying her. "Nonsense! The party would not be the same without you."

"I fail to see why any festivities would be at a disadvantage with me not being there."

Caroline really wasn't listening. "We are of about the same height. Your waist is not as tiny as mine, but the styles are high-waisted anyway. I am sure I can find something in my wardrobe that would suit you."

"You would do that for me?"

"There are always a few frocks I never cared for much, and you might as well have one."

"You are just being modest, my lady. You are indeed one of the most generous persons I have ever met."

Caroline smiled and nodded. "Be that as it may, we must now think about your hair." She frowned. "Well, I shall send Suzette in tomorrow to see if she can do anything with it. I hope that you have been practicing how to flirt."

"Oh, I have," Millicent said. "Every day."

"Then you are ready."

Millicent didn't get near enough to Caroline to speak to her all the next day. The overnight guests were arriving by droves. She met nearly everybody, but they all seemed in such a hurry that they had no time to chat. The servants and handymen were putting the last-minute finishes on the decorations in the ballroom. The musicians arrived and began practicing, while the grand dining room was being readied for the dinner to be served to forty-eight special guests.

Later in the day, Millicent went to visit Rupert. It had started snowing and she had thought that he might like to take a walk outside, but to her surprise she found him happily playing chess with Mrs. Peesbody. "She has the most monstrous stories about the French Revolution, Momma. She told me how the poor people knitted names secretly into their sweaters and things. She is even showing me how to knit."

Relieved that Rupert was content, Millicent returned to her bedroom, where she found three pretty dresses laid out on her bed. She tried on all of them, each one lovelier than the next, and finally decided on a bright green with apricot trim.

True to her word, Caroline not only sent Suzette to set her hair, but came herself to supervise. Two maids followed, one with a box of cosmetics, the other with a jewelry box.

"Now," Caroline said, "I have picked young Maudlin to be your first victim. He is the perfect specimen for you to practice what I have taught you. Harry is also a good catch on the marriage mart, deep in the pockets and not difficult to look at."

Millicent tried to think of a last-minute excuse not to go at all. "But I am four and twenty with a six-year-old son."

"Posh! It only proves you can breed—all the better for a family who has only one son. Shows them you can produce the next heir."

Millicent flushed. "Why don't you take him?"

"Being the daughter of an earl puts me far above a mere baronet. Besides my sights are set much higher than yours can ever be. But you, my dear, are well enough connected, given your tie to the Countess of Dankleish and being the sister-in-law of a baron, to make it a good match."

"I would not want to marry a man I did not love."

"You have other considerations now that you have a son. He needs a father."

Millicent had to agree. She must think of Rupert.

Caroline clipped on the emerald eardrops and stepped back to survey her creation. "Now you look quite presentable."

Millicent was almost afraid to look at herself in the cheval mirror. "Oh, do you really think so?"

"Remember what I have taught you and you will have Harry eating out of your hand in no time. I have arranged to have him escort you to dinner."

"You haven't! However did you manage that?"

"My dear, never ask another woman how she maneuvers."

"Oh, I am sorry."

"Think nothing of it," Caroline said with a flip of her pretty head. She then turned her protégée around to face her reflection.

Millicent gasped, her fingers clasping the delicate jewelry that adorned her neck. "My goodness! Will you look at me." She laughed. "Oh, my lady, I shall never be as clever as you."

Caroline straightened one of the folds in Millicent's gown. "Of course not. But if you do as I say, you will come off well enough. Now don't forget to bring your fan," she flung back, sailing out the door.

Millicent obediently picked up the fan, and after shyly taking one more peek at her reflection, descended to the drawing room where all the guests were assembled.

Wetherby had barely caught a glimpse of Millicent all day. He'd gone riding in the morning with friends, and he could scarcely be rude to his hostess, who kept putting one or the other of her daughters in his path wherever he ventured. But his luck took a turn for the better when he ran into an old acquaintance, Lord Bently—a middle-aged widower and country gentleman who was lonely but well enough off, his children all out on their own. "The perfect match," Wetherby said to himself. "The perfect match for Mrs. Copley." *What better news could he take to Copley than that his sister-in-law had received an offer from a distinguished gentleman before she arrived in Devonshire?*

However, he was not quite prepared for what he saw when Millicent entered the drawing room. In her green gown, she appeared to be a spring flower, her cheeks pink and petal-soft . . . her lips . . . ? He decided the idea that came most readily to mind was not a proper one, so he commanded his attention to travel upward. Her eyes looked like those of a mischievous child peeking into forbidden territory—even her hair piled atop her head only made her seem younger than she was. "Bently is way too old for her," Wetherby said to himself. "Definitely so." But he had already made the arrangements. He saw his lordship making his way toward her, and there was nothing he could do to stop him now.

"Mrs. Copley?" The words came from behind her.

Millicent whirled and found herself face-to-face with a pleasant-looking gentleman. "Lord Bently!"

"I did not mean to startle you, my dear lady, but I am flattered to find you remembered my name."

Millicent blushed and fanned herself—and it wasn't even warm out. "Of course I remember you, my lord. I did not mean to jump. It was just that . . ." *Oh, dear, she couldn't tell him she was expecting someone else.*

Lord Bently made a leg and bent over her hand. "Lord Wetherby has been so kind as to obtain permission for me to escort you into dinner."

"But I thought . . ." Millicent began, only to find Harry Maudlin standing at her elbow. She became so flustered that she dropped her fan.

Both men dove to retrieve it, and the resulting *thud* told Millicent that their heads had collided.

Millicent's hand flew to her mouth. "Oh, my goodness. How clumsy of me. I've made you hurt yourselves."

Both men quickly denied any great damage, and only glared at one another.

Lady Caroline seemed to appear from nowhere, picked up the fan, and handed it to Millicent. "I am sorry, Lord Bently, but Lady Maudlin has appointed Harry to be Mrs. Copley's partner for dinner."

Confusion showed in Bently's eyes, but he bowed once again. "Then, I do hope you will save a dance for me this evening, Mrs. Copley."

Millicent took a deep breath and collected herself. "Why of course I shall, Lord Bently. Are you sure you are all right?" she said, touching his forehead. "I am afraid you are going to have a nasty bruise there. Do you want me to get you a cold press?"

Lord Bently grasped her hand in both of his, his eyes aglaze with adoration. "A dance will be all that I need to set me aright, kind lady. I shall be looking forward to it," he said, bowing off.

Caroline gave Millicent a knowing look and took her leave.

"Ow!" moaned Harry, holding his head with a most pained expression on his face.

"Mr. Maudlin!" Millicent exclaimed, looking quite guilty. "I did not mean to neglect you. It is just that Lord Bently is such a much older man than you, and I felt I must tend to his injury first. Someone as young and strong as you can suffer an injury much better than an older man, can you not?"

Harry quit moaning immediately. "Of course, Mrs. Copley," he said, extending his arm to her. "A mere bump on the head is nothing to a round of fisticuffs at Gentleman Jackson's in London."

Millicent switched her fan into her left hand to take his arm and fell into step with the others entering the dining room. "My, you must be very brave to stand up to a strong opponent. Tell me all about it."

He glanced at the fan in her left hand and leaned closer, a gleam in his eye. "You did drop your fan for me then."

Millicent blinked. What was it Lady Caroline had said about dropping one's fan? *Oh, my goodness, I do believe it means a lady wants to be friends.* But what was it about carrying it in her left hand? Did it mean she wanted him more—or less? Millicent blushed. From the look in Mr. Maudlin's eyes, she'd given him an invitation to be familiar. But it was too late now to tell him differently, because he had her right hand imprisoned in the crook of his arm.

The ball commenced and to her surprise, Millicent found herself dancing every dance. She watched in amazement as the other ladies twisted and turned their fans so easily, raised and lowered their lashes, laughed in funny little birdlike trills, and still didn't make one mistake in their dance steps. She tried her hardest, but she feared she was doing everything poorly. She liked to look into people's eyes when she spoke to them. She poked her own face when she unfurled her fan, and even banged Sir Gifford in the nose with it. She was afraid Lady Caroline would be very disappointed in her. But regardless of her *faux pas,* both Mr. Maudlin and Lord Bently had asked her to stand up for two dances, and when she declined a third with Mr. Maudlin, he said, "Then permit me to find you a seat where we can talk."

Millicent was suddenly aware of her tired feet and laughed. "I would like that above all else." She found herself in a tiny little alcove with statues at the entrance and green ferns that made it look like a garden. "How lovely," she said, chattering on about her mother's indoor plants, until she suddenly became aware that Mr. Maudlin was saying nothing. *Oh, dear, she thought, Lady Caroline said men don't like women who jabber.* Millicent tapped her mouth with the handle of her fan to remind herself not to talk so much.

Mr. Maudlin moved quickly. "Oh, my dear Mrs. Copley, I had not hoped—" Harry began, drawing her into his arms and kissing her fervently.

"Mr. Maudlin, please," Millicent gasped, pushing with all her might against his chest.

"But you . . . your fan . . ." he stammered.

Millicent looked down at Caroline's fan, crushed all out of shape. What had she done? "I did not mean—" she started.

"Of course, you did not mean we should do it *here.* My passion for you made me forget all propriety. Forgive me, please, dear lady," he begged.

Her hair had come loose and was falling over her eyes. Mr. Maudlin made an attempt to push the curls back into place, which only wrought more havoc. With a final shove, Millicent broke free. Humiliation turned her cheeks scarlet. Holding up her fan to hide her face, Millicent rushed from the alcove across the ballroom. All she wanted to do was get to her room before anyone saw her disarray, but she nearly tripped over young Ascot Delphinny, then ran into Sir Richard. Mumbling her apologies, she rushed into the hallway and headed toward the stairs.

Lord Wetherby was just finishing a country set with Miss

Angelina when he saw Millicent streak past with three young men trailing her. "What the devil?" he spouted, taking out after them. It was outside of enough that she had come dressed like a coquette, but then she'd had to get young Harry Maudlin and Lord Bently scrapping over her at dinner. Now it looked as if a three-way fight was about to begin. He pushed past the trio and caught up with her on the stairs.

A curl covered one eye, and from the blush on her face and the swollen lips, Wetherby surmised that Mrs. Copley had just been kissed. Rage surged through him and he rounded on the three young bucks following her. His scowl soon sent them packing.

Millicent gave him a look that put him in the same category as her admirers, then turned and flounced up to the next floor landing.

Wetherby followed her. "Well, what did you think would happen after the outrageous way you have been flirting all evening?" He expected her to defend herself. Instead the tears began to flow down her cheeks, and to his surprise, he found his arms around her and her cheek against his chest. She didn't make a sound, but he could tell that she was crying. He stood for a moment not knowing what to do—an unheard-of circumstance for him when handling a female.

"Oh, I have made a mess of everything. I don't know how to flirt," she sobbed, giving him a good bang on the chest with her fist. "That is, I don't do a very good job of it, do I? Lady Caroline will be so disappointed with me."

"Caroline?" He should have known she'd have something to do with this. Wetherby held Millicent away from him and grappled for his handkerchief, which he handed to her. "Mrs. Copley," he said, "you were running through the room holding your fan in front of your face with your right hand."

Millicent looked at him blankly. "I didn't want anybody to recognize me, I was so ashamed."

Wetherby threw up his hands. "You were inviting every man you passed to follow you."

"I was?"

"You were."

The tears started again. "Oh, dear, what am I to do? Everyone will think me a fallen woman."

Wetherby had no choice but to fold her in his arms again.

# Nine

Wetherby held her away from him. "I should have kept an eye on you, but that is beside the point. Someone took advantage of you and I want to know who it was."

She looked him straight in the eyes. "I am not going to tell."

And Wetherby knew she wouldn't. "Then the first thing I want you to do is go to your room and fix your hair. I shall wait for you here. Then I will escort you down to the ballroom."

Millicent clasped her hands to her bosom. "I cannot go back down there!"

"You must. You cannot act the coward."

But that was exactly what she was, for she was wishing that he had been the one to have kissed her. "If I go back with you, they will think . . ."

Wetherby crooked an eyebrow. "They will think that you have just gone up to the retiring room to refresh yourself."

"No, my lord. With a reputation like yours, if I come back after such an interval, they will think that you are the one who has compromised me."

A knife struck the marquis in the stomach. He knew she was right. He watched her walk away from him, then returned to the ballroom by himself.

After her fiasco of the previous night, Millicent wanted to avoid having to face anyone in the household. Many of the guests were departing today, and she felt that she would not be missed. She rose late and had lunch with Rupert in the nursery, then took him outside for some fresh air. A thick layer of damp snow covered the ground, so they entertained themselves by walking in their own footsteps in and among the great trees that circled the gardens.

Now, Rupert patted out a large snowball and sent it flying toward a large oak—a satisfactory target for a while, but not for long. He scooped up another fistful and molded it carefully to just the right size. Eyeing his mother, who moved about the edge of the gravel path several feet away, he took aim and let go. The resulting squeal was quite satisfactory.

"You scamp!" she yelled, scooping up her own clump of snow. Her retaliating missile missed her retreating son—but her second one didn't, and caught him squarely between his shoulders.

Rupert yelped and hurried down a gravel path, his sword slapping against his leg with every step.

"You cannot get away from me," she called after him.

"Yes, I can."

Rupert ran around the side of the manor house and dove behind a thick tangle of rhododendron bushes to hide. He grabbed up a handful of snow and lay in wait for his mother to appear. But he'd no sooner settled himself than Lord Wetherby's familiar voice broke the silence on the other side of the hedge.

"Ah, my dear Miss Maudlin, you cannot ask me to decide which of all you lovely ladies was the most charming last night. Even Solomon was not as wise as that."

Several giggles accompanied his statement.

Rupert hunkered down and peeked under the bushes. If he was not mistaken, he spied not two skirts, but four surrounding the marquis's distinguishable fine leather boots that were coming his way. How was he ever to get Lord Wetherby to notice his mother when she was out in the woods and he was here with so many other women who demanded his attention?

Rupert rose, aimed, and fired. The snowball that he'd at first intended for his mother flew straight to its mark, and the resulting exclamation brought a smile of satisfaction to Rupert's face.

"What the deuce?" shouted Wetherby, as his high beaver hat flew off his head. Stooping to pick it up, he zeroed-in his gaze on the high bushes behind him. "Wait here, ladies. I believe I know where the culprit hides."

Rupert knew he was doomed, and was debating whether or not to make a run for it, when he heard a scream. Miss Maudlin's bonnet fell to one side of her head, and another snowball ripped through the air from the opposite side of the garden and hit Lord Wetherby full in the rear.

Rupert broke for the woods at the same time that he saw his mother speeding away along the outer edge of the formal gardens.

Coming to a stop under a stand of elms, Millicent raised her hands to her chest and gasped for air.

But Wetherby caught her.

Her blood had been pounding so loudly in her ears that she'd not heard his lordship's footsteps closing in behind her. From the stern look on his face, there was no telling what mayhem he intended, when a snowball smacked him in the side of the face.

Millicent fully expected a thrashing, but the eyes under the forbidding brows were laughing. "I surrender," he called out to his invisible foe.

Rupert came out of the trees, his sword raised, demanding, "Unhand that fair maiden, sir."

Before Wetherby released Millicent, he bent and whispered, "I really was quite bored to death with those schoolgirl misses, but I shall let Rupert think he rescued you. For no telling what your punishment would have been if he had not appeared when he had." He gave her a smile that she knew had probably been attracting women since he was in leading strings. A shiver of apprehension ran through Millicent. Oh, Lord Wetherby was indeed a dangerous man, for even she was becoming susceptible to his charms.

"Now," he said, wiping the snow from his face, "I believe we should be getting back to the manor house. It is, after all, our last evening at the Maudlins'."

Rupert sheathed his sword. "I hope you don't take offense, my lord."

"Oh, no . . . no, not at all. You did what you had to do to save the fair maiden. You have perfect aim."

Rupert let out a sigh of relief. "Momma, too. She can throw straighter than Jeremy Spitberry."

"Is that a fact?" Wetherby said, not missing the blush in her cheeks as he gave Millicent a sideways glance. "Well, Rupert, for your part in this afternoon's adventure, I believe you deserve a double star, for you rescued me as well as your mother." When he saw the question posed in Rupert's eyes, he laughed. "Some day you will understand what I mean."

The snow melted overnight, leaving no trace of its promised beauty. Jespers insisted he would ride up back with George, for the beginning of the journey, at least.

"We will have to travel most of the next two days to reach Tiverton," Wetherby announced as they climbed into their carriage the next morning.

His lordship was observing Millicent through shadowed eyes, and she had the horrible feeling that she was blushing. "We are not going straight on to Roxwealde Castle, my lord?"

There was a new sparkle in Mrs. Copley's eyes, and Wetherby prided himself to think that he might be the cause. He leaned back against the squabs with a sense of self-satisfaction. By the flirtatious looks the Maudlin sisters had been casting his way, he'd say that he'd had a successful trip so far to have captured three hearts in seven days. "Sir Jonathan Bridges and his sister live just beyond Tiverton and have invited us to stay over. From there it is only one day's journey to Roxwealde Castle."

"Oh, dear," Millicent said, "I still have presents to buy."

Wetherby tried to reassure her. "Tiverton is a wealthy wool town and has some fine shops."

Rupert eyed him intently.

Wetherby caught his thoughts and winked. "But if we see any interesting places along the way, we will stop," he said.

Rupert winked back, and felt quite pleased with his performance until he saw the look of disapproval on his mother's face.

Millicent glowered at Wetherby, and he was obliged to find something of great interest to study outside the window.

They visited two little villages that day. Millicent bought a little knitted cap for her nephew Percy, but Rupert found nothing of interest. "What if I cannot find a present for Momma, my lord?" he asked with a note of concern in his voice.

"We will find something, don't worry."

Wetherby tried to pass the time away by flirting with Mrs. Copley, but she seemed to have had enough of flirting. Maybe she wasn't as taken with him as he thought, and he began to fear that she was going to fall back into her habit of silence. For some reason the thought frightened him. Perhaps it was only to get her to smile, or to see her eyes light up, or wrinkle her nose the way she did when she was trying not to laugh—but he made a face at Rupert.

Rupert let out a *whoop* and proceeded to push up his nose and stick out his tongue.

Millicent turned horrified eyes first at her son, then at Wetherby.

The marquis found himself completely engrossed in the game. My God! He hadn't made faces for twenty years. Ignoring Millicent's glare. he pulled down his eyes and blew out his cheeks. "Nurse Jane used to hate that one," he said cheerfully.

Millicent felt the smile coming, in spite of the fact that she was using all her powers to stop it.

"See, Momma, his lordship can do it better than you."

The mirth rolled up from somewhere deep inside her, and Millicent broke into uncontrollable laughter. It wasn't until she realized that he was staring at her that she stiffened and tried to gain some semblance of dignity. But the tears kept coming.

Wetherby handed her his handkerchief.

Millicent dared a look at him. "Who was Nurse Jane?"

"She took care of my sister and me when we were at Orchid Hill." He saw the question on Millicent's face. "That was my mother's estate near Tunbridge Wells. The one I stay in most often now."

Millicent sat back and looked at him as if she really cared. No one had ever shown any interest in his upbringing before.

"Why there? The Lance family seat in Leicestershire is considered one of the most beautiful houses in England, and you must have accommodations in London."

"And an estate with twelve hundred acres in Kent, and many others which I cannot recall—" Wetherby added.

"Then why Orchid Hill?"

"It is mine. My mother left it to me when she died four years ago. My father bought the house for her when they were first married, because of its nearness to Tunbridge Wells. She found great solace in the waters and spent much of her last few years there. It was a small house, as houses go, and only a few dozen acres."

"That is a pretty name—Orchid Hill."

"Mother did not know of the orchids at first. She would bring my sister and me down with her when my father was in London. He hated the place. *Nothing to do,* as he put it. But Mother loved all the outdoors. One day while she was out walking, she came into a small gorge that was nearly hidden by the surrounding forest. There she discovered a surprisingly large array of rare orchids thriving on the chalk hillsides. She renamed the estate Orchid Hill."

Millicent's manner was now completely devoid of shyness. "It must be lovely to see in the spring."

"At one time, the conservatory attached to the house was filled with her orchids. I am afraid that it has been sadly neglected since she died."

Millicent looked into space as if she were viewing a picture. "What a pity. It must have been a sight to see."

Wetherby focused his gaze on Mrs. Copley. "Yes, it was."

They stayed the night in a crowded inn along the high road, and set out early the next morning. Wetherby insisted that Jespers ride inside with them now. It had started to snow sometime in the night, and it didn't look as if it were going to melt this time. The atmosphere was becoming much more Christmaslike wherever they went. They stopped at two towns to look in the shops, but Rupert found nothing for his mother.

It wasn't until the afternoon of the second day that Rupert saw the gift he was looking for. He tugged on Wetherby's arm to get his attention. It was a small shop called the Piddle-Dee-Dee, with mostly antique dishes and pottery strewn about the window. A dark oil painting was propped against the side, and in the corner was a china statue of a man and a woman in a court dress, embracing. "That's it," he said, pulling the marquis down to his level.

Wetherby thought a statue of two lovers an odd choice for a boy to make. "Are you sure you don't want to get her some jewelry?"

"No, no! That is the perfect gift for my Momma. It will remind her of Papa."

Wetherby swallowed hard. "If you are sure, I will see what I can do to distract your mother, and you can go in and have a closer look at it."

Rupert's eyes sparkled. "We'll fool her."

"By Jove! Right you are," Wetherby said, walking on up to Millicent. Jespers stood quietly behind. The marquis was glad he'd thought to have his valet come shopping with them. It took two to keep an eye on Mrs. Copley and her son, and Jespers seemed quite eager to accompany the young widow.

While they were talking, Rupert slipped into the shop. The clerk, however, didn't take kindly to a small boy wandering about his store, and Rupert was being led to the door by his ear when his lordship walked in.

"I am the Marquis of Wetherby," he said, much louder than was necessary, "and this young man is my charge."

"My lord," the clerk stuttered, giving Wetherby a frightened look before skittering off to the back of the shop. Barely a minute later, he returned with a skinny little man who was trying to tuck in his shirt, rake the few strands of hair over his bald head, and adjust his spectacles all at the same time.

"Your lordship," the man said. "How honored we are to have you in our store. Brixell's the name. Adam Brixell. Dealer in fine antiques."

Wetherby was actually surprised to see the fine quality of merchandise the man had. "We are interested in the china statue in the window."

Mr. Brixell hurried over to fetch the figurine, and handed it to Wetherby. "It is a fine piece, my lord. From the collection of a local squire who is needing to gain a little money."

To the shopkeeper's horror, Wetherby held the piece out to Rupert, who ran his finger over the delicate figures.

"Actually, it is Mr. Copley here who has the blunt and wishes to make the purchase," Wetherby said.

The shopkeeper looked from Rupert to the statue and swallowed hard. "And how much is Mr. Copley willing to pay?"

Rupert quickly pulled out his purse and began to dig out his coins, one by one. "I saved my allowance all year," he said proudly, as the little pile began to grow.

Mr. Brixell began to sputter.

Rupert looked startled. "Wait, I have a few more coins," he said anxiously.

Wetherby had the horrible feeling that if he didn't act swiftly, the little boy's heart would be devastated. "Mr. Brixell, I saw a snuff box over here that interests me very much. While Mr. Copley is getting his money, would you please show it to me?"

Five minutes later, they returned to an anxious Rupert, who showed them twelve neat stacks of coins.

"Now Mr. Brixell will count it and see if it is enough," Wetherby said, sticking a small package in his pocket.

Mr. Brixell's disposition had mellowed remarkably in the last few minutes, and he very carefully picked up and called out each coin.

"Is it the right amount?" Rupert asked, a worried look on his face.

"Well, not exactly," Mr. Brixell began. "Actually, I owe you two pence back."

Rupert let out such a sigh of relief that Wetherby was afraid he'd blow Mr. Brixell away.

"It is very delicate, you know," Wetherby said, frowning at the statue.

"I shall take very good care of it, your lordship," Rupert assured him.

"I can have it wrapped," Mr. Brixell said. "I shall see to it personally. And unless it is used as a ball in a game of cricket, I do not know how it can possibly be broken." He broke into a nervous little laugh.

When Mr. Brixell returned from the back room, Wetherby took the package. They were just coming out of the store when Millicent and Jespers came toward them. "I hope we were not too long. It was rather difficult finding the sort of biscuits you wanted, your lordship."

Wetherby winked at Rupert. "No, Mrs. Copley. You have not kept us waiting at all."

They had not traveled as far as Wetherby had wished that day. They had, of course, taken longer to shop than he'd planned, but he was glad that Rupert had found a gift for his mother. Wetherby had instructed John Coachman to leave the post road when they came to Chard and cut cross-country to Tiverton, but now he began to doubt the wisdom of that choice. The snow was slowing them down much more than he had anticipated. It really didn't matter all that much. He wasn't obligated to stop at Sir Jonathan's; he'd just said he would if he happened that way. They could go straightaway to Roxwealde Castle if he wished.

That night they found a comfortable inn, but because of the inclement weather, it was already filling up with the travelers who were trying to get in out of the snow. When Millicent wasn't looking, Wetherby slipped the wrapped statue to Rupert, who lovingly placed it in his portmanteau before he took it up to his room.

When Millicent and Rupert came down for supper, they found Wetherby already there.

"We were lucky to have gotten a private dining room," he said, pulling out a chair for Millicent. "From the ruckus out front, I would say that a lot of travelers will be sleeping on the floor tonight. I sent Jespers off to have something to eat." He turned to Rupert. "Everything go all right?"

Rupert nodded happily.

Millicent had been watching the signals passing back and forth between the two of them. She worried that the marquis was exhibiting far too much influence over her son, especially when Rupert wouldn't divulge what they had been whispering about all afternoon. Yesterday in the coach—the way Lord

Wetherby spoke of his mother and her orchids—almost made him seem human—not at all a rake. It was hard to believe that he'd been a little boy at one time, making faces and playing jokes on his nurse. For a few brief moments, she'd looked back with him. She saw he remembered too, and she didn't think all the memories were bad. Heaven knows, she hadn't laughed so hard in a long time—not since—not that way. His maleness filled the room even now. How skillful he was in seducing without making any effort. Oh, dear, she thought, she was undeniably becoming attracted to Lord Wetherby.

The noise in the outer room was becoming more and more discordant, and, it seemed, was now even louder right outside their private room.

The resonance of the voice seemed distinctly familiar. All three pairs of eyes turned as the door crashed open and Lady Caroline threw herself into the room.

"My dears, you cannot imagine the terrible experience I have just had. It is a miracle that I am alive!"

Wetherby rose from his chair. For once even he was so jarred by her tone of voice that he forgot to ask her what she was doing there. "What has happened, Caro?"

Caroline threw herself into his arms. "It was devastating, my darling. My coach overturned on that dratted road out there."

Wetherby raised his eyebrows. Even Caroline's gentility slipped now and then into cant.

Millicent didn't seem to notice. "Was anyone hurt, my lady?"

"Only my pride," she said. "Oh, yes, my coachman has perhaps broken his leg, and one of the grooms was knocked unconscious. But Suzette is all right." Almost as an afterthought, she asked, "Where is Suzette?"

"I am here, *mademoiselle,*" the maid said, standing in the doorway.

Millicent immediately went to the woman, and taking her by the hand, led her to a chair and made her sit down.

Wetherby's mouth quirked into a half grin. Now that he looked closer, Caroline seemed as devastatingly beautiful as ever, and quite healthy, when it came right down to it. He called to a servant to fetch Jespers. "I shall get my coat and go see to the matter immediately, Caroline. Where is your carriage?"

"They got us uprighted and dragged the miserable contraption here. Something about a crooked wheel or something." Caroline pulled out a handkerchief and dabbed her eyes. "You aren't going to leave me, are you, Ernest?"

"Millicent will stay here with you," Wetherby said, with a certain suspicion beginning to creep into his voice. "I shall see that there is a room prepared for you and your maid."

Rupert, who until now had remained silent, picked up a glass of wine from the serving table and offered it to Caroline. "Here, my lady, perhaps this will refresh you."

Caroline glanced toward the door, saw that the marquis was nowhere in sight, and sighed. She'd heard the disbelief in his voice. "I am beginning to think you are the only true gentleman here, Master Rupert."

Rupert fell to his knees. "I shall be your humble servant forever, my lady."

"Well, it looks as if you may be the only one. Is there any food left? I'm starved."

"I shall call for more," Millicent said. "Isn't it a wonderful coincidence that you have stopped at the same inn? Are you going to visit someone near here?"

"As a matter of fact, I am due at Karkingham Hall just past Wellington, day after tomorrow." Caroline omitted to say how many miles *past* the town. "Lady Karkingham shall be terribly disappointed if I do not arrive. She is planning a large party for me," Caroline said. "But that, of course, would probably be out of the way to take me with you."

"I don't know why we couldn't. Now that his lordship says it is unlikely we shall be going to Tiverton, I'm sure we can adjust."

Rupert jumped up. "It would be jolly fun if she could go with us, wouldn't it, Momma?"

When it came to helping someone, it took no time at all for Millicent to make a decision. "Why, yes, it would. I shall speak to Lord Wetherby. He cannot possibly have any objection."

# *Ten*

An hour later, Lady Caroline and her maid were settled in a room. Rupert had gone upstairs with Jespers, and Wetherby had just come in from speaking to the local apothecary about the injured coachman. His broken leg had been set, and the groom had sustained a slight concussion. Both were resting comfortably in rooms over the stables. A wheelwright was to come out in the morning to inspect the carriage. Millicent was still in the private dining room, eagerly waiting to inform the marquis of their plans.

Wetherby stared at her as if she had just come down from the attic. "Good God, madam! Where do you suggest we put her? On the roof?" *What was it about the woman that drove him to profanity?* He was glad Rupert was not around, or he'd have another *X* in his journal. "The carriage is crowded now with four of us inside, and our luggage fills the top. I have never known Caroline to travel with anything less than half a dozen trunks."

Millicent was beginning to realize what an obstinate man the marquis was. "But Lady Caroline says she must be at her friend's house in Wellington by day after tomorrow, or she will miss a party. She enjoys them so much. Surely it won't be much out of the way if we carry her with us. She says it is only about seven miles from here."

Wetherby ran his fingers through his hair. "Have you seen the snow outside? Of course you haven't. We may not get out ourselves tomorrow."

"Oh, dear, we are behind a day now, but surely if we are not going to Sir Jonathan's in Tiverton we can just as easily go by way of Wellington. Rupert is so afraid he will be late for Christmas Day at his Uncle Andy's." She could see that the marquis was not in an accommodating mood, even when she explained things to him logically.

Wetherby attempted to be reasonable. "We will stay here one more night and see what the morrow brings. I shall send a messenger ahead to Copley to let him know that we may be delayed. After all, the holiday season runs on for twelve days. One day more or less will make little difference. We must make the best of it."

"I suppose so, but it will be difficult to explain to a six-year-old. It has been a most unordinary trip for him."

"Madam, nothing has been ordinary about this dem . . . this unusual holiday, for you or for me." He smiled in spite of himself. Rupert would be proud that he'd managed to bypass a swear word.

Later that night in their room, Millicent sat with her hands folded in her lap, straining to hear Rupert's prayers. "Speak up, dear, I can't hear you."

"His lordship doesn't have anyone to say his prayers with tonight, Momma."

Millicent couldn't imagine that bothering the marquis too much. "Well, you say yours, so you can get to bed."

Rupert mumbled a little louder.

"Do you have a toothache, dear?"

"That is the way Lord Wetherby says them."

"His lordship said his prayers with you?"

"Well, yes, but I couldn't hear him very well."

"Well, no wonder if he mumbled."

"I asked Lord Wetherby about that."

"What did he say?"

"Lord Wetherby said he was sure God hears our prayers

whether we say them out loud or to ourselves. He said that maybe we would be more honest if no one else heard them."

"Well, perhaps he is right, but I think God likes little boys to be very clear."

"I wish you wouldn't call me a little boy, Momma. Lord Wetherby treats me like a grown-up."

Long after Rupert had fallen asleep, Millicent lay in her bed trying to picture Lord Wetherby saying his prayers. It was difficult to do. She felt that the marquis was exhibiting far too much influence over her son, especially when Rupert wouldn't divulge what the two of them had been whispering about so much lately. What terrible things could he be teaching her son? Millicent pondered everything Rupert had told her tonight. Perhaps she'd have to start from the beginning to rethink her opinions about the man. Was he a sinner but a little bit of a saint, or was he a saint but a little bit of a sinner? No matter how much she agonized over the gossip she'd heard about him, she found that she was becoming undeniably attracted to the man.

They awakened the next morning to another six inches of snow. Wetherby sent a messenger on to Roxwealde Castle to inform the baron of their possible delay.

They passed the day entertaining themselves with reading, games of chess and cards, and staring morosely out the window, wishing the weather would clear.

The wheelwright said Caroline's coach would need some minor repairs that would take another two days to complete. She was still hinting for a ride to Wellington, but Wetherby had made it clear that they didn't have room. She'd just have to miss her party and wait until her coach was fixed. He still thought it odd that she had turned up at two of the same residences as he had—and now this inn in a way-out corner of Somerset.

The following morning brought no better news. They were having breakfast when the proprietor told them that a traveler arriving at the inn had warned him that the storm of the previous night had made many of the roads impassable.

"We will have to stay another day, then," Wetherby said. "I shall have John Coachman return the carriage and cattle back to the stables."

Rupert was becoming visibly upset. "But, if we don't leave now, we will miss Christmas Day with Uncle Andy, Momma."

Seeing the disappointment in Rupert's eyes was too much for Millicent. "I agree with my son, my lord. We must go on. The horses have been resting for two days. Surely if we are careful they can make it to the higher road."

Wetherby knew he was defeated. Thank God Caroline had stayed abed and he didn't have to contend with her also. "All right," he said. "Can you be ready and out front in half an hour?"

"Yes, my lord," Rupert said, jumping down from his chair. "Thank you, my lord." He raced for the door and just as he reached it, ran headlong into Lady Caroline.

After separating herself from a most apologetic little boy, she said, "I saw your coach in the courtyard, Wetherby. Were you planning on leaving without me?"

"Caroline," Wetherby said, rising. "I have told you we have no room."

"You are always telling me what a great whip you are, why don't you take the ribbons? After all, it is only seven miles to Wellington. My carriage will be ready to travel tomorrow. My driver is in no condition to handle four horses. If I sacrifice my maid, and you your valet, your coachman can drive it up tomorrow with the rest of my servants and their luggage. I know that the Karkinghams will think nothing of putting you up for a night or two. A marquis is always welcome, don't you find?"

Millicent clapped her hands. "That would be the perfect solution. Then you will not have to miss your party and we will be so much nearer to Roxwealde."

Caroline, Millicent, and Rupert all looked at him expectantly.

Wetherby accepted defeat. "All right, Caro, you may come." He turned to Millicent. "You had better go to your room and get your wraps. I had the trunks put on earlier, taking the chance that we would go."

As soon as mother and son left, Wetherby rounded on Caroline. "I have agreed that you may come, but I see no reason for putting my servants out. You will ride inside with Mrs. Copley and Rupert. My valet is not strong enough to take the cold and will ride with you. I will be up front with my driver, for it may take two of us to handle the horses. You will have to make do with one trunk. That can be squeezed into the rumble seat with my groom. That is my last word on the matter. We have already wasted ten minutes in this discussion. If you are not ready, we leave without you. Is that clear?"

Caroline smiled smugly. "You promise you will be off in twenty minutes, my lord?"

An uneasy feeling shredded through Wetherby, but he wasn't going to back down. "You now have less than twenty minutes, my lady."

"Actually, I am ready," she said. "When I saw your coach outside, I had my things carried on."

Wetherby's eyes narrowed. He should have wondered at her heightened color, her pink cheeks. She'd been outside. "What do you mean, you had your things loaded?"

"I have already talked to your coachman. He said he would take care of my man and bring him along tomorrow. My groom is still weak and cannot possibly handle the ribbons." She started out the door. "I am afraid my trunks are already strapped down and there is no room in the rumble seat for anyone. If you don't want your valet to sit up front with you, he will have to come with the others in my carriage." Caroline sailed out the door. "I only have to fetch my coat and bonnet, and I will be ready."

She was gone before he found his voice. By the time Wetherby got to the coach, all three of his passengers were inside surrounded by bags and packages. Caroline held a large leather case on her lap. The rumble seat was full, and there was even a large trunk up on the high driver's seat.

"Isn't this jolly?" Rupert said.

Caroline smiled. "Don't look so down in the mouth, Wetherby, it is only a short distance." She wouldn't tell him how many miles outside of Wellington the Karkinghams lived until they got to the town.

Wetherby slammed shut the coach door and climbed into the driver's seat. He told John he planned to follow their scheduled route as if he was going to Tiverton, then the innkeeper directed him, "After about four miles, turn north onto Catscow Lane to catch the road to Wellington."

With a curse that would surely give him at least five *X*'s in Rupert's book, he cracked the whip over the horses' heads and off they went.

The snow kept falling, eventually rising to such heights alongside the hedgerows that it was difficult for Wetherby to make out the signposts at the cross lanes. Finally, he stopped the horses and went back to the carriage. "I shall need Rupert's eyes to help me find Catscow Lane," he said.

"Yes, your lordship," Rupert cried.

"Impossible," said his mother.

"Madam, I need your son—we all need him."

Rupert eyed his mother intently.

Millicent was acutely afraid that she was losing control over her son. "All right, but you be sure you wrap your muffler tightly around your neck, dear."

"Oh, Momma."

Caroline pouted. "Can't we stop at an inn and get something to eat. Wetherby? I am starving."

"You should have thought of that before you suggested this insane escapade," Wetherby snapped.

"Well, you don't have to be so touchy," Caroline huffed.

Wetherby shut the door with a bang and marched back to the front of the coach.

Rupert was too happy at being allowed up top with his lordship to give any deep thought to his mother's finickiness. "Women worry a lot, don't they?"

"Hmph," was the only answer he got until they were both seated, then the marquis pulled up a blanket from the floor. "I have a fur rug here," he said, tucking it in around Rupert's legs. "Now wrap your muffler around your neck and pull your hat down over your ears."

"We men have to take care of the fair maidens, don't we, Lord Wetherby?"

"Right," he said, slapping the horses with the reins. Actually, Wetherby was frightened. He had the responsibility of two women and a child. He hadn't seen a snowstorm like this since the freeze of 1814.

They had been on the road a good three hours and Wetherby had no idea of where he was. A few lines on a sheet of paper were different than what he was now seeing. It seemed strange that not one crossroad had a sign posted. But Rupert hadn't been in his seat more than five minutes before he pointed. "I see a sign ahead," he shouted.

It sat high above the snow bank, as if someone had just planted it in the snowdrift.

"It's Catscow Lane, my lord. It points to the right."

"Right you are," Wetherby laughed. "Thank God!"

"That's praying, isn't it, my lord?"

"Yes, my boy, that's praying."

"We aren't lost anymore, are we?"

Wetherby laughed. "No, son, we aren't lost anymore." He stopped the coach and went back to inform the women. "It shan't be long before we are on the road to Wellington."

"Well, it has taken long enough for you to get there," Caroline complained. "You are just fortunate that Mrs. Copley and I are so patient."

Wetherby was too relieved to be upset. He guided the horses to the right. The lane was so narrow that the hedges scraped the sides of the carriage. He was just thinking that there would be no way to turn around if they met another vehicle, when the lead horse shied and reared up.

A log lay across the entire road, blocking their path. Behind it stood an imposing, blackhooded figure, a gun in his gloved hand.

His voice, deep and extremely polite, drowned out the howling wind. "Lord Wetherby, I believe? How accommodating of you to drive yourself right into my trap." With a wave of his arm, a great hulking figure appeared from the dense white fog and took hold of the lead horse.

Wetherby placed his arm protectively around Rupert. "Who are you and what do you want? If it is money, you can have all that I have with me."

"Ah, that would not suffice, I'm afraid. I am after much richer gain. You are familiar with the Christmas kidnappings, are you not?"

Wetherby sucked in his breath. "The Bandit King."

"So I hear I am called."

"You, sir, are a coward."

"Don't think you can provoke me, my lord. Mine is merely a useful profession."

"I would call it stealing."

"And I would not take a farthing from someone who has earned his money by the sweat of his own brow. I only harvest from those who have done nothing for their riches."

"Than you are no better than they," challenged Wetherby.

Rupert began to shiver.

"Ah, I don't know where you came upon such a small driver, Wetherby, but if you don't wish him to freeze, you will get back into your coach with your fellow travelers, and I will have one of my men drive you to your destination."

As if on cue, four more men appeared. Three of them, heavily coated and muffled to their eyes, began to remove the log. The other, dressed all in blue with a scarf hiding his features, stepped forward, brandishing a gun. He silently motioned for Wetherby to come down from the high seat.

"What are we going to do, my lord?" Rupert whispered.

"When you have two guns pointed at you, the wise thing is to do as they say," Wetherby said, climbing down. Before he could reach for Rupert, two of the men had his arms pinned to his sides.

"You don't mind if I bind you, my lord, and place a blindfold over your eyes. It is just a precaution."

Rupert jumped to the ground and ran to stand by the marquis. "You will have to bind me too, you scoundrel, or I will run you through." Rupert was sorry now that he'd left his sword inside the coach.

"You have a faithful vassal I see, my lord, and I agree with his suggestion. I will have to tie you both, or he will cut you free the minute I am not looking."

One of the robbers pulled Rupert's arms behind his back and had just begun to wrap a leather thong around his wrists, when the coach door flew open and Millicent jumped out. "You beast!" she screamed, running at the man and pounding him with her fists. "Let go of my son!"

The man crossed his arms over his face to protect himself.

"Hold her!" the Bandit King barked. The man wrapped his arms around Millicent from behind. If she could have bitten him, she would have.

As they struggled, Caroline stepped down daintily from the coach and threw her shawl around her face the minute she felt the cold air. She sized up the situation and faced the masked man. "What is the meaning of this, sir? How dare you accost Mrs. Copley!"

The bandit seemed taken aback for a moment. "I had not expected women to be with you, Lord Wetherby. A pity, but they will just have to come with us, I am afraid."

Caroline's voice was muffled, but she made herself clear. "I cannot come with you. I have a party to attend tomorrow night."

"You will just have to miss it, my lady. Now I order you to be silent and keep your servant under control, and no harm will come to either of you." He then went to the coach and looked inside. "I am surprised, my lord, that you would travel without any men. Quite unwise, don't you think?" He still held his gun, and he motioned again to one of the thieves. "Under these unexpected circumstances, you will all have to be bound and blindfolded. We have some distance to go before we reach our destination. There you will be my guest until I can notify the Duke of Loude that his son has been borrowed for a short time."

It seemed hours before the coach stopped. Raucous voices were heard as the horses were unharnessed and speculations were made about the contents of the baggage. Millicent was terrified, but she managed somehow to keep hold of Rupert's hands, even though they were tied behind him. They were led into a building and their blindfolds removed. It was a large, cavernous kitchen, the thick air filled with odors of food cooking, that were coming from a large iron pot that hung from a chain in the largest fireplace. Herbs and pots hung on pegs around the walls. A manor house, she decided, ancient and long neglected, by the looks of the chipped brick walls and uneven flagstones. There were three fireplaces, one large enough to walk into, and two smaller ones at opposite ends of the room. A long trestle table with several stools around it sat in the middle of the room, already set with large wooden trenchers and bottles of wine, as if someone were expected for dinner.

Upon their entrance, a tiny man with a large wooden ladle in his hand came running, the ladle dripping a path of liquid in its wake. Thin spikes of silver sprang out of his head as if he'd been electrified. He came to a skidding stop a few feet from them, his bright little shoe-button eyes surveying the entire parade with interest.

"Peen," the masked bandit said, "we have some unexpected guests for supper."

The little man nodded eagerly.

Their captor strode to the wide hearth and stood with his back to the blazing logs—a black silhouette, his mask hiding all of his face. Even the slits for his eyes didn't reveal what lay behind them.

Two of the men, both burly with unkempt beards and foul-smelling clothes, accompanied them. They shed their coats and threw them on the table.

Millicent winced.

"Tooter, untie the women and boy," the bandit ordered. "But you, my lord," he said to Wetherby, "will remain bound until you are locked in the room where you will stay until your father comes up with your ransom."

The second man, a wide grin on his face, pushed the marquis down onto a straight-backed spindle chair.

"Now, now, Boggles. That will never do." Then, tapping his chin with his riding crop, the tall man studied the women as they rubbed their wrists. "I shall have to figure out what to do with you and your maid," he said to Caroline.

When she saw that Caroline was about to repudiate him, Millicent put her hand on her arm. "Let him think I am your abigail, or he may separate us," she whispered.

Caroline turned around, motioning to the little man to help her off with her coat.

"Peen," the bandit said, and nodded for him to oblige her.

Caroline carefully removed her bonnet and patted her hair. The ringlets shown like pure gold in the reflecting light of the fire.

Rupert thought she was the most beautiful lady he had ever seen. He declared to himself right then and there that come what may, he would protect her with his life. But his thoughts were interrupted when the kidnapper walked toward her.

"Why, 'tis Lady Caroline Cavendish, I believe," he said, taking Caroline's chin in his hand, and turning her around to face him.

For one of the few times in her life, Caroline had no retort.

His voice was low, but everyone in the room heard every word. "One would think that I had captured a double prize. However, it has come to my ears that your father is unfortunately quite empty in the pockets. So, my dear lady, I must claim my reward in another way." He raised his mask and lowered his lips to hers so quickly that no one saw his face.

Wetherby growled through his gag and struggled to gain his feet. Millicent tried to free herself from Tooter's grip. And, alas, poor Rupert saw that his princess was being attacked by the villain. Oh, that he had his sword, but it had been left in the coach. However, he was a resourceful boy, and not devoid of innovation. He ran to the cavernous hearth and grabbing the end of a stick ablaze, whacked the blackguard across his backside. "Unhand the fair maiden, you knave," he yelled, brandishing his weapon.

The Bandit King dropped Caroline. Whirling about, he snatched the burning stick and hurled it across the room. It struck the far wall and fell sizzling to the stone floor.

Rupert glared, but stood his ground with shaking fists clutched at his sides.

The man in black saluted the angry boy. Even though she was not inclined to let him touch her, he took Caroline by the hand and lifted her up. "It seems, my lady, that you have a champion. I shall have to watch my back from now on."

Ignoring the disdainful look she cast his way, the bandit addressed Rupert. "Fear not, brave knight, I shan't kiss your lady again. I have far more important things to tend to. Now it is time to see Lord Wetherby to his room. In the morning, I shall decide what fate awaits my three uninvited guests."

# Eleven

Tooter dropped Millicent's arm and rushed pell-mell toward the marquis. "Can we take his lordship to his cell now?"

The Bandit King put up his hand. "Words, Tooter. Watch your words. You will frighten the ladies. Remember, we have prepared nice accommodations for his lordship."

Rupert didn't like the renegade's tone of voice. "I won't let you put Lord Wetherby in a dungeon," he challenged.

Millicent pulled her son protectively to her.

The masked bandit laughed. "Boldly said, young man, but I am afraid your imagination is running to the medieval. All these old farmhouses have a spiderweb of underground cellars. I have chosen one small room. It may be a bit cold and damp, but a brazier warms at least a corner of his chamber. Under the circumstances, I doubt his lordship will be wandering about and catching a chill."

Wetherby let out a frustrated growl and with his teeth, ripped at the cloth that was twisted tightly over his mouth.

The Bandit King bowed and with a voice as soft as velvet, said, "Tooter and Boggles will now escort you to your room, my lord."

In his enthusiasm to beat Tooter to the prize, Boggles tripped over his own feet and fell onto Wetherby's lap, pinning him to the chair. Swearing a string of oaths, the bumbling fellow pushed himself off the marquis's legs, only to slip again and fall flat on the stone floor.

Tooter slapped his knees and guffawed like a donkey.

Glowering, Boggles struggled to his feet and fisted Tooter in the nose. "You noddy. A gud lick o' the chops will wipe that grin offen that bracket-face of yers."

Millicent put her hands over Rupert's ears, while the little man named Peen stood timidly, wringing his hands, oohing and ahhing behind her.

The bandit's voice cut the air like a bullet. "Boggles! Tooter! Do you want our guests to think we are barbarians?"

The two fustians sheepishly dropped their arms to their sides and shook their heads vigorously.

The Bandit King grasped Wetherby under one arm and hoisted him to an upright position. "If his lordship wishes to rise, he may."

His gag now loosened, Wetherby had a few choice words of his own, which were easily heard through the tattered cloth.

"My lord!" the Bandit King said in mock astonishment. "Where are your manners? There are ladies present."

Wetherby was a man of good height and well muscled, yet his abductor towered a full head over him. He wanted to wish the bandit to hell, but with his hands still tied behind his back, he couldn't very well fight.

The bandit said smoothly, "I am sorry, my lord, but as you can see, my men are loyal to me, but easily provoked. I beg you to remember that fact when I am not here to see that they behave."

The two women and Rupert all glared at him.

"Surely you are not going to keep him bound and gagged," Millicent said, finally gaining her tongue.

"Never fear, Mrs. Copley. His bindings will be removed as soon as he is safely in his room." The bandit turned back to Wetherby. "I hope you don't mind the inconvenience, your lordship, but after a couple of the other young men were so foolish as to try to escape my hospitality, I am afraid it will be necessary to keep one of your ankles chained to a wooden post."

Millicent and Caroline passed sidelong glances between them.

The masked bandit seemed to read their minds. "I suggest that you do not waste your time trying to unlock his chains. Boggles keeps the key fastened to his belt at all times."

Boggles, a wide, toothless grin splitting his face, lifted up the sloppy folds of his shirt and showed them the large key which was fastened by a leather thong to his belt.

"Peen," their host called, "bring the lantern."

The little man scurried across to a table and lit a lantern, then ran back and handed it to Tooter.

The bandit grabbed a torch from a sconce on the wall, and in a few long strides, covered the distance to a brick wall on the other side of the large fireplace. "Now if you will come this way, Lord Wetherby, we will escort you to your chambers." Holding the torch high, he removed a brick that revealed a metal ring. One quick pull, and a door swung outward. He bowed. "I hope you find your accommodations to your liking, my lord. They may not be quite what you would expect at Grillon's, but there are many in this kingdom who would call themselves fortunate to have a roof over their heads on a night like this."

Millicent put her hand to her mouth. She had to think of something.

The bandit turned his head her way. "I am sure none of you will be so foolish as to try to leave while we are in the cellar, Mrs. Copley. My partner is standing guard in the courtyard. Even if you did manage to reach the gate, the snow is still falling, and we are miles from any inn or town. You would freeze to death in a short time. I shall deal with you when I see that his lordship is comfortably settled."

Wetherby quickly glanced at Millicent's and Caroline's startled faces. With a growl, he lunged head first at the blackhearted jackanape, but Boggles caught him with one giant hand and stopped his flight.

"Ah, Lord Wetherby, no heroics please," the bandit said.

"You need have no concern for the ladies and the boy." He laughed. "I assure you, I will see to their accommodations personally." Then stepping aside, he gestured for Boggles to take the marquis below.

Millicent's worried eyes watched Wetherby disappear into the dark hole in the wall. "Are you sure he will be warm enough?"

Caroline placed her hands on her hips. "Oh, this is outside of enough. I will not permit you, sir, to continue this abominable behavior. I demand that you bring Lord Wetherby back up here and release us now."

The Bandit King held up his hands in supplication. "Ah, ladies, 'tis a pity that I shall be here only one night. You would have provided much needed amusement. But as to setting his lordship free, I am afraid that is impossible. Where will I get my income for this next year?"

Millicent put her arm around Caroline.

Rupert, knees quaking, bravely planted himself in front of the two women and recited over and over to himself, "*Women are frail things to be protected.*"

"You are a scoundrel, sir," Millicent said.

"You are near the mark, madam," the bandit agreed. "But now I must think of something to keep you entertained and out of trouble while I am gone. Of course, there will be a few rules you will have to follow, but we shall speak of those in the morning when my men come in for breakfast."

"Your men?"

"My cohort will leave with me, but I have two stablemen who come for their meals. Peen, Tooter, and Boggles will remain inside the house."

The three men nodded their agreement.

Caroline stamped her foot. "I want to be shown to my bedchamber now."

Amusement colored his words. "You are in it, my lady."

Everyone took a sweeping look around the large open room.

The masked man looked at Caroline. "I suggest, your ladyship, that you count your blessings. I assure you, you would find the stables far more uncomfortable."

Caroline sniffed. "How dare you suggest I sleep in a kitchen? This is a big house. There must be nearly fifty rooms."

"And they are all uninhabitable," the bandit said. "There is no furniture, and the chimneys probably have not been cleaned in forty years. You would have to carry your own luggage, you know, for I will not have my men waiting on you. Why do you think I came to an abandoned house in the middle of nowhere? Each year, I choose a new hiding place in a different part of the country. One where no one would think to search. You may fix yourselves a space at the other side of the room by that small fireplace."

They all looked to where he pointed.

Millicent brought her hand to her throat. "But there is no privacy."

"I told the stablemen to fetch a couple of horse blankets to cut off a corner of the room."

As if on cue, a blast of cold air shot through the kitchen door. Two snowdusted men carrying ropes and blankets blew in just as Tooter and Boggles returned from the cellar.

The Bandit King motioned the men to the far end of the room. "Tooter and Boggles have been persuaded to give up their straw mattresses to you ladies. You will find your coach rugs over by the luggage."

By their scowls, the two men in question didn't appear to be the least bit pleased, but they, as well as the others, looked to where the tall man pointed. True enough, while they had been occupied with their concerns for Lord Wetherby, all the trunks and boxes from the coach had been brought in and tossed willy-nilly against the wall just inside the kitchen courtyard door.

"Where do you intend to sleep?" Caroline asked, eyeing him suspiciously.

"My partner and I have a space by the other small fireplace. We take turns being on watch during the night hours. Peen sleeps by his pots and pans. Tooter and Boggles have orders to stay where they can keep an eye on the door to the cellar. Do not fear, ladies, you will be amply protected."

Caroline commented with a questionable word under her breath.

The bandit paid no mind to her protest. "Breakfast will be at dawn. My partner and I plan to leave at first light."

"I never get up that early," Caroline complained.

"That is up to you. Peen serves two meals a day. If you miss breakfast, you will not eat again until nightfall. Now, ladies, I see that the blankets are hung and the men have dragged the pads over for you. I suggest you get settled in quickly. Peen seems to have supper about ready."

"I will need my night bag and the green trunk," Caroline said peevishly.

"You know where they are. You are free to help yourself."

Millicent coaxed Caroline over to the baggage. "Come, my lady, we only need our portmanteaux tonight. I think I shall feel much safer sleeping in my clothes, anyway. Tomorrow we can sort things out."

They hurriedly searched for their bags and carried them to their corner behind the blankets.

The stablemen, Tooter, and Boggles were already seated, as was Rupert. Millicent was glad to see that Peen had removed the men's coats from the table before he placed the food on it.

"Bring my meal over by the fire, Peen," Caroline said.

The bandit strode over to her. "You will eat at the table with everyone else, or not at all, Lady Caroline."

Caroline pursed her lips and seated herself near Millicent and Rupert.

Millicent smiled encouragingly. "You must be famished, my lady. You haven't eaten since this morning."

Caroline stared at the crusted food clinging to the rim of the bowl. "This is disgusting!"

The bandit stood behind her. "Fie on you, Lady Caroline. You are too critical of poor Peen. He tries his best to put tasty meals on the table. Did it never occur to you that servants have feelings?"

Caroline snorted.

"If you had to work all day meeting the demands of those in command, you might change your opinion."

"Well, thank goodness, I don't have to."

There was a loud silence behind her.

Caroline gritted her teeth. "Well if I must eat here, why are you taking *your* plate away?"

"Because, dear lady, I permit no one to see my face. My friend will come in soon to eat, and I will take over the watch. He, too, does not wish to have his identity known." With that the bandit walked to the far side of the room, and sitting with his back to them, raised his mask and began to eat.

Caroline daintily picked a piece of meat out of the stew, then dropped it back in. Without a word, she left the table and, pouting, marched behind the hanging blankets.

There was nothing Millicent could do to stop her.

Rupert had no such compulsions, and was attacking his meal enthusiastically.

Millicent picked up a sticky spoon and placed it back down on the table. She decided it was far safer to eat with her fingers and sip the gravy from the bowl like the men were doing. The thick porridge, with huge hunks of meat and what could have been corn floating in it, was tasteless, but after looking at the cook's eager expression, she didn't have the heart to say so. Instead she smiled and said kindly, "It is most interesting, Mr. Peen."

The little man's eyes lit up and he offered her some bread. It proved hard, gritty, and burnt on the bottom, but she found it somewhat palatable when dipped into the broth and softened.

When she finished all that she could, Millicent broke off a chunk of bread, and scraping off as much of the black crust as possible, wrapped it in her handkerchief. Perhaps she could persuade Lady Caroline to eat a little. It was all they had.

Earlier, Millicent had seen Tooter go down the stairs to the cellar carrying a tray with a trencher and mug, and she wondered if Lord Wetherby was having as much difficulty as she in swallowing his meal. She yawned. Oh, dear, there had to be a way out of their difficulty, but now she was too tired to think clearly. Tomorrow. Tomorrow when she was rested, she would surely figure some way to see for herself if he was all right.

She found a bucket to use as a chamber pot and filled a bowl of water for Lady Caroline to wash in. She and Rupert would have to share a mattress. "I think it wiser if we keep our beds as close together as possible," Millicent whispered.

Caroline didn't object, and let Millicent lug her pad over nearer theirs.

Rupert ran over to the hodgepodge of trunks and boxes. He located his sword and his portmanteau, which he opened quickly. With a sigh of relief, he found the box with his mother's present still carefully wrapped among his nightclothes. He touched his journal. My, Lord Wetherby would have a lot of stars beside his name when they finished this adventure.

Running back across the cold floor, Rupert placed his sword beside the straw mattress and crawled under the fur robe beside his mother.

Caroline reached out from under her coach rug to the adjoining mattress. "Good night," she said, with a little tremor in her voice.

Millicent patted her hand. "Good night, my lady."

Rupert felt his mother's arms encircle him. "Don't be frightened, Momma," he said softly. "I shall take care of you." Millicent's arms tightened, and he snuggled closer. He had two fair ladies to protect now. It was a great responsibility, and he tried to think what his lordship would want him to do.

A few minutes passed. "We didn't say our prayers, Momma," Rupert whispered.

Millicent was mindful of the masculine voices murmuring only a few feet away. "Perhaps, tonight, we will say them to ourselves," Millicent said. "Like Lord Wetherby does."

In the cold cell below, Wetherby was not in a prayerful mood. He couldn't tell if it were day or night, the food had been atrocious, and he'd only eaten because he was near to starvation. Unless he practically sat on top of the brazier, he had to stay under the covers with his coat on to keep from freezing. His hands were no longer bound, but the chain on his ankle gave him little freedom to move about. They'd given him some candles, but nothing to read. There was no hope of breaking the lock. Even if he had a saw to cut through the pole that supported the beam, he'd only bring down the ceiling on top of himself.

Whatever possessed him to let himself be persuaded to take that spoiled, high-fashioned, clothes-horse Caroline to Wellington? They could have been safely on their way to Roxwealde Castle. One woman was bad enough, but being confronted by two—and a very determined little boy—he'd been overwhelmed. Who said women were frail things to be protected? It was men who needed assistance to resist them.

He cringed to think how foolish he'd been to send that message off to Copley telling him not to be upset if they were held up for a few days. There was no one, no one at all who would be concerned about them for as much as another week. By then, his father would have received the ransom note. The irascible old skinflint would probably refuse to pay the price and let him rot in this hellhole for the rest of his life.

He worried, too. Worried that Rupert would get himself into

trouble. Worried that Caroline would provoke the bandit once too often. But most of all, he worried that he'd failed miserably in his commitment to guard that unpredictable woman he'd promised to protect on her journey to her brother-in-law's. He realized how much he'd gotten used to her. Her chatter. The way she wrinkled her nose when she was trying not to laugh. Even the way she scolded him with her eyes when he said *one of those words*, as her son put it. Demme! If those imbeciles laid a hand on them, he'd kill them.

His thoughts turned to Rupert. Wetherby couldn't help but think how disappointed the little fellow must be in him—or how many *X*'s he was probably marking down in his ledger for failing to uphold the Code.

The next morning, the smell of bacon, burnt bread, and strong coffee awakened Caroline, Millicent, and Rupert. It was still dark, but they were all ravenous. They came out cautiously, not knowing what their reception would be. Tooter and Boggles lay snoring on one side of the big fireplace. The Bandit King and his masked companion were sitting at the table conversing in low tones. Their empty plates showed that they'd already eaten.

Caroline took herself to the very end of the table, as far away as possible from them. Millicent and Rupert followed suit and took seats beside her. Peen came running with an overflowing bowl of porridge, and in his eagerness to place it in front of Caroline, he slipped on the greasy, stone floor and spilled half of it down the front of her dress.

Caroline screeched.

"Oh, my goodness," Millicent said, handing Caroline her handkerchief.

Caroline pushed the crusted dish away. "Bring me a clean bowl and spoon," she demanded. "This is not fit for a pig to eat out of."

Peen screwed up his face and looked in horror at the havoc he'd caused.

A deep voice traveled down the length of the table. "If you are not satisfied with Peen's cooking, Lady Caroline, perhaps you would like to take over that job yourself."

Tooter and Boggles woke up to the noise. Like two hungry dogs, they hurried to the table, seating themselves across from the women.

Caroline glared at them.

Boggles gave her a gap-toothed grin.

The bandit continued, "You need a lesson in manners, Lady Caroline. While I am gone, you will cook and wait upon my men when they come in for their meals."

Tooter hooted and nudged Boggles, who was already stuffing his mouth with food.

Caroline raised her chin defiantly. "I will do no such thing."

The bandit spoke cooly. "In any house of mine, everyone receives the rewards of their efforts. If you do not cook, you do not eat. It is as simple as that."

As that thought sunk in, Caroline's eyes widened. "But I don't know how to cook," she said miserably, her eyes glistening with tears.

Pity filled Millicent as she looked at Caroline, her hair rumpled, her fine dress stained with the porridge. "I do," Millicent said impulsively. "I will help Mr. Peen."

A chuckle came from behind the mask. "Ah . . . *Mr.* Peen, do you hear that? You have a kitchen helper."

The little man looked as if he wanted to jump up and down with ecstasy.

Caroline let out a sigh of relief and thanked Millicent with her eyes.

However, their host was not as benevolent. He walked over and picked up a large black kettle from the worktable. "Since you cannot cook, my lady, and you have such a disgust for the state of the cookware, then perhaps you should be the one to clean it." He plunked the kettle right under Caroline's nose before seating himself once again.

Caroline pulled away from the food-encrusted pot. "I won't do it."

His voice became as smooth as honey. "Ah, but I think you will. If any one of you three does not do something for his or her keep, then all must suffer. *Mr.* Peen," he said, "remove Master Rupert's and Mrs. Copley's bowls, please."

The little man complied reluctantly. He even took the spoon filled with porridge from Rupert just as he was about to put it in his mouth.

Rupert watched his bowl being carried away, then looked sadly at Caroline.

"I think her ladyship is about to discover that any one person's selfish deeds affect those around her," the bandit said.

"Wait! Wait!" Caroline called desperately to Peen. "I'll do it—only give Rupert back his breakfast."

The masked man leaned back from the table and steepled his fingers. "Just think, Mr. Peen. In a single morning, you have acquired a kitchen helper and a scullery maid to clean your pots and pans. And, I might add, someone to scrub the floor clean, too. The way everyone has been slipping on the greasy flagstones, 'tis a miracle no one has broken a leg."

Caroline made a little choking sound.

Rupert had had enough of this bullying. "You cannot make Lady Caroline do such a thing," he said.

"Ah, but I can, because I am King here, you see. Isn't that right, Lady Caroline? In your household, you never question your right to order your servants about, do you?"

Rupert studied the black-robed man and leaned over toward Caroline. "I shall help you," he whispered hoarsely.

"You have loyal friends, my lady. I hope you realize how fortunate you are." He turned to the boy. "That is very generous of you, Master Rupert. You may help the new scullery maid if you wish, but she must not shirk her duties. In fact, Mr. Peen, if any one of the three does not perform to my aspirations, you will refuse food to all. Is that clear?"

Peen wrung his hands and nodded.

The bandit pushed back from the table. "And here I was worried that I would not be a good host and couldn't find something to keep you all entertained while I was gone. Now you will not have a dull moment until I return from my errand."

"What about Lord Wetherby?" Millicent asked. "Surely you are not going to make him stay in the cellar all the time you are gone!"

"Alas, I feel that is necessary. I cannot have any of you getting in trouble by trying to help him escape. No, he will stay chained. I visited his lordship this morning. He has eaten well. Although he had some disagreement with what I am doing, I think he will eventually see reason in adjusting to his situation. Now if you will excuse me, we shall be leaving."

The bandit drew on his black coat with its several capes. As soon as he had pulled on his gloves, he exited with his henchman, leaving Caroline and Millicent looking helplessly at each other.

# Twelve

Millicent was glad to have something to keep her busy. She suggested to Mr. Peen that he melt buckets of snow by the fire and fill a barrel to provide an unlimited supply of water for all their needs. She showed Rupert and Lady Caroline how to scour the pots and pans with sand, then rinse them with water. However, there seemed to be few foods to work with, and Peen prepared most of the dinner that proved to be as skimpy as that of the night before.

The next morning, Boggles fell down the cellar steps, splattering Lord Wetherby's food everywhere. Poor Caroline was given a bucket of water and a rag and told to clean it up. Tooter held a lantern over her head to light the stairs, giggling all the time. She could have killed him.

However, Millicent had her own concerns. "Mr. Peen," she asked politely, "will you please show me what supplies you have on hand?"

He led her to several sacks that were pushed against the wall.

"Dear heaven, that does not seem much to feed several hungry men. What is in them?"

He shrugged helplessly.

Millicent pulled one of the bags out. "It says barley, Mr. Peen. You had the words facing backward." She then turned all the bundles around. "Wheat flour, cornmeal, millet. See, someone has labeled all of them for you."

The little man studied the sacks hard and turned scarlet. "Don't make no difference. Can't read."

Millicent cringed when she thought of the flat, rock-hard bread they'd been served the night before. She began to suspect that he didn't know how to cook, either. "Surely there are more supplies."

Mr. Peen led her to a small, cold storage room off the kitchen. Mutton, chickens, and beef hung from hooks. She also discovered a barrel of apples and sacks of potatoes and other vegetables. The Bandit King had evidently planned for a long stay. She'd already noticed the herbs in the kitchen the night before. "What oils do you have?"

Peen took a cruet down from a shelf.

Millicent stuck in a finger for a sample. "It is a cooking oil of some kind. I'm not sure what, but it is not grease." She opened several other crocks and found brown sugar and molasses, honey, vinegar, and salt. "Oh, my, you have a good stock here."

Peen watched her with anticipation.

One look into those questioning eyes, and Millicent knew for certain that the timid soul knew nothing about preparing food. "I am sure you have your own way of doing things, Mr. Peen, but perhaps I can suggest a few recipes that our cook, Mrs. Woodhouse, taught me," she said.

He nodded happily, a little crooked smile lighting up his face.

"While you are busy chopping up some meat and potatoes for the evening meal, I can relieve you of the bread-making."

No argument came from Peen, who scurried out to the storage hut to get the needed supplies.

Thinking of how gritty Mr. Peen's bread had been, Millicent dug out the remnant of her torn veil to make a sieve. She sifted the flour into a large wooden bowl, fetched the kettle from the fireplace, and poured in hot water to make dough. "Now just a pinch of salt."

Suddenly, Millicent realized that she had an audience. Mr. Peen had returned, and couldn't hide his curiosity. Caroline stood close, peering over Millicent's shoulder, and Rupert kept jumping up and down at her elbow.

"Momma, are you going to make some crumpets?"

She laughed. "No, we will simply start with unleavened bread."

Caroline set down her bucket of dirty water and wiped her forehead with the back of her hand. Her favorite velvet traveling dress was ruined: first by the porridge that Peen had spilled on her, and then because she'd torn the hem when she'd had to get down on her knees to scrub the slate floor. She now looked at the lump of flour and said, grimacing, "It looks a mess."

"But that is the fun of it," Rupert cried. "May I help, Momma?"

"Well, the dough has to be kneaded three hundred times, so you all can help by counting with me. When we reach one hundred, one of you may step in and take my place," Millicent said, watching Mr. Peen from the corner of her eye. His mouth formed a big *O*.

"May I be second, Momma?"

"First we will ask Lady Caroline and Mr. Peen if they want to knead the bread."

Mr. Peen, his eyes now like saucers, chewed on his lower lip and nodded.

Rupert tried not to look disappointed, but he failed miserably.

Caroline sniffed. "He can have my turn."

Rupert's smile returned.

While Millicent punched the dough, she and Rupert counted out loud. When it came Peen's turn to knead, he kept his gaze on Millicent's lips. He waited until she called out the number, then he repeated it in a near shout.

Finally, Lady Caroline's soft voice joined them.

As soon as Rupert finished his turn, Millicent retrieved a linen towel from her portmanteau and soaked it in water. This she stretched over the bowl before setting it on the hearth.

Caroline, her eyebrows raised, followed her.

"Now," Millicent said, "we must wait until the dough rises before we knead it again. In the meantime, while Mr. Peen is putting the meat and vegetables in the cooking kettle, I might just make up an apple pudding to have with dinner."

Mr. Peen suddenly remembered his chopping chores and rushed back to the potatoes and other vegetables.

"How did you ever learn to do all that?" Caroline asked. "Didn't you have a cook?"

Millicent laughed. "The best. Mrs. Woodhouse started me out making biscuits and gingerbread men when I was a little girl."

"Goodness," Caroline said, "didn't your mother object to your working like a servant?"

"No, she thought it kept me busy and out of trouble. My father is mayor of our village and we had a steady stream of people coming to consult him. Mother often had to entertain them and their wives."

A few hours later, Caroline watched, fascinated, as Millicent plumped up the dough to just the right shapes to fit into two huge, oiled skillets. She then cut the tops lengthwise. "We must let them proof for an hour before we set them to bake."

"It swelled up," Caroline said, in awe.

Millicent laughed. "Would you like to try to make some bread?"

Caroline wiped her hands down the sides of her once-beautiful frock. "Do you really think I could?"

"You will never know unless you try," Millicent said kindly.

"I want to do it all by myself," Caroline said as she chose her flours and made her mixture. Rupert helped her count to three hundred.

Caroline's first loaf was hard as a rock, because she kept taking off the towel to peek. Her second burned because she left it in the skillet too long. But her third loaf was just right, a hard crust with a soft and tasty center.

"Perfect," exclaimed Millicent.

Caroline brought her hand to her mouth, her eyes sparkling. "It is just, isn't it?" she said proudly, as the men devoured every bite.

"Now," Millicent said, "we will mix another batch so it will be ready to bake in the morning."

That evening after supper, Boggles, full of good food and too much ale, tripped over a stool, once again spilling Wetherby's food.

For the second time in one day, Peen had to fill the trencher all over again. The cook handed Boggles the lantern and told Millicent, "From now on, he can light your way, and ye will take Lord Wetherby's meals to him."

Boggles pouted, but went ahead to open the door of Wetherby's room for her. As soon as she was inside, he deliberately slammed the door, bolted it from the outside, and stomped back up the steps.

Wetherby couldn't believe his eyes. "Mrs. Copley?" She looked like an angel standing in the reflected light of the small brazier. He leaped to his feet and walked toward her as far as his chain permitted. "Here," he said, taking the tray and placing it on the floor. "I am afraid the only place for you to sit down is on my pad."

The room was cold. A candle flickered on the floor, and he wore his coat. After she'd settled herself Indian-fashion on the straw mattress, she was still shivering. "That odious man! I have been so afraid he might have hurt you."

Wetherby was moved by her concern, and settling beside her, pulled a wool blanket up over her shoulders. He searched for the words to set her mind at ease. "He will not harm me. The Bandit King would not allow it. Whatever else the renegade is, he has never hurt any of the gentlemen he kidnapped. Of course, I don't know what he will do if my father refuses to pay my ransom," he said, trying for a bit of humor to lighten the conversation. However, she didn't seem to get the point.

"My lord! Do not say such a terrible thing. Surely the duke will pay."

"Yes, well, I suppose he will. I am his only son . . . it is just that—"

"It is just what?"

"You might say we have had a few disagreements—mostly about my finding a wife of impeccable bloodlines to produce the next heir to the Lance family empire."

Millicent's heart fell. "Yes, I suppose you must marry *someday.*"

Wetherby began to eat. "It just seems so disagreeable—being shackled to one woman for the rest of my life."

Millicent pondered that for a moment. "I cannot imagine my mother and father living apart from each other."

"You mean day after day, year after year?"

"Why, yes. Occasionally there have been times—like when my mother went to care for her sick sister up in Ashford. Mama was gone for two whole months, and we missed her sorely. Papa especially. But she said that Aunt Milly—I am named after her—needed her more."

He considered his mother's last illness, which kept her abed for months, and the fact that his father had visited her only twice. Wetherby had come more than that—three times. And yet, he'd considered that His Grace held his wife in high regard. He was always saying so. Hadn't he hired the best of physicians to attend her, and seen she had plenty of servants to supply her every need? But seeing the same face every day across the table, around the house, without becoming bored? That was a different matter altogether.

He suddenly realized how quiet Millicent had become. "I am sorry, forgive me. You were about to say something else, and I am afraid my mind wandered."

Millicent looked down at her hands. "I just said that I had expected Bertie and me to live the same sort of life when the war was over."

He didn't know why, but he took her hands in his. "I knew Captain Copley quite well. I have never known a more amiable, worthwhile fellow."

She glanced up at him, her eyes glistening with unshed tears. "You are a very kind man, Lord Wetherby. I am sure you will find a woman to love someday."

He was afraid it was getting to be a habit, but he wanted to kiss her, even though he knew he'd be taking advantage of her vulnerability. *Someone of your ilk probably would,* she'd said. He was totally reprehensible. No, not totally. He fought off the urge to take her in his arms, patted her hands instead, and placed them back on her lap.

She gave a nervous little laugh. "Did you like your meal?"

Wetherby looked at the empty plate. He'd eaten every bite without realizing it. "It certainly was an improvement over breakfast. Almost as if another person had cooked it."

"I told Mr. Peen I would help him. He is a very sweet man."

Wetherby looked to see if she'd become addled by this upsetting experience. "Sweet man? You jest."

"No, really. He has not had an easy life, my lord. He has told me all about it."

Wetherby really didn't want to hear about Peen. He wanted to hear more about *her,* but he would listen to anything—even take one of her scoldings—to keep her with him a bit longer. It was lonely down in this dark cell all by himself. "Tell me about him."

Millicent folded her hands in her lap. He was glad to see that she didn't seem any more eager to leave than he did to see her go.

"Mr. Peen told me he was orphaned when he was a child and was taken in by a family of smugglers on the Devonshire coast. His foster parents made him work like a slave, and since he was so small, the older boys beat him and made fun of him. They sometimes lent him out to farmers and then took every penny he earned away from him. He said that the Bandit King gave him his first honest job."

Wetherby made a choking sound.

"Are you all right?" Millicent cried with alarm. When Wetherby assured her that he was, she continued, "Mr. Peen allowed that he fibbed a bit, for he really did not know how to cook."

That was obvious to Wetherby by the first meal he'd been forced to eat. So Mrs. Copley could cook. "Now I know why the quality improved so greatly from one meal to the next. But it is you three that I am concerned about. They haven't made you do anything you didn't want to, have they? I mean . . . no one has forced you . . ."

Millicent cocked her head. "Well, Caroline may disagree with what I say, but no, I would not say that they have."

Wetherby stiffened. "What do you mean? Has Caroline not been treated well?"

"The Bandit King said she had to scrub pots."

Wetherby almost laughed. "Scrub pots? No one could ever make Caroline scrub pots."

"He left orders that if she does not, she gets no food." Millicent didn't add that neither would she or Rupert.

Wetherby guffawed with relief. "Thank God she was not hurt. If any of those scoundrels dares put a hand on her—"

A strange feeling of melancholy descended upon Millicent. She had guessed that Lord Wetherby was very fond of Lady Caroline, now she knew it. What man would not be? She was so beautiful—genteel—friendly. A diamond of the first water. Giving a nervous laugh, she said, "Well, I see that you have eaten all your supper. If I stay any longer, Mr. Peen may not let me bring you your meals."

No sooner had she said that than there was a pounding on the door. Boggles's irritated voice barked from the other side. "Ain't he finished with his meal yet?"

Millicent made to rise, and Wetherby jumped up to assist her.

He handed her the tray. When she reached the door, he tried to think of something to hold her longer. "How is Rupert?"

"Oh," she laughed, "he insists on helping Lady Caroline with her chores. He is quite taken by her, I am afraid."

Wetherby was surprised at how much he missed the little rascal. "Perhaps you can think of an excuse for him to come with you next time you bring my meal."

Millicent's eyes sparkled in the lantern light. "Rupert would like that above all else, your lordship. I shall have to think of something to get Mr. Peen to allow him to come."

The pounding resumed, louder this time.

"Yes, Mr. Boggles. I am ready to go," Millicent called out.

They heard the latch being lifted.

Wetherby was afraid he was beginning to feel sorry for himself. "I don't suppose you have anything I could read. It gets terribly dull having to converse only with oneself."

"Oh, it must," she said, sympathetically. "I have a book by Sir Walter Scott in one of my trunks that I think you may enjoy. *Rob Roy.* I shall look for it."

Boggles raised the lantern over his head and peered into the room. The lantern cast strange shadows upon his ugly face.

Wetherby watched Millicent go. It would be another twelve hours before he ate again . . . before he would see her again.

The following morning, Millicent brought Wetherby his breakfast. This time she knew enough to wear her wool pelisse. "I have not asked Mr. Peen yet whether Rupert can come. But I have brought you the book I spoke of." She settled down and waited for him to eat.

"Rupert said to tell you that he will put a star in the journal for you every night that you are in the dungeon. He said you would know what he was talking about." Millicent waited for Lord Wetherby to give her a clue as to what her son had meant, but she soon realized that he wasn't going to.

Instead, he bypassed the subject completely. "How is Caroline?"

A trifle disappointed, she shrugged. "She is all right, though Boggles said she must scrub the stones in front of the hearth where he sleeps. I don't think she was too happy about that, because she has all the pots and pans from breakfast to clean yet."

Wetherby laughed outright for the first time since Millicent had brought him his meal. "I daresay Caroline hasn't done a useful thing in her life."

"It is outside of enough that you should make light of poor Lady Caroline's position. You just do not appreciate her hidden talents."

"I am afraid Caro has been spoon-fed since the day she was born."

Millicent raised her nose a trifle. "Did you like your bread, my lord?"

"What has that to do with Caroline?"

"She baked it." Millicent watched with satisfaction as disbelief, and then suspicion, passed quickly over his face.

"Good lord! Caro?" Wetherby guffawed. "I cannot believe it."

"I daresay, she was quite proud of her achievement, too," Millicent said smugly.

Boggles began pounding and shouting obscenities at the door.

Millicent held her ears. "That impossible man! I must think of a way for me to bring Rupert and get rid of Boggles all at the same time," she whispered, holding out her hands for the tray.

"I shall see you this evening," he said, kissing the inside of her wrist.

A shiver went through her. She was glad to see the sparkle back in his lordship's eyes, but, oh, he was still a rogue. Loving one woman, while kissing another. The terrible thing was, she wanted him to do it.

* * *

That evening, Boggles and Tooter were already impossibly drunk by the time they had finished eating and went to sit beside the warm hearth. There they continued to drink, belch, and sing the most outrageous songs, calling to Caroline to come fill their tankards with ale as quickly as they emptied them. They laughed uproariously when she reluctantly complied.

Mr. Peen finished filling Wetherby's tray with food and looked helplessly at the two fustians.

Millicent saw her chance to have Rupert accompany her. "Both men are foxed, and in no condition to carry the lantern into the cellar," she said convincingly. "If either of them fell, the house would be set afire. My son is a strong lad, he can carry the light."

Rupert hurried to his mother's side. "I am that, Mr. Peen."

One look at Boggles and Tooter, and Peen agreed.

Rupert ran behind the curtain to get his sword. He took his responsibility seriously, and proceeded to lead his mother down the stairs. The corridor opened up into a much larger room, and off it were several doors—some closed—most hanging on broken hinges, or missing altogether. In the blackness of it all, some black holes seemed to go on forever.

" 'Tis the door on the right," Millicent whispered, as if she were afraid someone were listening.

Rupert had to put the lantern on the dirt floor and stand on tiptoe to reach the latch. With a bit of trepidation, he slowly opened the door. Once his eyes became accustomed to the dim light, he was overjoyed to see that Lord Wetherby was neither hanging by his toes from the ceiling nor being stretched on a torture rack. Only chained to a post, which really wasn't so bad when Rupert considered the alternatives. Relief shot through him, loosening his tongue, and neither adult got a word in edgewise for the first several minutes.

Then Lord Wetherby and his mother began to talk about grown-up things, and Rupert's imagination kept being drawn to the shadows on the walls and the black holes he'd seen running off the big storage room.

"Momma, may I go out in the passageway?"

Millicent started to protest, when Wetherby placed his hand on her arm. "What harm is there in it? He is getting restless." He then spoke authoritatively to Rupert. "Loyal knight, go outside and guard the entrance to my quarters."

Rupert snapped to attention, his eyes sparkling. "Aye, my lord. Code Number Two. Right?"

Millicent frowned. "Stay near, Rupert, and take the lantern, so I know you are there."

"Yes, Momma. I am not afraid of the dark, but may I have some candles, too? That will give even more light."

"Certainly," Wetherby said, handing him three tapers.

Rupert picked up the lantern and bowed his way out the door.

Millicent still wasn't sure it was a good idea. "He may hurt himself."

Wetherby assured her, "It is just a large, empty room. What harm can come to him?"

Millicent relaxed and waited for Wetherby to finish his meal. While she kept her eye on the yellow light outside the door, they talked about *Rob Roy.* They didn't stop until Millicent realized that the glow in the corridor hadn't fluctuated. If Rupert were using the lantern, the light and shadows would be moving, wouldn't they?

She didn't want Lord Wetherby to think her missish, succumbing to vapors. She said her good-byes, and taking the tray, left the room. The lantern sat about four feet from the door. There were no candles, and no little boy in sight. She quickly set the tray at the foot of the stairs and went back to bolt the door. Boggles was sure to check soon to see that she had done so.

"Rupert?" she whispered. There was no answer in the cellar,

but sounds of a peppery commotion whirled down from the kitchen above. A shiver of apprehension ran through her. Picking up the lantern, Millicent turned in all directions. "Rupert!" she hissed, louder.

From above, Millicent heard Boggles bellowing like a bull, but it was Mr. Peen's shrill voice that called from the stairwell. "Mrs. Copley? Where are ye, Mrs. Copley?"

Millicent was beginning to have a terrible feeling that something awful was going to happen, when she saw the tiny flickering light of a candle growing larger as it made its way toward her.

"Momma! Momma!"

Millicent splayed a hand over her heart. "Rupert? My goodness, you did give me a start."

"I'm sorry, Momma."

"Wherever have you been?"

"I found a passageway."

"Well, after this, if you are going to have an adventure, I want to go with you. Is that understood?"

"Yes, Momma. But come, I must show you. It may lead to a way out of here."

Millicent held the lantern high. Several doorways opened off the wide room, but at the far end, it narrowed to a single corridor where she could see that the opening split into two directions. Curiosity and desire to investigate were about to win her over when there was a terrible crash.

Mr. Peen had tripped over the tray, scattering dishes everywhere. "Mrs. Copley!" came his frantic cry.

"Coming, Mr. Peen." Millicent put her face down near Rupert's. "I cannot come with you now. We must go back to the kitchen. I fear they are having a frightful row. Here, take the lantern, we must help Mr. Peen."

Millicent was assisting the little man up from where he lay sprawled on the floor when a woman's scream spiraled down from the room above. It was followed by deep raucous laughter, then a loud crack, which sounded considerably like splintering wood.

"Oh, please, Mrs. Copley," Peen whimpered, "come at once, or I do believe she is going to kill them."

# Thirteen

As the loud, boisterous voices rumbled down the cellar steps, Millicent leaned closer to Rupert. "I don't believe it wise to investigate just now, dear. If we delay much longer, the men may become suspicious and not allow you to come with me again. Perhaps we can explore further tomorrow, after we have brought Lord Wetherby his breakfast. You say you think there may be a way out of here?"

"I am sure of it, Momma."

A little shiver of expectation ran down Millicent's spine. "Tomorrow it is, then. Now we must get back upstairs. We cannot leave Lady Caroline alone with those men."

"No, Momma, we cannot, but I have my sword. They shall not harm my lady."

Millicent and Rupert followed the agitated Peen to the kitchen, where they found Boggles and Tooter circling Caroline. She sat squarely on her jewelry box in the middle of her mattress, wielding a butcher knife, daring them to touch her.

As soon as the cowardly Tooter spied the others, he ran out to seek safety in the center of the large room. Boggles, however, continued to dance around Caroline just beyond her reach, spewing childish chants and holding Rupert's portmanteau in front of him in case she decided to test her aim. Trunks were open, clothing strewn helter-skelter. It was obvious that the men had been going through their belongings.

Rupert's eyes widened as he recognized his bag. He ran toward Boggles, shouting, "Put that down, you ruffian!"

"Ho!" guffawed the big fustian. "The brat says this is his, Mr. Tooter."

To his horror, Rupert saw the portmanteau fly over his head into the outer room. Tooter caught it. Rupert reversed his course, but again as he reached for his bag, Tooter whisked it back through the air to Boggles. Both women rounded on the renegade. The clumsy man tripped and turned a backward somersault over a stool. Rupert watched helplessly as his bag sailed over their heads and crashed against the bricks of the smaller fireplace.

While Peen stood in the background wringing his hands, Millicent and Caroline chased the big oaf from their sleeping quarters.

Rupert retrieved his portmanteau, then sat down on the hearth and opened it. With shaking hands, he unraveled the package. Shattered pieces of china fell onto his lap. He picked up a little hand and tried to fix it back on the pretty lady's wrist.

"Are you all right, Rupert?" Millicent called from the other side of the horse blanket.

"Yes, Momma," he replied, trying to block the pain from his voice. Rupert wiped a tear from his eye and looked around the room. What was he to do now? His mother's Christmas present was ruined beyond repair. He had to hide it. He couldn't take the chance of her asking questions, so he lovingly placed each chard back in the box, and stuffed it behind the pile of kindling that was stacked beside the fireplace. He'd no sooner finished concealing the package than his mother and Lady Caroline came back around the curtain and began to prepare for bed.

That night Rupert wrote his sad thoughts in his journal, then blowing out his candle, stuffed the book under the straw mattress and crawled into bed. For a long time, he tossed and turned. His heart was heavy over the destruction of his mother's gift. The fact that he wasn't able to tell anyone about his loss only added to his misery, and he felt very much alone—even in his mother's arms. He couldn't help thinking how unhappy and lonely Lord Wetherby must be, too, down in the dark cellar all by himself. His mother and Lady Caroline, exhausted from their ordeal, slept soundly beside him. The thunderous snores of Boggle and Tooter and the high-pitched whistling twills from Mr. Peen told him that the men were not likely to awaken until morning unless the roof caved in upon them.

Carefully, Rupert wiggled out from under his blankets. He stuffed the journal inside his coat, put a pencil in his pocket, and quietly lit a candle. Boggles always left the cellar door open a crack so that he could listen for any suspicious noises from below. Rupert squeezed through the opening and made his way down the stairs. It didn't take him long to unlatch the door to Wetherby's cell.

Wetherby, growing more and more offended over his powerlessness, always slept battle-alert, one eye open, ears tuned to hear the slightest of sounds. The fire in the brazier burned low, but he could see that the figure silhouetted in the doorway was too small to be any one of the adults. He sat up. "Rupert?"

"I thought you might like to work on our journal," Rupert whispered, pulling out the book as he came nearer.

Wetherby raised his eyebrows. "I take it no one knows you are down here."

Rupert shuffled his feet.

"It will not go well with you if those barbarians find that you are not in your bed," Wetherby said, not unkindly.

"They won't wake up for hours. They are too drunk."

Wetherby winced. The lad was too young to know about the excesses of men. "Well, you are here now, and indeed I would like a bit of company. Light these candles in the fire and sit beside me," he said, patting the mattress.

Rupert happily did as he was told, and when the tapers were wedged into the dirt on the floor, he settled in and opened the ledger. For several minutes, the two heads leaned over the pages as Rupert explained what he had written. "My spelling may not be so good," he said hesitantly.

Wetherby was quite astounded with what he saw. There were no *X's* beside his own name—only stars. "You make stars quite well," he said. "It must have taken a lot of time to draw so many."

Rupert pulled out his pencil. "Mr. Tipple taught me. See," he said, going up and over until he'd made five points.

"Isn't that something?" said Wetherby.

"Would you like me to teach you how, your lordship?"

"I would like that very much," Wetherby said, trying to keep a straight face.

Rupert showed him again. "Now you try it," he said, watching as Wetherby painstakingly traced over Rupert's bold marks.

"Oh, that is good," Rupert said reassuringly, "for your first try."

"You are an excellent teacher." Wetherby replied.

Rupert smiled proudly and wriggled a little closer.

Wetherby closed the journal, and Rupert was afraid he was going to be dismissed. "I am sure you have had many great adventures in your life, my lord. Would you tell me about some of them?" Rupert saw by the look on Lord Wetherby's face that he was too modest to brag. "Or perhaps you can tell me another story about the brave knights of old?"

That seemed to please his lordship more, because he immediately commenced weaving a daring tale about a young knight named Sir Jerome. He had fallen in love with the lovely Princess Alicia, who was being kept captive in a tower by a wicked gnome.

Rupert wished the knight had been called Wetherby and the princess Millicent, but he feared he might cause his lordship embarrassment if he suggested it. Alas, all good things do have to come to an end, and as soon as the fair maiden was rescued against enormous odds and obstacles too numerous to relate in one short visit, Wetherby said, "I believe you had better go upstairs now before your mother discovers you are gone and rings an alarm."

Rupert nodded, hurriedly gathering up all that he'd brought. He had only taken a couple of steps toward the door, when he paused and held out the ledger to the marquis. "Would you like to keep the journal, your lordship? It would give you something to read."

Wetherby realized the honor the boy was according him. "Thank you. I shall keep it safe," he said. He watched as the door closed. Then, running his hands over the weathered leather, he lay the book beside his mattress and fell into a restful sleep.

The next morning as soon as Wetherby had finished his breakfast, Millicent and Rupert set out to explore the passageways at the end of the cellar. The one to the right led only a short way before it ended, sealed off completely by fallen debris. The one to the left proved more promising until they came to a barrier of fallen dirt and rock, similar to the first.

Millicent's heart sank. " 'Tis no use, Rupert. It is the same as the other. Probably sealed off for years."

Rupert looked at his candle. "Momma! See the flame flickering? A draft is coming from up there," he said, making his way over the rocks. "Bring the lantern. I do believe I see a hole."

Sure enough, a narrow crack appeared. He started to wriggle through.

"Wait!" Millicent cried. "It may be dangerous."

Rupert's voice echoed back. "I am quite sure there are no dragons anymore for you to be afraid of, Momma. I've really known that all along." He hesitated a moment. "But I suppose there might be some pirates."

Millicent held the lantern high over her head. The beam revealed stairs going upward. "I doubt that, dear. However, I don't think you should . . ."

But Rupert had already crawled through the opening, his candle throwing only a small light on his surroundings.

"Wait for me," she ordered, just barely squeezing through the crevice.

Upward they went, excitement hurrying their every step, until they came to a small wooden door. Millicent placed the lantern on the landing and struggled with the latch until the rusty hinges, squeaking and groaning, gave way. A rush of cool, fresh air caught them in its grasp.

Millicent shivered as she peeked out onto a patchwork of brown and white. Much of the snow that had plagued them only a few days ago had melted. "You were right, Rupert. It is a way out. We must tell Lady Caroline and Lord Wetherby that we have found a way out of here."

"But Lord Wetherby is chained, Momma. He cannot escape," Rupert said, his growing anxiety showing on his face.

Millicent bit her lip. "Oh, dear. That is so."

"His lordship is a chivalrous warrior. He would tell us to be brave and go without him."

Millicent couldn't explain the sense of loss she felt when she contemplated leaving Lord Wetherby behind. "Yes, he would. There is no telling what those thugs would do if we were not here to protect him." Then and there she knew she had no intention of escaping without him. "We will consult Lady Caroline." she said with determination. "Surely between the three of us we can come up with a scheme to free Lord Wetherby from those jackanapes. But now 'tis better we go back. We dare not let Boggles discover us snooping around, or he will raise Cain."

Later, while all three prisoners were doing their morning chores, Millicent reported their discovery to Caroline.

"But we don't have the key to unlock his chains," Rupert lamented.

"If we can get the key—what then?" Caroline whispered, studying her red, callused hands with disgust.

Millicent saw the spark in Caroline's eyes and knew her faith in the fine lady had been well-founded. "Then we could all escape."

Caroline's eyes narrowed. "You leave that to me," she said, looking toward Boggles. "Now here is my plan . . ."

Millicent and Rupert listened with admiration as Lady Caroline outlined her scheme.

That evening, it took very little encouragement to get Boggles and Tooter totally foxed. As soon as she was certain the men were asleep, Caroline crept into the main room and easily cut the key from Boggles's belt.

Millicent and Rupert waited breathlessly behind the curtain for her to return. They had donned several layers of clothing: coats, capes, and walking boots. Millicent had made sure the door to the cellar was not closed completely when she returned from taking Wetherby his supper. They'd decided not to reveal their plans to him, until they knew for sure that they had the key.

But now—that feat accomplished—the three culprits stealthily made their way down the dark stairwell. Rupert had his sword, and Millicent had the key and carried a lantern, which she intended to light with the fire from Wetherby's brazier. Caroline was burdened with her heavy jewelry box, but she refused to leave it behind.

A few minutes later, they entered the cell. It wasn't the creaking of the door as much as the gentle words, that awakened the marquis.

"Lord Wetherby?"

He knew he had to be dreaming. However, the familiar sweet voice that he waited for with such anticipation each morning and night continued to whisper his name. He watched the three specters advance toward his bed. He was about to call her name when a more demanding order startled him.

"Ernest! For heaven's sakes, wake up!"

Wetherby sprang to a sitting position. "God, Caro! What are you doing here?"

"Well, that is a fine reception. Good Lord! You look as if you haven't shaved in days."

Wetherby ran his hand along his rough jaw. "I haven't had access to the luxuries you have been enjoying," he said sarcastically, taking note of her straggly hair and less-than-impressionable jumble of clothing.

Millicent could see his lordship was not overly joyed to see them. "Shh," she admonished, lighting the lantern. "There is no time for arguing. We have come to rescue you, my lord."

Wetherby was now standing, and pointed to the chain on his ankle. "How, pray tell, do you propose to do that?"

Millicent set down the lantern and falling to her knees, turned the key in the lock. The iron ring fell free.

"I'm afraid to ask how you got that," he said.

"Lady Caroline did it," Millicent said, then in hushed tones proceeded to tell him of their discovery of the passageway and the door leading into the field.

"Did you give any idea to what would happen if we are discovered?" He held up his hand. "No, I can see you didn't. I only pray that you are right about the exit." Wetherby quickly pulled on his coat and was hurrying them to the door, when Caroline nearly dropped her heavy box.

"What is that?"

"My jewels, of course. I refuse to let that rude, masked thief have my valuables."

*Deliver me from the vanities of women,* Wetherby mumbled. "It will only slow us down and even cause us to be caught. You will leave it." He took the case and tossed it onto the mattress beside the ledger.

Caroline pouted, but complied.

Rupert, eyes pleading, picked up the journal and held it to his chest.

Wetherby started to shake his head, but on second thought took the book and stuffed it inside his coat. "It is not that big," he said gruffly. He handed Rupert a candle and lit one for himself. "Now, let us be gone before we are found out."

Millicent was already several paces ahead, carrying the lantern.

Wetherby caught up with her and reached for the light.

She refused to give it to him. "Rupert and I know the way," she said. "You and Lady Caroline do not. It would be more helpful if you brought up the rear to see that she doesn't fall."

Wetherby decided that now was not the time to argue, and upon reflection, it made more sense for him to stay behind in case their captors came in pursuit.

Which is exactly what happened.

Boggles's angry roar echoed through the hollow passageways, with Tooter's bugle call following close behind.

"Faster!" Wetherby urged.

Millicent looked back, and in so doing, stumbled over a fallen rock and pitched forward. The lantern crashed to the ground, the light going out with it.

"Momma!" Rupert cried in dismay.

Wetherby dropped his own candle as he leaped forward to catch Millicent.

She grimaced. "I am afraid I have sprained my ankle. Go on. Don't miss your chance to escape. I will be all right."

The angry voices of Boggles and Tooter sounded farther away than they had before.

"They have taken the wrong passageway," Rupert whispered.

"But not for long," Millicent said, the urgency showing in her voice. "They will soon discover their mistake."

Wetherby thought quickly. "Rupert, go on with Lady Caroline. I will not leave your mother. If the two of you escape, you can bring help." He handed Caroline his candle. "It will take Boggles and Tooter awhile before they find us. It is our only hope. Go!"

Rupert and Caroline hesitated only a minute, then fled down the final passageway, just as the thieves turned the corner and spotted them.

Wetherby raised his hands in surrender. He wouldn't take the chance of Millicent being hurt further.

"Hang it! The brat and the witch are getting away," shouted Boggles as he rounded on Wetherby and Millicent.

"The Guv woll have our heads if they escape," Tooter whimpered.

"Stoopid! Stay with these hoity-toities while I go after them other two," Boggles yelled at Tooter, before following the dim spot of light in the distance.

Up ahead, Rupert pointed with his candle and cried out, "Lady Caroline! There is the opening."

Caroline surveyed the black hole in alarm. "It is too narrow," she hissed. "I cannot possibly get through."

Rupert's faith in his princess was not deterred. "You can do it, Lady Caroline. I know you can!"

Caroline looked at the earnest little face below her. Yes, she very well might.

Rupert felt his heart thudding against his chest. "Quickly, I hear someone coming. I shall hold them off as long as I can," he said, handing her his candle.

Caroline looked with trepidation at the opening in the wall.

"There you are you, little brat," Boggles yelled, making a grab for Rupert.

Caroline climbed up over the pile of jagged rocks.

Rupert was quaking in his boots, but undaunted, he unsheathed his sword and faced his enemy. "On guard!" he cried, whacking Boggles across the shins with the wooden blade.

Swearing every foul oath he could think of, Boggles swatted

Rupert out of the way, then clambered up after Caroline—too late. She'd already squeezed through the crevice.

Boggles couldn't even get one of his beefy legs through the narrow opening. He raised the lantern only to see a tiny pin-point of light disappearing up the steps. Dragging Rupert by the scruff of his neck, he headed back toward Tooter and the other captives.

Rupert tried to break away. "Momma, are you all right?"

Millicent tried to reassure him. " 'Tis only a twisted ankle—but where is Lady Caroline?"

"She escaped," Rupert reported.

"Thank God!" Millicent said.

Wetherby could not believe what he'd heard. *She escaped.* Caro was showing a whole new side of herself. Perhaps his assessment of her had been wrong.

Boggles growled. "You," he ordered Wetherby, "make yer-self useful and carry the jade up to the kitchen." Tightening his grip on Rupert's arm, he continued to pull him, sword and all, along the corridor.

Wetherby would have gladly pulverized both men, but with a woman in his arms and Tooter's gun at his back, he had little choice in the matter.

Wrapping her arms around his neck, Millicent closed her eyes and let out her breath. "If it had not been for my stupid blunder, you would all be free by now. You should have left me," she said.

Wetherby climbed the steps and held her closer against his chest to hush her. "Let me hear no more of that rubbish, madam." He wondered how, at a time like this, he could even be contemplating the softness of her. It was as he laid her gently on her mattress a few minutes later that the journal fell out of his coat and plopped to the floor.

Rupert made a dive for it, but Tooter was faster. Hooting like a ninny, he kicked the book across the floor.

"Shet yer trap, Tooter," Boggles bellowed, pinning Wetherby's arms behind his back. "We ain't playing games. He'p me with this sprig or we're in big trouble."

Rupert threw his arms around Wetherby's waist and glared at the two men.

Before the boy could get himself into more mischief. Wetherby whispered hoarsely. "Hide the book or those simpletons will tear it apart."

As Boggles and Tooter dragged the marquis to the far side of the room, Rupert retrieved his journal. Then, when no one was watching, he stuffed it behind the same pile of kindling that hid the remains of his mother's gift. He would retrieve it later after the men were asleep.

But alas, it was not to be. No more than an hour later, the Bandit King returned to the farmhouse, alone. He strode in confidently as if expecting to find the establishment running like a well-oiled machine, only to hear a cock-and-bull story of chaos and utter confusion. The marquis was chained to an iron ring that protruded from the large fireplace. Some terrible odor rose up from the black kettle on the hearth, strangling his throat. Mrs. Copley lay on her mattress with a bandaged foot propped up, while her son stood beside her, ready to unsheath his sword.

Boggles and Tooter exchanged looks that were both apologetic and terrified, while Peen busied himself noisily banging his pots and pans.

The masked man roared, "What do you mean, Lady Caroline escaped? Why didn't you go after her?"

"It was his lordship you said was the bait," Boggles sputtered.

"You bumbling fools! Don't you realize that if she gets help, it will not matter one way or the other if we have the marquis?"

Boggles gave a sickly smile. "Shouldn't be no trouble fer you. You got a horse. She don't."

"Hasn't any one of you bothered to stick his nose outside today? Snow has been falling for the last eight hours."

Boggles and Tooter looked first at their feet, then at the rafters in the ceiling. Everywhere except at their employer.

The bandit whirled on them. the urgency in his deep, rumbling voice unmistakable. "I must go after Lady Caroline. 'Twill be a miracle if she survives in this weather." He ignored Millicent's gasp in the background and continued, "It will take another two days for my business transaction to be completed. You are not safe here anymore. 'Tis imperative you move to another location immediately." There was a crash as a crockpot shattered on the stone floor. "Peen, quit hiding behind your kettles and get over here. I want you to see that these imbeciles do as I tell them."

The little man ran over and wriggled into the lineup between Tooter and Boggles.

The Bandit King marched back and forth in front of them, pulling on his gloves. "I shall deal with the three of you later. But now, every evidence of our guests must be removed from this house—and don't forget Wetherby's cell. As soon as the coach is loaded, I want you to head south back toward Exeter. Take our guests to the old inn where we had our first meeting. Blind Daniel will not betray me. Stay there until I contact you. And . . . I don't want one hair on their heads hurt. Do you understand me?"

The three men nodded like puppets on a string.

The masked bandit's anger cut the air like a Saracen's sword. "I warn you if you bungle *this* assignment, you will not receive so much as a halfpenny." He stared at them for one more agonizing moment before he slammed out the door, his final words ringing in their ears. "I shall deal with you later."

# Fourteen

With the help of the two stablemen, the coach was loaded before daylight, and the three prisoners found themselves once again bound, gagged, blindfolded, and stuffed like sacks of flour among a jumble of trunks and boxes. Only Millicent had been given a small amount of consideration for her sprained ankle, and was carried to the carriage by Boggles—a humiliation she wished she hadn't had to endure.

Peen sent Tooter to clean out Wetherby's room in the cellar where he found Caroline's jewelry box. Squealing his delight, he ran up the steps two at a time to show Boggles. "Lor! Look yerr!" he giggled, his eyes shining brighter than the diamond necklace that he held up to the firelight.

Boggles smacked Tooter's hand, making him drop the necklace, then pawed through the collection of precious metals and sparkling gems himself. "I woll take care of these," he said, slamming shut the fine-tooled case and tucking it under his arm.

Tooter pouted but didn't challenge the larger man.

It was not long into the day before they were on the road leading from the old farm. When they came to the turn where they had posted the misleading signpost to Catscow Lane, Boggles dutifully turned the horses south.

Inside the carriage, Millicent found herself on the seat opposite Wetherby and Rupert. It was uncomfortable being seated with her arms bound behind her, and her ankle ached—especially every time Rupert's feet banged against hers. He was so young and impatient, but it seemed to her that he was bouncing about far more than was necessary, until she heard his squeal.

"Momma! I got my gag and blindfold off."

Millicent wanted to ask Rupert how in the world he'd done that, but her own mouth was still filled with the dirty rag Boggles had stuffed into it. It wasn't until she heard Wetherby's voice that she realized something was afoot.

"Press your back up against mine," Wetherby said. "Your fingers are the nimblest. See if you can undo the knot on the binding around my wrists."

Millicent strained to picture what was going on across from her. Suspense, hope, and helplessness collided in her imagination.

Then Wetherby's words rang out. "You did it, you little rascal."

She felt strong hands grasp her scarf and unwind it from her eyes and mouth. They were not gentle hands, but they were quick, and to Millicent they felt like those of a benevolent angel. She began to cry her relief, but before she could do so, Wetherby clamped his hand over her mouth.

"Do not make a sound. We don't want our captors to know that we have freed ourselves."

Millicent made out Wetherby's face in the dim light. It was so close, she could feel his breath on her cheek. The next moment she thought he was embracing her. A tremor ran through her and she waited breathlessly for him to tell her that everything was going to be all right. But alas, he'd only reached behind her to loosen the rope binding her wrists. She put her foolishness down to the excitement of the moment. However, now that she was free, she felt much more the thing and turned her attention to her son, who was still doing far too much jumping about. "Rupert," she hissed, "whatever you are doing, stop it. You are bumping my foot."

"I'm sorry, Momma. I was strapping on my sword. See? I found it on the floor of the carriage."

Sure enough, even in the dim light of the coach, Millicent could see Rupert confidently arming himself.

While the three prisoners consulted inside, an argument was crescendoing rapidly atop the high seat of the coach. Luckily, or unluckily—it depended on whose opinion one sought—Peen sat squeezed between the two men. Only his presence had so far kept his companions from being at each other's throats.

"It's all yer fault," Boggles spat out, cracking a whip over the heads of the four horses that were endeavoring to gain their footing in the rising snow.

"Ain't neither. If you weren't such a clumsy lummox—spilling everything you carry—that Jezebel wid never've gone down into the cellar in the first place."

Boggles reached over and tried to knock Tooter's hat off. "I told you he wud have our heads."

"Come, come, gentlemen," squeaked Peen from under their armpits. "We have a long way to go, and it is starting to snow harder."

Sure enough, the white flakes were descending with more and more rapidity, piling atop the already two feet that had accumulated over the night. But the struggling of the horses only made the men angrier, and the quarreling continued. Boggles reached over to smack Tooter again, and only ended up hitting Peen. As the little man grabbed for his hat, he jolted Boggles's arm, which made him jerk on the reins, sending the confused cattle off the now-invisible narrow lane and into a prickly hedgerow. The more they thrashed, the more entangled they became. The carriage tilted dangerously to one side, and was in danger of tipping over.

"See wot you done, Stoopid," Boggles bellowed. "Now we have to get them beasts out of this mess." With much maneuvering, he finally managed to get the frenzied horses to back up. "Get down and see if them nobs is still in one piece."

Tooter jumped off and ran back to the coach.

The minute the door opened, Wetherby came out fighting. Millicent thought he was magnificent. He landed a well-placed facer square on Tooter's nose, then rounded on the bellowing Boggles. Rupert grabbed his sword and followed. Tooter had recovered and lay siege to Wetherby from behind while trying to protect his backside from the whacking Rupert was giving him with his wooden stick.

It was not in Millicent's nature to stand idly by when she was needed. After all, she had an axe to grind with the ruffians as much as Rupert and Lord Wetherby did. With a flourish, she leaped to their rescue, only to find herself flat on her face beside the carriage. She'd forgotten her injured foot.

Poor Peen stood up on the high seat, rocking back and forth, wringing his hands, while his cohorts pounded the marquis into unconsciousness. "Oh, me, oh, my! Look what ye've done," he whimpered.

Both men stared down at the prostrate nobleman, blood running into the snow from the cut on his forehead. "The Guv will have our heads fer sure now," said Boggles, looking accusingly at Tooter.

"Oh, Momma! They have killed him," cried Rupert, kneeling beside his hero.

Millicent scooted over to Wetherby and cradled his head in her lap. His head was bloody, but he was breathing. "He has just been knocked unconscious, dear. He will be all right when he wakes up." She hoped she sounded convincing, but to hide her own worries, she rounded on the simpleton standing over her. "You were told no one was to be hurt," she scolded.

"Didn't mean to hit him so hard," Tooter whined, "but he was banging me face. He shouldn't have din that."

"Git into the carriage," Boggles demanded obnoxiously.

Millicent looked down at the lifeless face in her lap and swallowed uneasily. The indignity of it all brought back her courage.

"And how, may I ask, do you think we can do that when I am crippled and his lordship is unconscious?"

"Gah! Sharp-tongued females," was the only reply she got from Boggles.

By now, Peen had climbed down, and he and Tooter managed to get Rupert and Millicent into the carriage. Tossing the comatose marquis in after them, Boggles slammed the door shut.

They had proceeded for another half hour before Tooter broke the silence. "Don't seem fair that we has to do all the work, and don't get no money."

Boggles stopped the horses. "That's the first smart thing I heard you say all day," he said. He reached under the seat and pulled out the jewelry case. "There's enough loot in this box to set us up to live like kings fer the rest of our lives."

Tooter stuck out his lower lip. "The Guv wouldn't let us keep it, you dummy. He wud come right to Blind Daniel's and wring our necks."

"Not if we head north instead of south," said Boggles, backing the horses around and turning in the opposite direction. "We can be on the north coast of Devon by tonight. With all the smugglers I know, we'll be on a boat and far away by the time the Bandit King knows wot's wot."

"More likely any mates of yers will take all the jewels for themselves."

"Not if we hide all the good stuff in our boots. What they don't know won't hurt 'em. We'll hand over the coach and tell them they can have all the loot if they take us up the west coast."

"And what do we do with his lordship and the biddy and her chick?"

"Hmm," Boggles thought a minute. "I say we do away with them. Who's to know?"

Peen gasped. "Oh Lor! Thee cannot do that."

Boggles snapped, "And have them fetch the authorities on us?"

"Surely if thee just leaves them somewhere where they wid not be found for a while, it wid give us time to get away."

Tooter giggled. "Like in a snowbank?"

Peen pulled his muffler tighter around his face. "If thee did that, they wid freeze to death."

"Do you want us to throw *thee* out with 'em, Peen?" Boggles threatened.

Shuttering, the little man shrank further down into his collar.

Only once did they stop to get some food and rest the horses. Due to their shortsightedness, the men had failed to bring any provisions with them. Millicent knew it was at Mr. Peen's insistence that she be allowed to go into the inn to freshen up.

"Jest herself," said Boggles. "The boy and the nob stay outside. She won't cry foul if we have her calf."

It was an unsavory, dirty place, smelling of stale tobacco and unwashed men. A coating of soot from the smoldering logs and cooking odors clung to the plastered walls like mold on week-old bread. Just the fact that she was a woman drew several crude remarks and made Millicent draw her shawl more tightly around her face. A worse lot she'd never seen. The only females were serving girls, and they gave her no more than a passing glance. She thanked her stars that her own bedraggled clothing and tangled hair bespoke nothing of a lady. If she had any hopes of slipping a word to someone of her plight, they were soon dashed. She hurried to the back room off the kitchen that was indicated by a slatterly-looking woman who was slapping food into trenchers from a large iron pot boiling over the fire.

It seemed that spirits were most on Boggles's and Tooter's minds for when Millicent returned to the common room, both men had two bottles tucked under each arm. Mr. Peen had secured a large mug of hot gruel and some bread for her. Millicent gave him a grateful look. She took only a sip and carried the rest out to Rupert, who sat inside the coach with his nose pressed against the window, anxiously awaiting her return.

Wetherby was still unconscious, and only a groan now and then showed that he was still alive. Perhaps it was better in the long run, Millicent thought, because men seemed to have a propensity for making matters worse when they were angry, and she was sure his lordship would be anything but pleasant when he awakened.

It seemed to Rupert as though they'd been traveling for ever so long, and the snow was coming down so fast the horses struggled harder and harder to make their way. As the path became bumpier and the drifts higher, the ride became increasingly rougher. He wondered if they were even on a road at all. Then the air cleared. The clouds parted, stars shined through, and a half-moon smiled down, painting a deceptively fairylike picture. Once in awhile a scraggly clump of leafless trees loomed on the horizon, but for the most part it was a white, barren landscape. In the distance, he saw a tiny yellow eye of light flickering. Then the wind ceased. No sounds now except for the heaving snorts of the horses, the creaking of their leather harnesses, and the deep growling voices that floated down from the driver's seat.

"The snow has stopped, Momma," Rupert whispered, "but I don't see any buildings out there."

Millicent tried not to show her anxiety. "Lie down and try to sleep, dear. Like his lordship," she added, trying to sound natural. "We must be rested for tomorrow." The marquis lay sprawled over the baggage on the floor, and she was not strong enough to lift him. She'd wrapped a cloth over his wound and covered him with the fur coach rug, hoping that when they reached their destination she would be able to persuade Mr. Peen to find a doctor for him. She tried to hold Rupert, but he wriggled free to look out the window.

"Do you think Lady Caroline is safe?"

"I am sure she is warm and cozy in someone's fine house," Millicent replied as reassuringly as she could. "The authorities are probably looking for us already."

Rupert didn't say anything for a few minutes, then sighed. "We are not going to get to Uncle Andy's for Christmas, are we, Momma?"

"There is still time, dear. I am sure the bandit will let us go as soon as he has his money."

"But Christmas is day after tomorrow."

Before she could answer, the coach came to a staggering halt. There was a commotion outside and the door flew open.

Millicent gave a sigh of relief. "Are we there?" she asked, hopefully.

Boggles laughed, a much more wicked laugh than Millicent liked to hear. "This is the end of the line, my lady," he said, grabbing her around the waist and heaving her from the vehicle. She tried to maintain her balance, but her ankle gave way and she tumbled into a snowbank. Rupert followed, his exit a little rougher.

"That was uncalled for, sir," she said, trying without success to rise. Millicent wasn't ready for what happened next, or she would have protested harder. Before she knew it, Wetherby was dragged through the door, coach rug and all, and dumped into the snow beside her, knocking her flat once more. With a great deal of effort, she held her indignation in check. After all, one couldn't expect much else from a fustian like Boggles, and any opposition from her would surely provoke him to more disgusting behavior. The important thing was to get Lord Wetherby into the warm inn. She looked about the bleak landscape in confusion.

The odious Boggles, still laughing, jumped back up to the driver's seat and with a shout to the horses, left the three travelers sitting alone in the snowbank beside a pitiful stand of trees.

As they rode away, she heard a high-pitched, protesting squeal from Mr. Peen.

Occupied as she had been in searching for a dwelling—which she soon saw didn't exist—Millicent realized with a sinking heart that she'd failed to interpret Boggles's true intention. The bounder had meant all along to leave them there. She watched helplessly as the coach disappeared over the roadless hills into the starry night, carrying with it all their clothing and Christmas gifts.

So there they sat in the snow: a little boy, an unconscious man, and a crippled woman. Only one day before Christmas, and heaven knew where they were. They would surely freeze if they didn't get aid. Millicent held Wetherby's head gently to her chest and did the best she could to tuck the coach robe over both their legs. He was so still. If anything happened to him . . . It was then that Millicent recognized the warm sensation sweeping through her heart for what it was. Love. She'd fallen in love with Ernest Lance, the Marquis of Wetherby. She didn't want anything bad to happen to him any more than to her son.

But Rupert, clapping his hands together to keep them warm, was on his feet staring into the distance. "Momma, we must find help."

"Dearest, we will have to wait until daylight. I have no idea of where we are, and I cannot walk—and his lordship . . ." She didn't want to frighten Rupert with what she really thought. 'Twould be a miracle if anyone found us on a night like this.

"Oh, Momma, you are right. It *is* the time of year for miracles, is it not?" A moment of silence prevailed, broken only by Rupert's sigh. "But, I suppose God is quite busy tonight getting ready for all the holiday services."

Millicent held her breath in anticipation of what her son would think of next.

"Maybe God could use some help."

"Rupert, get over here and under this blanket before you catch your death," Millicent admonished, more quickly than was necessary.

He squared his shoulders. "No. I will have to be the one to go," he said, a little waver in his voice.

Millicent watched the struggle on her son's face. "My goodness! Do not speak such foolishness. You are . . ." she started to say *only a little boy,* when she saw the look of defiance in his eyes. "What would his lordship say if he knew you planned such nonsense?" she said in a last desperate attempt to dissuade him from his folly.

"It is Code One, the most important of all—Faithfulness to one's God. Lord Wetherby knows all about that," Rupert finished, with a note of male superiority.

Knowing she was losing the argument, Millicent said a little defensively, "You are not dressed warmly enough. Besides, where would you go?"

Rupert looked back in the direction from which they had come. "I remember seeing a light from the coach back aways. It must have been a house. I shall follow the carriage tracks and ask for help."

The idea of letting her child out of her sight terrified Millicent.

Rupert made sure his sword was tucked securely in his belt. "I will be grown soon, Momma. Think how brave Lord Wetherby was when he was chained in that dark cellar all by himself. Think how hard he fought for us. I must show him that I can be brave too. You cannot go because you hurt your leg." He hesitated telling her that she was a frail woman and had to be protected, because that was a part of The Code that he still had trouble understanding. But now he had other, more important, things to attend to. "I shall not fail you."

Wetherby groaned and twisted restlessly.

Millicent drew him closer to try to warm him with her own body heat. She knew in her heart that there was no alternative but for Rupert to go if they were to get help for Lord Wetherby. "Then I shall pray for your safe return," she said, trying to keep her voice steady. "And, Rupert," she called after him, "pull your sleeves down over your hands to keep them warm."

Rupert did not hear her, for his thoughts were filled with the outlandish tales of gallantry that Lord Wetherby had spun for him. Fancying himself a knight of old, he stoically marched across the lonely countryside with only the moon and stars to light his way and the tracks of the coach to guide him.

Millicent's eyes strained to watch the small figure until he was no more than a speck of dust that disappeared over a snowbank.

Twenty minutes later, a very tired and cold little boy stumbled across a humble crofter's cottage that was overflowing with children's laughter. When the kindly farmer's wife opened the door, there were so many curious faces surrounding her that Rupert could not count them all. The family was getting ready for Christmas and the home was filled with the delicious odors of honey cakes, pies, and puddings.

Upon hearing Rupert's story of woe, Mr. Potter, a robust man with a thick red beard and arms as thick as oak trees, called to his two equally strapping sons, "Joshua . . . Samuel . . . don your coats and mufflers. Someone here needs help."

Taking no thought of their own discomfort, they came with Rupert to rescue the poor lad's parents, *Mr. and Mrs. Lance,* whom the boy said were freezing in the snow after having been set upon by thieves. Rupert thought the *parent part,* which he added to his already embellished tale of misfortune, was a very clever bit of frosting on the cake. Oh, yes. His bones may have been chilled, but his wit was only sharpened by all the excitement and adventure.

In no more time than it took a star to wink, Millicent found herself and Wetherby wrapped in thick, woolen blankets and carried into the comfortable cottage. As the warmth infused itself through her body, Millicent was only barely aware of all the activity their entrance had aroused. On the opposite side of the large room, a fireplace blazed invitingly. A long table and benches took up much of the floor space. She could hear the bleating of sheep and the lowing of cows through the walls.

Mrs. Potter shooed the younger children away and appointed the older ones to run errands. "Mary and Martha, fetch some bread and stew for the brave lad."

The brown-haired twins, round and sassy and already taller than their mother, good-naturedly did as they were told.

Rupert hailed that idea with much enthusiasm, and discarding his wraps, climbed onto the bench and fell to eating.

The woman then turned to Millicent, who'd been carried to a rocking chair near the hearth. "Now, don't thee be worrying yerself, dear. Yer son has told us all about your terrible ordeal. He is already eating a hearty meal—nothing wrong with his appetite—and my men are taking good care of yer man's wound."

Not until she heard that Rupert and Wetherby were being attended to was Mrs. Potter able to persuade Millicent into an adjoining bedroom where a small blaze burned in a stone fireplace. She undressed her as if she were a child and helped her into one of her own night rails. After *oohing* and *ahhing* over her bruised foot, Mrs. Potter redressed the swollen ankle before tucking her into the soft, toasty bed. She once more offered her guest a bowl of soup.

Millicent was too tired to take more than a few sips, and assured again that the other two were safe in the next room, she quickly fell into an exhausted sleep.

When Millicent awakened the next morning, she found herself staring up at an unfamiliar whitewashed low ceiling, crisscrossed by dark, hand-hewn beams. She let her gaze pan from one corner to the other. Last night she thought she'd never be warm again. Now, she felt as though she lay in a field of clover on a summer day. She heard the crackling of fire. Someone had already been in to light it. Slowly her memory returned. A woman's pleasant voice softly hummed "Hark! The Herald Angels Sing" in the next room. Children giggled. Then she recognized Rupert's runaway tongue. A sense of peace ran through her, and savoring the softness of the thick feather mattress, she snuggled down and tried to pull the comforter tighter around her. But it wouldn't budge. Millicent gave it another tug, then rolled over to see what held it. She gasped.

Tucked in beside her, a very familiar face lay upon the adjoining pillow, brown eyes watching her inquisitively. His head was bandaged and one eye nearly swollen shut, but still an insufferable, half-cocked grin was spreading across his face. Millicent sat upright. "You!" she exclaimed. A humiliating realization struck her. She had spent the night snug in bed with Lord Wetherby.

# Fifteen

Millicent sealed her lips. She would never forgive him. Neither would she give way to a fit of the vapors, like some missish green girl. How dare he try to compromise her? She was no lightskirt. On second thought, Lord Wetherby had been unconscious when they had arrived at the cottage last night. There had to be another explanation of how he came to be in her bed.

Wetherby spoke from the right side of his mouth, which gave him a slight slur. "I shought for a minute that pr'haps I'd died and gone t'heaven."

Millicent eyed him suspiciously. It was plain as a pikestaff that if she was going to get a sensible answer, it wasn't going to come from his lordship. Yet, the jackanapes didn't seem the least disturbed at finding himself in bed with *her.* Millicent's gaze ran over his bruised face. It appeared that he might have a permanent wink etched upon his handsome features. She hoped not. What a disastrous happenstance that would be if his masculine beauty were marred. However, the comical picture of Rupert trying to imitate Wetherby's present lopsided expression triggered a totally unexpected response, forcing her to turn away from him to keep from giggling. She was becoming as addlepated as his lordship.

Perhaps she was being unfair. It had to be the delirium. After the hit on the head, he was not himself. Millicent would have to satisfy herself with that—for the time being. The fault was that she'd had no previous experience with rakes before she'd met Lord Wetherby, and therefore was amiss as to how to react to one who was obviously demented. So as not to unbalance him further, she decided the best course was to treat the whole situation lightly. Millicent cast Wetherby a sideways look.

The minute she glanced his way, he held his ribs, groaning, "Dashed funny—didn't notice a shing a minute ago—now, I feel like a coach and four hash run me over." His eyes closed and his head fell limp to one side.

Millicent, ashamed of her callousness in regard to all the bravery he had shown them during their perilous journey, leaned forward, letting the coverlet drop to her waist.

Wetherby's eyes popped open. "Did shoo know Mrs. Copley—'scuse the 'spression—shoo are a demmed attractive woman in th'morning?"

Millicent clutched her night rail at the neck. Of course, he didn't know what he was saying, she reminded herself. *Answer as if nothing is helter-skelter,* she told herself. "Lah! No more handsome than you, my lord."

Wetherby gingerly felt his swollen eye. "*Touche!*" he said, trying to sit up, only to fall back onto his pillow once more, his face turning white.

Panic gripped her, and Millicent began to massage one of his hands. "Please, don't try to get up. You are not at all well."

He began to stare at her in the oddest way. "Shoo will 'scuse me, Milli-shent . . . I may call you Milli-shent, may I not? It does seem that under the circumstances *Mrs. Copley* is a trifle formal."

Millicent quickly stopped her rubbing and jerked her hands away. He was laughing at her. Even after being knocked senseless, his lordship still remained a rascal. She was searching her brain for what to say next, when he furrowed his brow.

"I seem to have a vacant spot in my memory. I remember . . ." Wetherby threw off the coverlet and sat upright. "Good God! Those runagates. Rupert! Is he all right?"

Millicent lunged across him just in time to grasp the edge of the comforter before it fell to the floor. "Rupert is fine," she gasped, frantically trying to cover his legs back up. "After Boggles and Tooter left us in the snow, Rupert insisted on going for help. He came across these good people, the Potters, who rescued us. We are in their cottage now."

Wetherby sank back onto his pillow with a sigh of relief. "Rupert did that? Hee'sh but a child."

"You should have thought of that before you filled his head with all those tales of derring-do, my lord," she scolded. "He just may have died out there in the cold." The thought of her innocent son made Millicent more aware than ever of her compromising predicament. She dare not let Rupert see her. What explanation could she possibly give a little boy for his mother being in bed with a man who was not her husband?

Her question was interrupted by a knock. Mrs. Potter's face appeared around the door. "Ah, prithee! Thee are awake, Mrs. Lance."

Millicent pulled the covers up around her chin. "*Mrs. Lance?*" she repeated dumbly.

The crofter's wife, her arms laden with a tray of sweetcakes and a pot of coffee, thrust the door open with her ample hips. "Yer son has been very worried about thee and his papa.

"His *papa?*" Millicent knew that she was beginning to sound like a parrot, but she could think of nothing else to say. To make things worse, the marquis lay beside her, hands locked behind his head, grinning like an idiot. His attitude certainly wasn't helping the situation one bit. Well, as soon as she was alone with Mrs. Potter, she'd set things to rights. But how could she possibly do that without making her own position look worse?

Before Millicent could utter a coherent word, Rupert came bounding into the room. "Momma, Papa, you must get up and see the Nativity Joshua and Samuel are setting up. Tommy says that Samuel carved it. Each year he makes a new figure and won't tell them what it is until they set up the whole scene and they are making bows and braids to put on the windows and Mrs. Potter says I may help decorate." He stopped to catch his breath.

Millicent stared at her son.

Chuckling, Mrs. Potter made way for the excited boy. Then, setting the tray on a table by the side of the bed, she checked Wetherby's bandage. "Now, now," she chided, "yer papa is in no condition to be gallivanting about. Hem had quite a beating."

"Come here, son," Wetherby said, exerting great effort to make both sides of his mouth turn upward at the same time. He failed.

Warily, Rupert looked back and forth between the two adults in the bed. He had called him *son.* It was only make-believe, of course, but his lordship seemed willing to play the game. He glanced hopefully at his mother.

Millicent pursed her lips and said nothing. So this was Rupert's doing. There was nothing she could do now—but just wait until she got him alone.

Rupert swallowed hard. From the warning in his mother's eye, he knew he had to move quickly before she spilled the beans.

Wetherby held out his hand like a lifeline and Rupert, grinning gleefully, ran to him. If Mrs. Potter hadn't been present, he would have jumped into bed with them. Then, they would be as they should be—a family. A momma on one side of him and a papa on the other.

Wetherby tossled Rupert's hair.

"You look terrible," Rupert said, frowning.

" 'Tish but a trifle inconvenience," Wetherby said. "A warrior muth 'spect a few battle scars."

Rupert stood up straighter and nodded solemnly. "I shall remember that," he said.

While Mrs. Potter turned her attention to Millicent, Wetherby whispered, "From the reports of shur brave and daring deeds, I do believe that another shtar will be forthcoming in your book, wouldn't shoo say?"

Rupert looked down at his feet. "I am afraid the journal got left behind at the farmhouse."

Wetherby placed his arm around Rupert's shoulder and gave him a hug.

By now, Mrs. Potter had rounded the bed to Millicent's side. "How's yer foot, Mrs. Lance?"

Surprisingly, Millicent had forgotten all about her sprained ankle. The swelling had gone down and with the new binding, she felt little discomfort. This knowledge made her disposition improve immeasurably, and she felt more inclined to let matters stand as they appeared for the moment. She looked warmly upon the kind woman.

"I thought thee would like something to eat in bed," Mrs. Potter said cheerfully. " 'Tis nearly noon. Thee has slept through the morning."

The smell of food raised Wetherby's spirits. "Are shoo as hungry as I am, m'dear?" he said. "I feel I haven't eaten for a week."

Millicent would not give him the satisfaction of looking at him. "Oh, no, Mrs. Potter, I prefer to eat in the other room," she said, springing from the bed only to look down in dismay at her night rail.

"Now, now," Mrs. Potter clucked. "Don't thee be worrying about yer clothes, dear. They were quite worn. I am sure 'twas due to yer terrible ordeal. Martha washed them this morning. Yer husband's, too. They are hanging by the fire. Thee are welcome to wear something of mine until yers dry." She took a gown and an apron from a peg on the wall and handed them to Millicent. "I'll leave now," she said, "so thee can dress. I know thee will be wanting to take care of yer husband's needs, too. The pot is here under the bed," she said, pulling the large lidded crockery out in full view.

Millicent's face turned crimson.

Without a backward glance, Rupert dashed out of the room ahead of Mrs. Potter.

Holding the garments, Millicent looked about frantically. There wasn't even a screen to hide behind.

"I shall close my eyes while shoo change," Wetherby said quite seriously, pulling a pillow down over his face to emphasize his sincerity.

Millicent flushed from head to toe. She didn't trust him one whit and as she dressed, kept looking back nervously over her shoulder. Her hair was quite hopeless. She stuffed as much of it as she could under the mobcap that Mrs. Potter had left for her. She had just started for the door, but she hesitated. Taking care of a man in delirium was one thing, but was he able to get out of bed by himself? "Do you want me to . . . to pour you a cup of coffee—or anything else?" she said, confused as how to finish.

"Just leave . . . Millish . . . Mrs." he mumbled some almost indistinguishable syllables from under the pillow, which she was sure she didn't want to hear anyway. "Whether shoo believe it or not, I am quite capable of taking care of m'self."

"Yes, my lord," she said, scurrying from the room, not at all certain of anything.

As soon as she left the room, Wetherby let out a low growl—a decidedly animal growl. Then the truth struck him senseless. He was in love. When had it happened? Was it this morning, when he had awakened to find her beside him? Or had it been in that dismal cell, when he'd counted every minute until he'd see her again? Or perhaps when he'd watched her give her money to a beggar? No, it had to be when she'd hit him with the snowball.

Who would have ever believed it? He, Ernest Lance, the Marquis of Wetherby, had fallen in love. He'd found a woman he not only desired like no other before her, but whom he wanted to make his wife.

Surely his father would come round once he'd met Millie. *Millie*. It was the first time he'd permitted himself to think of her in such a personal way. He realized how much he would want to see that face next to his when he awakened each morning for the rest of his life. But from the way she'd glared at him, she obviously was not of the same opinion. How could he blame her?

Wetherby's head was spinning, and every time he opened his mouth he sounded like an idiot. Wincing, he tried to move his jaw from side to side. Boggle's facer had surely dislocated it. How could she possibly think of him favorably, looking like a ruffian dragged in off the streets? His courtship of Mrs. Copley would have to wait. Wait until he could do it properly. He never realized how much he depended upon his valet. He'd wait until Jespers had him shaved and dressed to the eyes—like a respectable gentleman. Then, he'd tell her how much she'd come to mean to him. He'd even get down on one knee to propose to her. Hell! Who was he fooling? He knew his father wouldn't give one inch in his requirements for his heir's wife.

*Impeccable bloodlines, son. Make sure she's an heiress in her own right. Don't want a woman who is in awe of the title and wealth that will be yours someday.*

Wetherby was afraid no amount of persuasion would ever change the old stick-in-the-mud, and he could see that his charm wasn't working any wonders on Mrs. Copley, either. What was it he'd said or done to put her in such a dither? He winced to think that at first when he'd awakened, he'd started to accuse her of deliberately crawling under the covers with him. The ploy had been used before, and as out-of-it as he'd been, he wouldn't have known the difference until too late. But she'd seemed as surprised as he had been to find them in the same bed—and he doubted that Mrs. Copley was capable of such fabrication.

At least she wasn't indifferent to him. He'd seen the flush creep up her neck. In fact, he'd watched it spread all the way to her toes. No pillow was going to rob him of that pleasure. He let out a whoop of laughter. If she'd known that he'd been peeking, he really would have been in the stew.

Now, Rupert—he was another matter altogether. There was the culprit, he was positive. His deceptively angelic face was like looking into a mirror. Wetherby had been accused of similar tomfoolery often enough when he was younger. The little devil would need watching when he got older, or he'd wreak havoc wherever he went. But the first thing Wetherby had to do was tell the Potters who he really was and find out where they were.

Millicent had no sooner shut the door than she heard the earthy howl. Such cavalier behavior! Ordering her to leave. The man had no conscience. That was outside of enough. What was he so out of countenance about? After all, it was *her* reputation that was in jeopardy. How could she have been so noodleheaded to even think she could possibly entertain tender feelings for such a rogue? If she hadn't known better, she'd have thought he was foxed, for a more disreputable countenance she'd never seen. Hair askew, four days of beard covering his face, one eye swollen shut like a bloody pirate. *Heaven help her! Even her language was becoming common.* She was beyond redemption. And now, trying to interpret the wild sounds he was making behind that door, she could only conclude that his mind wandered as well.

Suddenly, a sadness enveloped her like mist on a gloomy day. Even if she had felt any affection for the rascal, or he for her—a most unlikely occurrence—she knew that his father would never approve of a serious relationship between them. True, she was sister-in-law to a baron and her own father had a connection to a countess, but that was of little consequence to the likes of the Duke of Loude. Her family was not of the peerage, and the duke would say that she was not worthy of marrying into the Lance dynasty.

Millicent set her lips firmly and limped into the kitchen area.

Who did the duke think he was to decide that a man like her father was not worthy? Edgar Francis Huxley, Esquire, was a good man. He'd been elected by the people of Cross-in-Hand to be their mayor. The duke hadn't been elected to anything. He'd only come by his title because it had been handed down to him. Well, if that was what the nobility judged a man's worth by—title and wealth—she wanted nothing to do with it.

By now, Millicent was in quite a state, and when she came upon Mrs. Potter coming up from the cellar, a sack of potatoes in her arms, she spoke a little more adamantly than she'd meant to. "I want to help you with the cooking today."

Mrs. Potter glanced down at Millicent's bandaged foot. If she thought her guest out of line, her round, ruddy face showed no sign of irritation. "Now, wouldn't that be nice. If thee truly want to be helpful, sit by the fire and stir the batter for the Christmas cake. But first, you'll be needing some breakfast. Martha," she called, "set the kettle to boil for Mrs. Lance. Mary, spoon up some porridge." The twins, as jolly and pink-cheeked as their mother, hurried to do as they were told.

The farmer's wife seemed determined to have her guest sit down, and taking her arm, steered Millicent toward the huge fireplace. "Now when thee has had something to eat, thee can tell me all that brought yer family to this sad state of affairs."

Millicent's ankle proved not to be as well mended as she'd first thought, and after only a few minutes of standing, she found herself grateful to lower herself into the rocking chair. Mary brought her a large bowl and spoon, the smell of cinnamon and steaming cereal coming with her.

Millicent waved to Rupert, who was on the far side of the room playing with Tommy. She had the feeling her son was trying to avoid her—and for good reason, she had to admit. He kept swinging his sword, while Tommy flailed the air with a long stick. Finally he acknowledged her, and with dragging feet, started across the room. Tommy and his sisters followed.

Mrs. Potter leaned forward. "I am glad to see thee are feeling better this morning. But yer mister?" She clucked her tongue. "I am afraid he was not looking quite the thing, his face all swollen up like that. Last night, me mister kept hem up walking a bit before he put hem to bed. He also had me fix a posset to help hem sleep. I always keep barley water and herbs handy to tend me own. In fact, Mr. Potter insisted I make up a tisane, too—said it would take away the pain."

Millicent's eyebrows shot up. A mixture of an alcoholic drink and milk and another of herbs and barley water? A combination that would surely make an elephant noddy. No wonder his lordship was acting the clown this morning. But she would never think to be so boorish as to mention her suspicions to her hostess. She accepted the steaming bowl of porridge from Mary with a smile, and nodded as Martha placed a mug of hot liquid on the stool beside her. "You were all so kind to rescue us."

"Now, dear heart, 'twas nought. Thee are welcome to stay as long as it takes for Mr. Lance to get his senses back," Mrs. Potter said, seating herself on a highbacked, wooden settle, and facing Millicent. " 'Tis nought that us would not have done for any poor folk like us. Yer husband did sound a bit dotty, though, rattling on so," she said, with the lift of an eyebrow.

"He isn't like that all the time," Millicent hurried to assure her.

The good woman gave Millicent a sympathetic look. "Of course not, dear heart. It was getting his noggin cracked, I am sure. But, my oh my, someone certainly darkened his daylights. Such a mess—blood all over."

Millicent choked, spilling her drink.

"Oh, do watch yer coffee," Mrs. Potter warned. "I don't want thee to scald yerself."

Millicent took a deep breath to calm her stomach. "I'm sorry we put you to so much trouble. It was more than enough to ask."

Mrs. Potter threw up her hands. "Landsakes, child! With two growed sons as stiff-rumped as their father, I've patched up more broken heads than thee will ever see in yer lifetime. I did no more than wash and bandage yer man. Me mister stripped hem down and put hem in one of his nightshirts. I reckoned a good night's sleep was what he needed," she said, nodding knowingly. " 'Cept for the bruises on hes face, I'm sure hem will soon be feeling fit as a fiddle." She nodded toward her two sons and five younger daughters, who were coming toward them. Mrs. Potter put her arm around the littlest girl, Ruthie who snuggled up against her mother's skirt. "I'm just thankful I'm having a little respite before Tommy starts thinking hem has to lick every bully who crosses his path." Her eyes glowed with pride. "But, I suppose hem will take after hes father, too. Rough and tumble—me mister—but with a heart twice as big as any ordinary man. That's why hem said us dasn't think of letting thee leave until yer husband gets hes wits back."

They were interrupted by Mr. Potter's deep voice booming from the back doorway as he and his two big sons tramped in from the outdoors with armloads of kindling. " 'Twould be a sin against the Good Lord to cast strangers out into the snow on the eve of Christmas."

" 'Twould indeed," agreed Mrs. Potter, watching her older boys start to forage for any oddments left over from breakfast. "Joshua," she said, "before thee eat up all of the porridge, go knock on Mr. Lance's door and see if hem feels well enough to come out."

With a good-natured shrug, the young man laid down the bowl he was scraping, and headed for the bedroom door.

"Momma!"

Millicent jumped, startled to find Rupert standing at her elbow.

"Even if we cannot be with Uncle Andy for Christmas, being with the Potters is the next best thing—don't you agree, Momma?"

Mr. Potter looked back over his shoulder as he held his

hands to the fire. "Thee were expected somewhere for Christmas, Mrs. Lance?"

Millicent put her finger on Rupert's lips to stop him from saying more. "Actually," she said, "we . . . we were headed for a residence in Devonshire—Roxwealde Castle. There was a party planned, you see."

"At Baron Copley's?" asked Mr. Potter.

Millicent was at a loss as to how the simple crofters would know of her brother-in-law. "Why, yes. I would have not expected you to have heard of him this far south."

"But us be in the north of Devonshire, Mrs. Lance."

Millicent mulled this over for a moment in her mind. "How can that be? I heard our abductor say that we were to be taken to a place near Exeter."

"My oh my! Yer man does muddle up things, don't hem? Poor man!" Mrs. Potter said sympathetically. "Why, thee are in the Devon moors on the border of the Copley property. Us are tenants of the baron's." Mrs. Potter clasped her hands to her bosom as a new insight presented itself. "Thee were going to a new situation at Roxwealde, were thee not? Us heard that they had opened up the old castle and were hiring new help."

Mr. Potter tightened his muffler and started out the door with Samuel. "Jobs be hard to come by in these parts. Me son here went up to apply for carpentry work, but they said they had already filled all the positions."

Samuel nodded.

Frowning, Millicent watched Joshua disappear into the bedroom.

Mrs. Potter shooed the children away. "Now, dear heart," she said, "I can see something is bothering thee. Do you wish to tell us what it is?"

Whether or not the Potters thought them a married couple or not, Millicent knew she must think quickly for some excuse not to spend another night in bed with his lordship. "Mrs. Potter, I wanted to talk to you about our sleeping arrangements," she whispered.

Mrs. Potter leaned closer to hear her. "Ay?"

Millicent took a deep breath. "May I have another room tonight? My husband is still not well, and he would sleep much better in a bed by himself. I worry that if I bump him, I may cause further injury." She thought that sounded plausible enough to take care of the situation, but she was mistaken.

"Oh, my! I am afraid that is impossible. We gave thee our bedroom, last night. 'Tis the only one in the house. See," Mrs. Potter said, emphasizing her point with a wide sweep of her arm.

Confused, Millicent took another look around her. The room was of good size, but there seemed to be children filling every crack and cranny. Near to where Tommy and Rupert were once again fighting imaginary dragons, the five littlest girls laughed and giggled as they strung brightly colored ropes around the windows. Mary and Martha chattered happily in the kitchen, and either Joshua or Samuel came stomping in and out of the barn, bringing in the aroma of livestock as he carried fresh straw to place around the Nativity scene. Besides the door to the animal shelter, there was the front entrance, and the door that led to the bedroom. Another exit off the kitchen area had to lead to the backyard. There could be no other rooms. "Then where did you sleep last night, Mrs. Potter?"

"In the loft with the girls," she said, pointing to the steep ladder-like steps leading to an opening in the ceiling. At Millicent's wide-eyed expression, Mrs. Potter laughed. "Now don't thee pay no nevermind about that," she said. "It brought back memories. 'Twasn't until us had five sprouts of our own before Mr. Potter added on that little room. Until then, the older children slept up above, and the mister and me stayed in this room with the new babe. It seemed large enough until our sixth little lamb came along. Now that Joshua and Samuel are growed men, they have made themselves a corner in the barn."

"It must be frigid out there."

"My goodness, no. 'Tis cozy as a mouse's nest up against the back of the fireplace. I can tell thee, they much prefer the company of critters to the chattering of their seven sisters and pesky little brother." With pride shining in her eyes, she looked across the room at the five little girls now playing ring-around-the-rosy with their ropes. "Poor Tommy. Hem ain't allowed to stay in the barn with his older brothers, and in his opinion, 'tis an insult to sleep with girls. So he makes his bed all by hemself down here. I tell thee, 'tis a rare treat for hem to have a lad his own age to play with. Hem and yer son slept on the hearth last night."

"How can we ever thank you for all your family has done for us?"

Mrs. Potter's robust laughter filled the room. "Yer husband should thank the Lord hem has such an understanding wife." She glanced around at the children and gave Millicent a wink. "I know what a temptation these men are. I will give thee some extra pillows to put down the middle of the bed, then thee won't have to fear hurting yer man."

Millicent tried to hide her embarrassment by intently scraping the last of the porridge from her bowl. "That will be very kind of you, Mrs. Potter." *Oh dear, now what was she to do?* Until Lord Wetherby recovered his wits, she could do nothing about her compromising situation. She would just have to keep herself busy and hope that a solution occurred to her by nightfall. She rose, casting a worried eye toward the bedroom door. "Mrs. Potter, I really do want to help in the kitchen."

Mrs. Potter gathered up her sewing bag and settled into her rocking chair by the fire. "Ain't that nice," she said. " 'Tis like I've gained another daughter. Now, I shall have time to get on with me knitting." Which is exactly what she did, and with needles clacking, she pursed her lips and concentrated on the pretty blue-and-green scarf she was making.

* * *

It was amazing what clean clothes and a hot meal did for one's constitution, Wetherby thought. Someone had even mended the tear in his breeches. By late afternoon, he announced that he felt well enough to come out of the bedroom, or so it seemed at first. But upon rising, his head spun and he nearly fell flat on the floor. The surprisingly gentle giants, Joshua and Samuel, were glad to help him dress. They did the best they could, but they weren't Jespers. Then supporting him between themselves, they saw him comfortably seated on the settle by the hearth.

Wetherby smiled and nodded magnanimously as one or the other of the girls left off readying the table for supper and brought a blanket and pillows to tuck around him. With a giggle here and a whisper there, they shyly stood watching his every move, as if they were expecting him to do something. He couldn't quite imagine what. Probably they had never entertained a member of the *ton* before.

"May I get thee something to drink, Mr. Lance?" Mary asked.

He shook his head, grinning his crazy, crooked grin.

"Or another pillow," Martha added. This time he nodded and indicated his right side, which rested against the arm of the settle.

Two of the younger girls raced to answer his request. Even Ruthie offered him her doll, a very used one from the looks of it, with its mouth gone and only one button eye.

"Her name is Bridget," she said.

At first he didn't know what to do with the doll, but as soon as he placed it on his knee, the child nodded solemnly. Then she stood, fascinated, her eyes never leaving his lips, while he told Bridget a story. Soon they were all laughing—for what reason Wetherby wasn't clear. To his own amazement, he found he was quite enjoying himself and made his stories more and more implausible, delighting in their reactions.

Rupert inched closer and closer, until Wetherby pulled him

to his side. "How would you and Tommy like to hear about some very fierce dragons that I fought?"

The boys nodded eagerly, and as the girls pressed nearer, Wetherby added princesses to his tale. He knew his mouth was working faster on one side than the other, but it didn't seem to bother the children, who listened enthralled at every word he said. Soon he had them all *oohing* and *ahhing,* and clapping their hands. In wide-eyed wonderment, Ruthie leaned against his knee, never letting her gaze leave his face.

Millicent worked alongside Mrs. Potter and the twins in the kitchen. She was watching Wetherby so intently that she spilled gravy all down the front of her apron. She glared at him. From the way the girls were acting, she knew immediately that they were going to spoil him insufferably—the way he expected all females to do, no doubt. She banged the lid down on the kettle, but even that didn't get his attention. He only raised an eyebrow and went on entertaining his rapt audience. Well, she had to warn him that not only did the Potters believe them to be married, but now they thought them to be domestics going to Roxwealde to fill new positions.

On the pretense of rekindling the fire, Millicent hurried toward Wetherby. "Don't tell them who we really are—" She managed no more than a beginning to her waspy entreaty, before Mr. Potter, Joshua, and Samuel came in to supper. With a squeal of delight, Ruthie rushed to greet her father. And as little ones will do, she was waylaid halfway to her destination by the sight of her mother filling a plate with gingerbreads.

"Dash my buttons! Lance is up," Mr. Potter said, patting his smallest daughter on the head as he passed on to where Wetherby sat. "Thought thee looked too hearty a man to be kept down by a few blows."

With a sharp look at Wetherby and a shrug of her shoulders, Millicent retreated to the cooking area. He still chose to ignore her. Dreadful man!

"Potter, I believe?" Wetherby said, holding Ruthie's doll with one hand, while extending his other one to the farmer. "We are beholden to you, sir."

"Pithee, let's hear no more o'at." Mr. Potter said, eyeing the doll quizzically.

Wetherby shook his head. " 'Tis more than enough what you have done for us. It was not my intention to be such a burden to you. We will be on our way as soon as we can obtain transportation."

"Thee will stay until 'ee are well enough to go on," replied the farmer gruffly.

Millicent waved a wooden spoon in the air, trying to signal Wetherby from the kitchen. It seemed that so far he had not said anything about their situation to paint her as a fallen woman. She was thankful for that. But that didn't mean the obstinate man wouldn't make a slip of the tongue and somehow reveal their true identities. Then the Potters would know that they weren't man and wife. Wetherby was being impossible, of course.

It was right then and there that the devil sat down on Millicent's shoulder and suggested the appropriate solution in her ear. She glanced demurely at her hands. "Mrs. Potter?"

"Eh?" Mrs. Potter said, letting Ruthie help herself to a gingerbread.

The little girl stuffed the pastry into her mouth, then stealthily looked back and forth between the two women before she dared pilfer another.

Millicent lowered her voice. "There is something I must tell you about my husband."

Mrs. Potter placed a finger over her lips. "Say on, Mrs. Lance. Yer secret be safe with me."

With a gleam in her eye, Millicent leaned closer and spoke softly.

# Sixteen

"Mrs. Potter, my husband is a simple man."

"So I concluded, dear heart. Thee need not hang yer head in shame. God makes some quicker than others, but I am sure Mr. Lance has many good qualities," she said, looking over at Wetherby.

Millicent sucked in her breath. "What I wanted you to understand, Mrs. Potter, is that he may say things at times that seem a little outlandish. I would not want him to frighten the children."

Mrs. Potter placed a finger to her lips. "Don't thee be worrying yerself now. The children are used to playing with Charlie Doodleby. He's a big lad—nearly four and thirty. Simple and quite harmless. I'll warn me mister to pay no nevermind to a word Mr. Lance says."

A slight smirk graced Millicent's lips. That brought a perplexed expression to his lordship's face, she was pleased to see. She smiled back. *That should put a spoke in his wheel,* she thought, turning her back on him to hide her laughter.

"Thou't's the spirit," Mrs. Potter said. "Always look on the bright side."

Millicent peered up meekly. "Oh, thank you, Mrs. Potter. I am so glad you understand." *Now let his lordship try to wiggle out of that one,* she thought smugly, chancing a quick glance at Wetherby where he sat looking like a large hairy bird nestled in its nest.

He grinned back crookedly.

To hide her amusement, Millicent made a pretext of wiping perspiration from her forehead with the sleeve of her dress.

This gesture consumed Wetherby with guilt. Odsbodikins! It did not sit well with him to admit to his weaknesses. He had refused to acknowledge to the Potters as well as to himself how badly he'd been hurt. He would have jumped up immediately to help her with the heavy chores, if he hadn't feared he would disgrace himself by falling flat on his face.

He admired Mrs. Copley for trying to put the best face on a difficult situation, when it was plain to see that she was shaking with fatigue. Had there ever been such a sweet and giving soul to grace the earth? It was almost more than Wetherby could bear to see her toiling like a kitchen drudge. He wanted to take her in his arms and tell her everything would be all right. When she became his wife, she would never work again. He would see that his sweet marchioness was clothed in the finest silks, and she would have a dozen handmaidens to wait upon her hand and foot.

Mrs. Potter picked up a large serving spoon and started toward the head of the table, where Mr. Potter was already sitting in his highback, beautifully carved chair. "Come, everyone," she called, "time to gather around for supper. 'Twill be a simple meal tonight. Bread and stew. Us don't want to spoil our appetites for tomorrow's yule feast."

Wetherby saw that matters had to be righted. He could clear up his own identity to insure that Mrs. Copley be treated properly, and still not reveal that she was not his wife. "Wait," he called, "I want to tell you who I really am."

Millicent, her face barely showing over the large crockery pot she held, shook her head violently. Her mouth formed a big round *No!* He could not help but notice her, so she could only surmise that he was purposely doing exactly what she didn't want him to do. Arrogant man!

Forcing himself up from the settle, Wetherby willed himself

not to waver. "I am afraid I have allowed you all to be misled. I am really the Marquis of Wetherby, the son of the Duke of Loude." He was glad to see that in spite of Mrs. Copley's theatrics, all eyes turned politely his way. Aye, he may have never known anyone with such a kind and willing nature, but he feared that if Millicent continued her strange performance, the Potters would think her unbalanced.

Ruthie, her cheeks smeared with dough, stood staring sweetly up at Wetherby. "You're daft, aren't you?"

Mrs. Potter exchanged a quick glance with her husband. "Now, now, Ruthie, sweeting. Don't thee be pestering his *lordship.*" Then with no more than an if-you-please, she called over her shoulder, "Martha, bring the bread before you sit down."

Wetherby watched the younger children scramble over the benches. The adults were strangely silent. In shock, Wetherby looked toward Millicent, who was finding something of uncommon interest in the depth of the pot. *No one had believed a word he'd said.*

The little girls began to giggle; Tommy looked at Rupert, who sat with his mouth open; and the older boys elbowed each other.

Mr. Potter's strict glare silenced them. He then pushed back his chair, and rising, turned to Wetherby with a benevolent smile. "Come, my good man. A stomach full of Mrs. Potter's victuals will make thee right as rain. Josh—Samuel—help our guest to my chair. His lordship cannot be expected to climb over a bench, now can hem?"

Millicent looked everywhere but at Lord Wetherby. What had she done? Well, it served him right, the scoundrel. The man had no conscience.

Rupert squirmed for most of the meal, studying the situation, not daring to look at his mother. Things were going terribly wrong. He didn't know why she wouldn't play the game. She used to be so much fun. From the look of disbelief he'd seen on Lord Wetherby's face when he'd made his announcement, Rupert wondered how he could ever again raise his lordship's consequence in the eyes of the Potters . . . and most of all, his mother's.

Only Ruthie seemed unmoved by all the hubbub. "Hem tells good stories," she said, looking with unbiased admiration at Wetherby. "Better than Charlie Doodleby."

The other children hailed their agreement.

Mr. Potter nodded to Wetherby. "See? The Good Lord gives everyone a talent. Thee need not try to be someone thou were not meant to be."

Mrs. Potter added her accolades with hearty enthusiasm. "Hem is right, *yer lordship*. No one needs to be ashamed of what hem do best." Then she frowned and looked at her husband. "But it do seem a shame that the Lances may lose their positions because of their bad fortune. Can us do nothing to let Lord Copley know that the Lances are here and will come along as soon as they are well enough to travel?"

*Lord Copley?* It took all of Wetherby's powers of self-control to steel himself from choking on the bite of food he had just put in his mouth. Someone had set him up, and he knew it wasn't Rupert this time. His eyes zeroed in on Millicent, but she refused to meet his gaze.

"These are not easy times for the likes of us," Mrs. Potter commiserated. "Us poor have to help each other. The Quality have no such fears, do they?" she said, looking at Wetherby sympathetically. "They don't know what it is like to scratch a living out of the thin soil or dirty their hands in the service of others. But I do not envy them, for us are so much more fortunate," she said, looking about proudly at her children. "I hear their mommas give over the care of their wee ones to nurses, and the papas send their sons away to school when they are no older than our Tommy and yer Rupert. I pity them."

Millicent smiled weakly.

While Wetherby was trying to make sense out of this strange commentary on his peers, Samuel spoke up for the first time since their repast had begun. "I will go, Mama."

Mrs. Potter shook her head. " 'Tis not even possible for us to get to the church in Danbury Wells for services this Christmas Eve."

"N'ought tonight," the young man said. "I can ride to the castle tomorrow to inform the baron that his new servants have met with a mishap."

Wetherby protested profusely. "What nonsense say you, Samuel? Tomorrow is Christmas. I will not permit you to miss your Christmas feast."

"I will leave after," Samuel said. "Old Darby can plow through a snowdrift as easily as he can through the moor's rocky soil. The castle is only a couple of hours away, and I can be back before dark."

A new idea presented itself to Wetherby, and he asked, "Do you have something to write on, so I can send a note to the baron?"

Mr. Potter's chest swelled. "My boy Joshua has writing materials. He has been studying with the vicar at Danbury Wells. Go fetch them, Josh. He can pen whatever thee tells him."

"I can write," Wetherby said, somewhat testily.

Mr. Potter blinked a couple of times, but nevertheless, finally nodded to Joshua, who brought Mr. Lance paper and pen.

Wetherby tapped his chin with the quill pen for a few minutes, contemplating what he should write. Then, setting down a few lines, he folded the paper and sealed it with wax from a candle that Mrs. Potter handed him. "You are not to let go of this paper until you can place it in the hands of Lord Copley himself. No one else. Is that clear?"

Samuel seemed so taken by Mr. Lance's tone of authority, that after he took the missive, he automatically stepped away, pulling on his forelock.

Millicent watched with misgivings. Lord Wetherby would give it all away if he weren't careful.

But in spite of Millicent's apprehensions, the evening played out comfortably on a congenial note. As soon as the table was cleared, they sang Christmas carols and Wetherby was persuaded to tell another tale.

Then Samuel brought out his newest figure for the Nativity. It was a lamb, beautifully carved in the finest of detail, so real that it looked as though it were breathing.

Ruthie was given the honor of placing it wherever she wished. After much deep contemplation, she set the animal atop the baby Jesus in his cradle, and stepped back with great satisfaction.

Everyone applauded—Wetherby most enthusiastically of all.

Mrs. Potter sat for a while, knitting, but as the hour grew late and Ruthie showed signs of falling asleep in Mr. Lance's arms, the good woman rose. Setting aside her needlework, she went into the kitchen area. "I do believe mugs of warm, spiced milk are called for. 'Tis a custom we have on Christmas Eve," she explained to Millicent. "The children expect it."

Within minutes, she returned with several cups upon a platter, and passed them around to the children. Finally—and not without protest—the girls were bundled off to bed. A second trayful was brought for the grown-ups, and they all raised their cups and wished each other merry. Soon after, Mrs. Potter climbed the ladder to tuck her daughters in and hear their prayers. The older boys excused themselves and left for their quarters in the animal shelter. Mr. Potter followed to give one final check to his livestock. Although they tried to stay awake, Tommy and Rupert were soon asleep on their straw mattress off to the side of the hearth.

Millicent sat on a stool facing the fire and slowly sipped the hot, spicy drink, trying to ignore the fact that she was alone with his lordship.

When he was assured that the boys were sleeping, Wetherby,

still enthroned on the settle, tried to get Millicent's attention by staring a hole in the back of her neck. "And now, madam, would you mind telling me why you did not tell me we were on your brother-in-law's property?"

"How, pray tell, could I do that when you did everything within your power to ignore the signals I sent your way?"

Wetherby waved his arms about in the air. "You called these signals? I thought you were practicing for a pantomime at a country fair."

Millicent decided not to acknowledge his rude remark.

Wetherby thought he was being quite reasonable. "All I am asking is that before I believe I truly *am* ready for Bedlam, I would like an explanation of this farce. And, pray tell, whatever possessed you to tell them we were domestics? I've never heard anything so addlebrained in my life." One side of his mouth curled up as he spoke. "Though I have to admit—you did look rather fetching with that smudge of flour on your nose, *Mrs. Lance.*"

Millicent's hand went involuntarily to her nose. "You are disgusting," she said, turning her face away from him.

He chuckled. He *knew* that would nettle her. "I know," he said, shaking his head to keep from yawning.

Millicent bit her lip.

"Mrs. Copley? Are you laughing?"

Millicent fought the urge to giggle. There certainly was nothing funny about the situation. "Of course not. You are depraved."

"I agree," he said, putting his hand to his head. He was beginning to feel quite strange. He was sure he'd heard a muffled laugh.

"Truly, my lord, I did not know myself until this afternoon that we were on Andersen's estate. When Mrs. Potter mentioned it, one thing led to another, and she took it into her head that we were going to the castle to take on new situations."

Wetherby stared at her down his aristocratic nose. "Madam, how came you to think Mrs. Potter could believe such an absurdity?"

"How can you blame her? When did you last look in a mirror, Lord Wetherby? You do not exactly look like a member of the *haut ton.*"

Wetherby cocked his head to one side. "*Touche* again, *madame.*"

Millicent set her mug down on the hearth. "Oh, do be serioush," she lisped, hiccoughing.

Wetherby raised his eyebrows. "I assure you, madam, I am serious—and now I want to hear the all of it."

"There is no time, Mrs. Potter is back," Millicent hissed, glancing over to where the farm wife had just checked the two little boys before coming their way.

Mrs. Potter sat down in her rocking chair and once more resumed her knitting. "I can see yer son has his father's eyes," laughed Mrs. Potter, looking at Wetherby. "Big and round and brown as chestnuts. Hem is such a comely child, I am surprised thee don't have more."

Two spots of pink appeared on Millicent's cheeks.

She looked so charming that Wetherby's good spirits returned. "Oh, we do plan on many more, Mrs. Potter, don't we, my dear?" He thought his quip quite clever, but Mrs. Copley didn't seem to see the humor in his jest, so he decided it wise to let the matter drop.

Suddenly, Millicent yawned.

"It sounds as though thee are about ready for bed."

Millicent made an effort to keep her eyes open. "That is a very good suggestion, Mrs. Potter," she said, rising unsteadily. "If you will excuse me, madam . . . your lordship . . . I do believe I shall retire."

Heading entirely in the wrong direction, Millicent became confused and started to open the door to the barn, when Mr.

Potter came in. With a little assistance, she finally found the bedroom and entered. "Good night, everyone," she called back over her shoulder.

Millicent stared at the mound of pillows down the middle of the bed. As Mrs. Potter had promised, two large feather pillows divided the bed in half. It dawned on Millicent that she'd forgotten to tell Lord Wetherby that there was only one bedroom. She quickly changed into her night rail. Well, it would serve him right when he found out he had to sleep on the floor in the other room.

But Millicent misjudged his lordship, for soon after, a male form stood silhouetted in the doorway. The scoundrel wove about in a disconcerted way, finally making his way to the bed. Millicent peered over the covers and held her breath. If she yelled, the jig would be up.

"What the hell is that?" Wetherby spouted. "It seems a mountain ridge has sprouted up across the bedscape."

As far as Millicent was concerned, a mountain the height of Mount Everest would not be sufficient. "Mrs. Potter put them there. She was only thinking of you, my lord."

"Of me? I doubt that she got the idea all by herself, Mrs. Copley."

"I told her I was afraid of bumping into you in the night and causing you more harm."

He sighed most pitifully. "You don't trust me."

"Not likely, my lord, especially after you had the affrontery to brag that we would have more children."

"Don't you want more children?"

"Yes, I would like more children—but that is not the point. We are not married."

"But you let them think we were," he said accusingly. "Even to telling them that we are domestics going into service at the castle."

Millicent bit her lip as she felt the jolt as he sat down on the bed. "I did not tell them that. Mrs. Potter only assumed."

His voice carried over the pillows. "Don't deny it. I heard you. Hah! Won't Copley have a laugh over that."

"You wouldn't dare tell him."

"Wouldn't I?"

She thought about that. "Well," she harrumphed, "you started it first by letting them think we were married. I had to think of something after they put us in the same bed."

"And talking of tall tales, how, pray tell, did the Potters *assume* that I was a noodlehead?"

"Well—that just happened." Millicent tried to stifle a laugh, but with no success. "I am sorry." she said burrowing her head into her pillow to hide the sound, but only making the bed shake more. "I am beginning to feel very strange."

Wetherby snorted, then burst out laughing.

"Shh," she hissed. "They will hear us."

"If I am any judge of people," said Wetherby, "the Potters will just think that you have overcome the barrier and climbed the mountain."

"Oh, you are disgusting!"

"I know that." Wetherby was not ready for the pillow that was flung over his face. "Mrs. Copley," he said, "if you do not stop this assault, I shall not take responsibility for the consequences."

A hand reached over the barrier to retrieve the pillow. Wetherby caught it and held it in his. He held his breath, waiting for her to snatch it away, but she did not. Slowly, he released her hand and watched it disappear onto her side.

For a few minutes the only sounds were sparks popping out of the ashes in the fireplace.

"Millicent? I . . . I would like to call you that, if I may," he said, his voice so low and serious that she could hardly stand it.

The sparks continued to crackle as they flew up the chimney. "Y . . . you may," she said, suddenly feeling very drowsy.

Wetherby yawned. "I want you to know that I would never hurt you. Do you believe me?"

Millicent nuzzled into the soft down pillow between them. "Yes . . . and you know what else?" He didn't answer, and she was not quite certain he'd forgiven her for making him out to be a noodlehead. "I want you to know that I truly appreciated your trying to protect Rupert and me from those dreadful men—getting beaten up the way you were. That was a brave and very dangerous thing for you to do. And I want to thank your lordship, too, for not revealing that we are not man and wife," she confessed, shyly. "The Potters gave up their bed to us and are sleeping with the children in the cold loft. Did you know that?"

The maddenly stubborn man still lay on his side of the barrier, refusing to answer her. Here she was trying to tell him of her fears that he might die—ready to confess how much he'd come to mean to her—and the odious man didn't even have the manners to answer. It was more than enough. Millicent sat bolt upright and peered over the pillows. "Lord Wetherby!"

The dying embers in the fireplace reflected across his still form, his eyes closed and mouth slightly open.

"Lord Wetherby?" His steady breathing was like the steady rolling of ocean waves, and just as hypnotic. Strangely, Millicent's head seemed to disconnect from her body and fly about the room in dizzying circles. She flopped back onto her pillow and was asleep in a matter of minutes.

In the next room, Mr. and Mrs. Potter sat contentedly before the fire—she with her knitting, he with his pipe.

She looked up. "That Mrs. Lance—now there is a clever girl, don't ye agree, Mister Potter? She will do well in any kitchen anywhere. Lady Copley will be lucky to hire her." Mrs. Potter shook her head. "But Mr. Lance? Pool soul, I'm not so sure about hem."

"Hem will do well enough."

Mrs. Potter smiled a wee smile and began to hum.

Mr. Potter narrowed his eyes. "Mrs. Potter, I do believe ye have been up to yer tricks again."

"Now, Mister Potter, why ever would ye be saying such a thing?"

"Because, I know thee better than ye know yerself. I saw them young folks, weaving and a-yawning. Ye gave them a posset *and* a tisane all together."

"Well, I say that if they are to be getting on the right side of Lord and Lady Copley tomorrow, they needs a good night's sleep. Thee don't want them off on the wrong foot with their new employers, now do ye?"

Mr. Potter took a few more puffs on his pipe. "No. But now, Mrs. Potter, I do believe 'tis time us go to bed."

Mrs. Potter held the finished scarf up for inspection. Then, satisfied, rolled it up carefully and tucked it away in her basket. "I do believe 'tis," she said, glancing at her husband out of the corner of her eye.

A few minutes later, Mr. Potter gave his wife a push up the ladder. "I hope thee gave me one too, Mrs. Potter, or 'tis sorry ye may be that ye didn't."

# Seventeen

Christmas morning began with a song. Wetherby heard someone in the other room singing "God Rest Ye Merry Gentlemen," accompanied by an orchestra of rich aromas that sneaked under the bedroom door. He opened his eyes to find himself looking at a sleeping figure beside him, so close that her hair touched his face. Somehow the pillows that divided them when they went to bed had ended up on the floor. Carefully, he removed her arm, which lay over him, and withdrew his own from under her. No matter how innocent he had been in the matter, he knew Millicent would have his head if she should find herself in his arms. He lay there watching her for a minute, when a wicked gleam appeared in his eyes, and he leaned over and kissed her. A little smile spread across her face, but she didn't waken. Rising stealthily, he replaced the pillows to their original line of demarcation, then made haste to dress before she awakened.

Wetherby rewound his bandage as well as he could and tucked the loose strands of cloth up off his forehead. Thank goodness, his brain no longer felt as if it were being squeezed in a vice, and the swelling around his eye had diminished. But each time he pulled a garment over his ribs, he grimaced. Wishing Boggles and Tooter to Hades, he silently slipped out the door into the main room of the cottage—only to find himself swept along by a whirlwind of yuletide activity.

Chirping bird songs—which sounded very much like children's voices—flitted about from somewhere on the far side of the room, and Mary and Martha bustled in and out of the kitchen area, now singing "Come All Ye Faithful." Fat dripped and popped from the goose roasting over the open fire, while the perfume of spiced muffins filled the air.

Wetherby targeted the wooden bench by the fire as his goal, hoping he could make the journey across the room without knocking into something. First he looked about to make sure Joshua and Samuel weren't in sight. He could not tolerate being coddled, as if he were a baby in leading strings, one more day. Then, boldly setting one foot in front of the other, he managed to reach his destination without falling on his face.

As he shuffled past her, Mrs. Potter raised her head out of the flour bin and called cheerily, "Merry Christmas, Mr. Lance. Did thee sleep well?"

Wetherby sucked in a deep breath. It was a mistake. Pain seared through his midsection, and the room seemed to slant crazily to one side. To save himself from pitching forward, he grabbed the arm of the settle. Once anchored to something stable, he felt much more the thing. Swallowing the less-than-polite expletive on the tip of his tongue, he forced a smile. "Never better, Mrs. Potter, never better."

"Glad I be to hear it. As soon as the pudding be finished, I will put a clean wrap on yer head. Thee made a mess of it, didn't thee?" she scolded. "In the meantime, do sit down by the fire and one of the girls will bring a bowl of hot porridge and cream. Hemself will be in a'fore long to keep thee company."

Wetherby had no sooner eased himself down than Mr. Potter emerged from the barn, stomped the straw off his boots, and took the space beside him on the settle. The younger girls raced to see who would be the first to reach their father, and Rupert and Tommy came over to inspect him.

"Your eye is open," Rupert said, matter-of-factly.

Wetherby's fingers went immediately to that area. "So it is," he said, smiling.

Tommy nodded. "Yer mouth ain't so crooked either."

"Thank you," Wetherby answered, not exactly knowing what the appropriate reply should be.

On the heels of the children, Millicent emerged from the bedroom, looking a little confused, a little sleepy, and strangely shy. Her hair flowed down her back and her clothes were the same as the day before. In fact, they had been the same for several days now. So it wasn't her attire that made her so appealing to Wetherby. But for some reason he couldn't explain, she appeared to him the loveliest woman he'd ever seen. He ran his hand over his stubble of beard. He would, of course, have to wait until he got to Roxwealde to be washed and shaved—dressed once more as a gentleman should be. Then, when he looked his most presentable, he would ask her to be his wife.

Millicent's cheeks burned. She knew that Wetherby was trying to get her attention, but she bowed her head and scurried into the cooking area. She remembered having the strangest dream during the night, but she was bound if she could recall what it was. She only remembered that she'd felt so warm and . . . and—Oh, my goodness, she couldn't admit which feelings had rushed through her, even to herself. Then she had awakened to find herself quite alone in the bed, hugging a pillow. She knew then that it had all been a dream. Lord Wetherby had not been there at all. But now, she dared not look at him, because she was afraid that her eyes would reveal what she was thinking.

Before Wetherby had time to refine on Millicent's behavior, Samuel and Joshua, loaded down with bundles of furze for the fire, blew in with a gust of cold air.

"Merry Christmas to all," Joshua shouted. "The snow has stopped. 'Twill be a bright day."

"No doubt o'at," Samuel agreed. "As soon as us eat, I be a-go to the castle."

Ruthie pulled on her father's sweater. "Me open presents first."

"And so thee shall, my little bug," her father said, turning his attention to his youngest daughter.

A multitude of *ayes* proclaimed that to be by far the most popular suggestion. Pandemonium followed, and bundles of oddly wrapped objects appeared magically from the most surprising places: from the loft, from behind the woodpile, and even from inside the bread bin; all accompanied by giggles and grins.

Tommy let out a yelp when he unwrapped two miniature carved horses. "Samuel made a wagon for me last year," he explained to Rupert. "Now I have the cattle to pull it."

Samuel had a lovely carved box for his mother, and for his father, a new axe handle. Joshua, from his small earnings at the vicarage, had provided the axe head, buttons and ribbons for his sisters, a new knife for Samuel, and a belt for Tommy. To his mother, he proudly gave a linen handkerchief trimmed with lace.

The men measured their heavy woolen sweaters across their chests. There were dresses and aprons for the girls, knitted gloves for Wetherby and Rupert. There were toys, of course: tops and whirly-gigs, a checkerboard and doll clothes. All homely objects, all handmade with care. All received with love.

Wetherby ticked off in his head the expensive gifts he'd bought over the years for his nieces and nephews. All ended up abandoned on shelves, neglected, broken, or discarded for something new in a few weeks' time.

Finally, Mrs. Potter presented Millicent with a lovely green-and-blue knitted shawl.

Millicent fingered the warm, durable wrap. "Oh, dear, I am afraid we have nothing to give to you."

Mrs. Potter brushed that aside with a wave of her hand. "Pooh! Pooh! Don't thee be worrying yerself about that, dear heart. Thee lost everything— but not each other. That is of more import."

Wetherby held his breath as he watched a fleeting change come over Millicent's face, and for an instant their eyes met and held—or so he thought. But he must have been mistaken in his interpretation, because he realized that her gaze had settled on her son, not on him. A feeling of disappointment ran through him.

But his despondency was short-lived when Mr. Potter handed Ruthie a doll, one with *two* eyes and a painted smile. He explained to her, "Samuel carved the wooden head, and yer Mama made her cloth body. Joshua bought the laces, yer sisters sewed her fine gown, and Tommy painted her eyes and hair and gave her a happy face."

After a close inspection of the doll's eyes, the little knitted shoes, and a peek under her skirt, Ruthie held her up for Wetherby to see.

"She is very pretty," he said. "What is her name?"

"Elizabeth!" scolded Ruthie, "Thee should know that."

"Of course. I stand corrected," Wetherby apologized, wondering what would happen to poor Bridget now. Then as he watched the child introduce Elizabeth, with great pomp and ceremony, to the older doll, his heart experienced a strange twist. He knew for certain that the less-than-beautiful Bridget would not be cast out or forsaken. The little mop-haired mother would love and cherish the used-up doll for the rest of her raggedy life.

Next, Mr. Potter cleared his throat and handed his wife a decorative ivory comb for her hair.

Mrs. Potter clapped her hands. "Did thee ever see the like?" she exclaimed, as though she'd been presented with the crown jewels.

Wetherby thought of the multitude of expensive baubles worth a fortune, which he'd lavished carelessly on his mistresses over the years. They'd thanked him in many ways most pleasant, none had ever looked at him the way Mrs. Potter looked now at her rough-hewn husband. A disturbing thought crossed Wetherby's mind. He, the son of a duke, was envying a rustic.

After the gifts were distributed, everyone gathered around the table, and Mr. Potter said a prayer. The Christmas feast began, and continued until one and all cried that they would surely burst if they ate one bite more.

There were only a few more hours of daylight left. Samuel hastily prepared for his ride to the castle.

"We are obliged," Wetherby said. "Don't forget my letter—and Samuel—see if Lord Copley can have someone come for us tomorrow."

The young man looked anxiously at his mother and father. Mr. Potter placed his hand on Wetherby's shoulder, Mrs. Potter shook her head, and Millicent, as Wetherby should have expected, began sending her nick-ninny signals again from the kitchen.

Enough was enough! Wetherby had about had it with the theatrics and he'd just decided to end the farce, when Mrs. Potter spoke. "There, there, now, Mr. Lance. Don't thee be fretting yerself. I'm sure his lordship will hold yer post. Thee know yer welcome to stay here 'til the snow melts. When yer well again, the mister will hitch up the wagon and carry thee all to Roxwealde."

Millicent hurried to his side. "I will take care of him, Mrs. Potter. It's all the excitement," she said, her eyes daring him to say more. "Come, dear, let us be reasonable and sit down."

*Reasonable?* She wasn't the one being made out to be a simpleton. Wetherby's sentiments of a few minutes ago took a quick turnabout, and he tried his hardest to give the termagant a set down with his eyes. But she obviously failed to see it, for she was too busy tugging at his sleeve. Wetherby said a few choice words under his breath, but nevertheless returned to the settle.

Mr. Potter pulled up a stool by the fire and took out his pipe. "Have thee ever farmed, young man?"

Taken aback by the question, Wetherby tried to think why

Mr. Potter would think a marquis should be required to work in the dirt. Then the reality of his situation struck him, and he reminded himself that he was playing a role. However, as insulting as he felt the inference to be, a picture of his mother's neglected conservatory suddenly came back to haunt him. Drooping orchids, brown ferns, and spidery, leafless vines danced before him. The duchess would ring a peal over his head if she saw it today. "I have not been very successful with plants," he conceded.

"Houseman, then?"

Wetherby riveted Millicent with his eyes but she was again looking the other way. He was quite sorry she missed his censure. "No, sir," he sputtered.

Tommy held up one of his new wooden horses. "I'm going to be a woodworker like Samuel when I grow up. Can thee carve?"

"Why, no. I never have," Wetherby replied, wondering from whence the next attack on his ego would come.

"Never?"

Wetherby frowned. Although he'd attended Eton and Cambridge, he was beginning to feel that his education had been sadly lacking in some ways.

Potter shook his head. "Whatever do thee plan to do at the castle, then?"

Ruthie gave him an exasperated look. "Can thee not do anything?"

Rupert stepped to Wetherby's side. "He beats up ruffians, and he can tell stories," he said, defensively.

Wetherby looked at the clinched fists, the belligerent expression. Had he sunk so low that he had to be championed by a six-year-old boy? Enough was enough! Wetherby was about to set the whole fiasco straight when Ruthie said sweetly, "Tell us another story."

One of Wetherby's admitted faults was that he never could resist the request of a pretty woman. At first an uncomfortable feeling flooded through him, and he asked himself how he'd been reduced to an itinerant performer. Then he looked at the cloud of expectant faces surrounding him, and something happened within him. A wonderful thing. He didn't know where it came from, but he started to laugh and threw up his hands in mock surrender. He was rewarded by *hurrahs* all around. Even Joshua came to sit by the hearth to listen.

Wetherby glanced over at Mr. Potter and recalled the pride shining in the rugged crofter's eyes when he told him that his son Joshua was learning to read and write. Guiltily, Wetherby thought of how he'd wasted his salad days at Cambridge. Surely it would count for something when he occasionally took his seat in the House of Lords. However, Wetherby doubted that the practical Potters would look upon that as much of an accomplishment.

At least as a teller of tales, he had gained some degree of favor in their eyes. He looked about to see if Mrs. Copley was noting his popularity, but he was disappointed to see that she was so absorbed in washing the tableware that she seemed unaware that he even existed. He wondered what it was he had to do to gain her approval.

Ruthie raised her arms to be lifted up, and as soon as she and Bridget and Elizabeth were settled on his knee, Wetherby began his story. "Once upon a time there was a mean and terrible dragon who threatened to take Christmas away from a whole village in Devonshire. There was a family of brothers and sisters named Rettop. That is Potter backward," he explained, "and they vowed that they would drive the dragon away."

To his amazement, Wetherby found he was enjoying himself. Who would have ever thought that the Marquis of Wetherby would tolerate being surrounded by fidgeting children and holding a wiggly child on his knee? Maybe he *was* going daft. If so, it didn't seem to be any deterrent to his being considered top-o-the-trees by the Potter children. He could even see Mrs.

Potter where she stood scrubbing the table, cocking her head to hear every tittle of the story he was relating. He grinned and looked over Ruthie's head to see if Mrs. Copley was listening. Unfortunately, she was now engrossed in sweeping the floor.

He looked down at Ruthie. She held her two dolls in her arms, her curly head bobbing up and down, her wide-eyed gaze never leaving his face. For what purpose, he did not know. Wetherby was beginning to feel as though he were being sized up by a stricter judge than any of the distinguished members on the King's Bench. When he finished his tale, the bigger children drifted away. After silently evaluating him for another long uncomfortable minute, Ruthie held out her raggedy doll to Wetherby.

"Ruthie wants thee to have Bridget," she said, looking up at him through her long lashes.

Overwhelmed by the gesture, Wetherby realized the honor and trust the little girl bestowed upon him. "Thank you," he said with great solemnity. He then settled the pitiful-looking doll atop his other knee, where it immediately fell over on its back. No amount of propping up could induce Bridget to sit upright, so he left her sprawled where she lay, her skirt in shocking dishabille. Undaunted by this display of unladylike behavior, Wetherby placed his right hand over his heart and continued his acceptance speech. "I shall cherish Bridget always, and I promise—on a knight's oath—to honor and protect her."

Ruthie hugged her new doll to her chest and with a snort, slid off his lap. "I wanted to get rid of her anyway," she whispered, with a smirk.

Wetherby blinked. He'd been duped by a three-year-old hoyden.

With not even a backward glance, Ruthie skipped across the room with Elizabeth and was seen introducing her to baby Jesus.

Wetherby glanced down at the disheveled doll lying limp over his knee, her black button eye staring blindly back at him.

"At least, my dear Bridget, you are one female I don't have to worry about being fickle."

Millicent watched the entire scene surreptitiously. When she had seen Ruthie hold up her arms to Lord Wetherby, she'd held her breath. Oh, she had no doubt that he'd come back with some rebuttal that he thought quite witty. Instead, to her surprise, he'd lifted Ruthie up on his knee as if it were the most natural thing in the world for him to do. Millicent's heart leapt within her. But it was when Wetherby had accepted Ruthie's doll that Millicent knew she had fallen in love all over again with Lord Wetherby—at least the part of him that could captivate the heart of a little girl. How sweet to see the child whisper some secret to him and to see her innocent smile as she ran off to play. Millicent brushed a tear away with the back of her hand. She had been so overcome by her emotions that she dared not look his lordship in the eye. Silly woman. How could she even dream that he could hold her in affection in the same way?

It was outside of enough for her even to think of such a possibility. She'd heard that the Duke of Loude was a hard man, stiff-rumped and a stickler for the proprieties. He would never accept a wife of lower rank for his only son and heir. After all, Lord Wetherby must marry someone high in the instep. Someone like beautiful Lady Caroline.

Hopefully, tomorrow they would be at Roxwealde, and he would again be the Marquis of Wetherby, heir to a dukedom.

And she? Millicent sighed. She would still be the plain widow Copley. The daughter of a small village squire, the mother of a six-year-old boy who would one day go off into the world to seek his fortune, and she would be all alone.

A good many hours passed and darkness was nearly upon them when Samuel was heard riding around and coming into the stables next to the house. As soon as he entered the cottage, he reported that he had done as he was instructed and had not given up the letter until he could place it in the hands of Lord Copley.

"His lordship insisted I start back right away. Hemself said he would instruct his coachman to follow my tracks and catch me up on the road. They cannot be far behind."

It was no longer than half an hour when a great commotion was heard outside the humble cottage. Tommy reached the window first and let out a whoop. "Mama, Papa, a great coach and four has stopped out front."

Rupert, arms flailing, made a dash for the door. Disregarding his sore ribs, Wetherby leapt from the settle and caught him. "Don't say a word," he whispered close to Rupert's ear. "In my letter, I asked your uncle not to reveal our identities to anyone, not even the servants. We still have a distance to go tonight, so do not say anything in front of the Potters or the coachman to make them think otherwise. If we are stopped, the coachman will say that they are only transporting domestics." He could see that Rupert was disappointed.

"I wanted to tell Tommy before I went away."

"Let us pretend for one more day. How does this sound to you? We shall be knights in disguise going on a quest for the king. Until we are safely at His Majesty's castle, we cannot tell anyone who we are."

Rupert's eyes sparkled. Lord Wetherby was his old self again. Rupert liked the idea of calling his Uncle Andy a king. "Oh, jolly good, your . . . sir," he whispered back. "And can Momma be a knight too?" he asked, looking over at Millicent.

Wetherby tried to keep a straight face. "I believe that under the circumstances, we can permit that."

"I shall have to tell Momma, so she won't spoil things."

Wetherby glanced at Millicent, who again was doing her dance and motioning to him, all at the same time. "I don't believe we need fear that your mother will give our plans away." *They may very likely take her to Bedlam instead.*

They didn't have much to gather up for their journey, and their only delay was in the Potters' reluctance to see their guests leave.

When Millicent was all buttoned into her coat, Mrs. Potter placed her new shawl over her shoulders and gave her a kiss on the cheek. "Thee hold yer head up, now, dear heart. Yer husband's a kindhearted man, and I'm sure hem will do just fine in his new position."

It was as Wetherby was wrapping Rupert's new muffler tighter around his neck that he noticed something amiss. "Where is your sword?"

Rupert shuffled his feet. "I gave it to Tommy."

"But it is the only thing you saved, and it meant so much to you."

"Don't you remember what Momma said? *A gift has more value if you give something that is dear to your heart.*" He fished around inside his coat and pulled out a wooden horse. "Tommy gave me this. I told him that he needed it to pull his wagon, but he said that it is better that I have it. That way, every time we play with the horses, we will think of each other."

Unexplainably, Wetherby felt a lump in his throat. "Come," he said gruffly, " 'tis time to take our leave."

After much hugging and shaking of hands, the three travelers made their way to the waiting coach.

Millicent was the first to enter and the first to see the dark-clothed figure in the far corner. However, before she could cry an alarm, a gloved hand clamped over her mouth. *Heaven help us! We are being kidnapped all over again,* she thought, struggling against her assailant. But his hands were too strong for her to break free.

Wetherby and Rupert boarded behind Millicent. Before their eyes became well enough adjusted to the dim interior to realize her dilemma, the door slammed shut and the horses leapt forward.

# Eighteen

Rupert was the first to get a good look at the other man. "Uncle Andy!" he shouted, throwing his arms around the baron's neck.

The moonlight coming through the small window was just bright enough for Lord Copley to make out his nephew's exuberant smile. "Well, I am glad someone recognizes me," he said, embracing the boy.

Everybody started speaking at once.

"Wait! Wait!" Copley laughed, trying to hug his sister-in-law, and at the same time shake the hand of his good friend.

Wetherby spoke first. "Samuel did not tell us you were in the coach."

"He did not know that I was. After that crazy letter of yours giving me your direction, then telling me not to reveal your true identity to the bearer, I feared more deviltry. I led the young man to believe it was only my servants who were bringing the coach to pick you up. Now tell me why you did not want the Potters to know who you really were. The family have been tenants of Roxwealde for several generations. You did not have to worry about their loyalty."

The coach bounced over a rut in the road. Wetherby hugged his ribs and tried not to think of the jolting they were taking. "It was not that, Copley," he said, through clenched teeth. "The Potters saved our lives. We will always be indebted to them. But at first, I did not know where we were, and, well . . ." He leaned slightly in Millicent's direction, the temptation to jog her out of her reticence compelling him to mischief. "One thing led to another and *somehow*—I cannot imagine why—the Potters came to the conclusion that we were going to the castle to seek positions there."

Millicent refused to rise to the bait. She merely cleared her throat and stared ahead—somewhere in the vicinity of her brother-in-law's chin.

Copley slapped his forehead with the heel of his hand and laughed. "Domestics? God! Ever since we received word that you had been kidnapped, we have been half out of our minds with worry, while all the time you were safely masquerading as ordinary servants?"

Rupert was happy to hear laughter again and eagerly added his opinion. "We had a great adventure, Uncle Andy."

Wetherby felt that they were not taking his injuries seriously enough. "It was not all that pleasant an experience," he muttered, as the coach proceeded along the gravelly road.

Millicent was inclined to be more to the point. "How *did* you know that we had been abducted, Andersen?"

"First, Jespers and your coachmen arrived with Lady Caroline's servants at Karkingham Hall outside Wellington. They were surprised that you were not there, but considered that you had stopped off at Sir Jonathan Bridges's. After all, you had planned originally to stay over. Three days later a farmer's wagon drew up at Karkingham with Caro wrapped in a horse blanket, perched atop a stack of straw."

Millicent clasped her hands, her voice full of concern. "Was she all right?"

Copley chuckled. "A bit bedraggled and quite angry, I understand. She does have a penchant for odd encounters, does she not, Wetherby?"

Wetherby exchanged glances with the baron, then began to shake with silent laughter.

Millicent gasped. It astonished her that the men found anything funny about poor Lady Caroline's narrow escape, but she also surmised that this was not the time to pursue their reason for hilarity. A man's sense of humor was vastly different from a woman's. From the corner of her eye. she caught Wetherby studying her. She tried to ignore the disturbing effect his closeness was having on her. "Go on, Andersen," she said primly.

Copley swallowed his laughter. "Caroline told the authorities the story of your abduction, but thought you had been carried south toward Exeter. That is where they have concentrated their efforts to find you. She has since returned to her father's house in Gloucester."

"Where she will most likely get a royal scold."

"Speaking of scolds, Wetherby. I thought you would like to know that your father paid the ransom, and I hear he is in a high dudgeon because you've caused him so much trouble. Now he is crying foul because you had disappeared and he is out the blunt."

"Poor Father. I doubt he will be any happier when he hears we have been rescued."

"The Karkinghams loaned Jespers and your men one of their vehicles so they could bring us the news."

Wetherby made no effort to hide his hostility. " 'Twas the Bandit King and his band."

"That is what Jespers said."

Wetherby shifted his weight to ease the soreness in his side. "It would give me great pleasure to track him down," he said through clenched teeth.

The baron could not have agreed more. "You and many others, but now tell me, why all the secrecy? You only wrote that you were well, and that I was not to reveal your true identities to the message-bearer. Did you fear that you were still in danger?"

Wetherby remembered Millicent's shock the morning she'd awakened next to him. "In a manner of speaking," he said, with a chuckle. He felt a kick against his ankle, but ignored it. She didn't seem the least bit impressed that he was trying to lighten the mood.

It was full night now, but as the moon rose higher, its light flooded the landscape. As if seeing him for the first time, Lord Copley narrowed his eyes and studied Wetherby. "When did you take to sporting a beard? And . . . God! Whatever did you do to your eye?" The baron leaned forward to better observe his friend. "I say, is that a bandage I see around your head?"

Copley's inquisition was annoying Wetherby, who thought his countenance had improved immeasurably over the last two days. Of course, he'd seen no mirror in the Potters' cottage, so how could he tell? He ran his hand over his face, dislodging the muffler that was wrapped around his head. Wetherby felt he'd suffered enough of Copley's scrutiny. "I feel fine." he snapped. " 'Tis the latest fashion in thieves' dens now, didn't you know? Beards and bandages."

"Cut line, Wetherby," the baron said, "I meant it well enough. Did they hurt you, Millie?"

"Momma sprained her ankle," Rupert reported happily, glad to have something of importance to add to the conversation.

The baron spoke sternly. "I want you to start from the beginning and tell me all."

For the next hour and a half, Copley heard a checkerboard recital—some from Wetherby, most from Rupert—of all that had happened since their abduction and rescue by the Potters. Millicent favored forgetting the whole incident and said so. However, for their own individual reasons, not one of the three confessed to the hoax that they had played on the Potters—that of letting them believe the Banbury Tale that they were the Lances: Papa, Momma, and son.

However, guilt was making Wetherby more and more aware of the woman beside him, and he lay his head back on the squabs and closed his eyes. But no matter how hard he tried, he couldn't shut out the sight of her. He had promised the baron that he would give his sister-in-law and her son safe passage to Devon. He'd failed miserably in his mission, he feared. She had never outwardly condemned him, but she'd barely spoken a word since they'd entered the coach. Now, he hoped her estimation of him had not been so badly tarnished that he would have no chance to redeem himself. Well, he had twelve days ahead of him to regain her approval. Plenty of time to charm her. He'd often done it in far less time. He didn't think she would reveal what had happened at the Potters', but there was no way of telling what Rupert was capable of spilling. If Copley found out that he'd been in bed with his sister-in-law, Wetherby knew the baron would demand that he do the right thing by her. But no matter how much Wetherby sought that very consequence, he wanted more for Millicent to come to him willingly. Perhaps his luck would turn at the castle.

The nearer they came to Roxwealde, the more he was reminded of Lord Copley's party almost two years ago. The Merry Five, they'd called themselves. They had planned a madcap weekend with some obliging little actresses from Drury Lane. But when Copley had discovered he'd lost his fortune and had only a few weeks to find himself a wealthy wife, he'd made a turnabout and invited, instead, some of the most sought-after young ladies of the *beau monde.* Lady Caroline had been one of these.

However, the old monstrosity that his ancestor, Lord Percival Copley, the first baron, had built to resemble a Norman castle, sat surrounded by rocky soil covered by bronzing bracken and mottled bramble, treacherous boglands, and granite outcroppings. Its sinister-looking twin towers were enough to terrify the bravest souls. Hardly a setting for romance, until a sensible, young squire's daughter, Sarah Greenwood, had switched identities with a notorious hostess. She'd not only transformed the castle into a winter flower garden, but she'd captured the heart of the baron as well.

The only thing that Lord Copley had failed to tell his guests was that his pet lion, named Dog, was loose in the castle. The baron, who had a soft spot for mistreated animals, had saved the beast from being put down at the Tower Zoo for being too old. Dog, being the social creature that he was, turned up one night in bed with Lady Caroline. Ah, yes, thought Wetherby, that was an evening to remember.

"There it is!" shouted Rupert, his nose pressed against the window. "There is your castle, Uncle Andy."

The baron exclaimed, "I daresay, that *is* a wonder. Would you believe? 'Tis right where I left it."

Rupert didn't take his gaze off the tall four-storied granite structure. "Oh, Uncle Andy. You know what I meant. Momma says it is a fairy castle."

The coach drove around another curve in the carriageway to reach the circular drive, and for a moment, the castle appeared on Millicent's side. Glad to have something to take her mind off the disturbing presence of the man beside her, Millicent turned her head to look out the window.

Wetherby caught his breath. The silvery light of the moon had transformed her face into something fey, and he thought her the loveliest creature he had ever seen. He remembered at Copley's party, the castle had indeed cast a spell on nearly every one there. Four of the Merry Five had succumbed to Cupid's arrow. Wetherby had thought himself fortunate at the time that he was not one of them. He could not imagine any man wanting to be put into shackles. Now that he'd found the lady whom he wished would do just that, she seemed to become more and more agitated with him.

The old castle had worked its magic for his friends. Would it do so for him, now?

Copley swatted his nephew's bottom. "Aye, I was only quizzing you, Rupert. However, I think I should warn you all that I told everyone before I left that you were coming. So be prepared for an enthusiastic welcome."

* * *

Their arrival was just that. A celebration. The minute old Mr. Proctor opened the massive arched doors of the castle, Lady Sarah Copley ran to embrace her sister-in-law, then Rupert, then Wetherby, who took the onslaught valiantly.

"I was so worried about you," Sarah cried.

Millicent and Rupert found themselves pulled in out of the cold and smothered in loving arms. Sarah's parents added their greetings to those of the servants who crowded around in the background.

Jespers was beside himself to discover that his master was still alive, and could not be faulted for shedding a tear or two.

When Wetherby was relieved of his muffler, Sarah spotted the bandage and blackened eye and exclaimed, "You look dreadful! Andersen, I insist you call a doctor."

Wetherby wished everyone would quit telling him how terrible he looked. "I've never felt fitter, my dear lady," he said, attempting to make a leg before his hostess. The truth was, Wetherby felt dizzy and swore that the floor curved up dangerously. He tilted his head to one side to make it straight.

His keen eyes narrowing, Lord Copley gripped his friend's arm when he saw him falter. "Come," he said, trying to hide any solicitous manner in his tone. "My wife will make milksops of us men if we let her." Then, tightening his hold, he directed Wetherby across the flagstone floor toward the fire.

Wetherby shook off Copley's hand. The long ride in the coach had done his injuries no good, and his head did feel queer, but if the women were not allowed to mollycoddle him, then neither was the baron. Wetherby glanced at Millicent as he passed her. She was lovely. He grinned at her. Yes, as soon as he was recovered and Jespers had transformed him into a figure of distinction once more, he'd court her in the style, with flowers and sweets and trips to the theater. He would take his time to make her love him. He would wine her and dine her and dance with her until the sun came up.

The Great Hall, with its flagstone floor, spread out before them. Christmas greenery festooned everything. Pine boughs, and sprigs of holly intertwined with red ribbons, encircled the columns that marched along both sides. Boughs of mistletoe were strung from doorways, and magic lanterns hung from poles extending from the balconies, casting their golden rays of enchantment over everyone.

Two dark oak stairways on either side of the hall spiraled up to the floors above, and at the far end, an immense fireplace spread almost the entire width of the room. It was said to be large enough to roast an ox in, but it now held a Yule log so big, it promised to burn far beyond the designated twelve days of Christmas.

Everyone was chattering at once, when they were all silenced by the roar of a wild beast. A great African lion raised his head from where he lay on the hearth.

"Dog!" shouted Rupert, running to hug his old friend. "You're still here."

The animal did not move from the spot. Beside him, a golden-haired child sat up from where he'd lain sleeping, his head pillowed in the thick mane.

Lord Copley laughed and picked up his son before handing him over to his nurse. "Dog is the only one with patience enough to put up with this rascal."

Sarah looked at Millicent's clothes and shook her head. "What a pity everything you had was stolen. Now, I know you will want to freshen up before we eat. As you see, we have been waiting for you to arrive before we had our Christmas feast." She indicated the other side of the fireplace where a long trestle table, draped with a white cloth, was already being covered with bowls of fruit and various dishes. "We have only opened the West Wing for the holidays, so you will all be on the same floor as my parents. I will let Jespers show you to your rooms while I select some clean clothing. One of Mrs. Potter's nieces is waiting abovestairs to attend you."

* * *

Wetherby's quarters were at the far end of the long hall. Big red bows decorated all the doors, and rope garlands of evergreens looped from side to side from the ceiling, along the entire length of the corridor.

It turned out that Wetherby and Copley were of a like size, and the clothes brought in fit him well. "I shall have to wait until tomorrow to shave, Jespers. A trim will have to do. Dinner is to be served shortly."

After he had dressed, Wetherby looked at himself in the mirror and was quite pleased with what he saw. Yes, he cut a fine figure. Mrs. Copley should be impressed. And now that he was going to reform and curb his wild ways, she should have no objections to his courtship whatsoever. "You know, Jespers, the beard does not look half bad. Rather gives me a pirate look, don't you think?"

So happy was Jespers to see his lordship, that he would have agreed if Wetherby's hair had hung to his ankles. He picked up Wetherby's dirty clothes with his fingertips and held them out at arm's length. "What do you wish me to do with these, your lordship?"

Wetherby wrinkled his nose. "Throw them out, Jespers."

The servant gave them a shake, and as he did so, a dirty cloth fell out. "What is this, my lord?"

Wetherby's eyes lit up. "What does it look like, Jespers?"

The valet turned it around. "A . . . a rag doll, my lord?"

"By Jove! You have hit it on the head, Jespers. 'Tis a memento to the fickleness of the female sex."

Jespers almost raised an eyebrow. "Do you wish me to discard it with the rest of your things, my lord?"

"Good heavens! No!"

Jespers, tip-top servant that he was, made no further comment and set the relic on top of the chest of drawers. The doll promptly fell over, face in her skirt.

Wetherby gave his cravat one last inspection in the mirror, then started for the door. "Oh, by the by, her name is Bridget," he said, leaving the room.

Millicent had just entered the hallway and was standing under the kissing bough. She looked lovely in a bright blue velvet dress, her shoulders covered by, of all things, Mrs. Potter's shawl. The knowledge of its simple origin and the honor she bestowed upon the friendship of a farmer's wife only made Wetherby love her more. He wanted to take her in his arms and smother her with kisses. But—he reminded himself that he was a reformed man now. Nothing on earth could move him to do anything to give her a dislike of him.

"Good evening, Mrs. Copley," he said, looking up for one whole minute at the clump of greenery above them. "Our hostess has very attractive decorations, would you not say?" Her gaze followed his, he was glad to see. Now she would realize what a true pattern-saint he was.

Millicent stared at the mistletoe. She knew full well what his lordship was thinking to do. Did the man have no idea of how humiliating it was to be grabbed and kissed with no more than a by-your-leave? A gentleman might—but a rake of Wetherby's ilk—no, never. If a man were so assaulted, he'd undoubtedly wish to place a facer square in the mouth of the offending party.

His lordship needed to be taught a lesson.

Millicent threw her arms around Wetherby's neck and pulled his head down until his lips met hers. She was not very strong, but she was determined—and—she had the advantage of surprise. She kissed Wetherby until she had no more breath in her and had to let him go.

His eyes showed shock, then wonderment.

Millicent was so jarred by what she had done, that she could do no more than clamp her hand over her mouth and dash for the stairs. She could not believe she'd had the courage to do it.

Well, at least she had taught him a lesson. "There!" she threw back at him before running down the steps.

Wetherby stood stock-still, staring after her. "There? There, what?" he called after her, but she was already out of sight. Well, he'd done it now. He'd broken his resolve before he'd even implemented his plan, and lost any chance of getting her to believe that he was reformed. But wait! He hadn't kissed her. She'd kissed him! "Damn!" Now he wanted her more than ever.

Just before Millicent reached the Great Hall, she paused to collect herself. Her purpose, she told herself, had been to show him how disconcerting it was to have someone—someone of the opposite sex—someone handsome and witty and altogether too charming—forever kissing you for no reason whatsoever. But she had not considered the consequences on her heart. Taking a deep breath, she put on a pleasant face and took the last step to the flagstone floor.

After they had eaten, they all gathered around the fire. Percival, the Copley's baby, was brought down again for the opening of the presents.

Rupert sat on the floor at Millicent's feet. "I'm sorry, Momma, that I lost your gift. Lord Wetherby helped me pick it out, you know."

No, she had not known. His lordship had helped select her present? How had that come to be? Then she remembered all the whispering and confiding in the small villages they had passed through. And here she had thought his lordship was filling her son's mind with all sorts of unmentionable subjects. Had she misjudged him? Perhaps he wasn't as bad as she had made him out to be. She gave Rupert a hug. "That is all right, dear. Remember what Mrs. Potter said? *We have each other.*"

Millicent turned to give Wetherby a smile, but alas, he didn't see her. He was watching the baron pluck his son from his nurse's arms.

Lord Copley sat down on the settle and after balancing the baby on his foot, began riding him up and down.

Wetherby guffawed. "I never thought I'd see the day that Andersen Copley would be bouncing a baby."

"You know, Wetherby, it isn't all that bad. You ought to think about getting married yourself."

"I have."

"Well, well. Someone has finally captured the king of hearts. And may I ask what the lady's name is who has caught your fancy?"

Wetherby scowled. "No!"

"Ah," Copley said, winking at his wife, "I do believe his lordship wants us to play a guessing game. Is she beautiful?"

"Very . . ." Wetherby said. "The loveliest woman I have ever seen—and the most humble person ever to grace my life—and that is all I will say." But that was not all that he had to say. "She is also generous to a fault."

"Then she must not be suitable, if you are reluctant to name her."

Wetherby rose to the bait. "She is more suitable than any woman I have ever met—and—the bravest."

"Ah! A regular amazon."

Wetherby started to rise.

The baron chuckled. "A bit out of curl, are we?"

Sarah scolded her husband. "Now Andersen, leave the man be. You are embarrassing him."

"Hah!" said Copley. "That is just what I am trying to do, my dear. How many times has he had me at a disadvantage? Now, my friend, if you have found such a paragon, why do you not tell us her name?"

"Because she is so far above me that I do not know if she will accept my suit." From the comer of his eye, Wetherby saw

Millicent stiffen. He couldn't interpret the expression on her face. She had to know he was speaking of her, so why didn't she look pleased? Any ordinary woman would be delighted to receive his praise. But, of course, Mrs. Copley was no ordinary woman. She chased dragons and threw snowballs, rode neck-or-nothing in a donkey cart, and outwitted thieves.

The baron was enjoying himself. "Well, now, we shall just have to make a list, Sarah, my dear—you are so good at that. Of all the eligible young debutantes who came out last year which one do you suppose would be willing to have such a rake for a husband?"

Wetherby winced. All the schemes he'd made to court Millicent were exploding like fireworks. When he had gone to Cross-in-Hand to fetch her, he'd wondered how she had come to take such an aversion to him. His encounter with her in London had been no more than an introduction, so who could have advised her otherwise? Now he knew. His so-called friend Baron Copley had been spreading lies about him.

Millicent looked down at Rupert's golden curls and fought back the tears. How could she stand to be around his lordship for the next twelve days and not reveal her feelings for him? He didn't have to name the object of his affections. 'Twas obvious to anyone who knew her. "Lord Wetherby loves . . . he loves . . . Lady Caroline," she said softly.

Rupert looked up with a start, thinking his mother was speaking to him. But her eyes were on some distant point among the evergreens hanging from the balcony. But he had heard, nonetheless. Why was she saying that Lord Wetherby was in love with Lady Caroline?

Millicent didn't notice her son's restlessness. Her mind was on the shocking revelation she'd just heard. But she had to agree with his lordship. He couldn't have found anyone more beautiful, or generous, than Lady Caroline. The fine lady had shared her gowns and jewelry with Millicent, and although the task was quite hopeless, she'd even tried to teach Millicent to flirt.

Rupert sat in a daze, surrounded by his own hopelessness. All his scheming had served no purpose. All he'd hoped for, and prayed for—everything—was going wrong. And it was all his fault.

# Nineteen

Lord Copley handed Percy to his nurse to take back to the nursery. "I don't know of any woman who would be brave enough to marry you, Wetherby."

Millicent flatly refused to hang her head. She knew that it was her ladyship of whom he spoke. Lady Caroline had been stouthearted enough to steal a key from a robber three times her size, and fearless enough to face the freezing cold to go for help. In Millicent's eyes there was no lady she thought braver.

Wetherby could take the jesting about his beloved no longer, especially when she sat in the very same room with them. Copley was acting abominably. 'Twas an aggravation to have a man who bounced a baby on his foot, telling his friend that *he* was not man enough to take charge of his life. There was a point when a gentleman had to declare himself. Wetherby narrowed his eyes. "You know, Copley, I just may propose to the lady and see if she will have me."

Rupert looked back and forth in desperation between the two adults he loved the most until he could stand it no longer. He didn't understand why people had to get married, for it seemed it certainly complicated matters. He'd chosen Lady Caroline for himself when he grew up. He had wanted Lord Wetherby for his mother. Now he knew he wanted his lordship for himself as well. He would have to sacrifice one or the other—Lady Caroline or Lord Wetherby. He loved his mother more than anybody in the world. He wanted her to be happy. His lovely gift that he'd saved for so long had been smashed. Now he could give her only one thing. Lord Wetherby.

Rupert had figured out a solution, but he knew he had to act quickly if all was not to be lost. He jumped up and cried, "Wait!"

All eyes followed him as he approached Wetherby. He tried hard to stand straight, hold his shoulders back, and not shuffle his feet. "My lord."

Wetherby glanced at the boy, not unkindly. "Yes, Rupert, what is it?"

Rupert bit his lower lip and tried to look his lordship straight in the eye, man to man, so to speak. "I am strong for my age, and I don't take up too much room, and I could help Jespers take care of you." He paused to catch his breath.

Wetherby's eyebrows shot up, then down again.

Rupert was not quite sure how one went about proposing. He reckoned it was sort of like praying. He fell upon his knees and steepled his fingers. "Lord Wetherby, if you will not marry Momma, will you marry me?"

Millicent's gasp was heard all the way across the room.

The look on Wetherby's face could not be described.

Confusion colored Rupert's cheeks scarlet, but he gathered his strength and continued, "Momma said that if two people liked each other well enough, they can sign a paper and live together for the rest of their lives. She said it is not hard when you love someone. And I love you."

As Rupert paused to catch his breath, Millicent's hand flew to her throat.

Wetherby looked over Rupert's head to where Millicent sat frozen to her seat. "I love you, too," he said.

Then, much to the amusement of everyone, Wetherby drew the distraught boy onto his lap and said, "I want you to know that I am very honored by your proposal, Rupert, but that is not exactly how it works."

"I am afraid I handled it very badly."

"Not at all, son."

*Son! He called him son.* Rupert could hardly contain his excitement.

Wetherby cast a warning look at Copley. "Since you are the head male of your family now, 'tis I who have to ask *you* for permission to address your mother."

It didn't take Rupert long to think the matter over. "Oh, yes, your lordship. I give it. I do. I told Momma that I wanted a father for Christmas, but she has not found anyone yet. But I am sure that I can persuade her to have *you,* my lord. You would make the best of fathers."

Wetherby was still watching Millicent, who was looking everywhere in the room except at him.

Millicent was beginning to wonder if all men took such a roundabout way to get to the point. If Lord Wetherby did not soon hurry over to where she sat, she was going to go to him.

While Rupert was trying hard to fight his inclination to throw his arms around Lord Wetherby's neck, that gentleman addressed the blushing Millicent. "Madam," he called quite loudly, "I do believe your son is sadly in need of a father. There is no telling what mischief the lad's ideas will lead him into if you do not obtain one for him in the very near future."

Millicent just knew that his lordship was in a delirium again. She tried to signal him to stop. That got no response. Then trying to hide her concern, she smiled vacantly at everybody in the room, including Dog. What would Andersen think? What would Sarah think? What would the entire world think?

Afraid that Mrs. Copley was going to go into one of her whirling dervish performances, Wetherby turned his attentions back to Rupert. "Master Rupert, I believe your mother is in a state of shock. So I shall have to ask you. May I apply for the position of being your father?"

Rupert threw his arms around Wetherby's neck. "Oh, yes, your lordship. I should like that above all else."

"Well, now that we have settled that, do you think we should go ask your mother if she will marry me?"

"Oh, yes, sir," Rupert said, hopping down. "I think that it would be best if you do."

Wetherby stood, and taking Rupert's hand, walked over to where Millicent sat. He was very glad to see that Lord Copley was speechless for once in his life. He suspected Millicent was laughing at him, and it made him a little uneasy. But the die was cast, and he couldn't very well act the coward in front of his new son-to-be. He knelt on one knee in front of Millicent. Watching Wetherby carefully, Rupert did the same, making sure that this time he put only one knee down.

Wetherby took Millicent's hand in his and put his other arm around Rupert. "My dearest Millicent, will you do me the honor of becoming my wife?"

"Yes," she said simply.

Wetherby kissed her hand and winked at Rupert.

Rupert could contain himself no longer, and popping up like a jack-in-the-box, shouted, "Oh, Momma. This *has* been a special Christmas, has it not? We did find a father for me after all!" He hugged Wetherby and his mother, then ran to his aunt and uncle, who were just rising to come over to congratulate the newly engaged couple. Mrs. Greenwood wiped her eyes, and Mr. Greenwood had the look of a man who still didn't comprehend what was happening. Dog yawned and lay his head back down on the warm hearth.

Wetherby rose, and pulling Millicent up to stand by his side, whispered in her ear, "Before we are inundated by our well-wishers, I want to tell you that you have made me the happiest of men. Not often is a man so lucky as to get a bride and a son at the same time. Merry Christmas, my darling."

* * *

Over a week had gone by, and Twelfth Night was still two days away.

Wetherby caught hold of Millicent under a sprig of mistletoe and kissed her soundly. A sudden donging of a clock made his head snap up. "Where is Rupert?"

Millicent sighed and placed her head on his chest. "I do believe he and Dog are hunting dragons belowstairs in the vicinity of the kitchen, although I suspect Dog's interest is more in Mrs. Proctor's hot cinnamon buns than in finding fire-breathing creatures."

Wetherby passed through an archway and started down the corridor. "I sometimes feel that even on cloudy days, I possess a second shadow. Do you suppose Copley will let us borrow the lion to keep tabs on our son for a while so we could go on a wedding trip?"

Millicent laughed. "I do not believe that will be necessary, my lord. Rupert needs to get back to his schooling. I received a letter from my mother yesterday, and they miss him."

Wetherby looked up at the mistletoe hanging from a banner pole. "I do not know if I can survive the next few days, my dear, if we stay here. There is a kissing bough in each room and several along every hallway. Even though I have complained profusely, Copley flatly refuses to take them down until after Twelfth Night."

"That is only day after tomorrow. We can leave from Danbury Wells right after the church service."

Wetherby took Millicent's hand and led her toward the library. "If it is all right with you, we will journey straight to Leicestershire, so you can meet my father. I want to get married as soon as possible."

"I confess, I do not think I can wait either. But, Ernest, I am so afraid His Grace will not approve our alliance."

Wetherby made sure that they were positioned directly under the mistletoe before he kissed the tip of her nose. "It will not matter one way or another."

"How can you say so?"

I have made my decision. I *will* have you. He cannot change the sucession." He gave her a long look. "You know, my darling, the first time we kissed—really kissed—I had the most peculiar sensation that we had done it before."

Millicent gave a half-smile. "Perhaps we had, my lord."

Wetherby tapped her chin with his finger. "I warn you. If we stay here, I will not be held responsible for my ungentlemanly behavior. Your lips do more to cause delirium than Boggles's and Tooter's fists ever did."

Millicent kept her arms around Wetherby's neck. "Then I shall just have to hold you in my arms for the next two days to make sure you do no harm to yourself."

"The agony will be worth it," he said, pulling her once more to him for another kiss. And when that one was over, another.

# Epilogue

Before the Copley party departed Roxwealde Castle, a basket arrived addressed to Rupert. Inside was an automaton made of two exquisitely sculpted porcelain figurines, a man and a woman in court dress, embracing. When the mechanism was turned on, they whirled in a circle, dancing to the strains of a Viennese waltz. The present was a hundred times the worth of the little statue that Rupert had purchased. A short note in bold handwriting told him that the sender hoped it made up for the one destroyed. There was no signature. Rupert proudly presented it to his mother. He also found his journal lying at the bottom of the package, and immediately began adding stars to Lord Wetherby's list of brave and chivalrous deeds.

When Millicent and Wetherby visited the Lance family seat in Leicestershire, Millicent, with her sweet disposition and her endless patience, completely captured the heart of Wetherby's stuffy father. The duke said he had never been so well looked-after by his own flesh and blood. He challenged Wetherby by saying that if he did not marry the fair Mrs. Copley, soon, he would marry her himself. Being the obedient son that he was, and not wanting to cause his father any undue stress, Lord Wetherby made Millicent his wife as soon as he obtained a license.

Lady Caroline returned to London after a visit to her father's estate in Gloucestershire. Unfortunately, she did not recover her jewels. A short time later, a small package was delivered to her town house. Inside she found a perfectly formed black pearl.

The Bandit King was not caught, but neither was any other young nobleman kidnapped that holiday season.

Dear Reader,

Born and raised in Indiana, I now live with my husband in Maitland, Florida. I fell in love with Ireland and the British Isles when I visited in search of my genealogical roots.

In *A Father for Christmas,* I brought back John Teagardner, a character from my Zebra Regency *Lord Wakeford's Gold Watch,* published in June 1995. More importantly, my hero, the Marquis of Wetherby, my heroine, Millicent Copley, and especially, Master Rupert, came from my Regency *Charade of Hearts,* March 1995. Also brought back were Baron Copley and his wife Sarah, the hostess with the mostest. And, of course, I could not leave out Dog, the lovable lion. I hope everyone met my Irish heroine, Caitlin O'Mullan, the fairy sprite, in the short story, "A Matter of Honor," from the Anthology *Lords and Ladies,* May 1996, where she took the English Duke of Maitland on a merry chase.

Elegantly,
Paula Tanner Girard

# A Husband for Christmas

# *One*

"I declare, Suzette, I am bored to death!" Lady Caroline exclaimed, emphasizing her point with a toss of her golden curls.

If the sudden movement caused a perfectly coiled ringlet to bounce loose from her impeccable coiffure and drop down over her smooth and flawless forehead, it had done so because she wished it to; for not a hair on Lady Caroline's head would dare disgrace so privileged a lady by falling out of place.

"I do believe I shall become a pirate or perhaps a highwayman."

The little French woman heeded her mistress with mock horror. "Oh, do not even consider it, *mademoiselle.* I am afraid you would not be able to find a competent modiste to your satisfaction, or hairdresser, who would be willing to take up life upon a ship, or spend nights riding on dark paths through the forests."

"That is true," Caroline said after some consideration. "I suppose that means I could not persuade you to join me?"

"No, *mademoiselle,* you could not."

"But, I am finding life as the Incomparable becoming so exceedingly dull of late," Caroline complained, as her gaze swept the large ballroom. "It seems that the only men in London this Season are pups, prigs, or noddies, and I have come to the sad conclusion that they have all congregated here at Almack's this evening."

"Does *mademoiselle* wish Suzette to fetch her wraps?" the petite, dark-haired woman at her side asked, quite unruffled by her mistress's lapse into colorful cant.

"Fie on you, girl. Did I not express my feelings clearly enough that I wish to go home? I do believe the clumsy dolts have danced more on *my* feet than they have upon their own. It is amazing my frock has not been ruined as well in the crush."

Suzette doubted her mistress could ever look anything but *elegante.* Lady Caroline's glittering gown was, as always, made of an exquisite gossamer fabric sewn into the latest design. Suzette watched as Lady Caroline unconsciously fingered the black-pearl pendant which hung from a dainty filigreed silver chain around her neck. She needed no other adornment to complete her toilette and Suzette knew that her ladyship was well aware of it.

"I cannot think of one gentleman I have met this evening who has warranted my notice."

"*Mademoiselle* is too particular."

Lady Caroline shrugged her pretty shoulders. "And you are getting too uppish for your own good, Suzette. You watch your ways or I shall have to turn you out."

The scold had little effect on the woman. "But it is true, my lady. You are the Incomparable. You could have had any gentleman you wanted since your debut three years ago, but you were too critical."

Caroline glanced about the room and wrinkled her nose at the sight of the men she saw. "That is nonsense, Suzette, and you know it. I am beginning to believe that the married state is not as desirable as it is made out to be. After all, I do have an income from my mother's estate; and now that my father isn't pressing me to help recover his debts, I see no reason to be at the beck and call of some self-centered male."

"That would certainly be unbearable," Suzette said with a sigh which belied her agreement with her ladyship's opinion.

Caroline would have pouted, but she knew it would only put unbecoming crinkles around her mouth. "Now go, you silly girl, and fetch my cloak."

"*Oui, mademoiselle,*" Suzette said, biting her lower lip to keep from showing her amusement.

"And hurry, you lazy thing, before some overzealous upstart asks me to stand up with him again."

Caroline watched the young woman weave her way gracefully through thc crowd toward the exit. A year ago she would have liked to box Suzette's ears for being so impertinent.

Lady Caroline's father, the Earl of Favor, deeply dipped into dun territory at the time, had only hired the little French refugee because she was willing and thankful to work for half what an English subject would. Now, Caroline could not imagine doing without her; once Suzette had been merely a servant. Now Caroline thought of her as a companion.

When she needed the latest tittle-tattle concerning behind-the-doors goings-on of other members of the *ton,* she could always depend upon Suzette to supply it. The coquettish handmaid had proven to possess a remarkable talent for gleaning tidbits of useful gossip from the most unlikely sources.

Although not of a malicious character. Lady Caroline was quite aware of her own consequence and what it required of a lady of quality to maintain her position atop the Fashionable World.

Unfortunately, she harbored a curious nature and an impetuosity which often led to disastrous consequences: as when she found that she'd climbed into bed with Baron Copley's pet lion, instead of his lordship at his castle in Devonshire two years ago. She should have known better for no matter how many harebrained schemes her father concocted, the baron had not come up to scratch.

Again, in her unsuccessful pursuit to leg-shackle the Marquis of Wetherby this December past, she'd had the unfortunate experience of being kidnapped with him by the notorious Bandit King, terror of the last four Christmas seasons and abductor of young noblemen for ransom.

As she remembered how she'd bested the black-masked thief by escaping his clutches and thereby foiling his plans, Caroline felt the thrill of her derring-do pulse through her veins. But her freedom had not come until after that bold bandit had stolen a kiss. Then as if that were not enough, his henchmen had made off with her collection of jewelry.

Later the mysterious bandit had sent her a single black pearl. *For what purpose?* she still puzzled. Of a certainty, the Social Season in London was definitely dull by comparison.

Caroline's fingers automatically raised the small pendant to her lips. She had no idea why she wore the bauble so often, except that it always brought her a great deal of attention and cast her into the role of a heroine, which she found to be much to her liking. However, she vowed that if she ever should meet the scoundrel again, she'd give him his just desserts.

Ordinarily these two misadventures alone would have discouraged a frailer maiden from hatching any further plots, but Caroline had spent much of her youth stealthfully circumventing most of the orders of her bombastic, pompous, unconscionable father, Lord Favor. This exercise in roundaboutation had by itself built a stronger and more stubborn will, which would have been more characteristic of a male heir to the earldom if there had been one.

So it was that Caroline looked upon these plans gone awry as no more than vexing delays in finding an up to the mark husband worthy of her elevated consequence. However, to her disappointment, each passing Season seemed to hold fewer and fewer possibilities of her hopes ever being fulfilled. She began to think it not worth the battle. What a rattle.

Suzette was no sooner lost from sight than Caroline was startled from her reverie by a gentle but firm hand upon her arm.

"Surely you are not planning on leaving us so soon, Lady Caroline."

"Lady Sefton," Caroline said, showing none of the loss of

composure she felt upon seeing the softspoken patroness smiling at her side.

"I have someone who wishes to meet you, my dear."

Caroline looked about her but saw no one of any unexceptionable significance to attract her.

Lady Sefton leaned closer and whispered. "Before I call him over, I want to tell you that I will take it as a special favor to me if you will honor him with a dance. He is the Earl of Blackmere."

"I don't believe I have ever heard of him," Caroline said, glancing about to discover the whereabouts of this unknown gentleman.

"He comes to Town only thrice a year from his family seat somewhere north of London. Sefton says Sir Harry told him that old Clifton Morley said that the Earls of Blackmere live in a castle built at the time of the Conqueror," Lady Sefton continued.

Caroline's eyes lit up with interest.

"Sefton brought Lord Blackmere home from White's to partake of dinner with us two nights ago. My husband insists the earl is tenacious in character and quite indifferent to women—but I don't believe a word of it. I think the poor soul is only lonely. After all, his limited social life when he does come to Town seems to be centered around those stuffy men's clubs. It was all I could do to persuade him to attend the assembly this evening; and if he does not have at least one agreeable partner—and you are still in my opinion the loveliest, my dear—I am afraid we shall never coax him out of his shell again."

Caroline was not without heart, no matter how spoiled and privileged; and she did, after all, feel that she had a reputation to uphold. There were too many young snippets coming out this Season, scheming to unseat her as the Incomparable. One more dance, she decided, would not kill her. Besides, one did not say "no" to any of the patronesses of Almack's.

"Lady Caroline, may I present Lord Blackmere?"

Caroline looked with faint surprise at the slightly heavy, mustachioed gentleman who shuffled toward them, shoulders slightly stooped. Sixtyish, she judged. If she was wont to feel a slight frisson of disappointment, she hid it well.

He came to a halt within a few feet of her and made a leg. A cotton-white wig sadly in need of a combing covered his head completely, and his hedgerow brows—drawn together in a scowl—were so thick that she could make out little of his features. His long dark coat, knee breeches and stockinged legs were the required costume for Almack's, but she surmised from what she saw that this was his usual wardrobe and not put on singularly for his appearance this evening.

Caroline sighed and held out her fingers.

The man bowed even deeper, taking her hand so gingerly that for a moment she feared he would drop it.

The fiddlers began to play a few bars of music to announce the next dance.

"Oh, dear," Lady Sefton said in an aside to Caroline, "I do fear we are to have a waltz. You will, I know, take his lordship's years into consideration and not expect too much of the pretty from him."

Caroline glanced down at the nobleman's arm extended from his side, awaiting her hand. A sigh escaped her lips. Her slippers would have to suffer one more thrashing. She smiled bravely. "I shall be honored to stand up with you, Lord Blackmere."

With the merest of nods, his lordship silently led her onto the floor. Only when he hesitantly placed his hand at her side did his gaze settle on the black pearl nestled against her chest.

For a split second his shaggy brows shot upwards and Caroline found herself staring into the greenest eyes she had ever seen.

Quickly, he turned his face away, grasped her waist—his large hand nearly encompassing it—and whirled her across the floor.

Caroline gasped. Her heart pounded, and for the next several minutes, she was to swear later, that her feet had not once touched the floor.

Not a word or even a smile broke the planes of Lord Blackmere's expressionless face. Even after he—with no more than a by-your-leave—planted the speechless Caroline in front of Suzette, who stood holding her ladyship's cape. He bowed, turned about, and left.

Caroline watched the elderly man, shoulders still stooped, make his hesitant progress around the perimeter of the room until he melted into the crowd.

Her hand flew to her throat. "Well, my goodness!" she said breathlessly.

"Well, *what*, my lady?" her little maid asked, observing Caroline's pink countenance with raised brows and no little amount of curiosity brought on by seeing her mistress's frustration.

"If I am obliged to say *well* that is entirely up to me is it not, miss? In fact, I shall say as many *wells* as I wish. Well, well, and—well!"

"*Oui, mademoiselle.*"

"I am glad that is finally understood. Now shall we go home?"

"*Oui, mademoiselle,*" Suzette said, a puzzled expression on her face as she placed the cloak around Caroline's shoulders. "Your carriage has arrived."

The Earl of Favor's magnificent green and gold town-coach was waiting at the curb. A footman, resplendent in his matching livery, stood ready to open the lacquered door emblazoned with the Cavendish coat-of-arms. Lady Caroline climbed inside, took a deep breath, and settled back into the soft squabs.

Who would have thought that a spin around the dance floor in the arms of an elderly gentleman would precipitate such heady feelings of excitement. It was beyond all reason.

Caroline smiled and caressed the tiny black pearl which lay lightly upon the bare skin of her bosom. She had seen the way

Lord Blackmere stared at it. The sight of the singular black stone had gained her the attention of other men too. That was why she enjoyed wearing it, and for an instant her thoughts went to the masked rogue who had sent it to her after she had returned home.

Three days later Lady Caroline sat at her dainty cherry wood escritoire going over her day's invitations when two letters arrived in the morning post. She saw by the handwriting and the Cavendish stamp that the first was from her stepmother, the Countess of Favor. She pushed it to one side of the desk and reached for the other.

Only a slight shrug of Suzette's shoulders indicated her disapproval of the snub.

The second missive her ladyship opened. A slow smile graced her face as she scanned the page. "Hah," said Caroline, running her gaze down the paper as she unfolded it. "It's a note from Lady Sefton. It seems I have a new admirer, Suzette."

"That is nothing out of the ordinary, *mademoiselle.* You break hearts wherever you go."

"Of course, I do," Caroline said, "but this I did not expect. She says Lord Blackmere wants to see me again."

"Why are you so surprised by that?"

"Don't be ridiculous, Suzette. The man is older than my father."

"So?"

"Lord Blackmere didn't speak one word to me the entire time he was with me."

"He would not be the first gentleman to be struck speechless by your beauty."

Lady Caroline was unable to stop herself from preening until she saw the amusement in the little French woman's eyes. "Oh, you are an impossible girl," she said, laughing. "Listen to what Lady Sefton says.

*My dear Caroline,*

*You made quite a conquest at Almack's the other evening. Lord Blackmere did not dance again after you left the Assembly Rooms. He found a spot along the wall and there he stayed.*

*He seemed neither bored nor uncomfortable at being in company with others; yet he spoke not a word to anyone.*

*There he remained quietly observing the crowd from beneath those puzzling brows like some ancient sage. Only after the guests began to leave did he approach me, speaking so softly that I had to ask him to repeat himself twice.*

*I do believe I have never encountered such a shy gentleman. He wanted to know if I thought you would be willing to welcome him if he called upon you at your house. He sounded so eager to have my assistance that I did not have the heart to refuse his request to intercede on his behalf.*

*In the meantime, I queried Sefton on Lord Blackmere's background. Strange to say, he blustered about a bit before finally saying that he saw no reason for you not to receive Lord Blackmere. So, my dear, I sent word around to his lordship's lodgings telling him that I would be pleased to have him escort me to Cavendish House in the Square tomorrow afternoon when I come to call on you.*

"Wasn't that the old man with the permanent scowl?" Suzette broke in. "Surely, you would not want him dangling after you, would you, *mademoiselle?* He would frighten away all the eligible young men."

Caroline was about to agree with her maid until she scanned the last paragraph of Lady Sefton's letter. Her eyes twinkled.

"Why not?" Caroline asked. Silently reading the final paragraph of the letter to herself with more thoroughness, she smiled a secret smile.

*I know Lord Blackmere is quite up in years, my dear, but he is from an old distinguished family. His title goes back several generations. Lord Sefton did hint that he must be quite wealthy, for he owns a great deal of property, he has never been seen to gamble, nor has he ever been married. Therefore, my dear, I do not think it would hurt your reputation to show the* tonnish *set that you have turned the head of so distinguished a nobleman.*

Caroline put down the letter. "I see no reason why I should not welcome him, Suzette."

Her maid looked at her as if she'd suddenly taken leave of her senses.

Caroline ignored the look. Yes, why not? she thought to herself, as a plan began to unfold in her mind. If my father sees no harm in making a fool of himself over a girl one-third his age, I shall put the shoe on the other foot and show him how ridiculous it looks for a man old enough to be my grandfather makes a fool over me.

"You haven't read your stepmother's letter yet," Suzette admonished, casting a knowing glance at the missive still sitting on the escritoire.

"Oh, do not say so, you exasperating girl. Is it not enough that my father married a seventeen year old straight out of the schoolroom that you have to call her my stepmother?"

"Well, like it or not, my lady, that is what she is. Your father seems quite content in his marriage," she scolded. "She is also the Countess of Favor and soon to be the mother of your new baby brother or sister."

"But she is so very . . ." Caroline studied her image in the mirror. "My mother was the Incomparable of her day—the Toast of London Society . . . and Mary is so . . . so . . ."

"So very sweet," finished Suzette.

Caroline sniffed. "I was going to say that with the dowry her father settled upon her, she is wealthy as the Queen of Sheba."

"And you would not be sitting here in this lovely refurbished house if it were not for her money," Suzette scolded.

As much as Caroline was inclined not to admit it, Mary's exorbitant dowry, which Mr. Bennington offered with all seven of his daughters, had enabled the earl to open up Cavendish House in London once more. It had been this residence in which Caroline had spent many happy hours when she was little, for her mother had much preferred the glittering life in the city to what she considered dull country living.

Her father's extravagant ways after his wife died had forced him to close it down. But now since his marriage to the young daughter of a wealthy country cit, Lord Favor seemed to prefer life at his family seat in Gloucester. Heaven knows, he'd spent a fortune on renovations for his new bride—with her fortune, of course.

"They seem to rub along well together," said Suzette. "I have not seen your father so happy in years."

"Happy? Dotty . . . chuckleheaded . . . foggy in the crumpet is what I call it," Caroline remonstrated. "Only the king's fool would cavort about the manor in front of the servants like a mooncalf. Good heavens, Suzette, the man is four-and-fifty. I shall never go back there. I shall find an excuse to stay in London."

"Well, I still say you should read the countess's letter."

"I don't need to. I already know what it says."

"How can you know what it says if you have not read it?"

"I receive the exact same letter every Tuesday, do I not? She will ask very politely when we are going to visit. Then she will beg me to look after her little brother Elroy while he is in Town, because she fears he will be led into all the pitfalls that confront an innocent schoolboy in the city. The gamesters, the gambling hells, and unscrupulous painted women who are certain to entice a fresh-faced defenseless cock-robin, such as her brother, into the dens of inequity."

"Oh, my lady!" expostulated Suzette clasping her hands to her cheeks in an attempt to look shocked. "You should not know of such things."

"Don't pretend to be missish, Suzette. I did not live in my father's house all those years without overhearing what he and his rapscallion cronies talked about—and I am certain I am not saying anything that you have not heard yourself. Besides, if I read the signs correctly, her little brother Elroy lost his innocence at Baron Copley's country party in Devonshire a year and a half ago."

Suzette bit her lower lip to keep from smiling.

"It is most likely true and you know it," said Caroline, trying not to succumb to her maid's exaggerated expressions. "I am quite determined about this, Suzette. I have no intentions of playing nursemaid to a foolish, young popinjay who blindly follows every blackguard and gamester in London."

# Two

The following afternoon, Lady Sefton arrived at Cavendish House in the Square with Lord Blackmere in tow. They had to wade through a forest of flowers which lined the entrance hall leading to the receiving room.

"My goodness, Lady Caroline has so many admirers," Lady Sefton exclaimed cheerfully, watching for his lordship's reaction as they followed the butler. A suit of armor, spear in hand, stood stiffly guarding the doorway of the Green Salon which they found was already overflowing with callers.

"Invitations to Cavendish House on the Square are jealously sought after," Lady Sefton said, in an aside to Lord Blackmere before she stepped into the room.

His lordship hesitated and looked around in confusion.

Lady Caroline did not let on that she saw them. She sat upon a green satin Grecian couch, smiling first at one and then another of the young men vying for her attention, while at the same time studying Lord Blackmere from the corner of her eye. Lord Featherstone stood behind her, whispering some nonsense in her ear. She pretended to be amused, and at the same time fluttered her fan at Jamie Stessels, who was practically on his knees making an idiot of himself with his pleas to ride with him in Hyde Park sometime soon. Two young ladies and another gentlemen made up their immediate group, all showing their adulation by parroting everything their hostess said.

Caroline was certain that Lord Blackmere could not help but be impressed with her popularity.

Only when Driggs announced the new guests did Caroline turn and greet them with an expression of delighted surprise. Rising, she held out her hands to Lady Sefton.

Maria Sefton, the sweetest of Almack's hostesses, looked lovely as usual and started across the room toward her. The Earl of Blackmere, however, had to be coaxed with a tug on his sleeve before he would put one foot in front of the other.

He still carried his walking stick and Caroline would have sworn the black coat and breeches were the ones he'd worn at Almack's. The same frothy wig sat on his head, and the lower part of his face was nearly covered by his walrus mustache; both wig and mustache appeared to be no better combed than the first time she'd seen them. Lord Blackmere's valet had to be very slipshod indeed to allow his master to appear so shamefully ill-dressed.

The Countess of Sefton always incited interest wherever she appeared, but it was the earl whom everyone's eyes followed. A newcomer was grist for the mill, thought Caroline.

"Lady Sefton," Caroline said warmly as the two women kissed each other on the cheek.

"You remember Lord Blackmere, my dear," Lady Sefton said, stepping aside to reveal his lordship hiding behind her.

The earl bowed over Caroline's hand and for an instant, she once again had a glimpse of those green eyes. Then with a gentlemanly nod, he stepped back a pace to give the ladies a moment to converse.

"Lah, I half believed you were not coming," said Caroline with a practiced flourish of her hand, which would have done honor to a dancer of the opera ballet. The graceful motion was completely wasted on Lord Blackmere, because he was leaning on his walking stick, staring at the floor. Botheration! She could see Lord Blackmere was going to be more difficult to impress than she'd thought. Caroline turned her attention back to Lady Sefton.

"You know I must be fashionably late," the patroness was saying with a tinkle of laughter. She leaned closer to Caroline. "Actually it was because, up to the last minute I was afraid I was not going to get his lordship to come. It did take a bit of persuading, even after my coach arrived at his hotel."

"Well, Lord Blackmere must come sit by me," Caroline said, preparing her most devastating smile, the one which had always gotten the daughter of the Earl of Favor anything she wanted. Anticipating the look of adoration she expected to see in his eyes, she turned to where his lordship had been standing. But—the spot stood empty. "For heavens sakes, Maria! Where is the earl?"

Lady Sefton covered her mouth with her hand. "My goodness! He has disappeared, hasn't he?"

"There he is," Caroline said, pointing with her fan.

All eyes in the room turned to watch his lordship, a black silhouette, making his way across the room to the farthest wall. There he carefully chose a straight-backed chair. He pushed it slowly to a spot in front of the tall window, laboriously seated himself, and leaning forward, planted his hands firmly on the head of his walking stick. There he remained staring out at the room until Lady Sefton prepared to leave.

Lady Sefton apologized humbly. "I am sorry, my dear, that things did not go as well as I expected with Lord Blackmere."

Caroline, still a little bewildered because nothing had gone as she had planned either, smiled graciously. "You must not read romance into everything others say and do, Maria."

"I just want people to be happy as I am," Lady Sefton said with a sigh.

It was true, as Caroline well knew, that Lord and Lady Sefton had a close relationship. "Well, this time you were totally mistaken about his lordship's attachment. No matter how many times I sent the servants over, he accepted neither food nor drink. Nor would he talk to anyone."

"But he seemed so genuinely interested in you when he asked me if you would receive him."

"Well, I think it was very rude of him just to sit there as though he was attending the theater and we were the performers here for his amusement."

"I think he was overwhelmed by the crush. My husband says that the Blackmere family seat is in a very isolated area somewhere outside of London. So I suppose there must not be many social activities. His lordship doesn't stay long on these visits, so I suppose he will be leaving London soon."

Lord Blackmere had seemed so completely disinterested on his first visit to Cavendish House on the Square that it was with some amazement one week later that Caroline found him entering her salon with Lady Sefton.

Caroline said as much to Lady Sefton. "I see no change in his behavior. He still will not accept any refreshments and he refuses to join in conversation with my circle of friends. I was speaking to Lady Tewilliger and Mrs. Browne about my father's vast library and Mrs. Browne kept pressuring me to invite Lord Blackmere to participate in our discussion."

Lady Sefton laughed. "Mrs. Browne, for all her robust charms, is also on the lookout for her fourth husband. That is enough to frighten any bachelor over forty."

"I well know that Mrs. Browne is worse than last year's turnips, but I fear that the glare he cast her way will be enough to set her tongue to wagging. You know it takes little to set her on her ear."

"I would not repine much on it, dear."

Caroline tried to sort the puzzle out in her mind. "I don't understand why he bothered to come at all. Why, he hasn't said one word to me since he arrived."

Lady Sefton thought about that a moment. "That is very

strange, because Lord Blackmere speaks quite readily to me when we are in the carriage."

Caroline looked at her incredulously. "He never!"

"Why, yes. He talks articulately, although at times it is difficult to understand him because he speaks so softly. It is almost like hearing a low wind through the pines," she said, cocking her head to one side as if trying to listen.

"Well, why doesn't he say something to me?"

Lady Sefton smiled, knowingly. "Perhaps he will, someday. A man likes to know that he is being listened to."

All of Lady Caroline's guests had come, stayed their allotted time, and left; or so she thought until she turned and nearly fell over Lady Sefton, who stood twisting her handkerchief in her hands and looking quite agitated.

"My goodness! I thought you had left some time ago. What has happened to distress you?"

"Oh, my dear Caroline, I fear I have misplaced Lord Blackmere," Lady Sefton said, tears shining in her eyes.

Caroline's gaze flew swiftly to the corner where she had last seen the earl. The chair was empty. "Perhaps he is waiting for you outside."

"No, I have looked. None of the servants can find him either."

"Have you ever misplaced an escort before?"

"No, never. This is the first time."

"I am sure he has just accepted a ride with someone else who left earlier," Caroline offered.

"Do you think so?"

"I am certain of it. He is likely safe and sound back at his hotel."

"You may be right. Lord Blackmere seems a little confused at times, but you have relieved my mind, dear," Lady Sefton said brightly, giving Caroline's hand a pat.

Lady Sefton had no sooner departed than the butler, eyes blinking, cheeks puffing in and out, appeared at the salon door.

Seldom if ever did Lady Caroline see Driggs lose his composure. "Yes, what is it?"

"There is a *person* in the bookroom. my lady," he said, indignantly.

Caroline's eyebrows shot up. "A person? What sort of a person?"

"That odd person dressed in black. The one with the ill-powdered wig."

"Lord Blackmere?"

"I believe that is his name, my lady. I was checking the rooms to see that your guests didn't leave anything of value behind."

Caroline knit her brows, forgetting in her puzzlement that such a reaction would put wrinkles in her forehead. "Well, obviously, Lady Sefton did, but I persuaded her that she hadn't. We came to the conclusion that Lord Blackmere had requested a ride from someone earlier."

"Well, he certainly didn't, because he is very much here."

"Whatever is he doing in the library?"

"He appeared to be reading a book, my lady."

"How very unusual. No one has ever read books in the library before."

"I know it sounds strange, but that is what he appeared to be doing. He was so absorbed that he didn't hear me open the door. To tell the truth, my lady, I was that surprised that I didn't say anything either, but came straight to you."

"You did the right thing, Driggs."

"Your callers often leave a cane or a hat, but this is the first time that I recall someone has left a person behind. Do you wish me to see him out?"

"No, no, Driggs." Caroline fought a compulsion to laugh. What flummery was his lordship trying to put over on her?

Could it be, she thought with a bit of self-satisfaction, that I have his lordship in my pocket already?

"I just now remembered that I did mention something about my father's large collection of books in polite conversation to Lady Tewilliger and Mrs. Browne. Lord Blackmere was seated nearby. He must have overheard and, for some reason, decided to have a look. I shall see him out."

"Is there anything else, my lady?"

"I don't believe the earl has any transportation now. Have my carriage sent round to fetch him."

As soon as Driggs was off on his errand, Caroline hurried to the library. The room was dark: dark wood, dark carpets, dark furniture. She found the earl mounted on a low stool, reaching for a book on a shelf above his head. Regardless of the thousands of volumes lining the shelves, the room was seldom used for anything more than a place to store the guests' wraps.

Caroline approached cautiously. "Lord Blackmere?" she queried.

He jumped. The stool tipped. The book flew out of his hand, and his lordship sat down with a thud on the floor.

Caroline's hands flew to her mouth.

Lord Blackmere, legs outstretched, wig nearly covering one eye, stared at her for a moment trying to orient himself.

"Oh, my goodness! I didn't mean to startle you, my lord," Caroline cried, rushing forward to help him up.

Lord Blackmere raised his arms to make it easier for Lady Caroline to slip her hands around his chest from behind.

His lordship was very heavy to lift. Even after he twisted a bit to enable himself to put his arm around her neck, it took several tugs and a few false starts before Lord Blackmere managed to gain his footing.

"Are you all right?" she asked, breathing heavily, as Lord Blackmere leaned down to retrieve the book he had dropped.

He patted each arm and lifted his feet one at a time. Seemingly satisfied, he nodded.

"Oh, I am so glad," she said, straightening his wig. "Lady Sefton feared she had misplaced you. It was so late that I persuaded her that you had already accepted a ride in someone else's carriage."

He looked around the room for a moment, then reached into his pocket and pulled out his watch. He took turns holding it to his ear, then shaking it. Finally, he abandoned that effort and once more glanced here and there, as if trying to find something.

"I am afraid we don't keep any clocks in the library," Caroline said, interpreting his bewilderment. "At least any that are working. The room is so seldom used."

"Incredulous!" he said, his voice no louder than a husky whisper.

Caroline moved closer to hear. "Did you say something, my lord?"

"You must excuse an old man for his idiosyncrasies."

"You are not old," she blurted out for no reason that she could think of.

He blinked several times. She couldn't tell if he was smiling or not. It was hard to tell with that monstrous mustache nearly covering his entire mouth.

"Were you looking for anything in particular, my lord?"

He nodded again and pointed to the red leather book in his hand. "Do you know if there is a second volume to this?" he rasped.

Caroline believed it was the longest sentence she'd heard Lord Blackmere utter since they had been introduced. His voice sounded more like a man with a bad sore throat than wind in the pines. Obviously, Lady Sefton's interpretation was more romantic than hers.

She looked closer at the title. *The Reverend Algernon Pick-*

*worth's Adventures Among the Heathen of the Malay Archipelago.* "Oh, my," she laughed. "If my father purchased a pair of those, there is no telling where the other is. I am afraid this library is rather topsy-turvy."

Caroline always wondered why her father kept buying so many books when she never saw him read anything except the morning papers. "Father never had any of his libraries cataloged."

Lord Blackmere shook his head and sighed. "A pity," she thought she heard him say.

At that moment, Driggs appeared with his lordship's hat.

"My carriage will carry you back to your hotel, my lord," Caroline said.

Lord Blackmere's expression was impossible to read, but Caroline saw the way his fingers caressed the red leather volume.

"You may borrow that if you wish, and please feel welcome to come at any time to look for your other book."

After Driggs showed Lord Blackmere out, Caroline made her way back to the Green Salon.

The minute she entered, she was met by an anxious Suzette.

"*Mademoiselle,* where have you been? Suzette was worried about you."

"I was in the library," Caroline said. She chose one of the more comfortable chairs to sit in and commenced to relate what had happened.

Suzette shook a finger at Caroline. "Shame on you, *mademoiselle.* You should not have been in there alone with a man. It is not proper."

"Oh, posh and bother, Suzette. He is a harmless old gentleman."

"No man is harmless, *mademoiselle.* Now . . . have you forgotten that you are attending the theater tonight? You must get ready."

"You go up and see to my bath and choose what I am to wear. I shall sit here a moment to catch my breath."

"*Oui, mademoiselle,*" Suzette said, hurrying from the room.

Caroline sank back into the chair. My, oh, my, she'd never met such a shy man as his lordship. He needed someone to encourage him to speak out. Lord Blackmere was really a very nice man when one got to know him, and Caroline determined that she would get his lordship to talk to her the same way that he did to Maria Sefton.

As Lord Blackmere left Cavendish House, a slender, not-too-tall young man, definitely a sprig of the latest fashion, sprang up the same steps, entered the house and handed his hat and cane to the butler. He flicked an imaginary piece of lint from his sleeve and tried to look like a man about town. He didn't.

"Afternoon, Driggs. Came to see her ladyship. I know she's here, so don't tell me she ain't."

Caroline hearing the altercation that ensued appeared in the doorway of the salon. "Do come in, Elroy, and quit badgering the servants."

"I say, wasn't that Lord Blackmere I saw climbing into your carriage, Caro?"

"I am *Lady Caroline* to you," she said, crisply.

"I dare say. It beats me why we have to stand on ceremony. It's not as if I'm asking you to call me *Uncle Elroy,* is it?" he said in a fit of snorts and barks of laughter which sounded not unlike a donkey braying. "It does seem rather silly, don't it, seeing that your stepmama is my sister and six years younger than you."

Caroline did not think that statement deserved a comment and turned about and walked back into the parlor.

"Well, five . . . four then," he said, dogging her footsteps. "Don't seem that a year or two should make that much difference. Nothing to tie yourself in knots about. Besides, I was asking you about Lord Blackmere. Very high *ton,* you know. No one in any of the clubs says nay to his lordship," he said, twisting his face into what Caroline took as an attempt at a suggestive wink.

Caroline wondered if acknowledging his antics was worth the effort, but now her curiosity got the better of her. "What can you possibly mean by that statement, Elroy? Lord Blackmere is a kind and considerate man. He may be conservative . . . and a little eccentric perhaps, but that is nothing to wink about, so don't you put him under a cloud."

"Dash it all, Caro . . . I mean, Caroline. It ain't something a gentleman lets on about to a proper lady," he said.

Caroline saw it was useless to remind him that he'd omitted her title. "Elroy, either tell me what *on dits* you have been spreading or quit making those monkey faces."

"Monkey see, monkey do," Elroy said stuffily.

At that moment, Driggs entered the room. "Your hat and cane, sir."

Elroy placed his beaver at a jaunty angle, and twirling his cane, pranced out of the room.

What a pickle. Caroline now acknowledged that if she had not been so quick to signal her servant to interrupt, she could have found out what it was about the shy Lord Blackmere that should cause Elroy to make such shameful hints. The mystery had now raised her curiosity, and Caroline decided that she would just have to count on other means to find out about what the exasperating boy had been hinting.

# Three

Lady Caroline's schedule remained a round of social calls and shopping during the day, parties and balls in the evenings. On returning to Cavendish House on the Square after a visit to her shoemaker in Oxford Street, she was met at the door by Driggs.

"Has anyone called or left a message?" she asked the butler, managing to remove her bonnet without displacing a single hair.

"Your messages are on the silver salver, my lady, and Lord Blackmere is in the library. Came an hour ago."

"My goodness! He gave no indication that he was coming. Whatever could he want?" Caroline said, with a bit of triumph showing in her voice. "Has he become upset waiting for me, Driggs?"

"Can't say that he has, my lady. He said that he came to work on cataloging your books."

A tinge of disappointment nettled Caroline. "Oh, do not say so. I fear the earl misinterpreted something I said. I did not mean that he should straighten out the bookroom."

Caroline couldn't believe that any gentleman who called would not be looking for her. Impossible! But neither had Lord Blackmere ever sent her flowers or written a pretty poem as her other admirers did. Yet, here he was. Surely that was a good sign, wasn't it? "Has he had any refreshments, Driggs?"

"He said he didn't want to be a bother, my lady."

"For heaven's sakes, something should have been offered him anyway. What will he think of us?"

"I'll see to it right away, my lady."

"Thank you, Driggs."

"This time I am coming with you, *mademoiselle,*" Suzette said, handing their hats and pelisses to a maid. "It is not proper for you to be in there without a chaperone."

"He is only an old man, Suzette," Caroline sniffed.

"You thought of your father as an old man, too. He did not start a new family by sitting in his chair drinking wine."

Caroline pondered that thought before replying. "Knowing my father the wine probably had a lot to do with it and I do not think that Lord Blackmere is a drinking man."

Suzette knew Lady Caroline had to get in the last word, but she had no intention of being left behind. She said nothing more and followed her mistress into the library.

They found his lordship seated at the large desk, bent over a large ledger contentedly writing. A stack of books was piled in front of him. On hearing them enter, he quickly removed his spectacles and pinching the bridge of his nose, rose from his chair.

"You must think us barbarians for not serving you better, my lord. Refreshments will be brought in shortly," Caroline said, holding her hand out to him.

Lord Blackmere rounded the desk and with a flourish bowed. His manners were correct and courteous; yet, Caroline could neither tell if he was annoyed at the interruption or delighted to see her.

Lady Caroline stepped aside and said, "May I present my companion, Mademoiselle Suzette."

"Charmed," responded the earl softly, bowing over her hand as nicely as he had done for Caroline only that he continued speaking to Suzette. "Did you know," he rasped, "that I have discovered several French classics?" He walked to a shelf and removed three little books. "Perhaps you would like to take them to the chair over there by the light to look at them."

"Oh, *merci!*" With a cry of delight, Suzette took the books and hurried over to the window.

Caroline puzzled over why his lordship conversed with Suzette at some length and not with her. "My lord," she said rather abruptly, "there is no need for you to try to straighten out this labyrinth of books. No one reads them anyway."

Lord Blackmere held up his hand to silence her. "It is a privilege, my lady."

Caroline could think of nothing duller than dusting off old books. "Nevertheless, my lord, I insist that you take a break from your labors," Caroline said, as two serving maids entered and placed a tea tray and a platter of sandwiches and biscuits upon a round table before the hearth. Caroline had been born to give orders in her own house and consequently moved toward the refreshments expecting Lord Blackmere to follow.

He did.

They seated themselves on the settee—Lady Caroline on one end and Lord Blackmere on the other, but after she handed him his cup and insisted that he take a biscuit, they both fell silent.

She knew he was studying her from under his heavy brows as she had seen him do before. It still unsettled her. She set down her own cup so she could let her fingers go to the small black pearl dangling from its silver chain around her neck.

Lord Blackmere's gaze followed as she knew it would.

A secret smile turned up the corners of Caroline's mouth. The black pearl was weaving its spell on his lordship as surely as it did on her younger admirers.

"Did you know that I was kidnapped last year by the notorious Bandit King?" she asked while watching for his reaction.

Lord Blackmere's eyebrows jumped to his hairline and Caroline was afraid she had quite alarmed him. "No!" he rasped, setting down his teacup upon the table with a *clank* and turning toward her.

"Oh, my lord, I didn't mean to frighten you!" Caroline cried, trying to hide her delight. It was not often now that she could find anyone who had not heard her tale of bravery.

"Well," she said, not daring to glance over at Suzette, who Caroline knew would most surely throw up her hands if she was made to hear the tale one more time. "Would you like to hear it?" she asked demurely, placing her hands in her lap.

Lord Blackmere's gaze remained riveted on Caroline's chest as he nodded. "Is he as terrible as they say?" he asked, his voice gruff with concern.

Caroline felt her face flush and she covered the pearl with her hand.

"Dreadful, my lord! At Christmastime he kidnaps the sons of wealthy noblemen, you know, then holds them for ransom. He has done it for four years now, so of course, families are terrified it will happen again."

"The authorities can't catch him?" He spoke so quietly that Caroline had to move closer to enable her to hear him clearly.

"They don't know where he will strike next, because he never carries out his dastardly tricks in any of the same places. The first year it was a nobleman's son in Yorkshire. Then a couple in Cheshire and Norfolk. Next Lord Duffmire's son right here in London. Last year it was Devonshire." She looked down at her hands then back up at him from under her lashes. "That is where he took us prisoner."

"My dear lady," Lord Blackmere said, his voice gruff with concern, "did you get a good look at him? That would help the authorities."

Caroline was quite moved by his lordship's sympathy. "No. He wore a hood the entire time. Except . . ."

"Yes?"

Caroline felt the flush rush to her face again. "Only briefly did he pull up his mask, but there was something obstructing my vision," she said, not daring to add that it had been the bandit's lips upon hers which had silenced her.

"A pity," Lord Blackmere said, shaking his head. "You must have been very frightened."

"Not in the least, my lord," Caroline answered. "The Marquis of Wetherby was his intended victim, but the wastrel found he had unwittingly kidnapped two women and a boy along with Lord Wetherby. That was his downfall."

Lord Blackmere chuckled.

Caroline felt quite pleased with herself that she had not only gotten his lordship to talk a little but to show some humor. She laughed along with him. "The Bandit King met his match, I can tell you. Outnumbered and out-foxed."

Eagerly, Caroline told him of her own ordeal and her part in stealing the key to the marquis's cell and her escape through an ancient tunnel under the manor house.

The expression on Caroline's face altered completely. "The rogue made me wash pots and scrub the stone floors."

Lord Blackmere looked shocked. "Cruel! Cruel!"

"It was almost too much to bear." She held her hands out toward him and to her surprise, Lord Blackmere took them in his and turned them over so that her palms were exposed.

Caroline swallowed hard. "They were quite dreadfully sore," she said, as she felt his hands tighten around hers. "I never realized how much a person's hands can hurt from being in soap and water all day," she said a little nervously.

Caroline thought for an instant that Lord Blackmere was going to kiss them, instead he released her hands, and she quickly folded them in her lap. "I . . . I have a stillroom maid who knows how to make herbal ointments, and I asked her to see that the serving maids in my house put some on their hands after they have put in a day's work," she stammered, not daring to look into those vibrant green eyes. "Suzette says that is kind of me."

When his lordship did not reply, Caroline gave him a quick sideways glance only to find to her surprise that he was rising from the settee.

Lord Blackmere excused himself most politely, said he

would call again, and was gone before Caroline could gather her wits about her.

"Aggravating man!" Caroline said after the door had closed behind him. "He didn't even tell me how unselfish I was."

"Suzette thought him most pleasant, *mademoiselle,*" said her maid. "It is my opinion that his lordship thinks that anyone as beautiful as you must by nature be charitable as well."

"Oh, do you think so, Suzette? Yes, that must be what he thinks. That means I don't need to be angry with his lordship after all."

As the days passed Lady Caroline was never quite sure when she would find Lord Blackmere in her library nor had she anticipated how much she looked forward to seeing him sitting at the desk piled high with books, scribbling in his ledger.

While Suzette sat by the window with a book or needlework, Caroline would order tea with sandwiches or pastries. Then she'd place Lord Blackmere's cup before him on the desk and pull up a chair for herself. While he worked, she told him funny tales about the parties she'd attended and the people she knew.

He encouraged her to continue with a nod of his head or a chuckle to show that he was listening.

One afternoon Lord Blackmere had been silent for some time, bent over, completely absorbed in his work. Caroline, having run out of anything new to relate to him about the latest goings-on of the *ton*nish set, now sat staring at the appalling white thatch atop his head. "Once I had an old shaggy dog named Dipper," she blurted out without thinking.

Lord Blackmere jerked up his head so quickly that Caroline feared his wig would fly off.

Her hand clapped over her mouth too late. "Of course, he wasn't always old, my lord," she cried, trying to make amends. "In fact, he was very-very young at one time." Oh, dear, what a muddle, she thought. I am only making things worse.

Lord Blackmere set down his pen, leaned back in his chair and folded his hands over his stomach. "I have been rude," he said, looking at her kindly. "Forgive me, my lady."

Caroline smiled weakly. She did not know what to make of his lordship. At one time she had thought he would be the perfect prize to dangle before her father to let him see how ridiculous it looked for an old man to woo a girl young enough to be his daughter. Now, she was not so sure of what his lordship's intentions were at all.

Lord Blackmere was again studying her with such intensity from under those rumpled brows, that his eyes reminded her more than ever of Dipper's. Not the color for the dog's eyes were brown, not green—but his lordship looked at her in the way that Dipper used to when he lay by the fire, his great shaggy head on his paws, gazing up at her with adoration.

"Now tell me about this dog of yours," he said in his low rasping voice.

Caroline was glad to see that Lord Blackmere did not hold what she had said against her and thus encouraged, she continued.

"I fished a tiny white puppy from the creek when I was a little girl. After Mother died, Father left me at Cavendish Hall in Gloucestershire and there were no other children for me to play with. I begged Miss Plunkett—she was my nurse—to let me keep him. I had already named him Dipper. I think Miss Plunkett felt sorry for me, so she agreed. After all, Dipper was no bigger than a rabbit and so timid that he cowered at the sight of a mouse."

Lord Blackmere watched in hidden amusement as the Incomparable Lady Caroline Cavendish so completely lost her consequence that she clapped her hands gleefully like a mischievous child, and laughed until the tears came.

"Of course, we expected Dipper to grow, but no one ever dreamed that he would continue to do so until he was nearly as big as my pony, Nibbles."

A low rumbling chuckle came up from somewhere deep inside Lord Blackmere, making his hands bounce up and down on his stomach.

Caroline didn't know why, but she was even beginning to find his raspy voice not unpleasant.

In the following weeks, Caroline became accustomed to looking into the library whenever she came home from one of her social activities.

Lord Blackmere's interest in the library seemed so genuine that it puzzled her and one day she ventured to ask him why anyone would want so many books. She told him that the romantics, which most of her acquaintances read, bored her.

"They are about beautiful people who live in fine mansions and heroines who are threatened by mysterious, sinister villains. Why should I want to read about places and people that I know already, my lord?"

He handed her a volume called *The Book of Marco Polo* to take to her room, and encouraged her to tell him what she thought of it when next she saw him.

For three days Caroline found she did not want to put the book down long enough to go out of the house. "My goodness, Suzette, I never knew reading could be so enjoyable. Lord Blackmere gave me this book which tells of traveling to a strange land named Cathay. That is what China was called long ago," she said. "And it has made me rethink my plans for my future."

"What is *mademoiselle* up to now?" Suzette asked warily.

"Have you ever ridden a camel, Suzette? I am thinking that I may join a caravan crossing the deserts of Mongolia."

"No, I have not and as to joining a caravan you cannot do that, *mademoiselle,* your calendar is too full. In fact, it is time that you start getting dressed for the Whistlewaites' Ball this evening."

With a sigh of disappointment, Caroline closed her book and placed it on the table. "You are right, Suzette. I had forgotten my engagement."

Suzette shook her head. It was not like her mistress to show the doldrums when she had a chance to get dressed up.

Mr. and Mrs. Portnoy Whistlewaite's terrace house was filled to capacity that night, the crush every hostess's dream. Miss Priscilla Whistlewaite being the reason for the reception only added to Mrs. Whistlewaite's hopes that her daughter would find a suitable attachment in her first Season. Her coming-out ball earlier in May had also been a resounding success and the proud parents had high hopes of their only child latching onto a Lord Somebody or Other. Anyone without a title was not encouraged to press their suit.

Lady Caroline was quite surprised to find Lord Blackmere there. Once, she had seen him at the theater in Lord and Lady Sefton's box, and another time at a musicale all by himself. But he seldom could be persuaded to attend a private party.

He had taken a seat at the far corner of the drawing room and refused every effort anyone made to get him to speak to them. Including Caroline.

"Impossible man!" she said just loud enough for him to hear and walked away.

Her thoughts were not at the height of charitableness or her spirits all sweetness and light when she passed a group of ladies gossiping.

"The man is an impossible bore," Mrs. Browne expounded quite with the purpose of having as many as could hear her.

"I agree, Persimmonie," Lady Tewilliger said just as loudly, and henceforth proceeded to list a number of other faults the earl possessed.

Now regardless of having used much the same wording only moments before, Caroline was incensed that anyone else should dare criticize his lordship. After all she had rather come to think of Lord Blackmere as her own personal domain.

"Lord Blackmere is no such thing! I think you are vastly unfair, Mrs. Browne. In fact, I find Lord Blackmere to be quite entertaining—and very knowledgeable in a number of things."

"Oh, Lady Caroline, how can you say so?" spouted Mrs. Browne huffily. "The man is an antidote. And those clothes!"

"I doubt he has a thought in his head either," Lady Tewilliger reiterated.

Throwing out her chest—which was considerable—Mrs. Browne rose to the occasion. "One cannot get a word out of him, no matter what one asks."

"Perhaps what you ask is not worth answering, Mrs. Browne. Now if you will excuse me, I do believe I see Lady Sefton signaling me," Caroline answered tartly, walking away.

"Well, I never!" said Lady Tewilliger turning scarlet.

"Is anything the matter, dear?" Lady Sefton asked as soon as Caroline joined her. "Is Persimmonie Browne too much for you?"

"Certainly not! I just think it vastly unfair for anyone to criticize someone they don't know."

Lady Sefton gave her a searching look. "Such as Lord Blackmere?"

"How did you know?"

"With your voice you would do well on the stage, my dear. I shall set you at ease and tell you that I saw Mrs. Browne get a good set down from his lordship earlier when she tried to exhibit her considerable charms for him. He would have none of it. I fear she is still burning."

"And well she should," Caroline said, quite relieved.

"Do you feel that you have gotten to know his lordship that well?"

"To tell the truth, I know him not at all. No matter how much I press, he reveals very little about himself. I know only that he is well versed in a good many world matters as well as history and geography."

"Do you wish to find out more about him?" Lady Sefton asked, giving her a sideways glance.

Now that Caroline knew that Mrs. Browne had been given her dues, she felt that she could safely return to criticizing Lord Blackmere herself. "Well, I think it not very nice that he should get me to tell him all about myself and he discloses nothing."

Lady Sefton lowered her voice. "It is the same with everyone, my dear. Although Lord Blackmere encourages me to speak my thoughts on many things, he is just as closed-lipped about himself. If I am curious about something, I gather information from other sources."

"What sources?"

"My husband, for instance," Lady Sefton said, sounding quite pleased with herself.

"Well at present I do not have a husband to consult," said Caroline, "and I am beginning to think that it is impossible to get meaningful information out of any man. They get you to tell them fribbles and nonsense and make you believe that they are interested in what you have to say."

Lady Sefton pulled Caroline to one side. "It is a matter of timing, my dear, a fact most wives learn if they wish to keep peace in the household. Now I have found Lord Sefton to be quite loquacious after his first cup of coffee in the morning, so this is the time of day I make subtle inquiries. He told me that Sir Blakey Deempster, they call him flakey Blakey," she said, laughing. "Well, Sir Blakey is about the only one old enough who remembers Lord Blackmere from his student days at Oxford. Although it does seem quite impossible in light of Lord Blackmere's present appearance and behavior, Sir Blakey paints his lordship as cutting quite a swath through town when he was a young blade."

Caroline tried to picture Lord Blackmere, white wig and all, as a bruising rider galloping through the streets, neck or nothing. "I don't believe it," she said.

Lady Sefton nodded. "I know but I am only repeating what I heard. Because of his family's position, his lordship was put up for membership in most of the important clubs at a very early age. When he succeeded to the earldom after his father's death, he returned to Blackmere Castle which is in some remote region northwest of London, I believe he said.

"Sir Blakey also told my husband that the Earl of Blackmere seldom took advantage of his London connections until about four or five years ago when he started coming to Town again after an absence of over twenty years, but he would only stay three or four days each time."

"My goodness, you mean one cup of coffee brought out all that information? I shall have to remember that," Caroline said.

"Two cups and Lord Sefton becomes a regular town crier," Lady Sefton confided.

"But why is Lord Blackmere staying so much longer this time?"

"I don't think we need look very far to see the reason why, my dear. It is not unusual for a man who has advanced beyond fame or fortune to realize he has reached his latter years with no one to carry on the family name. What better way than to seek a wife of good breeding who can give him an heir?"

Caroline glanced over to where Lord Blackmere still sat keeping his vigil. "Well, he must not be looking in the right places if he hasn't found one in all these years."

Lady Sefton looked at Caroline fondly. "He evidently is a very particular man. All I can surmise is that now something or someone is keeping him here."

"How could a young woman possibly consider an old man as a husband?" Caroline said, wrinkling her nose.

"It is not a bad choice when you look at the alternatives. Her husband would be past his reckless days, tired of gambling, and would be content to spoil a pretty young wife."

"Lord Blackmere has not brought me flowers or even a box of chocolates."

"Ah, but I notice things that you don't, and I have seen the way Lord Blackmere gazes at you when he thinks no one is looking. There are other actions that show largess, my dear. My husband told me that when Lord Blackmere appeared in Town four years ago, he announced at his clubs that when a certain young man from his shire appeared at their doors he was to be admitted as his lordship's personal guest even when he himself is not here to escort him. I suppose him to be the son of a country squire or local dignitary who the earl believes can benefit from acquiring a bit of Town Bronze. It only points to the good-heartedness of his lordship," Lady Sefton said, giving Caroline's hand a pat. "Yes, my dear, to find a husband who is not only kind, but considerate as well, is worth ten handsome colts who have not yet sown all their oats."

Caroline narrowed her eyes and tried harder to think of Lord Blackmere in that way, but the only image which came to mind was . . . old faithful Dipper.

"Some men of more advanced years still enjoy dancing, I am told," Lady Sefton said, with a slight raising of her brow.

Caroline thought back to the first time she'd met Lord Blackmere at Almack's. If she closed her eyes and thought of the way she'd felt when he whirled her around the ballroom. Perhaps . . . perhaps if she had met the earl when he was a young man, she would feel differently.

# Four

One day when Caroline managed to coax Lord Blackmere to leave his desk to sit on the settee for his tea, he pulled from his pocket an exquisite red enameled box inlaid with mother-of-pearl measuring no more than three inches square.

Lord Blackmere had never brought Lady Caroline a gift of any kind before, but there were certain things which were not proper for a young lady to receive.

Caroline's hand went to the black pearl pendant. "I cannot accept jewelry from a gentleman, Lord Blackmere," Caroline said, staring at the flat little box with no little amount of curiosity.

His lordship said nothing, but taking the box from her hands, he opened it.

"Why whatever is it?" she asked as she looked inside at the flat surface which consisted of fifteen tiny squares of ivory. The sixteenth square was empty. Into the fifteen squares were etched strange squiggly lines.

Lord Blackmere observed her reaction for a moment and then without saying a word, he began moving the little sections around. "It is a Chinese Puzzle Box," he said, finally breaking the silence.

"I never heard of such a thing!" said Caroline in astonishment as she watched his lordship change the position of one square after the other.

To Caroline's delight, the lines began to match up and before her very eyes a scene took shape—two figures standing under a tree. All in all, it could not have taken him more than a minute.

"Oh, my lord, may I try?" she asked eagerly. Intrigued, Caroline set about trying to master the puzzle, but it was not as easy as his lordship had made it appear. Caroline narrowed her eyes, thrust her tongue out the corner of her mouth and struggled on for several minutes more but to no avail.

She heard a chuckle begin to rise from somewhere deep within him. When he laughed aloud Caroline laughed, too. "Just you wait, my lord," she said, "I shall do it."

"I am sure you will, Lady Caroline," he said in his low raspy voice. "And when you do, you will realize that the accomplishment will stay longer with you than a bouquet of flowers."

Caroline stared at the little box. She had never given a thought to the idea—until now—that an accomplishment stayed with you forever. She sat up a little straighter. "You really don't believe that I can do it. I promise you, my lord, by the next time I see you, I shall have solved the puzzle."

"Lady Caroline," he said so suddenly and quietly that for a second Caroline thought she only imagined that he spoke. "Will you do me the honor of riding with me in Hyde Park this Friday next? Lady Sefton has graciously offered me the use of her carriage."

Caroline turned to stare at him. He looked so humble and hopeful that she could not think ill of him. If it were seen that Lady Sefton had given him her approval by use of her carriage and if it were noted by the *haute ton* that she had attracted the admiration of such a highly ranked gentleman as the Earl of Blackmere when no other lady had, wouldn't that only add to her consequence as the Incomparable and make her other admirers that much more eager to please her? "It would be my pleasure, my lord," she said.

Lord Blackmere rose and bowed over her hand. "Until Friday, my lady," he rasped.

* * *

"Zounds, Caroline, does that mean you're going to get leg-shackled after all? Everybody says the old man must have it in gobs for you to be interested."

Lady Caroline looked up in exasperation as her step-mother's brother settled himself into the most comfortable chair in her drawing-room. "For heaven's sake, Elroy, why ever would anyone believe such a preposterous taradiddle? I am only going for a carriage ride with the gentleman. I merely mentioned the fact that the reason I cannot take you to Mrs. Whistlewaite's on Friday is because I am riding in the Park with Lord Blackmere. Now thanks to you, all of London seems to know about it."

"Dash it all, *Lady* Caroline, everybody who is anybody knows he's been dangling after you; coming here all the time under the pretext of cataloging your books. Poindexter told me there are already wagers in the Betting Book at White's on when you'll tie the knot."

"Oh, do not say so!" cried Caroline. "Lord Blackmere is no more than a good friend." A dear old friend, she thought. Once again old Dipper came to mind. "The only thing I meant for you to understand was that you will have to find another way to see Priscilla Whistlewaite. You know her mama will only admit a man with a title into the house to see her."

"Well I almost have, don't I? Hell's bells! My sister is a countess. That should count for something. Come on, Caro . . ."

"It's no use, Elroy. The answer is *no*—and it's *Lady Caroline* to you," she added.

"Well, you don't have to ring a peal over me about it," replied Elroy testily while picking himself up out of his chair. "If you're going to get on your high ropes, I won't tell you the other things I found out about Lord Blackmere."

Caroline constrained herself from picking up one of the sofa pillows and hitting Elroy over the head. "Like what, Elroy? Do sit down and don't pout. It makes you look like a little boy who's had his sugarplum taken away from him."

Elroy pulled his lips in and sat back down, looking quite relieved that he could go on with his tittle-tattle. "Well, Poindexter said his grandfather had known Blackmere before he was the Earl of Blackmere when he was a viscount. He said his lordship raised quite a rumpus in his salad days."

"A lot of young men think they have to sow their oats before they settle down, Elroy."

"Well, Poindexter said that the viscount just kept on sowing, said he had no inclination to go home to that desolate old mound the Earls of Blackmere called their castle even though the family had lots of the ready rhino. No woman of any standing could bring him to scratch, which made his papa very angry, because he was the last of the line, so to speak."

"Then it is true that Lord Blackmere never asked any woman to marry him."

"Not as anyone knows. He only went home when he had to because his papa stuck his spoon in the wall and he was the new Earl of Blackmere. No one saw him again until he turned up in Town about four years ago."

"But he doesn't enjoy social events and Lady Sefton said that he has never been seen to gamble."

Elroy stuck his nose in the air. "Little you know about it. Poindexter said that his lordship comes to London every few months to make sure that his clubs admit a young man whom he says he's sponsoring. As soon as Blackmere makes the rounds, he goes home. So why ain't he going home this time?"

Caroline began to wonder if what Lady Sefton was hinting was right, Lord Blackmere was looking for a wife. "Just because I accepted a ride in the Park with a friend is no reason for rumors to start."

Elroy flicked his eyebrows in what was supposed to be a suggestive way. "Lord Featherstone and Jamie Stessels said they don't have a chance against an earl with a fortune and a castle. Featherstone claims that Miss Hughes has a good inheritance and don't have a buffle-headed father to go along with it. Stessels is really purse-purched and though Portia Duddlebury ain't as beautiful as you, her father *is* offering fifteen thousand pounds to take her off his hands. So there's no sense wasting their time dangling after you, now is there?"

"Lady Sefton's husband didn't tell her any of this."

"Well, let me inform you, there are other things you don't know either, *Lady* Caroline Cavendish. Men don't tell their wives everything," Elroy said smugly, going through the brow-flicking routine again.

As soon as Elroy left, Caroline sat immobile for a few minutes thinking about what he'd revealed. How had she been so wrong? The carriage ride which she thought would enhance her consequence was doing just the opposite. From what Elroy implied the on-dit was sending her other suitors running. What would she do for escorts if they all deserted her? She had to stop that from happening.

Caroline hurried into the library and sitting down at the desk took a sheet of paper from the drawer. She wrote quickly then pulled the bell cord to summon her footman.

"George, deliver this letter immediately to Lord Blackmere's hotel in Ryder Street."

Three days after she'd sent her refusal, Caroline still had heard nothing from Lord Blackmere, and she felt a little upset with him about that. She was sure that it was only a matter of time before he would appear in the library.

On the fourth day a letter was delivered by messenger to Lady Caroline Cavendish from Lady Sefton.

*My dearest Caroline,*

*I count you as one of my dearest friends, and because of that friendship, I cannot let another day pass without letting you know my feelings on the subject of one of our mutual acquaintances, whose name I shall not mention. I know you do not mean to be unkind, but sometimes we act too quickly before contemplating the hurt that we may do to others. You have done a grievous injustice in hurting someone I have come to hold most dear.*

*For whatever reason you feel that you were justified, I feel that you will not find contentment in your heart until you have righted this wrong.*

Caroline was sorry now that she had refused Lord Blackmere's invitation to ride with him in the Park. He did not call again. From the set down which Lady Sefton had given her, she feared she'd hurt his feelings, and this saddened her. Guilt was an uncustomary and unpleasant sensation for Caroline to experience, so she set her mind to forgetting Lord Blackmere and thinking of ways to enjoy herself.

But, alas, the Season was coming to a close, and already many of Caroline's friends were leaving the heat of the city for their country estates, or preparing to follow the Prince Regent to Brighton. Regardless of all the invitations she had received, Caroline had no heart to accept any of them.

Least of all, Caroline didn't want to admit to herself that not only was she homesick for her beloved Cavendish Hall, but for her nonsensical, twiddle-twaddling father as well. So in spite of her avowal that she would not return, Caroline and Suzette were soon in her coach on their way to Gloucestershire.

When they arrived at the Cavendish estate, Lord Favor and the young countess welcomed them with outstretched arms. At least Mary did. As to his lordship, who was every bit as round as his new wife, Caroline was not sure that he was as overjoyed to see his daughter as she was to be home.

"What a happy surprise," Mary cried, hurrying forward to greet her stepdaughter.

The picture her father and his child bride portrayed was ridiculous. Ridiculous and humiliating. Caroline's new stepmother—it pained her to even say the word—looked like a plump pudding. Very plump, and now that it was quite evident to anyone with eyes in his head that she was increasing, would become plumper by the day. More to her consternation, Mary's cheerful disposition seemed to add in some way to a singular glow in her countenance and a twinkle in her eyes since Caroline had seen her last.

"I shall go immediately and see to having your apartment opened and ready for you, dear. And I am so glad to see you too, Miss Suzette," she added. Mary never left out anyone. "You shall have your adjoining room as always. And now if you will all excuse me, I shall see to matters."

After the countess hurried out and Suzette left to direct the footmen where to carry the trunks, Caroline turned to her father. She had to call his attention to the fact that she still remained, for his wits—what was left of them—were completely diverted as his gaze followed Mary out of the room.

"You have not asked how things go with me, Father," Caroline said irritably.

"What, ho!" said his lordship, looking at her as if he was trying to recall how she had come to be there. He smiled idiotically, his eyes widening. "You look right as rain to me, gel."

"Are you not going to inquire if I have developed a tendre for anyone?"

"It don't make no nevermind to me if you have or haven't," Lord Favor said absently, his attention being pulled back to the portal through which Mary had disappeared.

"That's not what you told me when Baron Copley invited me to Roxwealde Castle two years ago," Caroline said with a certain peevishness.

"And you would have been married by now, if you'd followed my instructions, young lady."

With growing expectation of witnessing one of her father's famous temper tantrums, Caroline gleefully goaded her father. "More likely, your nodcock scheme would have ended with my being dinner for a hungry lion."

Lord Favor looked at her as though she were a naughty little girl saying a forbidden word. "Tch! Tch! Hasn't it been three Seasons since I paid for your come-out, my dear? All I can say is that if you haven't been able to bring a man up to scratch on your own yet, then it is most likely that you never will. But if you have a mind to try another Season, I have the blunt now to see you through," he said magnanimously.

Caroline's face turned red. "Well, I never!" But her outburst, which at one time would have brought on a spirited reprimand from her father, didn't even ignite a tiny spark of indignation.

"Now, now, my dear, don't get your dander up," the earl said absently, giving her hand a pat. "Not important anymore that you get yourself attached. My little wife has brought me all the happiness that I need. We'll take care of you."

With that his lordship held out his arms to Mary who was just re-entering the room. She hurried to his side. The earl placed his hand upon her stomach.

Caroline tried not to notice, but it was hard to do when half the household staff stood around gaping.

"The baby is due in December," he announced so loudly that Caroline was certain everybody in the manor as well as the entire shire could hear.

Mary blushed and giggled and nodded with enthusiasm. "It will be a wondrous Christmas. We would not think of celebrating the holidays without you, Caroline, dear. You must be here when the baby is born. Randy is hoping for an heir, of course, but I have told him that if he doesn't get his son, I am willing to start right off to have another try at it."

Caroline nearly choked. She managed to hold her tongue, however, until she and her companion were alone in her chambers. "I declare, Suzette, I have never been so mortified in my life."

"I am certain that just being able to share their happiness with you, they forgot for a moment who might overhear," Suzette soothed.

Unfortunately for Lady Caroline circumstances did not improve over the next two weeks.

"Their antics in front of the servants go against all sense of propriety," Caroline proclaimed in rather colorful terms as Suzette tied a yellow ribbon in her mistress's hair.

"But *mademoiselle,* everyone below stairs is all in a fever of excitement about the new babe. They are saying it will be wonderful to have a child in the house again. I have never seen the servants so happy."

Caroline had to admit it was true, but this made her more miserable than ever, for no matter how hard she tried, she couldn't find one thing to dislike about her father's bride.

And, her father? He kept staring at Mary with an idiotic, crooked grin on his face, working his mouth right along with every word which she spoke. It was more than any genteelly brought up daughter could stand.

Not much later, when a housemaid was bringing in the last of her ladyship's numerous gowns from being pressed, Caroline told her to have one of the manservants bring her trunks to her chambers.

Suzette looked at her mistress in dismay, "But, *mademoiselle,* I thought you said we were going to stay a month."

Caroline avoided the little Frenchwoman's eyes. "What has that to do with anything? I have decided to return to Town."

Their send-off the following day was a teary one, at least on Mary's part. She threw her arms around Caroline's neck and gave her a hearty kiss upon her cheek. "Please promise me you will come back for the holidays, dear. All of my family will be visiting. Even Elroy might be persuaded to leave London if you tell him you are willing to come, too."

The latter information alone was enough to keep Caroline away. "I don't believe I can," she said. "My winter schedule is quite full, you understand."

"Oh, yes. I am certain it must be," Mary agreed, smiling through her tears. "Elroy tells me you are the Incomparable."

"I would never think of missing the Countess of Dankleish's Holiday Masquerade. After all, it has always heralded the opening of the Winter Season, and my costume always wins the grand prize."

"Then you must not miss that," Mary agreed, looking quite downhearted.

"That's enough now. You've said your goodbyes to your stepmama," the earl boomed, hurrying his daughter into the coach—a little too eagerly it seemed to the disgruntled Caroline.

As the two women rode back to London, Suzette thought it best to say nothing until her mistress had turned everything over in her mind. For she knew in due course that Lady Caroline would want—nay would find it expedient—to voice her own views and opinions on any given subject which was uppermost in her thoughts.

Caroline plopped back onto her seat and stared out the window. The beautifully landscaped park slipped by: the stately elms bordering the carriageway, the magnificent spreading oaks that covered the path to the little silvery pond where her father had helped her catch her first fish, and the gently rolling hills where she'd ridden—and fallen off—her first pony, Nibbles.

She knew that she would be miserable in London. Everyone who was anyone would be away for several weeks yet. Society would pick up once again when the hunting season was over and the Quality began moving back to make ready for the opening of Parliament. But aside from the Masquerade Ball at

Lady Dankleish's country estate on the Thames, there wasn't much to really hold her attention during December.

Caroline hated to admit that she wanted to go home for Christmas. Ah, there was the rub. It was her father who had annoyed her. He didn't seem to care for her at all anymore. It was as if she had become invisible. She who had been the apple of his eye. Not once over the last week had he bellowed at her, ranted or raved about her impertinence, or scolded her for her lack of respect. He only had eyes for his adoring Mary. Caroline gave a very unladylike snort.

Suzette took that as her cue that her ladyship had come to some sort of decision. "Have you decided to accept Lady Favor's invitation to come to Cavendish Hall for Christmas?"

Caroline's eyes narrowed. "If you are trying to read my mind, Suzette, you are not even up to the mark. My father supports the opinion of many of his gender that a woman is of little import until she is married. My mind is firmly set. I will not return to Cavendish Hall . . ." Suddenly her face brightened. "Unless—"

The French woman cocked her head. "Unless, what?"

"Unless, I have a husband." Caroline sat bolt upright. "That is it, Suzette. I shall find myself a husband for Christmas. A husband who is so outstanding in character and presence that my father will have to take notice of me."

"But, *mademoiselle,* I thought you said you had no need of a husband."

"Where is it written that I cannot change my mind?"

Suzette shook her head. "But, how will you find this person you speak of in such a short time?"

"Hmph! That should not be difficult," Caroline said confidently. "There are men all over London forever begging me to marry them."

"But, *mademoiselle*, you keep looking for a man who is perfect."

"That is applesauce! I have very simple requirements for a husband."

Suzette examined her mistress's countenance to see if she was serious. She concluded she was. "And what may those simple requirements be, *mademoiselle?*"

"Only that he be titled, wealthy . . . and . . . possess a generous nature," she finished with a smile of satisfaction.

Eyes twinkling, Suzette nodded her head. "Indeed, one would not want a cheese-paring, pennypincher for a spouse."

Caroline tapped her cheek with her finger. "It would be well if he were a little daring also. I do not believe I could tolerate a dull stick."

"Oh, no, no, definitely not, *mademoiselle.* A pattern-saint would be unthinkable. One needs a little excitement and laughter in her life."

"Of course, it goes without saying that my husband will be so handsome that all other females will be jealous of me."

Suzette choked back a laugh. "Is that all?"

Lady Caroline raised her eyebrows.

Suzette looked down quickly at her hands. "*Oui, mademoiselle,* those are very practical wishes indeed."

"Is not that what I told you? I am disappointed in you, Suzette, that you should underestimate me," Caroline said pointedly.

"Suzette would never underestimate you, *mademoiselle.* You want an entertaining, attentive husband with wealth, beauty and an adventurous spirit."

"Don't forget *title.*"

"And, title," added Suzette.

Caroline nodded with satisfaction. "I hope I have made myself clear."

"Suzette understands you quite well, *mademoiselle,*" the little woman said fondly.

"Well, I'm glad that you do. Now that that is settled, I feel much relieved. I can relax and enjoy our journey back to London."

However, now that Caroline had decided on what her next venture would be, she found herself more restless than ever. She hunted in her reticule for her comb and mirror, and in so doing, discovered the little Chinese Puzzle box. She had forgotten she had placed it in the bag when she had anticipated Lord Blackmere's visit—which never came about. She removed her gloves and shuffled the tiny enameled squares around—and there it was—the picture of the couple under a tree.

"Oh, won't he think me clever?" Caroline said aloud, holding out the little box for her companion. "See, I have solved the puzzle."

"But his lordship may never call on you, *mademoiselle.*"

Disappointment filled Caroline and as she pictured his lordship watching her, she remembered how he willingly listened to her as if her opinions mattered to him. She was suddenly ashamed that she had behaved in so hurtful a manner. As she thought of Lord Blackmere a strange stirring took place in Caroline's heart and she realized how much she'd missed him.

Caroline decided then and there that as soon as she returned to London, she would send round a note to Lord Blackmere asking him to pay her a visit. She would just mention that she had solved the puzzle. He would want to see if she had, of course, and when he came she would apologize for her abrupt cancellation of his kind invitation to ride with him in the Park. She had no doubt that he would readily accept her apology. Caroline sat back contentedly savoring the moment of triumph that she would have when she showed his lordship the puzzle and proved to him that she was no empty-headed, silly goose of a girl.

# *Five*

As soon as Caroline was settled into Cavendish House in the Square, she called a footman to her chambers and gave him a letter to take round to Lord Blackmere's hotel, asking him to call.

But it was not to be.

"The clerk at the hotel said that Lord Blackmere left town a week ago, my lady," the man reported. "The proprietor said that he would hold the missive, but unless a guest wishes to offer the information, it is not his place to inquire as to his direction."

After the boy withdrew, Caroline tried to hide her disappointment from Suzette. "Well, that was not very considerate of him."

"Isn't that what you wished, *mademoiselle*? You yourself said that he was too old."

"I meant too old to have the members of Fashionable Society believe that I was taking him seriously as a suitor, you silly girl. I did not mean for him to withdraw from my company altogether."

"Was he to read your thoughts?"

"But, I believed him so sympathetic that he . . . that he would just know."

"How would you feel if someone without a by-your-leave abruptly turned down your invitation to drive in the Park after they had accepted it?"

Unhappily, Caroline considered the consequences of her actions. Had her words brought pain to the dear old man? She hoped not, but sadly she feared she had.

Suzette groped for a way to censure her mistress without sounding harsh. "My dear, you cannot expect others to always anticipate what you are thinking."

"Well, I have now changed my mind about having him drive me in the Park. It has occurred to me that we sometimes dwell too much on what others think is right. Do you not agree, Suzette?

"*Oui, mademoiselle.* It seems to Suzette that you are beginning to think for yourself."

Caroline's smile brightened her face. "I am certain that if I write him another note telling him that I am sorry, he will forgive me."

"But you don't know where he is."

Caroline's expression took a complete turnaround. "Where do you think he could have gone, Suzette?"

"Most likely back to his estate. Didn't I hear Lady Sefton say his lordship only came to Town occasionally?"

"Yes, but she also said that she now surmises that her husband was not telling her the all. Elroy kept hinting at something too, but the exasperating boy would only say that young ladies are not supposed to know about such things."

"It is indeed vexing, *mademoiselle,* but I fear that those who are tale-bearers have nothing more important to do."

Caroline knit her brows. "Well, I am certainly glad that I am not one to listen to idle gossip."

"Certainly not, *mademoiselle.* You would never do that."

Lady Caroline's good spirits returned. "So, tomorrow I shall write another invitation to Lord Blackmere and have it left at his hotel to be given to him when he returns."

"But he may not come back to Town for several weeks," Suzette said. "I heard Lady Sefton tell you that he goes away for months at a time."

"That is so," Caroline said impatiently drumming her fingers on her dressing table.

For a moment she stared out the window of her bedchamber, then turned slightly to give her companion a saucy look full of meaning.

Suzette knew that mischievous glint all too well. "So now, *mademoiselle* wishes Suzette to find out what the men wish to keep hidden from the ears of the ladies," the little maid said matter-of-factly.

"As only you can, Suzette," Caroline agreed with a saucy flip of her head and a glance in the mirror.

"And what does *mademoiselle* propose to do for the rest of the day?"

"It certainly will not do for me to sit around and fret over a harmless little indiscretion, will it? I think I shall go shopping for a new bonnet," she said in a much lighter tone.

Suzette was used to her mistress's quixotic turns of mind, but she couldn't help but comment on this one. "But, *mademoiselle,* you bought three new bonnets only last month."

"What has that to do with anything?" Caroline stated, discarding the blue hat while pointing to the one with tall pink plumes.

Suzette handed her the bonnet.

"A lady can never have too many hats," Caroline said, with a little less conviction.

The little maid gave her a sideways glance.

"Am I a mean person, Suzette?"

"No, no, *mademoiselle.* You must never think that."

"I am selfish then," Caroline said hesitantly, hoping that Suzette would say she was not.

"Yes, sometimes you are," she said quite frankly. Then seeing Lady Caroline's crestfallen countenance, she added quickly, "You have been brought up to expect privileges, *mademoiselle,* but remember you did give me three of your lovely frocks. That was very generous."

"And, I bought you a new bonnet in the spring, did I not?" Caroline said gaily.

"It was lovely, *mademoiselle.*"

Caroline's eyes brightened. "And this winter I am going to give all of my old shoes to the poor, Suzette. I learned last December what it is like to be out in the cold snow without adequate dress. It was a miracle I did not freeze to death. If those farmers had not found me after I escaped from the old farmhouse, I would have frozen."

"That is most charitable of you, *mademoiselle.* Life's lessons are only worthwhile if they teach us to be better persons."

"Oh, I do feel more the thing now, Suzette. It is fun spreading happiness to others, isn't it? I think that I shall also give away all my dancing slippers to the kitchen maids. What do you think of that?"

Suzette knew it would be futile to point out the impracticality of handing out satin slippers to young girls who labored all day on their knees scrubbing floors or were up to their elbows in suds washing linens.

Caroline clapped her hands. "Would you like another hat, Suzette?" Caroline asked, now quite filled with the giving spirit.

Suzette laughed. "No, no, *mademoiselle.* I have enough. But I am sure any of the maids would be most honored to have one of your lovely hats."

"I shall do that. Then I won't have to feel guilty when I buy new ones this afternoon. I am glad you thought of it, Suzette. But, now, I shall need new dancing slippers as well, won't I? Since I am ridding myself of the used ones."

The French woman only shook her head. "I think that if you keep being so generous you will soon need a whole new wardrobe."

Caroline looked at her companion with surprise, then laughed. "Oh, you are funning me, Suzette. Now, ring the bell.

I wish to tell Driggs to have my coach brought round at once. We are going shopping."

Kendale stood at the corner of New Bond Street and Bruton observing the hustle of shoppers with no more interest than a squirrel would have watching rabbits cavorting about a cabbage patch. He had neither the inclination nor leisure to follow the frivolous pursuits of the *beau monde,* and had just decided to make his way to St. James's Street to see if he could engage some reckless madcap in a game of whist at one of the men's clubs. Any game of cards would do, it made no difference to him, for he seldom if ever lost.

His well-tailored apparel was neither ostentatious or particularly modish as to bring unwanted attention to himself. However, no matter how much he tried to avoid appearing either priggish or overly conservative, his fine build and proud bearing did not go unnoticed by the ladies, while his reputation as an unbeatable, tenacious gamester led him to be held in awe by the male population of the Upper Orders, who insisted on constantly challenging him.

Kendale had no sooner stepped off the curb to cross the street than he was forced to jump back in order to avoid having the toes of his newly polished boots run over by a splendid green and gold coach as it pulled up to the walk.

A swarm of would-be ostlers came running from every nook and cranny vying for the privilege of holding the splendid pair of blacks.

A small boy with a mop of unruly blond curls swirling out from beneath an oversized cap won the race; not because of his size, for there were many others larger than he, but perhaps because he was swifter and more determined than the rest of the lot.

For a second Kendale felt a certain comradery with the sooty-faced lad, but his attention quickly turned to the liveried footman who jumped down to lower the step and open the door of the coach.

The fine equipage was quite familiar to Kendale for he had observed it often over the last few years. He recognized, too, the dainty, gloved hand which reached out for assistance, followed by a small foot in an embroidered silk pump. The lovely Lady Caroline Cavendish descended, and Kendale's heart stood still. Today she was a vision in pink. Yesterday it was blue. The tomorrows were always a surprise.

No matter how many times he saw her—and Kendale had watched her often enough—he never tired of the sight. A beauty such as Lady Caroline Cavendish was far above his reach, and he knew it. No matter how much of a fortune he accumulated, no matter how much a Town Bronze he acquired, he would always be a beggar child of the London slums. Nevertheless, he observed her unashamedly, quite boldly in fact, and swore she was the loveliest creature he had ever beheld.

Lady Caroline didn't see him, of course, for Kendale made sure he stood well back in the crowd by the time she stepped out of her carriage. He watched her and her companion until they entered a millinery shop and were lost to sight.

Kendale contemplated freshening up at the Stratford Hotel—a modest bachelor residence on Ryder Street near the clubs where Lord Blackmere let a small apartment to stay when he was in London. Kendale had used it for his main residence in the beginning, but later took additional lodgings in the basement apartment of an old house in Grace Church Street nearer his shipping business. The porter at the Stratford was quite used to the young man's comings and goings, so he never questioned him. But, damnation! The lure of plumping up his purse with a few more pounds was more compelling than washing his hands, Kendale decided, and whistling a lively sailor's ditty, he proceeded south toward Piccadilly and thence in the direction of St. James's Street.

* * *

Not even a nonpareil like Lady Caroline was entirely immune to a male's gallant gesture or flashing smile no matter what his age. This one she could not overlook as he shot out of nowhere, elbowed several fellow ragamuffins out of the way to grab the halter of the lead horse and at the same time managed to gallantly touch the bill of his oversized cap as she came past him on the way into the milliner's shop.

Lady Caroline had never particularly cared for children or necessarily wanted to be near them until she'd become acquainted with a curly-haired six-year-old knight named Rupert, who'd cast his heart at her feet some eight months ago. This one's smile triggered in her the same spirit of adventure which Rupert had done when he cheered her over the rocks of the underground tunnel to escape the clutches of her kidnappers.

She had been in the shop no more than ten minutes and seen and discarded seven bonnets when she said, "Suzette, I am bored with looking at hats."

"Where does *mademoiselle* wish to go?"

"Back to Cavendish House in the Square."

"What will you do there? You canceled your dinner engagement for this evening at Lord and Lady Brooknell's."

"I believe I will read a book," Caroline said decisively, tying the pink ribbon of her bonnet under her chin as she walked out the door. "Come, Suzette, do not stand there with your mouth open like a fish gasping for air."

The miniature ostler in his raggedy clothes still stood proudly in front of her two horses. He managed somehow to hold the harnesses with one hand, and stroke their noses with the other. Caroline paused and smiled at him just as she was about to enter the coach. "George," she said, addressing her footman, "how much do I give to the boy who minds the horses?"

"I give them a bob, my lady."

"Well, this one has done a more splendid job than most, don't you agree?"

"Yes, my lady."

"Then I believe twelve pence is not enough for one who is able to keep such spirited horses calm. His service deserves at least a crown."

George's air of aloofness which had been his mark of distinction was in grave danger of cracking. "I do not have that much blunt with me, my lady," he choked out.

"Why didn't you say so?" she said, digging several coins from her reticule and giving one to the startled servant. "Now, hand me up. I wish to go home."

There is in every city an area best forgotten where those unfortunate enough to be born without means or family are destined to live out their miserable lives with only the few crumbs which they can beg or glean from the discards of a more privileged Society.

Rows and rows of buildings without faces or identifying marks hide within their dismal walls tales best left untold. In one such room, up four flights of stairs, a young woman lay shivering under a ragged quilt helplessly listening to footsteps ascending the creaky steps to her garret under the eaves. The air was stifling from the summer heat, wreaking of mold and age. One soot-covered skylight over her bed gave only a faint view of the fast-darkening sky. The door squeaked open. A smudged face, nearly covered by a floppy cap, peeked in. "It is only I, Momma," the small person said, "and look what I brought you." With that Tommy pushed open the low door and began to unravel the coarse burlap bundle in his arms.

"Thank God, it is you, son."

"Mrs. Tumblewick has sent you a half-loaf and a pinch of cheese for your supper. She said it was all she could spare."

"Bless her heart." The young woman struggled to sit up, setting off a coughing spell which prevented her from saying more for a moment.

"That is not all, Momma," Tommy said, his cheerful reply covering his anxiety. He then retreated back out to the tiny landing, returning with a small crockpot. "Mrs. Tumblewick has sent some hot gruel for your cough. She said she'd have carried it herself, but she cannot climb up four flights of stairs on her crutch."

"And I would not expect her to," said Momma, savoring the warmth of the earthen container as she clutched it to her bosom with shaking hands.

"Mrs. Tumblewick said that if I can come to her lodgings before she sets off for market in the morning, she will have some hot porridge ready for you and Poppy." With that he looked around the tiny room. "Where is Poppy, Momma?"

"In her usual place," Momma whispered, inclining her head toward the low row of cupboard doors under the eaves. "We did not know it was you when we heard the footsteps on the stairs, and Baby knows what to do. She thinks it is a game."

Tommy grinned and holding his finger to his lips, tiptoed toward the slanted eaves. Leaning down, he jerked open the door. "Boo!" he called.

Out tumbled a heap of ragged calico with the face of a pixie, crowned with a mop of yellow curls. Cornflower blue eyes, made huge from their stay in the dark corner, opened even wider. "Boo!" she retaliated, managing to rise on her stubby legs just long enough to throw herself into her brother's arms. "Tom-tom," she babbled, giving him a wet kiss. "Poppy peek-a-boo."

"You are a good-un, Poppykins," Tommy said, giving his tiny sister a hug—only to stop midsentence to hold her out and away from him.

"Uh-oh," said the baby, looking down at the water puddling around her feet.

"Momma, where is the potty?" Tommy called frantically.

"It is too late for that now," Momma said. "Besides, she is

too young to understand. I try to sit her upon it, but I am afraid I have been too weak the last day or two to do it often enough. Take a rag from the pile in the corner and wipe her off. Then bring her to me so that I can feed her."

When Tommy returned to the bed, the young woman opened the front of her gown and began nursing Poppy. But it was not long before she pulled away and screwed up her face.

Tommy quickly tore off a chunk of bread and after dipping it into the gruel, held it out to the little girl. Poppy grabbed the soggy morsel and stuffed it into her mouth, smacking loudly. "I will feed her, Momma. Don't you fret now," he said, sitting his sister up so that her legs dangled over the side of the bed.

"Oh, son, what are we to do? I have no more milk to feed the baby, and I am so afraid that Mrs. Beetle has designs to steal her away when you are not here, and sell her."

"All the more reason why Poppy must learn to hide whenever she hears a noise on the steps. Even when it is I coming. Don't fret, Momma. You will be well soon, then we can move away from here. You and Poppy finish the soup now."

Tommy lit the stub of a candle which sat in a chipped saucer on a wooden crate beside the bed. Taking out his knife, he cut a slice of cheese and holding it over the small flame waited for it to melt before smearing it over a hunk of bread. This he handed to his mother. "I must leave now for the mews. Mr. Stubbs said I can polish the carriage lanterns tonight. You should see the coaches of the Quality, Momma. Some are splendid enough for the queen herself."

"It is too much for you to try to run errands all day and travel all the way across town to the mews so late at night."

"I'm strong, Momma. I usually fetch a good bob holding the gentry's cattle when they visit the shops along Bond and Oxford Streets, and there are always merchants who wish to hire a swift pair of legs to run errands.

"This afternoon," he said, trying to distract her, "I held a fine pair of blacks for the most beautiful lady I have ever seen. Her coach has green lacquered doors trimmed in gold with a splendid crest upon them. I have seen it before, for Mr. Stubbs keeps it at the mews. She smiled at me and when her footman started to give me a bob, she said I'd done such a good job at holding her cattle steady that he was to give me a crown. Oh, he was upset, I could see, but he couldn't disobey his mistress. Here, I was so busy worrying that I would spill your soup that I nearly forgot to give it to you," he said extracting the coin from his pocket.

"A whole crown," exclaimed Momma, cradling the coin in the palm of her hand.

"She wore pink feathers in her hat and lace around her face and her hair shone like it was the sun itself."

"She sounds very much the grand and generous lady," Momma said, lying back on the bare mattress.

"I really must go, now," he said, wiping the crumbs from Poppy's chin.

"Tommy, wait!" his mother cried, struggling to sit up again. "What if Mrs. Beetle should come in the night when you are gone and whisks Baby away? I could not bear it. Oh, I do wish you did not have to labor so long into the night."

"Just until you are well again, Momma, and you can find sewing to do."

"I am afraid, Tommy boy. What will become of our Poppy if something happens to me?"

"Do not fret so. It only keeps you from getting better."

Momma took his hand and placed the crown in it. "Listen carefully, son. Put this in the little blue teapot over on the shelf. You know that I told you about the coins I have been saving. This shall surely make it enough so that if something *should* happen to me—"

"Hush, Momma," Tommy said gently, brushing back the damp hair from his mother's feverish brow. "You know I shall always look after you and Poppy."

"No, you must tend to what I tell you. If something should happen to me, I want you to take the money from the pot and try to deliver Poppy to my sister Eliza's in Newport. She is little better off than we are with her seven children to care for and a husband who is more often at sea than at home, but at least he is alive and not killed in the war like your Papa. I know that they will do right by you both and give you a roof over your heads."

"If I do not go now, Mr. Stubbs will have my head," Tommy said, hurrying over to place the coin in the teapot. "Be sure to blow out the candle after a while, because there is not much left of it. I shall try to see if I can find some more broken sticks in the rubbish barrels behind the candlemaker's tomorrow."

"But you have not eaten a thing," said his mother with concern.

"Mr. Stubbs always sets aside some of his shepherd's pie. He says his missus packs a wicker hamper full of enough vittles to stuff a donkey and feed every drumbelo and bugher in the stables besides."

"Shame, Tommy," Momma scolded. "We may be poor, dear one, but our language need not be brought down also."

"I am sorry, Momma. But Mr. Stubbs does share his food with every poor creature that comes a-begging. Mrs. Stubbs's fruit tarts are quite famous, too. I will try to bring you a slice. Poppy would like it above all else, I know," he said cheerily, chucking his sister under her chin.

With the sound of his baby sister's giggles following him, Tommy hurried out the door.

# Six

Suzette looked into the library. "There you are, *mademoiselle.*"

Ever since they had returned to London from Gloucestershire, Lady Caroline had been in the doldrums. She claimed that it was because London was extremely dull toward the end of summer, but Suzette knew that was not so. *Mademoiselle* had no desire to go shopping, and she turned down several parties for no reason at all.

"Suzette has been looking all over for you." The truth of the matter was, the French woman knew exactly where she would find her mistress on an afternoon that they didn't make any calls.

"Where have you been?" scolded Caroline. "I sent you to Hatchards three hours ago to pick up the book I ordered."

Suzette handed Lady Caroline a brown-wrapped package and sat down in a chair facing her. "Suzette saw Lady Tewilliger's lady's maid behind one of the bookshelves, speaking to Filtersham, Lady Sefton's footman."

"Why did you waste time eavesdropping, you naughty girl? I wanted to read the book this afternoon."

"Suzette was only doing what you said she does best. *Re-con-noi-tering.* Is that not what you called it? You wanted her to find out what is Lord Blackmere's secret, yes?"

Caroline's attention was fully engaged now. "Yes! I am sorry I doubted your purpose, Suzette. What did you hear?"

"And you will trust Suzette's methods?"

"Yes! I trust your methods more than I would the Home

Office's undercover agents. Now do please stop the round-aboutation, Suzette. I am sure there is a quicker way of telling your story."

"No, there is not," Suzette stated with finality.

Caroline shrugged. She knew trying to rush Suzette when she had a tale to tell would only make it longer. "Go on."

"Well . . . your footman George is not immune to Suzette's charms to tell her things and Filtersham is a close chum of George's and Filtersham often accompanies his master Lord Sefton to his clubs on St. James's Street and there he hears a lot if he keeps his ears open," she said, stopping only long enough to take a deep breath.

Caroline raised her gaze to the ceiling and threw up her hands.

"*Mademoiselle* must practice the patience. Suzette is trying to show you that the point is not at the end of a straight line."

Caroline would have gladly strangled Suzette at that moment if it weren't that she was so eager to hear what she had found out.

"Your John Coachman is also making the friends with Sir Blakey's man, Harry, at the mews. George also has eyes for Sally in our kitchen and tells her things to make him look important in her eyes. Sally overhears things below the stairs that are being spread on the grapevine. Things that ladies of the Upper Orders would not hear above the stairs. Sally is a good girl and tells all to Suzette."

Caroline stared pointedly at Suzette, but it didn't hurry her. "Yes! Yes! I acknowledge you are a diamond of the first water, Suzette, but please get on with it."

The French woman sat back with a look of satisfaction. "Now that Suzette make it clear to you that her sources are the best, she will tell you what she learned."

"It's about time!" Caroline spouted impatiently.

Suzette leaned forward and lowered her voice. "There is a

certain young man whom Lord Blackmere fosters. Lord Blackmere insists he be admitted to the exclusive men's clubs where he himself is a member. The man's name is Kendale."

"Is that his Christian name, or his given name?"

"Kendale. No more, no less. Sir Blakey's man told George that this Kendale is in demeanor much like Lord Blackmere, a quiet man, intense. He is also a card sharp of remarkable abilities."

"A gambler?"

"*Oui!* It was put about years ago by Lord Blackmere himself that he had taken the lad under his wing when he was still the viscount right here in London. Picked him up on the docks, he said, and when Lord Blackmere's father died, he took the boy home with him to northern England. Sir Blakey's man said that he heard his master mention the times he and Lord Blackmere were hell-hatched young men riding *rantipole* through the river district."

"Whatever does that mean, Suzette?"

"Sally said it meant they belonged to a group of wild and noisy young bucks who frequented the establishments along the Thames, *mademoiselle.*"

"Lord Blackmere? I do not believe it. He is conservative and retiring, not wild and noisy. I cannot imagine him doing such things, let alone sponsor a gambler."

Suzette put her finger to her lips. "Lady Tewilliger's lady's maid told Filtersham that she learned from Mrs. Browne's abigail that there is some gossip that Lord Blackmere takes far more interest in his young protegee than is usual for a sponsor."

"Everyone knows that Mrs. Browne and Lady Tewilliger are two of the worst tattlemongers in London, Suzette. I wouldn't put it past Persimmonie Browne to have made the whole thing up because Lord Blackmere gave her such a setdown at the Thistlewaites'."

"That is not for me to say, *mademoiselle,*" Suzette said discreetly.

The nuance was not lost on Lady Caroline.

"Are you hiding something from me you naughty girl?" Caroline placed her hands on her hips. "Suzette?" she scolded.

"I said nothing," Suzette said innocently.

"That is exactly why I am angry with you. If you know something else about Lord Blackmere tell me right now."

"It is not what I heard, *mademoiselle,* but what I did not hear. No matter what their rank all men have a code among themselves, so even George wouldn't tell Sally more. All I know is what I have told you. Does it not seem strange that Lord Blackmere would insist that this Kendale—if he is just a waif—be admitted to all the finest clubs in St. James's Street?"

"You are right. Yes! Why would Lord Blackmere do that? You say that he found the boy on the docks?"

"That is only the story that Lord Blackmere spread about. Do you want to know what I think, *mademoiselle?* I think that Lord Blackmere does show far more interest in this young man than is natural for a lord and a beggar boy."

"Oh, do not say so!" Caroline knew full well that gentlemen deemed it a matter of honor to make some provisions for their by-blows. But Lord Blackmere to have had an affair with some woman of the dark alleys which produced a child? The idea was inconceivable. "I will hear no more about it, Suzette. I am sorry that I ask you to find out what the men have been hiding. It is known to everybody that they wager on the most ridiculous, nonsensical things."

"Suzette will say no more about the matter," she said contritely, sorry to see her mistress's distress. "Is mademoiselle going to stay in the room of books awhile longer?"

"I believe I will, Suzette." Caroline let her gaze move around the great room. She had become so accustomed to finding Lord Blackmere in the library in the afternoon that she couldn't break the habit of thinking she would find him there. She'd had everything in the room cleaned and polished, and with the new red-velvet curtains tied back to let in the light, she owned it was a very pleasant room to spend her time.

She really knew he wouldn't be there, but she'd hoped . . . just hoped that one afternoon when she peeked in he would be sitting behind the desk among the piles of books, writing in his ledger. As she always did, she would pick up something to read while he worked. Finally he would put down his pen and ask her to tell him about what she had been reading of late.

But once again, her curiosity had spoiled everything. Now she was sorry she had asked Suzette to find out what everyone was trying to keep from her. Only Lady Sefton remained convinced of Lord Blackmere's unexceptionable character. Knowing what she did now about Lord Blackmere, Caroline asked herself what would she do if he should return to London and find not one, but several letters of apology awaiting him and come to claim the ride in Hyde Park which she promised him?

Well, Caroline was not going to stay around London worrying about Lord Blackmere's turning up. But what was she to do?

At that moment, her butler entered through the open door. "The afternoon post, my lady," said Driggs setting the silver salver on the table beside her.

Caroline thanked him and halfheartedly began to open the letters. She had glanced over several invitations and her usual entreaty from Mary to come visit, when the seventh letter brought an, "Ahah!"

This one sound snapped Suzette to attention for it signaled to her that Lady Caroline was about to plot something anew.

"Here is our solution, Suzette," Caroline said, holding up the single sheet of paper.

"What is that, *mademoiselle?*"

"We are leaving London for Essex."

"We are?"

"Did I not say we were, you silly girl? I have decided to visit Miss Plunkett."

"She was your nurse when you were little, *mademoiselle?*"

"Yes. She retired to a cottage my father gave her on one of his holdings near Epping Forest. He renamed it Tallyho. My father is not an original man, Suzette. It has a small manor and only four hundred acres. He keeps it open with a staff of five to use during the hunting season, but no one has visited it for years. Miss Plunkett has often written that she is lonely and would love for me to visit her sometime when I am not too busy. Of course, my social calendar is always filled, but I am not one to be thinking only of myself, Suzette."

"You are most charitable, *mademoiselle.*"

"Thank you, Suzette."

"When do you want your trunks packed?"

"We will leave day after tomorrow. Tell Driggs that I want to see him, and then I will want to talk to my coachman to tell him that I wish to leave before daybreak so that we can make the journey in one day. I don't want to have to stay overnight at an inn."

Suzette rose from her chair.

"We will go visit Miss Plunkett and stay a long time," said Caroline. "So make sure I have clothing for chillier weather. It can get cold early in the year in the country."

It was near midnight and a foggy mist hung over the streets of London, but Tommy pressed on toward his rooming house. Mr. Stubbs had told him that after he'd had a bite to eat from the wicker hamper, he was to whisk the squabs and polish the gold trimming on one of the coaches. It was to go out before dawn, he said. But Tommy hadn't even taken time to eat for some strange feeling, almost like a voice on the wind warning him to hurry was pulling him back across town to their garret.

Momma had been getting worse the last few days and she was so weak she could barely raise her head to sip the gruel he would try to spoon into her. He would feed Poppy and tuck her into bed beside Momma before he left for the mews.

Before Tommy reached the second landing of the tenement house he heard the angry voices and drew back into the shadows under the stairwell. One lonely candle burned from a sconce outside Mrs. Beetle's doorway and caste an eerily yellow light on the two figures standing above him.

"Blast your purple gizzard, Gooch. The child is a pretty 'un and I oughta get more for her."

"So you say, Missus Beetle, but I haven't seen her yet, have I?" Gooch said in a smooth way that Tommy thought a snake would sound if it could speak. The man with his fancy tailored coat and brocaded waistcoat was known well in the district and the lads of the streets knew to stay clear of him.

"I'll get her for you after midnight. Her mam ain't for this world much longer. She won't put up a fight. Her coughings like to have torn her apart for two straight days now. Her little cub is off til near dawn every night, probably runs with a gang of footpads. It'll be easy as pie to slip in and carry away the baby."

"When Missus Beetle? My client is getting impatient. I promised her another female child and if I don't provide it, she'll take her business elsewhere."

"Tonight . . . after midnight. I have to wait until I'm sure no shitches will see me. Half my tenants are scabs and gullflushers and would as soon grab her and sell her themselves. Come an hour after midnight and I'll have the babe wrapped and ready for ye."

"All right then, here is the vile of laudenum. Only a drab or she'll be no good to us."

"I want a good gold coin, Gooch. No flimsies. You hear me?"

"Do you have any idea of how much it costs Madam Petuska to feed and cloth the wenches until they are old enough to let out to her customers? You will take what I give you or I'll have someone else come to get the brat."

"What about the boy?"

"I can catch him myself. He won't bring as much as a female-child, but there is high need of chimney sweeps. I can't keep up with the demand."

The landlady's reply was not for repeating, but Gooch only laughed. "Two hours, Missus Beetle. I have other accounts to settle and then I'll be back."

"I'll have her ready," she said, the wicked tone of her voice sending chills up Tommy's spine.

Gooch clumped out of the house right past Tommy without seeing him crouched beneath the stairs.

The minute the boy heard the landlady's door close, he tore up to the garret room. Momma had not put out the candle and the stub was nearly burned down to the saucer. "Momma," Tommy whispered, "Momma, I must take Poppy away."

Momma was silent.

Tommy lifted her arm gently from around Poppy. It fell lifelessly over the side of the bed. Tommy had no time to think, only act if he was to save his sister from being sold. "Poppykins," he said in her ear, trying not to startle her.

The baby sat up and rubbed her eyes. "Tom-tom," she babbled, throwing her arms around her brother's neck.

"Come, Poppykins. We are going to play a game."

"Peek-a-boo."

"No, Baby," he said lifting her swiftly from her warm nest. "Tommy is going to show you a new game." Of course he knew that Poppy didn't understand all that he was saying, but he prayed that her sweet nature and trust in him would keep her content.

While his ears listened for any sound of footsteps on the stairway. Tommy searched for something to wrap around his sister. The place was terribly bare. The only thing he saw of use was Momma's shawl, the one she said Poppa had given her before he went off to the war. Momma wouldn't be needing it any longer, he thought sorrowfully.

Tommy pressed his finger to Poppy's lips. "Shush now or you will spoil the game," he said, swaddling his sister from head to foot with the wrap. He heard a giggle from inside the bundle. He was not a big lad, even for ten years old, but his fear was so great that miraculously he found enough strength to pick up his sister and carry her down the four flights of stairs and out into the street. There were a good three miles between them and the mews, but it was the only place Tommy could think of to take her. If he could get her there, he would have the rest of the night to plan what to do.

In and out of the dark stagnant alleys which he knew so well, he ran. Down the narrow streets, between high, large neglected houses. When he had Poppy safe and sound, he would try to get help for his Momma. Now the important thing was to get his sister away from Gooch.

Tommy only carried Poppy so far before he saw what he was looking for. "We are going to play piggyback," he said, lifting her onto a wooden barrel. He coaxed her to put her arms around his neck and holding her legs to his waist, set off once again.

Their journey took a long time and Tommy had to stop often to rest. The bell in some distant clock tower was just striking three when they reached the mews.

He sneaked Poppy into an empty stall and covered her with the shawl. She was so exhausted that she quickly fell asleep in the straw. Mr. Stubbs had not yet arrived and the stableman left in charge was sleeping in a corner, his snores blending with the soft whinnying of the horses.

Hungrily, Tommy stuffed his mouth with a chunk of cheese and some leftover bread he found in the nearly empty hamper, then picking up his rag, began to rub the gold trim on the beautiful green coach til it shone. It belonged to his fairy princess; she who was the most beautiful, the most generous, and the kindest person in the whole world.

By the time he climbed inside the coach to whisk the seats, it was all Tommy could do to keep his eyes open. It was when he lay his weary head down on the soft seat and was just drifting off to sleep that the idea sprang into his brain. He awakened with a start and jumped out. He emptied Mrs. Stubb's hamper and got it up on the seat inside the coach. It wasn't an overly large basket, but Poppy wasn't very big either. He filled it with clean straw and tucked Mrs. Stubb's table linen over it. He heard men's voices at the front of the stables and knew he had to hurry or his plan would fail.

Poppy didn't awaken when he picked her up and carried her to the coach. He tucked her into the hamper and covered her with Momma's shawl. It was not much different from the tiny cupboard space she was used to hiding in for hours at a time.

She stirred but did not waken. "Poppy is going to play peek-a-boo," Tommy whispered in her ear. She smiled and stuck her thumb in her mouth. Tommy kissed her on the cheek and closed the hamper lid. He knew when his princess saw Poppy, she would love her with all her heart. Who could resist his little sister?

"Ho, there lad," a large man called. "Ye haven't been working all night have ye?"

"Just finishing up, Mr. Stubbs," Tommy said, backing away from the coach.

"Well, 'tis a fine job thee has done. I'm sure that Lady Caroline will be most pleased."

The stablehands were bringing out the pair of blacks and soon had them in their harnesses and all was ready to go.

"Better get yourself some sleep, lad. I have some saddles that will need waxing tonight. Off home with you now."

Tommy didn't go back to the tenement right away. He followed Lady Caroline's carriage to the Square and watched until several trunks were strapped on top and two ladies were helped inside. It was late in the morning by the time he arrived back at the garret. Momma was gone, her bed stripped of even the ragged blanket that had covered her. Tommy ran over to the little china teapot and looked inside. The coins were not there.

"I seen the brat go up the stairs, but if you catch him, Gooch, you have to pay me," a voice shouted from the landing. "What's right is right. She owes me the month's rent."

Tommy looked about frantically. The skylight was too far above for him to reach. He ran to Poppy's cupboard and squeezed inside, and lay there until he fell asleep. When he crawled out it was already nighttime. Trembling, Tommy stealthfully made his way down and out into the street. He had nowhere to go now unless Mr. Stubbs would let him stay at the mews. He would have to ask him.

They were well on their way into Essex when Caroline bumped her arm on the hamper. "Suzette, it was foolish of you to have food packed when you know we will be stopping at inns. It is not as if we were going to Cavendish Hall in Gloucestershire. We are only going thirty-five miles. John Coachman said he would drive the mail-coach road to Epping to save time. After that we will have to travel on winding country lanes and he doesn't know their condition. Nonetheless, we should be at Tallyho by nightfall."

"But, *mademoiselle.* Suzette thought it was you who had the hamper set in the coach."

"Oh, never mind. It is just such an annoyance having it take up so much space. It was probably Cook. She thinks everybody will starve to death if they do not have sustenance every hour or two."

"We can have the footmen strap it to the top of the coach when we reach the next inn."

Not more than thirty minutes had gone by when Suzette eyed the hamper hungrily. "I only had time for a cup of chocolate this morning, and Cook does bake such good pastries, *mademoiselle.* And I am sure that she had Driggs put in a bottle of your favorite wine, too."

"That is so," Caroline agreed. "I must admit I am quite hungry myself. I think a little refreshment would not be amiss. Let's see what Cook has prepared for us. Open the hamper."

With a look of anticipation on her face, Suzette unhooked the latch and lifted the lid. "It is odd that Cook would cover the food with such a pretty woven shawl," she said, folding back the cloth. Eyes wide, Suzette threw up her hands and screamed.

Up popped a head topped with tousled yellow curls, big blue eyes and a button of a nose. "Peek-a-boo!" Poppy shouted with a giggle.

Lady Caroline drew back. "Good heavens, Suzette! What is it?"

"I believe it is a baby, *mademoiselle,*" Suzette said, reaching for the child's outstretched arms. She lifted her out, but quickly held her away. "And it seems a very wet one."

# Seven

"Where could it have come from, Suzette?" Caroline exclaimed as she stared at the curly-headed moppet. She found a certain charm in some older children, but babies terrified her. "Who could have put it in here?"

"I do not know, *mademoiselle.* The hamper was already on the seat when we entered the coach. But right now, I believe we have more immediate concerns," Suzette said, standing the baby on the floor.

Caroline looked on mortified. "Whatever are you doing?"

"Suzette is taking off her damp frock, *mademoiselle* before she catches her death."

"Well, I will not have a naked child in my carriage. I shall have my coachman stop immediately," Caroline said, starting to raise her parasol to signal the halt.

Suzette looked out the window in horror at the congestion of coaches and slow moving wagons pulled by great hairy-heeled monsters. Horsemen on their fast flying chariots and a small boy trying to hurry his gaggle of geese across the busy road before they were trampled. "Does *mademoiselle* propose to throw the baby out onto the road to be run over?"

Poppy looked over at Caroline as if she too awaited her decision.

Caroline lowered her parasol. "Of course not," she said, suddenly feeling quite uncomfortable. "It was just that . . . I have never been presented with such a problem before. Escaping through darkened tunnels and outwitting thieves and smugglers excited me, but I know nothing about babies."

Suzette looked at her sympathetically. "No woman does until she cares for one, *mademoiselle.* Suzette had two younger brothers, and learned to take care of babies very early. Oh, *mademoiselle,* look," Suzette added. "It is a little girl. Is she not pretty?"

"For heaven's sakes, Suzette! Cover her with something."

Suzette discovered that the fringed shawl, a rich peacock blue interlaced with golden threads, had not gotten wet and wrapping it around the baby, drew her up onto her lap.

"Why this is a lovely shawl made of fine silk," Suzette said. "Much nicer than the pitiful little dress she was wearing."

Hooking her finger in her mouth, Poppy continued to stare at Caroline.

Caroline had the unsettling feeling that she was being judged and had somehow come up wanting. "Well, then, what are we to do with her? Someone must have put her in the coach between the time it left the mews and the time it arrived at Cavendish House. But we have come so far already that I refuse to turn back now."

"It seems someone didn't want her, *mademoiselle,* or else they had to get rid of her for some other reason," Suzette said, giving the baby a hug.

Relieved to see that Suzette had the situation well in hand, Caroline took time to study the child more closely. "Perhaps someone at the next inn would like to have her."

Poppy didn't take her gaze from Caroline's face.

"Oh, *mademoiselle.* How can you suggest such a terrible thing?" Suzette cried, pulling the baby closer.

Poppy covered her eyes with her hands, then flung her arms wide. "Poppy peek-a-boo," she called to Caroline, then closed her eyes tightly and giggled until the tears came.

Suzette laughed. "Well, one mystery has been cleared up. It seems her name is Poppy."

At the mention of her name, Poppy nodded happily. "Poppy num-num."

Caroline knit her brows.

"I believe Poppy is telling us that she is hungry, *mademoiselle.*"

Caroline looked at Suzette in amazement. "However could you tell that?"

"It is easy, *mademoiselle.* She is chewing on my gloves."

Caroline laughed. "And I will be too, if we do not stop soon." She signaled to her coachman and told him to pull into the coach yard of the next inn.

"The Four Sparrows is just ahead, my lady," he called down hopefully, for John Coachman knew that the proprietress, Mrs. Wriggles was famous up and down the post-road for her ale.

Soon they pulled into the busy courtyard of the inn.

The footman's expression underwent several startling changes as he tried desperately not to show his amazement when he opened the door expecting to help her ladyship down only to be handed a wrapped bundle, containing a pink face with big blue eyes peeking out at him. However, George was trained well and made no comment on the unusual happenstance, tucked the child against his chest with one arm, and still managed to assist the ladies from the coach.

Inside the inn they spoke for a private dining room where over a warm meal, Caroline reached the conclusion that there was only one person who could tell them what to do with the baby.

"Miss Plunkett is the answer," Caroline announced to Suzette. "Miss Plunkett will know what to do."

After all, didn't Miss Plunkett know all about babies? She'd cared for Caroline since she was born until she went away to boarding school. Perhaps she would know of some farm family who would take the child in.

When Mrs. Wriggles was informed of the situation, she generously found a frock for Poppy that one of her granddaughters had outgrown. It was a little large, but proved adequate until they could find something else. She also provided them with some scraps torn from worn out sheets to use to wrap around Poppy to keep her dry for the duration of their journey.

Due to the unexpected circumstances, the little party left the high road much later than had been expected. Caroline had sent word ahead the day before to alert the staff at the manor that she would be arriving.

"We will still be at Tallyho by nightfall, my lady," John Coachman said.

"That is good to hear. I certainly don't want to disappoint Miss Plunkett."

It was nearly two o'clock in the afternoon on that same day when Lord Blackmere appeared at the door of Cavendish House in the Square. He could stay away no longer—had to see her again—even though she had evidently taken a revulsion to him. Under the circumstances it was understandable, but to have turned him down so abruptly and then written that she was sorry, as she had done, only magnified his confusion. He should have left well enough alone, made his departure from London, and stayed out of her life altogether.

The door opened. "Good afternoon, Driggs. I have come to see Lady Caroline." Lord Blackmere fumbled about inside his coat until he found what he was looking for. "She sent a message asking me to call."

"I am so sorry, your lordship," Driggs said with true sympathy for the elderly peer. It was not for a servant to speculate on his mistress's whimsies. "Lady Caroline departed only this morning for one of the family estates in Essex to see her old nurse."

On hearing this news, Lord Blackmere seemed to suffer a setback. "Do you have any idea of when she will be returning?"

"She only said that she expected it would be an extended visit." Seeing his lordship's downcast expression, Driggs asked, "Have you come to work in the library, my lord?"

Lord Blackmere was tempted. At least he could be in her house for a while longer, but he decided against it. "No, Driggs. Thank you. There are other matters I need to tend to. Good day to you."

"Good day to you too, your lordship."

Lord Blackmere descended the steps and paused a moment. Then having made his decision, he hailed a hackney coach to carry him back to his lodgings. It was time for Lord Blackmere to exit London Town, he thought. He had remained far too long this time. All because of a lovely lady with golden hair and eyes which promised so much. He would have to leave the field to the younger Kendale.

The gateway into Tallyho's small park was not impressive but held a certain charm as its arched sign displayed the coat-of-arms and large iron letters announcing they had entered lands owned by the Cavendish Family. The great elms whose branches were once pruned back from the carriageway now grew where they pleased and John Coachman had to call on all his skills in handling the ribbons to drive in such a zigzag manner as to avoid having his hat knocked off.

A small herd of deer leaped across their path and disappeared into a wooded area just before the meadow that indicated they were nearing the old manor house.

It had not taken them more than twenty minutes from the gate before Lady Caroline's coach rounded the last turn and came to a halt at the front steps.

Miss Plunkett, tall, angular and proper had walked up from her cottage and was awaiting them at the entrance with Mr. and Mrs. Frisby and the rest of the staff when the coach arrived. She was dressed in gray as Caroline always remembered her; gray wool pelisse, gray frock, gray lace mobcap that held her gray hair in place under her gray bonnet, and to complete the ensemble, sensible gray shoes. Of course Lady Caroline's old nurse was overjoyed to welcome her Caro, but it was the sight of the baby that made her gray eyes light up.

"Wherever did this little angel come from?" she exclaimed, taking Poppy from Suzette.

The years dropped away as Caroline saw herself in Miss Plunkett's arms and heard the same words of endearment that had been crooned to her so long ago. "Would you believe me if I told you we found her in a picnic hamper?"

"You never! She is bamming me, is she not?" Miss Plunkett asked Suzette.

"*Mademoiselle* tells the truth," Suzette said.

Miss Plunkett was not satisfied with that tad of information and insisted right then and there that she be told the whole story.

When she finished telling her the tale, Lady Caroline told Mrs. Frisby to summon one of the serving maids to take the baby.

But Miss Plunkett would have none of it. It had been so long since she'd held a little girl that she quite stubbornly refused to hand Poppy over. While the trunks were being brought in and the young mistress settled in her chambers, she fed her, bathed her and washed her hair, until Poppy blossomed like a yellow flower with big blue eyes. After a nightshirt had been sequestered from one of the footboys, Miss Plunkett sighed and said to Caroline, "She looks so much like you did when you were a wee babe, that I would have thought I'd slipped back in time if I did not see my grownup Lady Caroline standing here beside her."

Poppy pulled back her head, stuck her finger in her mouth, and gave Miss Plunkett's face a solemn and very thorough study. Caroline was certain that the infant did not find the old nurse wanting, as she had done her in the coach.

Only when dinner was announced would Miss Plunkett allow the serving girl to take the baby up to bed.

Mrs. Frisby had prepared a delicious meal and Mr. Frisby brought up some of Lord Favor's wine from the cellar to celebrate the occasion. All during dinner Mrs. Plunkett listened enraptured to Carolyn's tales of London until she could hold her eyes open no longer.

After she promised Caroline that she would be up at the manor house for breakfast first thing in the morning, one of the footmen helped the exceedingly happy and tipsy Miss Plunkett back to her cottage.

As Caroline mounted the stairs to her chambers, she said to Suzette, "I forgot to ask Miss Plunkett to see if she could find a family in the village who would want to adopt the child. I shall have to remember to do it tomorrow."

Suzette wondered what Miss Plunkett would say to that.

At the same time that Lady Caroline was wondering what to do with Poppy, young Mr. Kendale was sitting comfortably on a sofa in his small apartment, flipping a gold coin into the air. Finally he pocketed it and laid his head back on the soft cushions. He'd walked several miles along the river that afternoon, and now, he planned to stretch his long legs out toward the fire and relax.

He could not recall how many times Lord Blackmere had told him that it was Destiny which had brought them together that cold, miserable, wet night along the London docks over twenty years ago.

"Yes, Destiny, my boy! There can be no other explanation," his lordship would say with deep conviction, thrusting out each arm one at a time to punctuate every word.

On the night mentioned, it had been the intention of a gang of little ruffians, to which Kendale proudly belonged, to make off with anything they could snatch, lift, fleece, or nip from the dandies, hell-rakers or sprigs of fashion who frequented the quayside gambling hells and pleasure houses along the wharf.

Although he never knew the date he was born, Kendale reckoned he could not have been more than seven or eight years old, perhaps younger. The River Rats as they were called—none of them knew any other name—hung out in the alleys, slept on rough planks in broken down tenement buildings, and teased the ladies at Lucianne's to feed them.

The young Viscount of Wickett and his cronies were frequent visitors at Lucianne's. When they came stumbling out into the street at dawn to find their way back to the fashionable section of London, they became excellent dupes for the little pickpockets.

Kendale remembered well the night that the River Rats lay in wait with bits and pieces of flotsam and jetsam, to trip, hobble, or whack the foolish young bloods as they made their way out of Lucianne's. Their plan worked better than expected and soon the cobblestones were littered with fallen bodies, arms and legs everywhere and a mighty scramble to acquire as much booty as the swift little hands and pockets could hold.

However, a fight had ensued among the River Rats themselves over a particularly shiny timepiece nipped from one of the fallen bucks. In his enthusiasm to gain the prize for himself, Kendale knocked the daylights out of the viscount with a long plank he'd yanked off a crate. All Kendale's pack scattered one way, the viscount's cronies another, leaving Kendale alone looking down at the man sprawled unconscious upon the wet, slippery cobbles.

Never before had Kendale seen one of his cullies fall over without getting up again in a matter of seconds. The viscount had never given them a scold for snitching a bit from his purse the way some of his highborn friend's did. And that night, Kendale had feared the young lord was beyond the pale, and it was all his fault. Then a strange transformation of thinking took place deep down inside the little River Rat. Something akin to a conscience surfaced. Confused by this new sensation and not knowing what else to do, Kendale ran to Lucianne for help.

"Look what you done to one of me best customers, you rascal," Lucianne scolded as she leaned down to inspect the viscount.

"The cove ain't dead, is he, Lucianne?" he had cried, sorely worried.

"Nah, but you sure planted him a facer," she said, laughing. After boxing Kendale on the ear for injuring one of her clientele, she dispensed two burly doormen to bring the viscount back into the house.

When the future Lord Blackmere awakened to find himself inside the establishment which he had thought to have exited the night before, he was amazed to find that in the light of day—and when he was no longer cup shot—that the ladies who in a haze of smoke and wine had seemed lovely beyond all reason, were anything but. His head was splitting and he vowed to give up spirits and women forever.

But when he heard that it was the skinny, green-eyed boy hovering over him who had sought help, he looked at him in a different light than he had the others. Holding his aching head, the viscount promised solemnly that someday he would return and reward the little beggar for saving his life.

Lucianne quickly squelched any hopes Kendale had when she told him, "A nobleman is the least likely of creatures to keep a promise, my dear."

So it was with much surprise to all the occupants of Lucianne's establishment of pleasure when the viscount did return later and carried the little River Rat away—all the way to Blackmere Castle.

The old earl has died, the viscount told Kendale. "And now that I am the new Earl of Blackmere, I shall do just as I please. What is your name, young man?"

"Don't have one, sir."

"Well, can't have you stirring around without a proper name. How does Kendale sound to you?"

"Sounds a good un to me, sir."

"Then Kendale it is."

That was so many years ago that it seemed a lifetime away.

Now it was time he rose and dressed for White's. Kendale had promised to meet Lord Farrington and two of his cronies in the card room for as long as the games lasted.

When Miss Plunkett arrived at the Tallyho manor house the next day for breakfast, she carried a satchel and insisted on seeing Poppy right away.

"When Betsy—she's my girl from the village—came this morning, I told her about the baby and her not having any clothes. She ran straight home and fetched some of her little sister's outgrown frocks. I have brought them with me."

The frocks were a bit large. but Poppy didn't seem to mind and managed to get them dirty as quickly as she would have done more fashionable gowns.

The next two weeks were spent exploring the estate, taking Miss Plunkett on carriage rides around the park and to a larger town to buy some books.

"Because," she complained, "there are no lending libraries in Beesbury."

But mostly they stayed in the park, had picnics and walked over the meadows and through the woods which were now lush with all the colors of autumn.

On one particularly warm day not long after they had come to Tallyho, Miss Plunkett suggested a picnic in the meadow. They saw a fox and a rabbit and flocks of birds flying south. Miss Plunkett had insisted that Poppy be brought with them, as she did every time they would not be going far from the manor house. Betsy came to tend her, but it was Miss Plunkett who held her the most.

Poppy had run off after the rabbit, Betsy close behind when Miss Plunkett asked offhandedly, "I don't suppose that the nursery is being used for anything at Cavendish House now?"

"No, but my father had it completely redecorated and jammed full of toys when he found that he was to be a papa again," Caroline said in what sounded suspiciously like a pout to Miss Plunkett.

Miss Plunkett looked pensive. "I suppose it will be a long time before he and the countess bring the baby to London."

"I certainly hope so," said Caroline. "I vow, I cannot abide even imagining the amount of dust that would stir up. Father insists on bringing all his own staff, and with Mary's maids and a nurse for the baby, I'm afraid I would have to move out."

"All the same, it does seem sad that such a lovely nursery is going unused when it is all ready for a child to enjoy." With hope in her eyes, Miss Plunkett asked, "And what are you going to do with the wee mite, my lady?"

Caroline thought this the perfect time to put forth her suggestion. "I suppose that until we know more about where she came from, we shall have to find her a home."

"And . . . ?"

"I told Suzette that you know everything about babies."

"Oh, yes, I do!" said Miss Plunkett, sitting forward eagerly.

"Well . . . I was thinking," said Caroline, "that you may know of a farmer's family or someone in the village who would be just right to adopt the child."

"Oh, my goodness! I thought . . . that is . . . for a moment there, I hoped . . ." Miss Plunkett was so embarrassed that she could not finish.

Caroline watched in bewilderment as her former nurse's face turned first white, then a brilliant pink. "My dear Miss Plunkett, are you all right?"

"Oh, yes, dear." Miss Plunkett's eyes turned in the direction that Poppy had taken. "You don't suppose that it would be possible . . . ? You wouldn't possibly consider . . . ? No, I suppose not," she finished, looking quite dazed.

Caroline reminded herself that Miss Plunkett was up in years now, but she had never expected her to come into her dotage so soon.

"If that is what you think you want to do, I shall ask the vicar next Sunday if he knows of a family. The thing is, it's so very lonely when one lives alone," explained Miss Plunkett. "Betsy is here every day to help, and I do go up to the manor house and talk to Mrs. Frisby—but she has her duties to perform."

"But, I thought your sister lived with you."

"Well, yes, she did for awhile. Her daughter lived in Harlow which was near enough for her to visit now and then. But her daughter's husband has been offered a position tutoring the sons of Lord Briskell in Nottingham. They have asked her to move with them. It would be too far away for her to travel to see them, of course, and she wanted to be near her grandchildren." Miss Plunkett sat back. "Things are best enjoyed when you have someone to share them with, my dear. I am sometimes sorry that I did not marry, but then nobody plans to be left alone, does one?" she said sighing.

"Now that you are older, I should think that you would enjoy the peace and quiet, Miss Plunkett."

"Just because I've added a few more birthdays does not mean that I wish to be counted as one of last year's cabbages. In fact, there is a family in Cambridge with six children—all under six years of age, I hear—that is looking for a nurse. I think I shall apply," said Miss Plunkett testily.

"Oh, Miss Plunkett! How can you even consider such a thing at your age?" Caroline cried.

"At least I would be of use to somebody."

"It would be your death."

Miss Plunkett stiffened her backbone. "I may be getting on in years, my lady, but I feel I have a lot of love to give a child."

Caroline did not think that Miss Plunkett realized the difficulties she would encounter. "Yes, one child might not be too much of a burden, but six children, Miss Plunkett! That is outside of enough! I beg you to reconsider."

"Betsy said she will go with me if I find a position. She would fetch and carry. Of course, a person never knows when more than one child at a time will get into trouble, does one?" Miss Plunkett said, nodding knowingly.

Caroline watched Poppy tumbling about in the grass, and recalled what she'd observed in the last couple of weeks. Poppy played peek-a-boo with everybody from the gardener to the stableboy and got lost twice doing so. She'd fallen down a flight of stairs before anyone could catch her and locked herself in a cupboard in the kitchen.

The child was only beginning to walk, but she thought she could run as fast or jump as high as every bird or rabbit that flitted or hopped across her path. She tried to collect every pebble on the ground or every pretty leaf that fell from a tree. Most of which ended up in her mouth. They didn't dare let her get near a pond. Caroline was exhausted just watching Betsy try to keep up with her. And if one child was so difficult to raise, what of the six children Miss Plunkett talked of caring for?

As they started to get ready to make their way back to the manor house, Caroline knew she had to find a way to keep her old nurse from going to Cambridge. That was all there was to it.

While Lady Caroline was instructing the servants to remove the chairs and food to the pony-wagon, Miss Plunkett confided in Suzette, "All there is to do here is to take a walk," she said dismally. "It is not the exercise that is displeasing to me, it is just not having something at the end of it that is of any interest. Every week it is the same. Friday mornings I ride in the wagon to Market with the housekeeper, Mrs. Frisby. On Sunday we go to the village for church services. In between I sew or tend a garden, neither of which ever caught my fancy. I have read all my books ten times over because there is no lending library near. I never painted nor do I have any desire to do so. I am only good at raising children."

"Then why don't you just ask *mademoiselle* if you can come back with us? I know that she likes Poppy. She is just afraid of the responsibilities of taking care of a child."

"How can anyone be afraid of such an angel? But Lady Caroline has a mind of her own. She has to think it is her own idea," Miss Plunkett said.

Suzette smiled. "*Oui, mademoiselle.* Perhaps if we help her a little she will think the idea is hers."

Miss Plunkett patted Suzette's hand. "I see that you know my little Caroline well."

Suzette looked at Miss Plunkett with amusement. "Suzette thinks she is beginning to know the woman who taught her too. Does the family who has offered Miss Plunkett a position really have six children?"

"No, of course not," said Miss Plunkett cheerfully. "There wasn't even one child—or even a family. I made that up."

"Miss Plunkett is even more sly like a fox than *mademoiselle,* I think."

"Of course, I am. I had to be to keep up with that imp when she was sprouting," said the older woman. "But this will be our secret, I hope, Miss Suzette."

"Suzette thinks *mademoiselle* has met her match," she said, laughing.

# Eight

Over the next few days, Miss Plunkett pretended to consult with a number of the village's leaders, and finally announced at the end of the week that Mrs. Frisby, the village clerk and the vicar of the local parish had said they could find no one to take Poppy.

"You will just have to carry her back to London with you, dear."

Caroline chewed on her lip and concentrated hard. "Oh, well," she said, brightening a bit. "It is only a day's journey. Suzette can care for her for that long and when I reach London I shall place her in a home there."

They had been nearly three weeks at Tallyho now. There were no balls, or theater, or shopping in Town. Boredom was threatening to overcome Caroline, which finally made her begin to understand Miss Plunkett's discontent. But the alternative frightened her more for she had not been able to dissuade Miss Plunkett from taking the position with the family in Cambridge.

That evening she spoke to Suzette about her concerns as she was preparing for bed. "I am very worried about Miss Plunkett. A woman her age cannot possibly keep up with a family of little children. They are probably all demons, too. I must find a way to stop her from doing something so foolish."

"Just because a person has grown older does not mean they want to be idle."

"That is exactly what Miss Plunkett said. But six children, Suzette. That is too much."

"Suzette knows that *mademoiselle* is so clever that she probably already has the perfect solution. Is that not true?"

Caroline did not want to admit that as yet she hadn't. "I am just working out the details."

"Suzette suspects she knows what *mademoiselle's* plan will be," the little maid said.

Caroline looked at her inquiringly. "You do?"

Suzette tapped her forehead with her finger. "*Oui, mademoiselle* is very clever. She is going to ask Miss Plunkett: who is to care for Poppy when we return to London if she takes a position in Cambridge?"

Caroline looked at Suzette with admiration. "That is exactly what I was thinking. To save Miss Plunkett, I must keep Poppy."

Suzette hid her smile. "That is a perfect solution, *mademoiselle.* And now she will find a way to persuade Miss Plunkett to her way of thinking?"

Caroline clapped her hands. "I will wait for just the right moment to ask her. Now," she said, "don't you let the cat out of the bag about what I am going to do."

"Oh, no, *mademoiselle.* Suzette's lips are sealed."

The next day Caroline cautiously set forth her proposal to Miss Plunkett, who, it proved, was not about to be thought so easily brought round.

"Let me think about it," she said, appearing to be giving the idea a considerable amount of concentration. Finally she shook her head slowly. "No, my dear, I am sure that I am too old to be of any use to you."

Caroline panicked. "Oh, I did not mean it when I said that you cannot be of help, Miss Plunkett. I don't know what I shall do if you do not come back with us," Caroline cried, trying to think what more she could do to persuade her old nurse to her way of thinking.

Miss Plunkett tapped her lips with her finger, wrinkled her

brow, and blinked her eyes a few times. Finally, she smiled and nodded her head.

Caroline sighed with relief. "Miss Plunkett is coming back to London with us," she called to Suzette. "Then we can have some time to think what we shall do with Poppy."

"My dear, I want to warn you that if we notify the authorities they may take Poppy away and put her in a workhouse."

George who was standing nearby cleared his throat loudly. "If I may say something, m'lady."

"Yes, George, what is it?"

"I have a cousin on me mother's side named Mortimer Digger. He has ambitions to be a Bow Street Runner. If you would like, I could ask him to look into the matter. Kind of . . . you know . . . mum's the word."

"That would be a splendid idea, George," Caroline said much relieved that she would not be blamed for sending the child off. "Ask him please."

"I will, m'lady, soon's we return to Town," the footman said, sounding quite pleased with himself.

It took only a few days for Miss Plunkett to settle her affairs and be ready to set out for London. She tacked up a notice in the village announcing that her cottage was for let and packed her wardrobe. Betsy collected her belongings and said goodbye to her family while the housekeeper, Mrs. Frisby and Sally's mother worked round the clock to sew suitable clothes for Poppy.

"Why does a little child need a bigger wardrobe than I have?" Caroline remonstrated as they made their way to the waiting coach where George was handing Suzette up.

There was a squeal nearby and both women turned to find the source.

"You will soon learn why," Miss Plunkett promised with a smile.

Caroline's hand flew to her mouth. "I have never seen anyone ruin frocks so quickly," she exclaimed as she watched Betsy drag a tattered Poppy from the bushes after chasing a rabbit. "Yesterday she chewed the pretty lace collar off the lovely dress Mrs. Frisby made. Is something wrong with her?"

"Hmph," Miss Plunkett said meaningfully. "You forget what you yourself did, my lady."

"I never!" said Caroline. "You are exaggerating. I am fastidious about my appearance."

Betsy was coming toward them carrying a very disappointed Poppy. "Hop-hop," she said, pointing back toward the bushes.

Miss Plunkett picked a leaf off Poppy's nose. "I was thinking of a bedraggled little girl who pulled a half-drowned puppy out of a pond."

Caroline laughed. "Imagine you remembering that."

Miss Plunkett's eyes twinkled. "I remember a great many things more, my lady, and don't you forget it."

"Well, I have quite outgrown such behavior, I assure you."

Betsy dusted the remaining leaves off Poppy's skirt and handed her to George who handed her up to Suzette who was already in the coach.

"Ah, yes," Miss Plunkett said as she settled in across from Betsy and the wriggling child. "This is lovely."

Poppy seemed quite pleased to be provided with so many laps to crawl over and was making the most of them.

Lady Caroline entered the coach and stared in horror. "Lovely?" she exclaimed, trying to draw her skirts out of the reach of the little girl. "One more day of this and we shall look as much a ragamuffin as she by the time we get back to London."

"Yes, Poppy reminds me more and more of you each day," Miss Plunkett said, sighing happily.

The welcoming atmosphere that pervaded the entrance hall at Cavendish House in the Square was one of expectation as the entire staff eagerly watched the arrival of their mistress and her guests. Lady Caroline's message to Driggs and the housekeeper had merely said that she was bringing Miss Plunkett and her maid back with her. Miss Plunkett was dearly loved, but it had been Lady Caroline's postscript which baffled them. It merely said that the housekeeper, Mrs. Newly, was to have the nursery cleaned and aired.

"Driggs," said Miss Plunkett cheerfully, holding out her hands. "And Mrs. Newly. How good it is to see everyone again." The smiles on all the faces, from footmen to kitchen maids, even the servants who had not known the woman before, showed that she was welcome.

But all eyes were now turned toward the young girl carrying the baby. "Miss Plunkett has a new charge," Caroline announced. "I hope that the nursery is ready, Mrs. Newly."

"What? Oh, yes, my lady," the housekeeper said, her gaze not leaving the beautiful, golden-haired child who had her hands pressed over her eyes.

Suddenly Poppy flung out her arms. "Peek-a-boo!" she squealed, melting into a fit of giggles in Betsy's arms.

After the nature of Poppy's mysterious appearance had been made known to the staff, the new members of the house were escorted to their aerie above stairs. Only then was the household at Cavendish House in the Square ready to settle down to run as it had before.

After everyone had been dispersed to their duties, Caroline asked Driggs to bring any correspondence to the desk in the library. "And the calling cards, also." As soon as he brought them, she quickly picked up and discarded each piece one by one. "Is this all that has come in?" she asked.

Bewildered, the butler stared at the mountain of missives on the tray and the silver bowl full of cards, wondering how anyone could want more. "Yes, that is all, my lady."

"Did anyone come to call who didn't leave a card?"

Driggs thought for a moment. "Come to think of it, my lady, Lord Blackmere called soon after you left for Tallyho."

Caroline tried to hide her excitement. "And?"

"He said you asked him to call. Showed me a letter."

"Did he say when he would come again?"

"No. He just said that he had things to tend to and then he left."

"Thank you, Driggs. That will be all."

Caroline stared a few minutes at the pile of letters, then rose and went up to her apartment. Lord Blackmere had come back to see her. Did it mean that she was forgiven?

Across the street, Kendale paused for a moment to look up at Cavendish House for the second time. He'd made it a habit to include this part of the city in his long walks and today luck was on his side. He had seen Lady Caroline's coach arrive and he'd circled the entire square to come round again. So the Incomparable was back. Not that he could approach her, but at least he could look forward to seeing her here and there about the city.

Humming a lively tune, Kendale continued to make his way back toward Town. The air was brisk, the sky a hazy blue-gray. It was not long before he smelled the river much sooner than he saw it, and with the first whiff, his mood changed. How strange a twist his life had taken.

After eleven years at sea, and jolly ones they had been, Kendale had returned to England with the greatest expectations; a ship of his own laden with goods from the Orient, the means to start his own company and the potential to buy more ships as his business grew. But greater than all this was his pride in knowing he would be able to thank the man who had not only rescued him from the gutter, but had given him the backing to go out in the world to seek his fortune. His champion, Lord Blackmere.

But alas when he had journeyed north to be united with his

benefactor—the man who had given him a home, educated him, and treated him more like a son than a servant—Kendale found Lord Blackmere had vanished.

The gates into the park were locked, the castle boarded up, No Trespassing signs warned strangers away. In Wickett, the village nearest the castle, Kendale was told that his lordship had not been seen for years. No one was quite sure how long exactly.

Kendale had returned to London in some confusion as to what to do. He took up lodgings in a modest apartment near the docks and commenced to set up his business, making inquiries wherever he could, but he had been away from England for so long and he did not know where to start.

Then one day as he was heading east along Upper Thames Street, Kendale had caught sight of a familiar face. It was only a glimpse, but that was all it took for him to recognize a long ago friend.

"Jon!" he called, but the man did not hear him.

The fellow had already turned and was heading in the opposite direction. He was about the same height as Kendale, but a good six stone heavier and had a large leather bag strapped on his back. When Kendale caught up to him, he called out his name once more.

"Jon Baskins!"

The man turned. Time had not aged the pink-cheeked fellow, only made him fuller and more jovial-looking, if that were possible.

"I knew it could be no one else but you," Kendale said, slapping him on the shoulder.

For a moment, the man had stared, then a wide grin spread across his thick jowled face. "Master Kendale! It is you. Bless me if it ain't you, Master Kendale. 'Pon my word, you're the last person I'd be expecting to see in Londontown. We thought when you sailed away to the other side of the world we would never lay eyes on you again."

"I'm back now, Jon. But I can't find Lord Blackmere. Do you know where he has gone?"

"That were the strangest thing," Jon said, slowing down to keep step with Kendale. "M'grandfather were getting up in years. He'd set aside a bit of a nest egg to buy a little cottage in Wickett when he became too old to be in service. His lordship hadn't said anything, but I were hoping I were to be the one to take over Grandfather's position as his lordship's gentleman's gentleman.

"When the time came Lord Blackmere said I could take as long as I needed to settle Grandfather. I were gone only two weeks and when I went back to the castle it were all boarded up. There weren't many of the staff left by that time and we found work elsewhere. His lordship hadn't let on, but I think he were deep into dun territory."

Kendale was having a difficult time trying to sort out this disturbing information. "And why are you in London, Jon?"

"I'm a peddler now," he said, pointing to the bag on his back. "I travel from town to town and can set up anywhere on a street. Grandfather died a few years back and when I'm not on the road, I have his cottage to abide in."

"We are not far from my lodgings. Do you have the time to stop? There is so much I would like to ask you."

"I'd like that, Mr. Kendale. I surely would."

It took no more than another fifteen minutes before the two men were settled in Kendale's small sitting room. A bottle of wine was opened and he poured them both a drink.

"Now," Kendale said, "you say no one knows the whereabouts of his lordship?"

"No, sir. Men came and boarded up the castle."

"Yes, I know, I have seen it. It is posted with No Trespassing signs. The fields are fallow, and I saw all the cottages are empty."

"Yes, sir. The sheriff said everybody were to move out."

"No one in London seems to know of this."

"I don't doubt that, sir. The old castle is so hidden, no large towns around. You know yourself, sir, that no guests ever came to Blackmere Castle. His lordship liked it that way. You remember how he used to go to Londontown once in awhile when you were here—I think it were to see his solicitor—but then soon after you left home he suddenly didn't go at all anymore. Said there was nothing there for him. Most of his old cronies were either leg-shackled or dead. That were when he started letting the staff go."

"Someone who knew him in London must know something of his whereabouts. That worries me, Jon. If he is into dun territory, I can help him. Do you know at all who his solicitor was?"

"No, sir. I don't know anything 'bout things like that. I'm sorry, sir."

"No, I suppose you don't. I shall inquire. But surely if he didn't have a feather to fly with, he certainly didn't go far. I must find him. I owe him a lot. I have come back with a ship full of spices, and silks and woods like you've never seen before. My profits should be substantial. He gave me a home and educated me—and you, too, Jon. Remember how he used to include you in my lessons?"

The big man smiled good-naturedly. "But I weren't as sharp-witted as you, Mr. Kendale."

It was true, Jon had the good nature whereas, Kendale had a thirst for knowledge that couldn't be satisfied. "You know as well as I, Jon, that he saved me from an early trip to the gallows if I'd remained where I was. If Lord Blackmere is living in poverty, I shall never forgive myself."

"Lord Blackmere is a good man, sir."

"I'm glad to hear you speak as if his lordship is alive, Jon. I don't know if I could bear to think that I will never see him again to thank him for all he did for me."

"Oh, no, sir," Jon said, "it is a terrible thought to think of his lordship as having stuck his spoon in the wall."

Kendale couldn't stand to see the distress in his old friend's eyes. "It will turn out all right, Jon. We will find Lord Blackmere and bring him back home. Now, what I am thinking is that between the two of us perhaps we can find out where he has gone. I have started making inquiries here in London. You travel the byways and know far more of the country towns than I do. While you journey, you can ask questions."

"Like what, sir?"

"Give people a good description of what Lord Blackmere looked like. Surely someone will know if a stranger has moved into their midst in the last ten years. Now that you know where I live, Jon, I want you to contact me whenever you are in London. We shall find him, don't you worry."

After his visit with Jon, Kendale threw all his efforts into his business. He had warehoused the cargo he'd brought back from the Orient and expected to make a good profit. As soon as his ship the *Archipelago* was once again put out to sea, he began his search for Lord Blackmere's solicitor.

Now as Kendale entered Upper Thames Street he remembered that it had been this very spot where he'd first run into Jon Baskins some four years ago and they had started their search for Lord Blackmere.

One evening three weeks after that, Kendale had arrived at his rooming house to find Jon waiting for him. "Come in," he'd said, opening the door.

The big man looked relieved. "I was afraid I'd missed you."

"From the look on your face, I fear you do not bring good news."

Jon shook his head. "I was in Oxfordshire the last two weeks. I asked about like you said, but I found out naught."

"Well, I have some hopeful information. I located the whereabouts of Lord Blackmere's solicitor. His name is Josiah Chumbley. He retired and is living south of London. I purchased a horse at Tattersall's this past week and it will be a good chance for me to see how he handles. I shall ride down to see the man tomorrow."

"You mean this Chumbley fellow ain't Lord Blackmere's lawyer anymore?"

"I don't know. When I inquired at the Temple I was given the information that many of Josiah Chumbley's clientele were transferred to other solicitors, but Lord Blackmere's name was not on that list."

"I hope Mr. Chumbley knows something about his lordship," Jon said, heaving his great bulk up from the chair.

"I hope so too, Jon. When will you be back in London?"

Jon screwed up his face as he tried to concentrate on his answer. "I don't know for sure, Mr. Kendale."

"Well, when I see you again, I hope to have better news."

The following day, Kendale had visited Mr. Chumbley. His house with its vine-covered walls and steep thatched roof so blended with the dense forest that at first Kendale thought it a living thing.

Mr. Chumbley resembled a gnome; thick set, his shapeless knit cap pulled down over his ears, and breeches of fustian tucked into knee-high boots. He was pleasant enough and while he emptied his pockets of bread crumbs for the squirrels which were scolding him from the trees, he told Kendale to tether his horse under an old beech tree and invited him inside the cottage to sit.

As Mr. Chumbley cleared a path to the hearth, he told Kendale that he and Lord Blackmere had had a row many years ago when the earl had refused to make out a will. "Said he didn't believe in them. However," the solicitor said, "he came to me later with a document that he'd written out himself and wanted me to make it legal. He said I was to keep a copy and the other he wanted to give to the local constable of his district. It had to do with closing down the castle, posting signs, and such if something should happen to him. I thought it was all foolishness until an anonymous letter arrived about mmm . . . let me see . . . five years ago telling me that Lord Blackmere had deserted his lands. When Lord Blackmere did not return and no more word was received from him, his orders were carried out. I sent word to the constable to have the house closed and boarded up. The servants had been dispensed, I was told, and I suppose took posts elsewhere."

"They did," said Kendale. "As soon as I docked in London, I journeyed at once to the castle. I visited Wickett, the village nearest the castle, to ask for information. No one there could believe it either that his lordship just left without a word. Then I came across one of Lord Blackmere's former servants soon after I arrived back in Town. He has told me the same sad tale."

Mr. Chumbley indicated to Kendale to sit down in the big stained chair which stood before the fireplace where a large log was burning. He then looked round as if trying to locate something. Finally he tramped over to a tall bookshelf which was filled more with boxes than with books. "Never have sorted out any of this since I moved in four years ago. I know I have all of his lordship's papers here somewhere."

He pulled out a box marked A-B-C and began rummaging inside until he pulled out and unrolled a large sheet of foolscap. "Always pays to be orderly," Mr. Chumbley said. He found his spectacles in the tinder box on top the mantelpiece, read over the paper, and handed it to Kendale.

"From what I hear, I am afraid that the castle fell into disrepair long before Lord Blackmere went away," Mr. Chumbley said, removing an orange cat from the only other chair by the fireplace before settling himself into it. "I thought that perhaps he'd merely done what many of the nobility did when he saw his circumstances go bad . . . escaped to the Continent."

"He couldn't have done. The war was still on. If it is as you believe that he didn't have a feather to fly with, how could he have gotten off the island?"

"You have a point there," Mr. Chumbley said.

"Did he have a man of business?" Kendale asked.

"Yes, Crenshaw was his name. Good man. Took care of the elder earl's affairs for over forty years. But the present Lord Blackmere was stubborn on that issue too. Said he didn't believe in any man investing his blunt for him. He dismissed Crenshaw. Invested in crazy things like raising silk worms in the American Colonies. Dumb fool! Just like the wrong trees James I planted, Lord Blackmere sent Black Mulberry to the colonists. If he'd done his research he'd have known that silk worms only flourish on White Mulberry. I told him right off he was a nincompoop. I don't think he cared much for my opinion. Lord Blackmere never consulted me again."

Kendale stared at the papers in his hands seeing little. He couldn't have been more than fourteen or fifteen years old when he went to sea. He knew Lord Blackmere had been a scholarly man. He remembered him as a bit eccentric; given to quick impulses, bought whatever he wanted, and spoiled Kendale unmercifully. However, Kendale couldn't picture his lordship as being so impractical as to go through all his inheritance in such a short time. The story just didn't fit his picture of his champion. Something was not right, but at that time Kendale couldn't put his finger on what it was.

He scanned the document once more. It was dated just six months before he arrived back in England.

"He made no mention of me in any of his papers?" Kendale asked.

"No, I am afraid not," answered the lawyer with a touch of

sympathy in his voice. "However, I remember his telling me quite proudly that he thought you would do well for yourself in the world. I hope that is true, Mr. Kendale, because I am afraid your master seems to have done poorly by himself."

"I did well enough," said Kendale not willing to reveal that he had the makings of a fortune tucked away. "Did he never say anything about receiving my letters? True. I could only write a few over the years, but I did write telling him that I was working hard and would someday return to repay him."

The solicitor fell into contemplation. "Yes, now that I come to think back on it, I do believe he once mentioned that he had received a letter from you. He seemed quite pleased that day. He remarked about what a bright lad you had turned out to be. That was several years ago."

"Then you probably don't know if he got my later letters telling him I was setting sail for England?"

"No, I'm sorry, I don't."

"If only I'd come back sooner," Kendale said sadly. "Is there something I can do about the castle?"

"Not until his lordship is declared legally dead, I am afraid. When that time comes we will of course try to notify his next of kin first; which could take quite some time, because he never indicated that he had any living relatives."

"So nothing can be done for another six years unless Lord Blackmere turns up?" Kendale asked.

"As to his lordship's estate, I'm afraid not. But that is a long time off, Mr. Kendale," he said, as a nuthatch flew in the open window. Mr. Chumbley watched contentedly as the tiny gray and rufous bird flitted about, teased the orange cat and finally, after picking up some seeds from a dish on the countertop, flew out again. "The reason I removed myself to the woods is so I could live a quiet and tranquil life. I would dislike having anything disturb it."

Kendale blinked, not quite sure of what he'd seen. "Then you don't intend to notify the authorities of Lord Blackmere's disappearance?"

"I have no desire to dig up a hornet's nest. I had enough of the idiosyncrasies of the Upper Orders when I practiced law in London. As for yourself, you can do anything you please."

Kendale remembered that he'd returned to London that day feeling that he had found out no more from Mr. Chumbley than he'd known already. Unless it was that his mentor had mistakenly thought that the American colonists could raise silk worms on Black Mulberry leaves.

Now, Kendale had reached his apartment and the sight of a familiar brown paper sticking out from under the door chased all thoughts of Mr. Chumbley from his mind. The threatening messages had been coming for four years now, and he and Jon were still no nearer to finding Lord Blackmere. He was afraid someone was only playing a cruel joke to lead them to believe that his lordship was still alive somewhere. Reluctantly he picked it up and took it inside where he tore open the seal. After reading the letter he crammed it into a box with the others.

Tonight he would dine at White's and enjoy a game or two of cards. The young bucks would probably beg him to escort them to some of the more forbidden realms along the docks. He just might oblige them; for no matter how hard Kendale tried to forget it, his roots kept drawing him back to the River Thames.

# Nine

"Now, my lady," Miss Plunkett said from her bed where she lay bundled up to her chin, her head covered with a nightcap, her nose a rosy red. "I know that you can handle it very well. I am asking you to do nothing more than take Poppy and Betsy with you when you go for your ride in the Park."

No sooner had word of Lady Caroline's return to Town reached the ears of the *haute ton* than the invitations had begun to pour into Cavendish House in the Square. Miss Plunkett had happily moved back into the nursery as if she had never gone away. In fact, things were running so smoothly that Caroline would have forgotten altogether that she had a child in the house, if it had not been for Miss Plunkett mentioning Poppy at dinner—that is—on the few occasions when Caroline was home of an evening.

Now she had been summoned to Miss Plunkett's room.

"Poppy has become accustomed to our taking her for an outing every day, and she will be so disappointed if she has to stay in," Miss Plunkett said, stopping to blow her nose.

Caroline's gaze darted to the doorway where Betsy stood holding Poppy in her arms. The infant seemed docile enough, but still nagging doubts remained.

"Can you not get one of the other maids to accompany them?" Caroline said.

"No," said Miss Plunkett adamantly. "I would not trust anyone else but you with my little darling. And don't say that you have another engagement this afternoon, because I know you do not. Betsy will have Poppy dressed and ready to go on time."

A flicker of a smile threatened to show itself on Caroline's lips. "Are you certain I should not call a doctor?"

"I only need a day or two in bed and I shall be right as rain," Miss Plunkett assured her. "Now tell me what you are wearing."

"Whatever difference does it—"

Miss Plunkett censured Caroline with an old familiar *look*.

"I shall wear my new French bonnet, I believe. It matches my lilac colored cassimere pelisse," she said obediently.

"Betsy will have Poppy in the hall at quarter before four."

"But that is too early," Caroline complained.

"It isn't early for Poppy. It is getting dark earlier and the fog begins to roll in now that fires are burning in the fireplaces all day. Betsy and I usually go for our ride before two o'clock."

Caroline knew that with so many of her acquaintances off to their country estates for the Hunting Season that there were fewer people riding in the Park at the fashionable hour anyway so it would not matter if she had the child with her.

"Quarter to four and don't be late."

"No, Miss Plunkett," Caroline said as she headed for the door. She didn't know why she felt she should hurry.

"Be sure to take a muff. It is getting chillier out," Miss Plunkett called after her.

If Lady Caroline had reservations about taking a child with her to the Park, they were dispersed as soon as her two-horse landau passed through Hyde Park Corner and onto Rotten Row. The day was not chilly, so they rode with the top down.

The postillion who was smartly dressed in the Cavendish green and gold, handled the high-stepping chestnuts to perfection. George, nose in the air, sat proudly in the high seat in back. Betsy ever alert to the antics of her young charge, faced the rear across from her mistress.

In the seat facing forward sat two ladies dressed identically. Both wore lilac-colored pelisses and bonnets. Both had golden ringlets framing their delicate faces. White fur muffs hid their hands. The only difference was in the ladies' size, one a tiny replica of the other.

Well, that really was not the only difference. The taller lady greeted passing carriages or riders with a slight nod of the head, or perhaps a personal greeting to close friends. But the smaller lady had a tendency to keep removing her hands from her muff to cover her eyes and shouting, "Peek-a-boo," to everyone she saw; from the arrogant Mrs. Drummond Burrell, to a lovely Cyprian, to the attractive Lord Sefton. Neither did she leave out the little tiger riding on the back of Lady Tewilliger's carriage.

Soon Lady Caroline's landau was surrounded by gentlemen, as well as ladies, seeking an introduction to . . . Poppy.

But unbeknownst to Caroline, there was someone who did not seek an audience. Kendale had kept his horse some distance back of Lady Caroline's carriage. When he was not riding he stabled his horse at the mews near the Park where it could be exercised regularly. He seldom rode his horse while he was in Town. When he did need transportation within the city he hired a hackney. However, he knew that Lady Caroline often took a carriage ride in the afternoon. After a tiring day of business, he counted it enough of a reward just to be able to watch her. She never disappointed him.

When Lady Caroline had returned to London, the news traveled swiftly that the Earl of Favor's daughter had—out of charitableness and goodness of her heart—taken in an orphan who otherwise would have been thrown into the workhouse. But never before had she appeared in public with her charge, so Kendale considered this a double treat.

From the comments circulating round him, instead of censure and ridicule, her ladyship seemed to be finding herself the darling of the *haute ton* once again, and her consequence so elevated that she was being heralded as an example worth emulating.

As Kendale began to pass Lady Caroline's carriage he dared to rein in his horse. She was facing away from him, speaking to someone on the other side. Beside her sat the tiny lady enjoying herself immensely, flirting unashamedly while her nursery-maid tried desperately to keep the minx from crawling out of the carriage altogether. Lady Caroline seemed so sublimely unaware of the activity going on beside her that Kendale's curiosity made him do a very foolish thing. Boldly he pulled his mount to a stop beside the landau and smiled down at the curly-haired seductress.

She returned his gaze, her lavender bonnet slightly askew, her gloves off and her muff on the floor of the carriage. Blue eyes appraised him.

His grin deepened, and he boldly winked at her.

She giggled and began to bounce up and down so energetically that the maid sitting opposite had to reach out quickly to keep her from sliding off the seat.

Kendale believed he was losing his heart.

The imp covered her face with her hands just as Lady Caroline began to turn in his direction. Kendale urged his horse forward before she could see his face.

"Is it possible," he said to himself, "to fall in love with two lovely ladies at the same time?"

Behind him, he heard a wee voice call, "Peek-a-boo!"

Then another, sweet and clear answer, "I vow, I do not know what I shall do with you, Poppy. You are an outrageous little flirt."

Kendale knew there was no reason for a lady of such high breeding to take notice of him, yet he felt the need to hurry. He urged his horse into a canter and crossed the Serpentine Bridge, circled around and came back to pass her from the opposite direction. Her carriage had not progressed very far only that now an entirely new selection of the Fashionable World surrounded her and the little imp sitting beside her.

Finally, Kendale pulled his horse to the side of the carriage road where he could quietly observe her. Near enough so that he could hear her voice, but far enough as not to attract attention.

Meanwhile Caroline was weighing the merits of Poppy's popularity overpowering hers when a highflyer phaeton was stopped by the traffic and pulled up beside hers. The seat was situated so far above her that she had to crane her neck to see the driver, which was not a fashionable young buck, nor a man of address, as one would expect, but Miss Priscilla Whistlewaite who confidently handled the ribbons of the two spirited greys.

Next to her sat Mrs. Whistlewaite who was clutching the side of the carriage and not looking nearly as confident as her daughter. They seemed to be having a heated discussion and were oblivious to all that went on around them.

"You should have an orphan, Priscilla. Look at all the attention it is getting Lady Caroline. If you would cease to ride this dangerous vehicle you talked your father into buying you and show a little more womanly frailties, you might attract some titled gentleman."

"Mama I have told you that I shall marry whom I please."

Caroline's opinion of Miss Whistlewaite rose at that moment. Although she was not a beauty, Priscilla was a spirited girl and Caroline could not blame Elroy for being attracted to her. But he was such a fribble. There was no way a young woman with gumption would look at him twice. Caroline suddenly found herself feeling sorry for Elroy.

"Oh, here comes Lord Featherstone," Mrs. Whistlewaite exclaimed. "I do believe he is coming this way. Now be nice to him, dear. There is no reason why Miss Hughes should catch him when your father has far more money."

With a determined look on her face, Priscilla started to maneuver her carriage around Caroline's.

"Mrs. Whistlewaite. Miss Whistlewaite."

"Lady Caroline," simpered the elder woman. "We did not see you, my dear."

Priscilla reined up.

"Peek-a-boo!" called Poppy.

"So this is the little unfortunate I've been hearing about?" Mrs. Whistlewaite simpered.

Caroline only nodded.

Poppy took one look at Mrs. Whistlewaite and insisted on climbing onto Betsy's lap. She put her hands into her muff and smiled up at her nursemaid.

"I was just admiring your phaeton," Caroline addressed Priscilla.

"You were?" Priscilla said with interest.

Mrs. Whistlewaite piped in, "Isn't that nice of her to say so Priscilla, dear?"

"I was just comparing it to the high-perch phaeton that Mr. Bennington is thinking of purchasing."

Priscilla blinked. "Mr. Bennington?"

"Yes, Mr. Elroy Bennington."

She frowned. "I don't believe I know the gentleman."

Caroline didn't want to tell her how easy it was to overlook Elroy. "I am surprised you have not heard of him. Crack-whip, you know. He is a great admirer of yours."

"Really? And he is thinking of purchasing a high-perch phaeton?"

"Yes, but he has been hoping to find someone knowledgeable enough to look it over and tell him if it is a good bargain."

"You called him *Mister* Bennington," Mrs. Whistlewaite broke in.

"Oh, Mama! He may be very nice."

"But not good enough for my daughter."

Caroline took a deep breath. She could not believe she was

backing Elroy. "Mr. Bennington's sister is the Countess of Favor. My new stepmother."

"He is still a *mister,* Priscilla. Oh, my. Lord Featherstone is almost here. Smile, dear."

Priscilla slapped the reins down hard, the horses sprang forward and the Whistlewaites carriage nearly flew away.

Caroline laughed and called to her postillion, "Peter, it is time to go home. And if you get us away before Lord Featherstone reaches us, you shall have an extra night off next month."

Oh dear, why in the world she had championed Elroy she would never know. Now she must get word to him to hurry posthaste to Tattersall's to see if he could find a high-perch phaeton to purchase before he next tried to see Priscilla Whistlewaite.

Kendale waited for Lady Caroline's landau to pass him before he rode out onto the bridle path and made his way back to the mews.

"Did you have a good time, dear?" Miss Plunkett was propped up in bed waiting to hear all about their outing. "Tell me everything."

Betsy carried Poppy off to the nursery after the infant had thrown Miss Plunkett a kiss from the doorway and Caroline pulled a chair up to the bed.

"The smile on your face tells me that you did," said Miss Plunkett. "Was Poppy a good girl? I hope so, because I have another favor to ask of you."

This was all said so fast that Caroline had no time to comment or add to the conversation and before she knew it, she had promised to take Poppy to St. James Park the next day.

"Betsy is a dependable girl and will take good care of Poppy, but it takes two adults to watch after a child."

To Caroline this seemed quite impossible to believe. After

all, how could a child with legs less than twelve inches long outrun an adult? But she nodded her agreement as Miss Plunkett chattered on.

"The park is much better for children and the pond is not nearly as long as the Serpentine. There are so many birds for them to watch too. You must go earlier though. It was almost dark by the time you got back this afternoon."

"You didn't tell me how you are feeling," said Caroline, changing the subject in the hopes that Miss Plunkett would forget any further suggestions.

"Oh, much better, dear. I am certain I shall be up in a day or two. Now, I know you have a dinner engagement tonight, so I will not keep you any longer. Suzette came up to see me and wanted to know when you would return. She said you were expected at the Farleys' at eight and she would have your bath ready and your clothes laid out."

Caroline should have known when she started for the door that Miss Plunkett would think of something else to say.

"Oh, Missy, I forgot to tell you. Poppy does love to feed the ducks, so you must remember to ask Cook to give you a bag full of bread scraps before you go tomorrow."

By two o'clock of the next afternoon the little party had reached their destination.

"George, it is ridiculous for you to follow us about. No one is going to rob us in St. James Park in broad daylight," Lady Caroline said for the third time.

"I am just following Miss Plunkett's orders, m'lady. She says it takes two big people to watch one little one."

"But I am here, George, and I am the one who pays your wages."

The footman looked embarrassed. "Of course, you are, m'lady."

"Now I insist you go back to the carriage and wait for us. If we need anything, I will send Betsy to fetch you."

George bowed and returned reluctantly to where the Cavendish landau stood at the edge of the park.

It had been some time since Caroline had taken a walk in St. James Park and she found she looked forward to it. The pond was filled with such a variety of ducks, geese, swans and gulls that their colorful array of feathers rivaled that of the autumn leaves which still remained on the trees and bushes encircling the water.

"Betsy, here are the bread scraps," Caroline said, handing her the ugly, drawstring bag.

"Quack-quack!" Poppy said, clapping her hands.

Since Betsy had her hands and lap full with Poppy in the carriage on their way across town, Lady Caroline had found herself the keeper of the duck's food until they reached the park. The day promised to be so pleasant that Caroline had decided they would ride in the landau with the top down again. She placed the bag on the floor of the carriage out of sight, but Poppy was upset when it had been placed where she could not see it.

The sprite had seemed to know exactly where they were going when they left Cavendish House in the Square. Each time she called out, "Duck-duck," she insisted that Caroline show her the bag with the bread scraps. Finally Caroline plunked the sack on her lap where the child could have it in full view all the time.

At first it bothered Caroline that the drab, coarse-woven bag looked hideous sitting on her stylish kerseymere pelisse with high collar and three capes, but when she saw the satisfied look in Poppy's eyes, she began to wonder if the child's happiness were not more important than the raised brows of those in the passing carriages.

"Duck-duck," Poppy kept repeating, her gaze riveted on the bag as if to make sure it didn't disappear again.

Now that they were in the park and Betsy was custodian of the food, the fickle child transferred her attention to the maid. Caroline didn't know why this should bother her.

Even though there was a chill in the air, it was a glorious day. The fog had dissipated somewhat and the browns and reds and yellows of the leaves made up for the gray sky.

Caroline was surprised to see so many people she recognized walking the paths, and she stopped to visit with many of them. It was a clever idea of Miss Plunkett's to have her and Poppy dress alike. Today they were in blue, and she knew it would be said that Lady Caroline had not lost her touch of elegance. She was still the Incomparable.

When she met some acquaintances she had not seen since she'd come back from Tallyho, she told Betsy, "You go ahead. I will catch up to you in a minute."

Now Lady Caroline was not knowingly self-centered any more than any of her class. But like many who are born to an exalted position, she had been waited upon, spoiled, and never taught to consider being on time a virtue when everyone accommodated her whims.

Therefore, by the time she left her friends and started along the path, she was surprised to find that Betsy and Poppy were nowhere in sight. She was becoming annoyed that she had been left alone, when she heard a screech coming from the bushes near the pond.

Caroline never thought of herself as a frail maiden who shrank from danger and with her parasol raised to strike the villain, she charged. She rounded the bush to find Betsy sitting upon the grass, wailing.

"Whatever are you doing, Betsy?" Caroline asked.

Hovering over her was George. He had Poppy tucked under one arm while at the same time trying to help the maid up with the other.

Betsy halfway rose, but fell back again, wailing louder than before. "Oh, my lady, I think I broke my ankle."

"Nonsense," Caroline scolded. "No one breaks anything walking in St. James Park. I'm sure they don't allow it."

However, it was soon evident that with George hanging onto the wiggly Poppy, and Betsy pulling on the footman, they were all going to fall over in a heap if something was not done.

"For heaven's sake!" said Caroline, removing Poppy from under George's arm. "Help the girl up."

"Duck-duck!" demanded Poppy, casting Caroline what appeared to her to be a very accusing look.

When Betsy was at least upright although leaning heavily on the footman for support, Caroline asked her what had happened.

"Poppy started such a racket, calling, 'Tom-tom, Tom-tom,' and pointing to the brush over there. I were trying to take some bread out of the bag for her to feed it—whatever it was she saw. Before I knew it, off she scampered. I reckon it were this root here I stumbled over," she said, pointing to the long protruding leg of the tree running along the ground.

"It was lucky that I happened to come by to see if you needed anything," George said, sounding suspiciously like someone who had been spying on them from the bushes all along.

"Don't be such a watering pot, girl," Caroline said with a little more feeling. "I'm not going to throw you out."

"Thankee, milady. I don't know what I'd do if you sent me home."

"Tom-tom," said Poppy, sticking out her lower lip.

"Now don't you start crying on me too," Caroline said. "Whatever is a Tom-tom, Betsy?"

"Don't know, milady. She comes up with new words every day and she may have started naming the ducks. I know she'll be disappointed if she don't get to feed them," Betsy said, starting to sob all over again.

"Well, we don't want to disappoint her now, do we," Caroline said.

"George, carry Betsy back to the carriage and I shall take Poppy to feed the ducks."

"Oh, no, my lady!" they cried in unison.

George seemed not to know which way to go. "I think it best if you come back with us, m'lady, and as soon as I have Betsy settled in the carriage, I can accompany you and Miss Poppy to feed the *you-know-whats.*"

"Duck-duck," Poppy said hopefully, looking at the footman.

Caroline chose to ignore the servants' exaggerated expressions of pending doom. "For heaven's sake! It doesn't take an army to watch one little girl. Now, George, do as I say."

"Oh, my lady!" Betsy wailed as George started to carry her off.

"Betsy, I do hope I shall not have to experience your crocodile tears every time I give you an order. Now where is the bread bag?" Caroline asked, looking around.

"I don't know, and that's the truth," Betsy replied from over George's shoulder. "It flew out of my hand when I tripped."

"Give it no never mind. I shall find it. Do get her back to the carriage, George."

The footman hesitated. "One of us needs to stay with you, milady."

"George! Carry the silly girl to the carriage, then come back. I shall wait for you here if you insist."

Poppy had become very quiet now, staring at the branches of a weeping willow tree which hung like a curtain near the pond.

"Now Miss Poppy wipe your tears. We shall get the bread and we will feed your ducks," Caroline said, setting Poppy on her feet.

But retrieving the bread scraps was not going to be as easy as Caroline thought. The bag had caught in the high branches of a bush and Caroline found she would have to reach over her head to untangle the string. That would scuff her soft leather half-boots and possibly tear her lovely kerseymere pelisse. She glanced about to see if she could find some gentleman to ask. But finding none that looked capable or would be willing to rip their own finery, Caroline had to come up with another solution.

Poppy stuck her finger in her mouth and stared at Caroline.

Caroline knew that she had to prove herself or forever feel herself a failure.

"You don't believe that I can do it, do you?" she said to Poppy as though the infant could understand. "Well, Caroline Cavendish is no green girl just out of the schoolroom. I have escaped from kidnappers, I'll have you know."

Poppy did not look impressed.

"Now what it comes down to is that we have to get the bread bag ourselves. All we need is a good long stick."

Caroline placed Poppy on a bench beside the path and began to search along the edge of the heavy brush and under the bushes and trees which lined the pond.

She finally saw what she wanted, a long forked branch with a hook on the end. But it took longer than she thought to retrieve the stick without tearing her coat.

"Now, young lady, let us get your bread," she said, proudly brandishing her tool. However, Caroline found she spoke to an empty bench. "Poppy?

Caroline experienced fright as she had never done before, and was near to calling for help when she saw a stranger coming toward her from the embankment of the pond. In his arms he carried a wet bedraggled bundle, her bonnet hanging by its ribbons, her curls soaked.

"Poppy!" Caroline ran toward them and frantically grabbed the child from his arms. "Oh, Poppy!"

Poppy twisted around, pointing back to the pond. "Tom-tom!" she said urgently. "Tom-tom!"

Her babbling made no sense at all to Caroline. All she could think of was holding the child tightly to her bosom to keep her safe.

A crowd had gathered and only after she'd felt Poppy all over, hugged her several times to convince herself that no great harm had been done, did Caroline say, "It's all right, She's fine."

Caroline had paid no attention to the man standing in front of her until he spoke:

"And who would have ever thought I'd find a wee pixie coming up out of the pond in St. James Park? 'Tis a sign for sure that the day of miracles is not passed after all."

The rhythmic cadence of his words made her cognizant of his presence, and she looked up to face the stranger. "You are most kind, sir," Caroline commenced, but she did not finish. Her mouth dropped open.

He was a tall man, his broad shoulders made larger by his many-caped coat, much of which was sodden and hanging with grasses from the pond. His hatless head revealed heavy dark hair in complete disarray. A devilish grin spread across his swarthy face, but it was his eyes which were regarding her so intently that startled her. Green! Green as the Irish Sea! Caroline would never have believed that there could be any two people in the whole world who had those same green eyes unless she had seen them herself.

# Ten

"I say, Caro," interrupted an irritating high-pitched voice.

The spell was broken. "Elroy!" Caroline said while trying with great difficulty to keep the wiggling Poppy from climbing back into the stranger's arms.

"Zounds! Whatever happened to you? Didn't anyone ever tell you it ain't healthy to take a plunge this time of year?"

Caroline glowered at him.

Her setdown had no effect on the popinjay. "Any fool can see it's way too cold. You talk about me being dippy in the noodle."

Before she could answer, Elroy had already turned to greet the man beside her. "Hey, if it ain't you too. Blessed if it ain't," Elroy said almost reverently as he looked the man up and down. "You was dry just a few minutes ago when I left you."

His solicitous tone of voice did not escape Caroline's notice. "Elroy," Caroline repeated between her teeth.

"Oh, yeh! Heh, heh. Right oh! May I present my *niece* Lady Caroline," Elroy said pompously, with his usual accompaniment of irritating noises. "This is Mr. Kendale."

"Kendale?" Caroline could say no more. This was the man Lord Blackmere was supposed to be sponsoring. She heard Lady Sefton's words. *"He's probably the son of a local squire, my dear."* No local squire's son would have those eyes . . . Not unless!

"I believe you should get the child home immediately and into dry clothes." The voice was clear and resonant and with a slight lilt or rhythmical cadence to it which she could not quite place. "Do you have a carriage rug to wrap around her?"

"What?" Caroline asked, shaking her head to clear the cobwebs.

"Do you have a carriage rug to wrap around her?"

"I don't know . . . that is, it seemed warm enough . . . I didn't think we needed one . . . ," she stammered.

Mr. Kendale had already removed his wet surtout and handed it to Elroy to hold while he divested himself of his riding coat. "Here, put this around her. It is dry and will keep her warm until you get her back to Cavendish House."

He wrapped his coat around Poppy. She stuck her finger in her mouth and stared up at Mr. Kendale over the collar of his blue superfine while she quietly studied the stranger in that contemplative way which Caroline now recognized so well. Then she smiled at him—not a shy little smile—but a big, wide, happy grin.

Poppy never smiled at her, Caroline thought. She smiled at Miss Plunkett, she smiled at Betsy, and Caroline noticed she had the giggles every time she saw Driggs. Of course that was understandable, Driggs always tickled her. But now she was giving a perfect stranger her gift of laughter. Why, Caroline wondered, didn't the child do the same with her?

Then she saw George, his expression a mixture of anxiety and relief, making his way toward them.

"Milady, what has happened? I heard people say a child had fallen into the pond. Betsy is quite upset. She said it could only be her little sprite doing such a thing."

"Oh, George! I am thankful that you have come. Take Poppy back to the carriage," she said, handing the dripping child to her footman. "I just want to thank Mr. Kendale here for . . ." Caroline turned and saw only Elroy.

"Why did Mr. Kendale leave? I did not dismiss him," Caroline said sharply to cover her embarrassment—or was it disappointment? It was all very confusing and she didn't even want to contemplate the feelings which were becoming all jumbled up inside of her.

"He ain't the sort who wants hoity-toity nobs fawning over him."

"I am not a hoity-toity nob, Elroy."

"Well, if you ain't, you certainly spend a lot of your time with the like. How would you feel if you had certain people flub you off because you don't have a title?" Elroy said, sticking out his lower lip.

"I was not going to *fawn* or *flub,* Elroy," Caroline said, surprising herself for feeling sympathy for the boy. "It is my duty to thank him, no matter what his station. It was rude of him to leave before I said he could. That is all I meant. Where does he come from anyway? I could not place his accent."

"Don't have the foggiest. Never heard him talk like that before. Must be his way when he's trying to come up sweet with a lady," Elroy said, guffawing obnoxiously.

Caroline wondered how she could have thought to intercede with Miss Whistlewaite on the behalf of this ninnyhammer. She had a mind not to tell him at all about purchasing a high-flyer phaeton. "Elroy, how could you attach yourself to such a . . . a person. Why, he is a known sharper."

"Just shows how much you know about such things. Mr. Kendale's a great gun, Caroline—knows how to turn a card all right. Says he learned the tricks in the Orient."

"The Orient?"

"He's been all over the world. Knows how to say thank you in twelve different languages."

"Well, I am glad to hear Mr. Kendale is so literate. That still doesn't excuse his ill manners or change the fact that you shouldn't be gambling, Elroy."

"Posh! You women don't enjoy life by half. I reckon if I watch him closely I'll soon pick up some of his tricks."

"And I suppose every other noddy of your circle of acquaintances has the same misconception."

"Well . . . maybe so . . . but Kendale's different. Besides I like to think *someone* likes me."

"He's only setting you up for the pickings, Elroy."

"No, he ain't! Poindexter and Lord Dribble will do anything to get him to take them to the hells along the waterfront. Mr. Kendale seems to know all the bang up ones. He asks me to come along because I don't toady up to him."

Caroline threw up her hands. "I'm sure he's attracted to your quick wit and savoir-faire. How much has he skinned you for, Elroy?"

"Now, don't get your dander up, Caro," he said, forgetting in the heat of the moment of how she'd forbidden him to use her shortened name. "I haven't lost but a couple centuries here and there. He always lets me try to win it back . . . at least most."

"But other gamblers may not be as generous."

"That shows how much you know. In fact, he warns me away from the real sharpers. I tell you, Kendale has saved me more than I've lost."

"Well, it isn't my worry. It's your father's," Caroline said. "You can lose everything you have as far as I'm concerned. I wash my hands of you *and* Mr. Kendale," Caroline said, turning toward the waiting carriage where she saw George handing Poppy to the anxious Betsy. "Now I am going home before Poppy catches her death."

"Well if you really want to know it all," Elroy said, dogging her steps, "Mr. Kendale didn't just ask me if I wanted to stop and stretch m'legs in the park. He took me with him to Tattersall's this morning to look at some carriages. He told me that what I needed was a phaeton. Not just any type, but a high-perch phaeton. They're all the crack now, you know."

Caroline stopped dead in her tracks.

"Never had a rig like that before. Well, what do you think?"

By now Caroline's mouth had fallen wide open.

"Ain't never seen you without something to say."

"That sounds . . . just the thing for you, Elroy," Caroline answered. "By the strangest coincidence, I . . . I overheard Miss Whistlewaite say only yesterday that she surely would be pleased to find a man who could drive a high-perch phaeton."

"She didn't."

"Yes, she did."

"Then I'll do it, Caro. I'll buy the bang up thing."

"You might seek Miss Whistlewaite's very good opinion first, Elroy. She rides in Hyde Park in the afternoons."

Caroline climbed into the carriage. She couldn't believe she'd done that. Actually aided Elroy.

"Well, I never. Did you see that, Persimmonie?"

"I certainly did. Disgraceful! It was that Kendale person, wasn't it?"

Lady Tewilliger and Mrs. Browne peered out of their carriage as it passed alongside St. James Park.

"She was talking to him right in public as if he were one of us."

"First, she made a spectacle of herself dangling after that rude Lord Blackmere, and now we see her with that gambler they say he sponsors. Do you think there is anything in it?"

"Where there is smoke there is fire, my dear," Lady Tewilliger said smugly. "You mark my words, Lady Caroline Cavendish had better watch her p's and q's, because if she persists in flouting the rules of the *haute ton,* she will find herself cut by Fashionable Society."

"Well what can one expect from the daughter of a coxcomb like Randolph Cavendish? Marrying a gel less than a third his age when there are so many more mature ladies of quality about," said Mrs. Browne with a sniff.

"And after you were so nice to him too," Lady Tewilliger said sympathetically.

"You are being silly," scolded Miss Plunkett from her rocking chair where she sat knitting in her room beside the nursery. "There is no reason why you cannot take Poppy out again. The child needs fresh air."

For three days after Poppy had fallen into the duck pond, Lady Caroline would not allow the child out of the house. She refused to admit that she was being foolish, or that she was to blame for what happened at St. James's Park. She only knew that she never wanted to experience the fear she had felt when she discovered that Poppy had disappeared. She convinced herself that the simplest way to avoid another near disaster was to keep the child locked up in the nursery, forever if need be.

But even that didn't seem to work.

There were two occasions during those days—once in her bedroom and once in the library—when Caroline had looked up to find the toddler standing in the doorway observing her. Both times, Caroline's discovery was followed by a distraught Betsy.

"Oh, milady, I don't know how the little rascal got here. I put her down for her nap. I thought she were asleep and went to check on Miss Plunkett. She will be so upset with me," the girl said, beginning to cry.

The remembrance of the horrendous sense of responsibility demanded by her old nurse suddenly overwhelmed Caroline, and for a frightening moment, she had found herself identifying with the quaking girl.

"I shall not report you to Miss Plunkett," Caroline had said, with some understanding of the girl's plight.

"Thankee, milady," replied Betsy, dabbing at her eyes. "But with Miss Plunkett in bed, I cannot keep up with the baby."

Now Caroline was standing in Miss Plunkett's room,

dressed in her bright blue carriage dress. "Suzette is waiting for me downstairs," she said, trying to avoid Miss Plunkett's riveting eyes.

"I see no reason if you are going to Hyde Park that you cannot take Poppy with you."

"But what if something should happen to her?" If she were so shattered by the thought of harm coming to Poppy, Caroline thought, what would she do if she really were hurt?

"She will not be running around there," Miss Plunkett said. "She will be in the carriage. By-the-by, has George's cousin, Mr. Diggers, found out anything about Poppy's background?" she asked hesitantly.

"No. He said that Mr. Stubbs at the mews told him that someone was on duty all round the clock that day—and there was no way that a baby could have gotten into the coach by herself. John Coachman insisted he'd not dilly-dallied anywhere after he'd driven out of the stables until he stopped in front of Cavendish House in the Square. We left the hamper at Tallyho, but Cook said that it was not one of hers because none were missing from the kitchen."

"Well, I suppose it will just have to remain a mystery," said Miss Plunkett trying hard to sound remorseful.

"Yes, I suppose it must," replied Caroline just as happily. Poppy had become so much a part of their lives that she could not imagine how she would feel if the little girl were taken away altogether.

"I will only agree to take her when you are well enough to accompany us."

"Well, then," said Miss Plunkett, throwing off the afghan lying across her knees. "I shall come too—and don't give me that *look,* my lady. The fresh air will probably do me more good than this smoke-filled room."

Thus persuaded, Caroline agreed. "I shall tell Betsy to get Poppy ready and that you are coming with me instead."

"Betsy will be distraught if she cannot come, my lady. She has taken it into her head that she is Poppy's sole guardian and thinks she mustn't let the child out of her sight."

"Nonsense, I am sure she will be very glad to have the rest of the afternoon to do as she pleases," Caroline said.

But when Betsy was informed that she would have to stay behind, she commenced such a caterwauling that Caroline had to put her hands over her ears.

"I don't think Betsy trusts you with Poppy after what happened at St. James Park," Miss Plunkett said, the light once more shining in her eyes.

"All right! All right, girl. You can come if you will only stop that blubbering."

"Thankee, milady," Betsy said, blowing her nose. "I shall have the baby ready in a trice."

So they all set out in the landau: Miss Plunkett in her winter hooded cape, a fur coach rug wrapped round her and her hands snug in a fur muff, Betsy and Suzette, Lady Caroline and Poppy. George proudly guarded the rear and Peter rode the lead horse. They made quite an interesting spectacle as they drove through the south entrance onto Rotten Row.

In spite of the brisk weather, there were still many riders and several carriages in the park—many of those enclosed—yet most stopped to wave greetings or pay their respects to Lady Caroline.

For some minutes Kendale had remained where he was, watching them. Supposing that Lady Caroline would not return to St. James Park any time soon after the child had fallen in the pond, he had been coming to Hyde Park every day since in the hopes of seeing his lady. Rewards came to those who persevered, he reminded himself. Now, as always, he was stunned by her beauty. But when he observed the odd assortment of passengers accompanying her, amusement replaced euphoria, and he urged his horse toward them.

Then, there he was—looking down at them from the great height of his high-stepping roan.

Poppy reacted first "Duck-duck!" she cried, crawling from one lap to the other to get to him.

His eyes sparkling like emeralds he said, "It's glad I am to see the wee sprite is no worse off for taking a bath in the pond."

Seven pairs of eyes turned upward to mark the man, but only the child moved. Her little hands and legs churned as fast as they could to take her to him. Six pairs of hands reached out to catch her—too late. Poppy tumbled over the side of the coach.

Kendale caught Poppy and raised her high in the air before passing her back to the waiting hands in the carriage. "Nabbed in the act, my little duckling," he said.

Poppy screamed with delight. "Quack-quack," she cried, looking back at him and flapping her arms.

"Quack-quack, yourself," he answered, and throwing back his head, laughed uproariously.

Caroline had gasped for breath when Poppy fell out of the carriage, but it was the sound of Mr. Kendale's laughter which made her think she'd stopped breathing altogether. A fascinating, confusing feeling ran through her as she gaped at his handsome face. His eyes sought hers and for a moment she sat mesmerized until he looked quickly away. But now everyone reached for the child, and Poppy was passed round to be hugged by all until she ended up in Caroline's lap.

All eyes now turned to Lady Caroline, who explained to Miss Plunkett and Suzette that Mr. Kendale was the man who had saved Poppy from drowning in St. James Park. Attention once again switched to the young man and smiles of gratitude were bestowed upon him by one and all.

"Mr. Kendale," Caroline began—then stopped. He was regarding her now through shadowed eyes. This confused her for she could not discern if he admired her or held her in contempt. In spite of the tremor shooting through her, she went on calmly,

"You left the park so quickly the other day that I was not able to thank you properly for saving my ward."

All during his rides over the last few days, Kendale had been rehearsing what he would say to her. Now that she was here, he could not think what that had been. So he said nothing.

Caroline cleared her throat. "Your coat was quite wet and wrinkled after you so graciously let us use it. It has been cleaned and pressed. If you will stop by Cavendish House in the Square you may pick it up. You need only ask for my butler, Driggs. He will fetch it for you."

Kendale inclined his head and backed his horse away from the landau.

His departure fueled an animated conversation between every one of its occupants—except one—all the way back to Cavendish House in the Square.

Caroline usually found men's minds to be so easily read. She wished she knew what Mr. Kendale had been thinking.

Across the carriage road a coach approached from the opposite direction. Inside two faces pressed against the small windows. "I told you, Persimmonie. That meeting is not a coincidence."

"You are right. He had to have been waiting. He came up and spoke to her just as bold as can be," Mrs. Browne agreed.

"It is fortunate that my coachman happened to go past Cavendish House this afternoon at the same time that Lady Caroline's carriage came out. The next thing you know she'll be inviting that here-and-therian into her house," Lady Tewilliger said, leaning back with a satisfied smile on her lips.

Rain fell heavily for the next two days. On the third, Lady Caroline looked out her bedroom window and declared that the skies did not appear to be so threatening.

"Suzette, it is the last day of the watercolor exhibit at the

Academy and I promised Miss Plunkett at breakfast that she should see it. While the coach is being brought round, I shall go up to see if she is ready."

At that same time, on the opposite side of the street from Cavendish House, Kendale was waiting for an approaching coach to pass him before he could cross over. His morning walk had brought him as usual to her house and what better excuse to stop than to pick up his riding coat. The coach rolled by, slowing down considerably before pulling over to the curb.

Just as Kendale was halfway up the steps of the splendid house it began to rain again. He hunched his shoulders and pulled on the knocker.

In the coach parked on the other side of the street, Lady Tewilliger rubbed a circle on the foggy window and peered out. Her coachman had gone round the square three times since she'd spotted that Kendale person.

Lady Tewilliger smacked her lips in anticipation as she watched the front door open, and who should be standing there to greet Mr. Kendale—not the butler nor even the footman—but the mistress of the house herself. She saw Lady Caroline smile and bid the man enter.

"Well," Lady Tewilliger said aloud to herself. "Wait until you hear that we were right, Persimmonie. My husband said I was barking up the wrong tree when I told him Lady Caroline would soon have that man in her house, but I can always tell the signs."

Late that evening, most of the tables in the card-room at White's were filled. Kendale's face remained a mask. Damn! He'd never had trouble before blocking out all distractions when he was involved in a game of chance.

Although Kendale's name was not mentioned, it was impossible for his three opponents not to hear the escalating argument in the next room. Poindexter Gray's sniveling innuendoes about the Incomparable Lady Caroline's fall from grace—having been seen several times consorting with a well-known rakehell—were being challenged by Elroy Bennington's incensed rebuttals of the remarks against his sister's family.

Kendale wondered what muck the busybodies had been spreading now. Some gossipmonger must have reported his visit to Cavendish House when he went to pick up his riding coat. A servant perhaps? News below stairs always spread fast. But the servants of Cavendish House would have known that their mistress had been standing in the hall with her companion and elderly nurse awaiting their coach. Lady Caroline had invited him in because it was raining. There had been no other purpose on her part. The ladies had departed moments later when their carriage had arrived. Then the butler had sent a boy to fetch a hired hackney for him.

But the damage had been done. No matter how accidental he tried to make his meetings with her appear—any association with him now could only bring further ruination, and that had not been his intention.

Kendale's opponents began to clear their throats, drum their fingers on the table, and finally find excuses to leave.

"I say, Kendale. You're a dull fellow tonight. You've been sitting there ten minutes staring into space," Lord Beary said, pushing back from the table.

Kendale merely nodded and continued shuffling the deck of cards. He had come too far to back out now for he sensed that the Incomparable Lady Caroline was warming to his society. He'd even made her laugh. And the way that she looked at the child tore at his heart. There was something in her expression that he'd not seen before.

Kendale slapped the cards down on the table. Who were they—the pompous—the high sticklers—the ones who called themselves the first class of Society—to say that he could not see her?

He'd fool them. They would not admit the plain Mr. Kendale into their parlors, so he would just have to become Lord Blackmere again.

Kendale pushed his chair back from the table and rose. "Ah," he said, " 'Tis a pity I did not take up acting as a career."

When he stepped out into the cold December air, Kendale thought the long walk back to his house on Grace Church Street would clear the anger from his guts; but to the contrary, the longer he dwelt on the tittle-tattle, the bombastic, insufferable, stuffy, self-righteous insinuations, the more determined he became to beat them at their game—and the more steadfast was his determination to call again at Cavendish House on the morrow.

Kendale entered his lodgings and began to pack his bags to move to Lord Blackmere's apartment in Ryder Street. He stuffed in the breeches, the scratchy knee-length stockings and the miserable old wig. Then he started to laugh. What would all those priggish aristocrats think if they knew that he had been pretending to be Lord Blackmere for four years now? They had begged him to join them in their theater boxes, in their mansions and at their balls. But once he removed these pitiful, pathetic, outdated clothes, they wouldn't even give him the time of day.

# Eleven

Kendale remembered exactly when it was that he'd gotten the idea of masquerading as Lord Blackmere. It was three weeks after his interview with Mr. Chumbley. That was over four years ago.

Jon had come to London, looking crestfallen. "I did as you told me, Master Kendale. The village folk either say they haven't seen anybody like Lord Blackmere, or else they ain't telling me if they did. I fear the village folk dasn't trust strangers overly much."

"I don't want to call the authorities to report him missing, Jon, because if his lordship is in trouble that will only make it worse."

Jon's eyes grew enormous.

Kendale almost laughed. "Do not fret, my friend. I believe I have come up with a better idea. If I were a member of the aristocracy, I could easily enter the stateliest houses of the *ton*nish world; I could meet and ask questions of Lord Blackmere's friends; I could even gain entrance to the hallowed male citadels such as White's and Watier's, which are gold mines of information."

"I always thought you were one of the Upper Orders, Mr. Kendale. Lord Blackmere treated you like one. I know his lordship thought you were smart enough to understand all that book-learning or he wouldn't have spent so many hours teaching you."

It was true, Kendale thought. Lord Blackmere had somehow transferred his own love of books to him and encouraged him to better himself. He was the kindest man Kendale had ever known. When his lordship learned of Kendale's fascination with the sea, hadn't he used his influence to obtain him a berth on a merchant ship sailing for the Orient.

"By the by, Jon, what did Lord Blackmere look like when you last saw him? You know; how did he wear his hair, had he put on weight, how did he dress? It's been over eleven years since I have seen him."

Jon had narrowed his eyes and chewed his lower lip, concentrating hard to conjure up a picture of Lord Blackmere. "He were a bit heavier. Grandfather said he always wore wigs because he was losing his hair."

Kendale could not help but smile. "Those crazy wigs," he said, laughing."I suppose I could inquire around the theaters to see where I can purchase such a costume."

Jon leaned forward eagerly. "Lord Blackmere used to give my grandfather his old clothes when he were through with them. Grandfather's trunk is still in the cottage. I didn't move anything after he died. I think I remember seeing one of his lordship's wigs," Jon added helpfully. "Grandfather used to like to put it on. He said it made him feel like a real gentleman," Jon said. "I am on my way back north now, Master Kendale. I'll be passing through Wickett and can take a look."

"You do that, Jon. Since no one in London except Chumbley has seen Lord Blackmere for twenty years or so, and if no one else remembers what he looked like, I see no reason why we cannot get away with the charade. But now to other matters. When Lord Blackmere is in Town, he must have a valet."

A look of confusion spread across Jon's simple face. "But we haven't found Lord Blackmere yet."

Kendale explained patiently. "I am referring to myself Jon. I will be Lord Blackmere."

Jon broke into a wide smile, nodding. "Oh, yes, sir. I understand, sir. Like the players at the country fair."

"That's right. We are going to be actors in a play. Now, you have always wanted to be a gentleman's gentleman. Do you think you can pretend to be one?"

Jon's face had turned a ruddy pink. "Oh, yes, sir, Master Kendale. My grandfather taught me to be the best." He looked down at his rough woven jacket, frowning. "I don't know that I have the clothes for looking the proper gentleman's gentleman though, sir."

"I shall buy you a most respectable suit, Jon. After all, we must both look up to the rigs. You shall be the envy of every valet in London."

A wide smile spread across Jon's face.

"Now off with you. The quicker you can fetch Lord Blackmere's clothing, the sooner we can begin our game."

For his first appearance in Town, Kendale had thought it better *ton* to settle Lord Blackmere at the Pultney in Piccadilly. A fashionable residence for his initial introduction seemed only fitting; besides, to do so fueled Kendale's sense of humor. God only knew, he needed some comedy in his life at this point.

Kendale had found his walrus mustache and bushy eyebrows in a costume maker's shop near Drury Lane. The wool knee-length stockings which Jon brought scratched his legs and the old wig made him look like a nincompoop, but the costume was so bizarre that it was accepted.

"I appreciate your helping me with this, Jon. It cannot be easy for you to keep up with your journeying and helping me, too."

"I would not think of abandoning you, sir. My devotion to you is only exceeded by my loyalty to his lordship."

Later Kendale had found a bachelor apartment for Lord Blackmere in Ryder Street near the clubs in St James Street. At first Kendale took advantage of this address himself, but his business expanded and a great deal more of his time became taken up with shipping matters.

Now for more convenience he'd moved to a furnished apartment in Grace Church Street near the waterfront and a short walk to both the Bank of England and the Royal Exchange. Only when he pretended to be Lord Blackmere did he move back to Ryder Street, as he planned to do tonight.

Kendale would have to think up some excuse for his valet's absence when he checked into the hotel in Ryder Street. Perhaps he'd invent a taradiddle about Jon having come down with a cold—he grinned—or he'd say his valet had to go to his grandfather's funeral.

Lady Caroline sat in a comfortable chair before the fire in her sitting room, reading her stepmother's usual Tuesday letter emploring her to come for Christmas. Mary also wrote that she'd had no word from her darling brother Elroy, and she wondered if Caroline would check on him. This put Caroline in more of the dismals than she had been. It was more than enough having the annoying jackanapes popping up like a jack-in-the-box when she least expected it, let alone asking her to seek him out.

Even Lord Featherstone had deserted her for Priscilla Whistlewaite. Elroy had been devastated that the object of his undying love had accepted another. Even his purchase of a high-flyer phaeton had not saved him. But then, falling out of it in front of Miss Whistlewaite when tooling neck or nothing along Rotten Row in Hyde Park had not added to his image of a crack whip.

There was a knock on the door of her chambers and Caroline gave her permission to enter.

It was Driggs. "There is a gentleman to see you, my lady."

No one of any consequence had come to call in over a week and for some reason she did not care. It was probably Jamie Stessels. He'd been making a pest of himself lately. He reminded her of a tart with a cherry for a nose—and so deep into Dun Territory that no sensible girl would have him.

"Tell the gentleman that I am indisposed, Driggs."

"Yes, my lady," the butler said, closing the door.

It had begun to worry Lady Caroline that no one had asked to escort her to Lady Dankleish's Masquerade Ball, and it was little more than a week away. Many of the Quality returned to Town just for that event, then it was off to their country estates for the rest of the Holiday Season.

Lady Caroline was determined to win Grand Prize for the most original couple as she had the past two years but she needed an outstanding partner to do that.

The picture of a tall, dark-haired young man with merry green eyes came to mind. What a splendid couple they would make at the ball. But a man of such questionable background—no matter how well-looking—would never be accepted at such a prestigious, *ton*nish event.

Caroline had taken Poppy to St. James's Park the previous day. Miss Plunkett told her that the only way to fight a fear was to face it. She, Miss Plunkett, Betsy and George had a pleasant time watching over Poppy while she fed the ducks, but that was not the real reason Caroline had returned to the park. She hoped that she might catch a glimpse of Mr. Kendale, but alas, he was not there.

There was another knock on the door.

It was the butler again. "I am sorry, my lady, but the gentleman insists on staying."

"Tell him that I have a megrim, or better still, I broke my leg," she said with a chuckle. "No, wait. Who is it, Driggs?"

"Lord Blackmere, my lady."

Caroline's hand went to her chest. "Lord Blackmere? Oh, my goodness!" She jumped up and rang the bell for Suzette. "Why didn't you say so? Don't just stand there, Driggs. Show his lordship into the gold salon."

"I believe he has already gone into the library, my lady."

Caroline ran to the mirror to see how she looked just as Suzette came in. She could not explain her elation. Had he forgiven her for her rude behavior? Oh, she hoped so.

"Hurry, Suzette! Lord Blackmere is here to see me."

Suzette had never seen her mistress in such a dither over a man, and she worked as quickly as she could to comb her hair.

Ten minutes later Lady Caroline swept into the library with her head high and held out her hand. "Lord Blackmere, what a pleasant surprise," she said a little breathlessly. Joy, relief, and, yes, affection mingled in her heart as she gazed at the endearing floppy wig and the ridiculous outdated clothes.

The eagerness in her tone and the sight of the little curl which had fallen out of place on the Incomparable's smooth, flawless forehead was not lost on the false Lord Blackmere. "Lady Caroline," he rasped, his lips lingering a little longer than need be on her fingers. She did not recoil at his touch, he noted. Then his gaze swept up to her throat. Her frock was more modest than usual and had a high collar. He couldn't tell if she were wearing the black pearl or not. He had seldom seen her without it

Suzette came in with the serving girl and a tray of refreshments. Since Lord Blackmere made no mention of her having turned down his invitation to ride in the Park, she didn't either. Suzette repaired to the corner with a book, and Caroline served him tea. Within a few minutes, Caroline felt that no time had passed at all since his lordship's last visit, and she asked if he would like to come to a dinner party that she was giving Thursday, next.

"I would be honored," he said.

"I believe you know Lord and Lady Beary and the Seftons. There will only be a few others." She didn't want to tell him that she was short one gentleman, or add that she had been turned down by several of her former suitors.

Caroline was about to tell him of finding a baby in her coach when her hand flew to her mouth. She had forgotten about the Chinese Puzzle box, but she was not sure where Suzette had put it. Suddenly more than anything, she wished to have Lord Blackmere's good opinion.

"Oh, my lord," she said, jumping up. "I have something I want to show you. It will only take me a minute to fetch it. Come Suzette, I will need you to help me." With that Caroline ran out the door. How clever Lord Blackmere would think her when she showed him how quickly she could solve the puzzle.

Chuckling to himself over his successful deception Kendale rose, and after adjusting the pillow under his belt, strode over to the shelves to scan the magnificent collection. He'd done a fair job of sorting out many of the books, but wished he'd had time to do more. He had not been alone but a minute when he heard a rustling coming from the direction of the doorway, but saw nothing. Then a curtain moved, he heard a giggle and a tiny face wreathed in yellow curls peered round. "Peek-a-boo!"

She came out then and stood there with a finger in her mouth, intently studying him.

Kendale had a horrible feeling in the pit of his stomach that disaster was about to strike. For what seemed like an eternity they stared at each other.

Then with a squeal, Poppy scampered across the room as fast as her little legs could carry her, and threw her arms around his knees, hobbling him. "Quack! Quack!" she shouted gleefully.

Something akin to panic ran through Kendale at that moment, and he had visions of his whole charade being unmasked. "No, sweetings," he said, dislodging her fingers from the back of his legs. "Come," he said, swinging her up and carrying her across to the sofa where he sat down and pulled her up onto his lap.

Poppy stared into his eyes and giggled. Then patted his wig and giggled again.

Good, lord! He hoped Lady Caroline did not take that moment to return. How could he explain the little duck's affectionate curiosity for him? At least she was quiet now, so Kendale let her touch his nose and stroke his mustache. He was safe. He could relax—or so he thought. There was a sharp, quick ripping sensation under his nose and Poppy proudly held up half of his mustache for him to see. Before he could catch her, she wiggled off his lap and scrambled for the door.

"You little rascal, are you in here?" came a distraught voice from the hallway. Betsy hurried into the room just as Poppy crashed into her. "You naughty girl," the maid said, picking the baby up and carrying her off. She did not even see the man in black who was watching helplessly as the little fist with a furry tail sticking out one end disappeared toward the stairway.

"Lord Blackmere?" Lady Caroline called, holding the Chinese Puzzle box behind her while she looked about the room. "I have a surprise for you."

In desperation, Kendale slapped his hand over the naked side of his face.

"Why whatever is the matter?" Caroline said with concern, as he turned his head from her. "Do you have a toothache?"

Kendale's brows shot up, and he nodded fervently.

"Is there anything I can do?" Caroline asked, handing Suzette the puzzle while she hurried to his side. "Let me see. Perhaps a hot press of tea leaves will relieve it."

He shook his head just as fervently as he had nodded it before. "I'd best be going," he rasped, and grabbing his hat from the stand, Lord Blackmere rushed out.

"The poor dear," Caroline said. "I know how terribly painful a toothache can be. But I do declare, Suzette, I am beginning to think that I shall never have a chance to show Lord Blackmere how clever I am."

In his hotel in Ryder Street, Kendale stuffed his costume into its bag. He could not believe that he'd been flummoxed by a little pixie only knee high. It was becoming too risky for him to play Lord Blackmere. He did not dare have his charade exposed now. Not while his mentor's life was still at stake.

As soon as it was dark, he would return to Grace Church Street. Jon should be turning up any day, and Kendale dreaded having to tell him that he had received another one of the disturbing letters written on brown paper.

That same evening high up in the Cavendish House nursery a struggle was going on. A very loud one from what Miss Plunkett was observing. "Whatever is the matter, Betsy?"

"Her nibs has something in her hand, ma'am, and won't give it up. Not even to have her supper or her sponge-off to go to bed."

Miss Plunkett looked at the fuzzy tip sticking out of Poppy's clenched fist. "What is it?"

"I don't know and that's for sure, ma'am."

"Well, it looks like a rabbit's foot. Mayhaps one of the servants gave it to her."

"A rabbit's foot is supposed to bring good luck. Isn't it, ma'am?"

One look at Poppy's defiant expression and the clinched fist, and Miss Plunkett smiled. "Yes, I hear it does, and we could all use a bit of that in our lives. Let her keep it. It can do no harm."

Poppy crawled into bed and went to sleep happily with the scrap of fur snuggled against her cheek.

"My goodness, Suzette, I cannot believe he would do such a thing." Lady Caroline perused again the message a serving maid had brought up to her dressing room.

The little French woman withdrew the comb which she'd picked up to repair the damage her mistress had done to her hair. "And *mademoiselle's* coiffure will look as if she has been holding onto an electrifying machine if she does not desist from running her fingers through it. Monsieur Damien just spent two hours arranging it for your dinner tonight."

"That is what I am talking about, Suzette. The dinner party. He isn't coming."

"Who is not coming, *mademoiselle?*"

"Lord Blackmere. He has sent a note refusing to come."

"Refusing?"

"Well, he does say he is sorry he cannot attend."

"Perhaps it is his tooth that is still hurting him."

"No, I believe he did it on purpose to punish me for what I did to him when I turned down his invitation to ride in the Park. What am I to do, Suzette? My seating arrangement is uneven again, and the guests will be arriving in another hour."

"You will just have to tell Driggs to have one of the settings removed."

Caroline had an uneasy feeling that something was going on and she couldn't put her finger on what it was. True, many of her friends left London for their country estates in December and only came back for such events as the Countess of Dankleish's Masquerade Ball, but for all that, she never had trouble filling her guest list. Members of *le beau monde* had always scrambled to receive an invitation to Cavendish House in the Square. Well, she would not let it disassemble her. She rang for Driggs.

Her hand had no sooner dropped the pull cord than there was a knock on the chamber door and there stood the butler.

"My goodness, Driggs, you are punctual," she said.

"I was on my way up to see you, my lady."

"Don't tell me someone else has cancelled for tonight. I don't think I could bear it."

"No, my lady. It is that *someone* not invited wishes to see you. I know you have instructed me to send him off if he calls, but he did seem so down in the dismals—never seen him so mumpish—even I felt sorry for him."

An uneasy feeling crept over Caroline. "Who in the world are you speaking of, Driggs?"

"Mr. Elroy Bennington, my lady. Now I know you have told me that you don't want him bothering you—but to tell the truth—I never seen him so well . . . he looks like he's about to come unhinged."

"For heaven's sakes! Elroy always looks as if he's coming

unhinged, but send him up anyway. I'll see him in my sitting room. I don't know what else can go wrong tonight." The butler was about to close the door when Caroline remembered why she'd rung for him. "Oh, Driggs, I nearly forgot, have one of the settings removed from the dinner table."

Five minutes later, Caroline had to watch as the lanky young man slumped and sloggled into her sitting room and collapsed into a contorted lump on the sofa, looking more like a dejected scarecrow than the pink of the ton as he tried to represent himself.

"Now, Elroy, why the Friday face?"

"Gad, Lady Caroline, there just ain't no use going on living is there?"

Caroline did not miss his use of her title. Elroy wanted sympathy. "I have a dinner party in just one hour. I have no time for theatrics."

"I just saw Lord Featherstone and Miss Whistlewaite coming out of her house. She was hanging onto his arm and throwing those sheep's eyes at him and he leaned down and bussed her on the cheek. It was enough to make a fellow sick."

"And what were you doing outside Miss Whistlewaite's house at this hour, Elroy?"

"I just happened to be going by in the hackney I'd hired."

"Her house is miles from your apartment."

"Well, dash it all, Caro. I don't know what she sees in him."

"Give it up, Elroy. Go to one of your clubs and lose lots of money or drink yourself under the table with some of your bucks and beaux."

"Don't want to. They're all talking about us . . . that is about my family and your father . . . and other things."

She looked at him suspiciously. "What other things, Elroy?"

"Don't make no difference. I'd just wish I could find somebody who liked me, that's all."

Caroline found herself empathizing with the boy and before

she knew it she'd said, "Elroy, do you think you could go home, dress and be back here in an hour? I need an extra man for my dinner party."

Elroy nearly flew off the sofa. "Do you really mean it, Caro? You're really a great gun, top of the trees, up the mark, stupendous. Be back in a trice," he said racing out the door.

Caroline supposed that was grand praise from Elroy. Well, at least she would have her table balanced. "Suzette," she said, "ring for Driggs and tell him to have the extra setting placed back on the table."

The next afternoon, Lady Caroline paced the floor of her chambers, waiting to find out if Suzette had been able to uncover any more information about the elusive Mr. Kendale and the whereabouts of Lord Blackmere,

Caroline had found out from Lady Sefton that she had a problem on her hands. How to handle it was another matter. What she needed was an escort to the Masquerade Ball and that possibility was fading fast.

Her dinner had gone as well as could be expected, much better than she could have hoped when she thought about what the potential had been just an hour before it began. But surprisingly, Elroy looked nice in his evening clothes and was so awed by the other guests that he kept quiet most of the meal.

Eventually the conversation had turned to the subject uppermost on everybody-who-was-anybody's minds at this time of year, the upcoming Masquerade Ball. The unattached young ladies and gentlemen were eager to announce who their partners were to be, but when they asked Caroline the same question, she only gave them a secretive smile. In her opinion it was nobody's business that she had not yet found an escort.

It was Lady Sefton's puzzling remarks later in the evening that began to shed some light on why of the thirty-eight people she had invited to dinner, only eighteen accepted. And eight of those were older married couples like the Seftons and Bearys who were friends of her family.

When the ladies had repaired to the drawing room while the men had their port and cigars, Lady Sefton had pulled her aside. "I must warn you, my dear, there are *on-dits* being spread round of the most disagreeable nature."

Caroline was surprised by Lady Sefton's allusion to gossip, because the gentle lady always made it clear that she would not take part in idle chatter.

"About whom?"

"You, my dear. That is why I am giving you a warning."

"What have I done that is improper?"

"It is not so much *what* but with *whom.* A certain young man is mentioned whom you have been observed meeting—more than once—even in this house. I am afraid, my dear, that Society's leaders do not deem him or your behavior acceptable."

Oh, my goodness, Caroline thought. She means Mr. Kendale.

"That is ridiculous," she said aloud. "He saved my Poppy from drowning. I only ran into him by chance and good manners dictated that I be civil. Besides, he *is* permitted into the best clubs."

"The men may accept him in their exclusive male world, but he would not be welcomed into their homes to mingle with their wives and daughters. If a young lady is thought not to be all that she should be, she will have no chance of a good marriage."

Caroline's ire was beginning to surface. "Well I declare. Who are the gossipmongers who started such tales?"

"I would not tell you if I did know, my dear. All I can say is that the stories grow more preposterous with each telling. Do not break any more rules. *Le beau monde* is very unforgiving to a young, unmarried woman who does not adhere strictly to their code. So conduct yourself with propriety and the whole incident will soon blow over and be forgotten."

# Twelve

Now that Caroline knew why she was being shunned by the women and avoided by the men, it only whetted her curiosity to learn more about the mysterious Mr. Kendale. Where had she read "Forbidden fruit is sweetest?"

A few minutes later there was a knock on the door and Suzette with her cheeks pink from the exercise of climbing the stairs, sailed in.

Caroline did not give her time to sit down. "Did you find out anything?"

"Suzette really didn't have to go beyond the kitchen. It is amazing what information is available right under us. You should go there sometime."

Caroline had only been belowstairs a couple times in her life, and those were when she was a little girl. "Suzette you are naughty to keep me waiting."

"George is a book of information for Suzette, and he sent one of the boys to inquire about things he did not know. Lord Blackmere left his hotel in Ryder Street and the proprietor does not know when he will be back.

"Suzette found out that Mr. Kendale is not all that he appears to be either. George says that he owns four ships and is having another made to his own plans. He trades in the Orient and the West Indies. He is considered to have accumulated quite a large fortune in the last few years. Yet, he lets a modest apartment somewhere near the Thames."

Caroline was surprised to hear this. She had thought he lived by the cards. No one would know by his appearance that Mr. Kendale was rich. His clothes were of good quality but not pretentious nor made by the best tailors like Weston, and now she found that he lived frugally. For a man who supposedly possessed a great fortune, he did not flaunt it. So what was he doing with his money?

She sighed to think of the waste. Not only was Mr. Kendale one of the most handsome men she had ever met, but she was finding that he was rich as well. If only he had a title, she could take him to the Masquerade Ball. She could picture Mr. Kendale dressed in the embroidered satin robes of the Emperor of old Cathay and she, his Empress in jeweled gown at his side. She would be the envy of every woman in the room. But he was not *ton* and perhaps he did not know how to dance. At least, Lord Blackmere knew how to waltz.

"I declare, Suzette, those two men have been causing me no end of trouble of late."

"Why do you fret about two, *mademoiselle,* when you have all the other men in London at your feet?"

"I do not and you know it. If Lord Blackmere had not deserted me, I would have allowed him to escort me to Lady Dankleish's Ball. But just because I was nice to Mr. Kendale, I am being shunned."

Suzette sat down and took Lady Caroline's hand. "It will not be for long. *Mademoiselle* is too beautiful for the young men to stay away."

"What is the use of being beautiful if no one likes me? It would be humiliating to go to the ball unescorted. I would be a laughingstock."

Suzette cocked her head and studied her mistress. She had never seen Lady Caroline so deep in the doldrums as this before. It was not the gay spirit she knew. "You and Mr. Elroy sound much alike," she said, sympathetically. "He does not think anybody loves him either."

Suddenly Caroline grabbed her maid and gave her a hug. "That is the solution, Suzette. Oh, you are a diamond of the first water. I shall tell Elroy that he is taking me to the ball." She frowned. "But I shall have to think of a costume that is so concealing that no one will recognize him, because he did not receive an invitation." She concentrated another moment, then jumped up, smiling. "If I am clever enough to figure out the Chinese Puzzle, then I can certainly think of costumes that will hide Elroy's identity and win me the Grand Prize as well."

Across town, Kendale stepped back to allow the large man into his Grace Church Street apartment. "Jon, come in. I have been expecting you."

"Has the letter arrived yet, Master Kendale?" Jon asked as he shrugged off the heavy leather bag from his shoulder and let it thud to the floor.

"Yes, it has," Kendale said. "I am afraid they are demanding a great deal more money this time. Sit down before the fire to warm yourself. I'll pour you a drink."

"You shouldn't be serving me, Master Kendale," Jon said humbly.

"Nonsense. We are together in this nightmare."

A few minutes later, divested of his heavy coat, Jon was settled in the largest chair in the room drinking from a mug filled with brandy.

As Kendale removed the box containing the letters from his desk, he recalled the first one which they had received over four years ago.

It had been less than a week after his visit to Mr. Chumbley's that he'd heard a heavy knocking on his door. When it was opened, Jon had pitched headlong into him.

"What's wrong, Jon? I thought you had left for the shires."

Trying to catch his breath, the big man had thrust a long sheet of foolscap into Kendale's hand. "It were the queerest thing, Mr. Kendale. I just checked into my room at the Tradesmen Hotel when this paper was stuffed under the door. It were addressed to you. I come running as fast as I could."

"It is not like you to get in such a quake over a letter. What does it say?"

Jon turned red. "It were addressed to you. I can't read all those words anyway. I thought it might be from someone who had news to tell us."

Kendale frowned as he read down the page. Then he crushed it in his fist. "My God! Lord Blackmere has been kidnapped!"

Astonishment was written all over Jon's face as he stared blankly at his host.

Kendale tried to straighten the crumbled paper and stared at the message once more. "Listen to this.

*My dear boy,*

*I was kidnapped by a band of cutthroats just before you were to come home. Somehow they must have intercepted your letter to me and read of your impending arrival in England. All my assets have been exhausted and now they want more. They are demanding that the ransom be delivered to them according to more detailed instructions which will be sent to you at a later date.*

*I beg that you follow their directions to the letter or else I fear I shall not see the light of day again. The money is to be placed in a leather pouch such as a tinker carries and given to the man named Jon. He will then deposit it at a place revealed to him somewhere along his known route.*

*They want me to assure you that I am well and have not been mistreated. I believe they are proud to be called cutthroats because they said they will allow that reference to them to remain in this letter to show how mean and clever they are.*

* * *

Kendale had recognized the handwriting and signature as the same that had been on the documents held by the solicitor. That had only been the beginning.

Now they sat here facing another Christmas Season and it seemed he and Jon were no nearer the solution than they had been four years ago. He wondered if his expectations of thanking his lordship were to be turned to naught? Lord Blackmere was in trouble and Kendale could do nothing about it except pay the ransom money until the dastardly kidnappers who held him prisoner should set him free.

Kendale poured himself a drink and sat down across from his friend. "They have evidently been having us watched all along, Jon. They know our every move; what I am doing and where you travel."

Jon's generous mouth formed a large "O" and he looked around as if he expected to find the culprit hiding in a corner of the room.

Kendale rubbed his forehead and stared into the fire. "It is just that Christmas seems such a cruel time of year to perpetuate such a hoax."

"I vow everybody in England knows about the Bandit King, Master Kendale. I hear them talking about him in the shires. The country folk say they are glad they ain't plump in the pockets so their sons won't be taken away."

"At least the wealthy young men who are kidnapped are returned unharmed after a week or so. Lord Blackmere has been suffering who knows what terrible depredations over the last four years. And he was not young anymore."

"Don't you believe his lordship when he writes each year that he is all right?' Jon said, wringing his hands.

Kendale didn't want to put any more stress on the simple man. "I'm sure he speaks the truth, Jon. Nonetheless, we will keep searching. Somewhere, sometime, the thieves will slip up and we will have Lord Blackmere back with us safe and sound. I promise you that."

"Aye, sir. I hope you are right and everything works out like you say it will. That surely would be a grand and joyful thing," Jon said, unfolding his hands.

Kendale was glad to see him relax. "Now, my friend. We must once again go over our instructions. The kidnappers are not patient men."

For two days Caroline turned one idea after another over in her mind of what costumes she and Elroy could possibly wear which would be different from anyone else's. Of course she had not yet informed Elroy of his part, but she would take care of that detail after she decided what they were to wear.

She had even made a trip to the attic to see what she could find. There were several of old clothes, lovely things that had belonged to many of the women in her family, but she would surely be recognized in those.

The secret to winning the Grand Prize was to not have anyone guess who you were. They could go in a donkey costume, but who would want to be bent over all evening, especially with a nodcap like Elroy?

"Suzette," she said, "I do believe if we go to the theater district and browse in some of the costume shops, I may come up with an idea."

In twenty minutes, Lady Caroline had called for her coach, changed to a fashionable, wine-colored carriage dress and cape, put on her plumed bonnet and started down the stairs to the ground floor. Bedlam greeted her.

Servants; maids, George, Driggs, Cook and footmen were running hither and thither, coming out, going in, looking under chairs, pots, curtains.

"Whatever is going on Betsy?" Lady Caroline asked, grabbing the girl as she went flying by.

"Oh, milady! I werc just trying to get her to give me her rabbit's foot so she could eat her porridge and she wouldn't open her fist and I ran to get Miss Plunkett to help and she must have got out then."

"Not again," said Caroline, not knowing whether to laugh, cry, or just be upset. "Did you look in all the cupboards in the nursery first? You know how she likes to hide."

"Oh, yes, ma'am. Cook even looked in the kitchen, because Poppy got down there once after she give her some sugar biscuits."

At that moment, Miss Plunkett hurried out of the Green Salon, a harried expression on her face. "I have looked behind and under every piece of furniture in that room," she said. "I cannot find her."

"Now," said Lady Caroline, her sense of responsibility coming to the fore, "we can surely find one little girl if we just stop and put our minds to it. We all know how Poppy loves to play peek-a-boo."

"Peek-a-boo," answered a tiny voice nearby.

"Why it came from somewhere here in the hall," said Miss Plunkett.

"Peek-a-boo!" said several voices at once.

"Peek-a-boo!" came the answer accompanied by a snicker.

"I beg your pardon, my lady," said Driggs, "but I believe Lord Favor's knight is giggling."

"Poppy!" Caroline admonished, pulling the little girl out from behind the coat of armor. "You are a naughty girl."

"Hug Poppy," she said, her lower lip quivering.

Looking a little embarrassed, Caroline glanced over at Miss Plunkett.

Miss Plunkett nodded.

Caroline leaned down and put her arms around Poppy. "Now what is it you won't give Betsy? Is it your rabbit's foot?"

Poppy held out her fist. All Caroline saw was a tuft of fur showing.

"She won't let go of it," said Miss Plunkett. "Even takes it to bed with her at night."

Caroline looked at the tiny clenched fist and thought of her own attachment to a black pearl which she had worn for nearly twelve months. Only in the last few weeks had she begun to hide it down inside her bodice where no one could see it. It was as if all of a sudden it had become hers and hers alone and she didn't want others staring at it.

"I have a suggestion," she said. "Poppy, would you like Lady Caroline to put your rabbit's foot on a ribbon so you can wear it around your neck?" And reaching inside her cape she pulled out the silver chain with the black pearl.

Caroline knew the child could not possibly understand all that she was saying, but Poppy's eyes grew round with wonder when she saw the pendant. She studied it for a minute then held out her prize to Caroline.

"Well, will you look at that," said Miss Plunkett. "She gave it to her ladyship right away."

Caroline stared at the fuzzy thing in her hand. "Why, it's not a rabbit's foot at all, but a scrap of fur. Wherever did she find that?"

Poppy's eyes grew wide with apprehension.

"But a promise is a promise," Caroline said. "Suzette fetch my ribbon box and a needle and thread."

Poppy's prize was soon attached to a pretty blue satin ribbon, tied around her neck, and placed down inside her frock. But Poppy would have none of that nonsense and pulled the swatch of fur out where it was displayed proudly on her chest. Her look of defiance dared anyone to tuck it in again.

After Poppy had been taken back up to the nursery and everyone else had returned to their duties, Lady Caroline stood in the hall studying the suit of armor. Suddenly a gleam came into her eye. "Suzette, we do not have to go out after all. I know exactly what my costume is going to be for Lady Dankleish's Masquerade Ball."

"Dash it all, I ain't going to do it, Caro!"

Lady Caroline stood with her hands on her hips and a determined gleam in her eye. "Oh, yes, you are, Elroy. You are going to escort me to Lady Dankleish's Masquerade Ball."

"They'll think me an odd-fish if I do what you want."

Elroy *was* an odd-fish, but Caroline wasn't going to tell him that now or he might act more stubborn than usual. "You won't get to attend otherwise because you didn't receive an invitation."

"But I promised m'mother and m'father that I would be at Cavendish Manor for Christmas. M'whole family is going. Anne and her husband Henry Smith, and all m'sisters. M'sister Mary wants us all there when her baby is born."

And my father's child, too, Caroline thought with a bit of rancor. She wondered if Lord Favor had been so excited about her birth as he was about this child. Probably not when she'd turned out to be a girl. "You will still have time to travel to Gloucestershire. The ball is two weeks before."

"Why ain't you going? Mary will be up in the boughs if you ain't there. After all, it's your brother she'll be having."

Caroline's hand went to the black pearl at her throat. "Oh, do not say so, Elroy!"

The boy slapped his forehead with the palm of his hand. "Egad, Caro! You don't think she's going to have a girl, do you?"

"That is not what I meant. And just what may I ask is wrong with a girl, Elroy?"

"Well, after all, look how long it took m'father to get me. Had to go through Anne and Dorothy and Mary before he got what he wanted. Then it didn't matter how many girls came after that because he already had me."

Caroline should have known she wouldn't get a sensible response from a scatterbrain like Elroy. "I shall be celebrating the holidays here with Miss Plunkett and Poppy. My Christmas shopping for everybody is finished so you can carry my gifts with you when you go."

"Sounds humdrum to me just having two and a half people," he said, going into one of his donkey laughs before he could finish. "They'd probably have a lot more fun in Gloucestershire than here. Anyway, m'father wants me where he can watch me. The Bandit King might be about again."

"For heaven's sakes! He only kidnaps peer's sons, Elroy. That should give you one good reason to rejoice in not being a member of the aristocracy."

Elroy chewed on this for awhile.

"Remember, Priscilla Whistlewaite will be at the ball and when you win the prize she will have to take notice of you."

"You really think so, Caro?"

"Of course she will, Elroy."

"By Jingo! I will go then. Tell me what I have to do."

It did not take long for Caroline to outline her plan. "We will go as a knight in shining armor and his lady," she said. "Only that I will be the knight and you will be the lady. Don't make faces, Elroy. You will have on a thick veil and no one will recognize you."

The boy's expression showed he didn't think that was foolproof. "I don't walk like a lady."

"I shall teach you. Now we are about of the same height and no one should be able to tell which is which. I have tried on the suit of armor that was beside the Green Salon. The men were shorter in those times—or at least that knight was—and Suzette is making me an undergarment of soft velvet so that I will be warm and the metal won't chaff me."

"What if someone sends their servants to spy on your house to see what your costume is going to be?"

"We'll arrive in separate coaches, so no one will guess who we are."

"That's silly. When a green and gold carriage comes driving up with the Cavendish coat-of-arms on the door, even a fool would know it's you."

"That is exactly what I am counting on. We will switch coaches. You will come to my house sometime during the day of the ball. You are always coming in and out so often that no one will give it a second thought. You can hire a closed hackney and have it park outside. My coach will pull up behind it. When we leave the house the knight will get into the hackney and the lady and her maid in my coach. Suzette will accompany you."

"You can't go alone to the Dankleish river palace."

"I won't be alone, Elroy. I will tell Driggs to choose one of the underfootmen to accompany me. It shall only be to the Dankleish estate. The ride should take no longer than two hours even if it snows. After the ball is over you can return to Town in the hackney, for I was invited to stay at the river palace overnight."

"Well, I ain't going to bring my man to see me in that getup, and I ain't going to go back to m'digs in Bury Street dressed like a doxy."

"George can help you dress, Elroy. I'll threaten to throw him out on the street without references if he says anything."

"Well, it still seems a rackety scheme that will only be a lot of trouble for nothing. You won't be able to dance in that piece of tin."

"Don't be so mulish Elroy. We cannot but help win the Grand Prize. There is no way that anyone will recognize us. Everyone will claim that you are me, and they won't be able to guess who the knight is because they don't even know you are coming. I'm going to change my costume after the unmasking at midnight. Just bring along a portmanteau for your clothes and we'll have it put in the hackney for you to change before you go back to Town."

Elroy scratched his head. "I'm all mixed up now."

"Trust me, Elroy. And while you are here, you can try on some of the lovely gowns I found in the attic. But first I shall show you how to walk."

"Dash it all, Caro. I know how to walk."

Caroline decided she'd rather not comment on that and instead glided gracefully across the room. "Put your shoulders back and raise your chin. Now go out and come back in correctly. Try to look like you are Quality and quit slumping."

"I don't slump," he fussed, slumping out of the room.

Caroline wondered if it was even worth the effort to go to the ball. But if she did not, the old gabble-grinders who were spreading tales about her would think that they had won the battle. And Caroline was not one to give up her position easily.

By the afternoon of the night of the ball, everything was in place for Lady Caroline's and Mr. Elroy Bennington's adventure. Elroy had visited a couple of days to practice being a lady. He reluctantly tried on several medieval gowns and conical henins with flowing veils for Caroline until she finally picked a deep blue velvet costume and a red wig.

Twice Poppy was discovered in the room in which he was dressing. The first being the most traumatic for Elroy because he did not see her until she'd popped out from behind the curtains crying, "Peek-a-boo!" just as he had removed his trousers. After that he looked behind, under, and around everywhere before he began to dress.

The second time was the very afternoon of the ball. Elroy appeared with a cumbersome, very worn wicker basket in his arms.

"What is that ugly thing?" exclaimed Caroline. "And where is your portmanteau?'

"Dash it all, Caro! This was all I could find on such short notice. I forgot I loaned m'bag to Timothy Botts a month ago and he ain't brought it back yet. So don't blame me. It would have looked stupid bringing my big traveling trunk just for my coat and one suit now wouldn't it?"

Caroline wrinkled her nose. "It looks and smells like a picnic hamper."

"That's because that's what it is. Bought it in October when we took some gels to the park, then thought it was foolish to throw it away and used it to throw my dirty linens in."

"And that's what you propose to put your change of clothes in?"

"What's wrong with it? A man don't have to take a whole trunk full of fancies like a woman does."

"It's just that I'm the one who is going to have to ride with it in the hackney." She threw up her hands. "Never mind, get up to your room and start changing into your costume. I hope you at least got an enclosed carriage for me to ride in."

Elroy looked hurt. "Of course I did. A two horse carriage too. I've hired the fellow before. He rides up and down right outside my hotel a lot, but he don't charge half what the other hackney drivers ask. He said he'd be glad to drive someone out to a big party, and agreed to wait and bring me back after the ball."

"Your father gives you enough of an allowance that you could buy the Tower if you wanted, Elroy. I don't know why you are such a pinchpenny when it comes to something so important. Now do get dressed. We don't have that much time."

Caroline entered her chambers where Suzette was ready to assist her into her cumbersome costume. She could hear snatches of song floating out from Elroy's room farther up the corridor when suddenly he let out a bellow loud enough to rattle the windows.

"Egads! She's in here again, Caro."

"Poppy!" both ladies cried at once and dashed out into the hall.

Betsy joined them.

"Don't you dare come in here, I ain't decent," Elroy fussed.

The door opened a crack and George, his face twitching in the most outlandish way handed Poppy out.

"She's in here hugging m'hamper and calling me Tom-tom like I was some fool cat," Elroy yelled from inside the room.

Betsy giggled and picked Poppy up. "I'm sorry, milady," she said trying hard to hide her mirth. "I will take her back to the nursery."

"I declare, Suzette," Caroline said as soon as they were back in her room, "the girl is getting too impertinent. I should have boxed her ears."

Suzette smiled. "I think *mademoiselle* would not box Betsy's ears, because *mademoiselle* has changed. The servants are not afraid anymore. They like her much better now and not one of them would think of betraying you by telling anyone about your costume."

Caroline weighed that statement thoughtfully while she dressed. She had always supposed it to be the opposite way. The staff would not obey a mistress they did not fear and now Suzette was telling her they liked her better for not scolding them.

Two hours later a fine lady and her maid departed Cavendish House in the Square in the splendid green and gold lacquered coach, a large trunk strapped to the back, George standing in the rear, and John Coachman handling the ribbons. Fifteen minutes after the first coach had left, a knight in shining armor left the same house and entered the hired hackney with the horrible hamper already inside and an underfootman on the box.

# Thirteen

It was already dark and the afternoon rain had turned to a light snow. The armor around Caroline was much heavier than she had imagined it would be. Thank heavens, the padded undergarments, two inches thick at the shoulders which Suzette had made, were warm. She removed her helmet carefully from over the padded sallet-cap enclosing her hair. She wondered how in the world the warriors of old could even move well enough to slay their dragons. But the discomfort would be well worth the effort just to see the surprise on the faces of the other guests when she took off her mask—or helmet as it was.

The steady rhythm of the horses' hoofbeats, the insulation of the metal casing enfolding her that was like sitting before a cozy fireplace, and Caroline found it not so uncomfortable after all. In fact, she found herself dozing off.

A sharp jolt jerked Caroline awake. The carriage rocked from side to side and finally came to a halt. Men's voices penetrated the silence. Then the door to the carriage opened to the pitch-black night.

"We only hit a rock in the road, sir. I wanted to check the wheels before we went on. Shouldn't be too long now," the man said and shut the door before Caroline could say anything.

He had called her *sir.* Then she remembered. The underfootman had been informed that he was not to reveal that it was his mistress who rode in the carriage and the driver would, of course, think that his passenger was still Mr. Bennington. So her scheme was working as planned, Caroline thought smugly as the coach got under way once again.

Caroline had no idea how long she had been asleep, it could have been five minutes, thirty, or even more, but she hoped it wouldn't be too much longer before they'd reach their destination. She wriggled the helmet down over her thick cap and pushed up the hinged visor to look out the window. No stars were showing, and since she'd lost all sense of time, Caroline had no idea of where they were.

She lowered the visor over her face and had settled back once more into the squabs when the carriage began to slow and finally came to a halt. The door burst open and a large figure leaped in. Before she could cry out a large hand covered the entire visor, she smelled a scent, sweet yet poignant . . . and then oblivion.

"You!" he growled, his deep voice muffled by the black hood covering his head.

A chill ran down Caroline's spine, but she wasn't about to let the renegade know it. "I should be the one shouting that," she said indignantly. She tried to sit up, but failed miserably. Her whole body felt like a lump of lead. She lay on some sort of cot in a darkened room, her hair falling about her shoulders, staring up at a hooded figure holding her helmet in his hands.

But although Caroline's arms and legs refused to respond, her mind did not seem affected. In fact, she was beginning to feel quite giddy. "I knew after your last efforts that you were completely unfit to be a bandit," she said, giggling in the most absurd way, considering the circumstances.

She was sure his mumbled response was not something she wished to hear.

The Bandit King whirled and strode over to the blue-frocked man standing at a far corner of the room. They looked like two giants from Hades; tall men, shoulders made to look a mile wider with their several capes and masked faces.

Caroline could only hear snatches of their conversation. She heard Elroy's name mentioned. "Oh, lord! You thought I was Elroy Bennington? You cheated," she laughed. "Elroy is not of the peerage."

She shivered a little as the Bandit King came back and not too gently took her by the shoulders and lifted her to her feet. This made her dizzy for a moment and she had the most terrible urge to laugh again. He pulled her toward him until her face was only a few inches from his hood. She could tell he was not too pleased with her from the way he sucked in his breath.

"Where is Mr. Bennington?" His deep voice rumbled through the small room.

Then it was true. Her masquerade had been so perfect that she had been mistakened for Elroy. Poor Elroy. The picture of him arriving at Lady Dankleish's ball dressed as a lady and without any clothes to change into brought on another fit of the whoops.

He dropped her. Or at least, he took his hands off her.

Caroline clattered to the floor where she managed to get up on her hands and knees but was too weighted down with the armor to stand.

"Get up," he said.

"I can't," she answered with another bubble of laughter.

"And stop laughing."

"I can't help it," she said, trying without success to stop the giggle that escaped from her throat.

"Where is the vial?" he said to his partner.

The man pulled a small bottle from his pocket and handed it to the bandit.

"Good lord, man! I told you all that was needed was a few drops on the rag."

"He . . . that is, she grabbed m'hand. It spilled."

"What did you do with the rag?"

"It flew onto the hamper there," the man in blue said, pointing to the large basket sitting on the wood-plank table a few feet from where Caroline still struggled to rise. A rag dangled from where it had caught on a jagged spike of wicker.

The Bandit King picked it up and sniffed it. "No wonder she was unconscious all night. We have traveled too far now to return to London. Come outside with me. We will have to think of another way to proceed."

"Aren't you going to help me up?" called Caroline.

"No," he said, slamming the door behind him.

"Insufferable man!" mumbled Caroline, finally managing to get herself into a sitting position. Although she still felt lightheaded, the temptation to laugh was beginning to leave her, and more serious thoughts were taking their place. She needed Suzette to help unhook the armor and she could see only one alternative if she were to be free of her encasement. No, she would never ever lower herself to ask the Bandit King to assist her.

Now that she was alone, Caroline looked about the room. It was small, no more than twelve by twenty feet at the most. The one window was shuttered and only the cracks between the slats emitted thin streaks of light. So it was as he said. She had slept through the night. And that could mean she was as much as eighty or even a hundred miles from London.

A fire burned in the small fireplace, a stack of wood beside it. Two beds, table and stools and dishes on shelves over a counter against the fireplace wall. There was only one door, and it had seemed to her when the two men had gone out that she had seen it open into a larger area and she heard a horse whinny. Knowing the Bandit King's habits, this was to have been Elroy's cell. A stable perhaps. At least it was a more pleasant place than the dungeon in which the Marquis of Wetherby had been imprisoned last winter.

But why had the thief chosen the son of a tradesman to kidnap this time? True, Mr. Bennington was far plumper in the pockets than many of the peerage. Perhaps that was the answer.

This time the runagate needed a great deal more money or perhaps he was just getting greedier.

Caroline's main concern now was how was she going to get out of her present predicament. More precisely and to the point what was the Bandit King going to do with her? However, her most pressing problem at the moment was to get up off the hard plank floor without making a fool of herself. She shuffled on hands and knees across to the bed and by grasping the bedpost managed to pull herself up. She was leaning against the side of the bed when her captor banged the door open and marched into the room.

"Now, madam," he said, "I have decided on your fate."

From the tone of his voice, Caroline was not quite certain she wanted to hear what that was.

"It seems you tangled yourself in my plans once before. That time you escaped. This time you will not. Neither will your father be freed from his responsibility. I should have taken advantage of your presence the last time I had you in my power. Softness of heart for the fairer sex has been the downfall of many a man."

Caroline gave a snort.

"But do not fear that I shall give in to that weakness twice. My guest was to have been Mr. Elroy. Not only is he an only son and heir, but his father is wealthy beyond most who consider themselves the first classes of Society. And now that I think of it, his daughter is now the countess of Favor, is she not? And I am certain Mr. Bennington will be just as willing to pay the amount which I am going to put on your pretty head if your father cannot. Don't you agree?"

"I demand that you let me go."

"How far do you think you will get in that suit of armor?"

He was right of course. If she let go of the bedpost she would most likely end in a heap on the floor again. "You are despicable."

"That may be, but it is not the point," he said. "My partner will be away tending to the business of the ransom. This time I planned on not letting my guest out of my sight."

Caroline's eyes grew round. "You mean we are going to stay in here together?"

"I had expected Mr. Bennington."

"Well, you will just have to find somewhere else to stay."

"I chose this hide-a-way because it is one place the authorities would not think to look. All provisions are here for our survival. Any movement out and around could be noticed and reported. No, I am afraid you will be stuck with me."

"I will not stay in here with you. I am leaving right now," said Caroline, taking her hand off the bed and straightening up. One step and she clattered to the floor. It was a pretty how-de-do. She felt fine as long as she was holding on to something but the minute she tried to walk, her head spun around like a top.

"I believe you need to be relieved of your armor, Lady Caroline," he said with a deep laugh, hauling her upright.

"Don't touch me!"

"As you say, your ladyship," he said.

She grabbed his arm. "Don't drop me again," she said, frantically. "All right, if you would just untie the cords or hooks or whatever my maid used to tie the sections together, I can get the armor off."

"I hope you brought a change of clothes with you," he said, as he took hold of her shoulders and turned her around. His touch was not as rough as she expected it to be.

With a sigh of resignation, Caroline raised her hair so he could reach the leather laces joining parts of her armor together in the back. She certainly wasn't going to have a fighting chance as long as she was in the suit of armor. "My trunk was in my carriage. If you'd been more astute in your abduction, you wouldn't have made such a hash of it."

She felt his hands tighten, but his voice remained calm. "I am sorry I did not anticipate your cunning, my lady," he said starting to remove the backplate, then stopped. "I hope you have something decent on under this."

"Of course I do," she said smartly as she pulled the breastplate off. "My companion made me a red velvet surcoat to go under the padding." She had thought at the time that the jacket was quite fashionable, but it was short—ending just above the knees—and she only had black stockings underneath.

"What is in the wicker hamper?" he asked as he added another piece of armor to the pile on the floor.

Caroline took off her knee-cops so she could sit down on a wooden bench by the table. "Elroy packed his coat and a change of clothes. He was going to switch from his costume after the ball. Now I am afraid he is left with only my dresses."

She heard him chuckle.

"It's nothing to laugh about," she said, trying with great difficulty to keep a straight face.

"You may have need of his clothes," he said. "I am afraid I have no ladies' gowns to offer you and I only have enough of my own for my use," he said, watching her remove the last solleret, the flexible steel shoe, from her foot.

Caroline wiggled her toes and began to take measure of the small room. "Your partner is evidently sleeping somewhere else. You can go stay with him."

"I am afraid not, Lady Caroline. He has already left to deliver the new ransom note I have written to your father. I will not be so foolish as to leave you by yourself."

Caroline was in a quandary as to what to do, but the Bandit King didn't seem the least concerned about the inappropriateness of his plans.

He walked over to the fireplace and stuck another log into the flames. "Now I suggest that you remove Mr. Bennington's coat out of the hamper. You may even find that his trousers will be welcome when night comes. It gets very chilly even in here."

Caroline eyed the hamper and decided that she would not

only put on everything Elroy had in the trunk, but even the suit of armor again if she had to. With that intention in mind, she approached the table. She put her hand over her nose. "Whatever is that sweet odor?"

"That, my lady, is what put you to sleep for half a day," he said, tossing the rag into the fire. "I am afraid my friend was a little overzealous in its use. It is also what made you giggle more than not."

"That certainly was not fair."

He laughed, but it was not in amusement. "Fair?" he said. "This is not a game, my lady. It enabled us to switch carriages and carry you for hours without your raising a rumpus. Albeit, we thought you were Mr. Elroy Bennington. That you were not was your own fault."

"My fault?" Caroline rounded on him. "I was going to a party—and I know I would have won the Grand Prize. Now, I find that instead of being the belle of the ball, I will be in a cold room wearing this," she cried, throwing back the lid of the wicker hamper.

"Peek-a-boo!" chirped Poppy, rising sleepily from where she lay swaddled in Elroy's large surcoat. She rubbed her eyes and giggled. "Poppy play peek-a-boo."

"Oh, Poppy!" Caroline said reaching for the child's outstretched arms. "Whatever have you done now?"

"What the devil?" said the man. "How did she get in there?"

"She likes to play hide and seek," Caroline said, lifting Poppy out of the hamper. "Oh, my goodness! Here, you take her," she cried.

Thrust at him unexpectedly, the Bandit King found himself now holding the child. "She's wet!" he said, handing her back to Caroline.

She didn't take her. "I know that!"

"Well, do something about it."

"Oh," said Poppy.

"I don't know what to do about it," Caroline snapped.

"What kind of a woman are you? You are supposed to know about things like that," he said, still holding the infant away from him.

Caroline looked into the hamper. "Elroy's coat seems to be dry, but I'm afraid everything else is *quite* damp." She tried to think of what Suzette had done in the carriage when they had found Poppy the first time. "It's cold in here, I need to get her clothes off. Stand her on the floor and pull that coverlet off the bed," she said.

He did as he was told, then grabbed more wood to put on the fire.

Caroline quickly divested Poppy of her damp clothing and wrapped the blanket around her, lucky amulet and all. The little girl was not about to let anyone remove the scrap of fur from around her neck.

"Now young lady," Caroline said, placing her on the warm hearth stones, "stay there." She turned back and looked at the pile of clothes on the wood floor.

"Do something with those," he growled.

"You don't expect me to take care of them."

"You will, my lady, or the little girl stays wrapped in your bed covering. There is a wooden tub under the counter, soap in the dish and hot water in the kettle on the hook over the fire. Now, I have business to discuss with my partner," he said, walking toward the door.

"Just like a man," she said accusingly. "Leave when things get difficult."

He turned when he reached the far end of the room. "By the by, Lady Caroline, I did not have a chance to tell you how charming I find your costume. Women should not be so reticent about showing their legs." With a bark of laughter he exited, shutting the door with a bang.

"You are insufferable," she yelled after him, then glanced

down at the black hose encasing her legs. She grabbed Elroy's great coat, rolled up the sleeves and put it on over her red velvet surcoat. It covered her to the floor.

Poppy sat contentedly on the warm hearth, playing with her fur piece; petting it, cooing to it and tickling her nose with it.

Caroline poured hot water into the wooden bowl, swished around the bar of soap and picking up Poppy's clothing, dropped them in. While she was at it, she reckoned she might as well wash Elroy's shirt.

These were all hung on stones protruding from the fireplace by the time the Bandit King came back into the room. He walked over to the hearth and handed a chunk of bread to Poppy, who immediately popped it into her mouth.

"I had planned on staying in this room with Mr. Bennington."

Caroline rounded on him. "You already said that, and I told you that you cannot stay in here with me."

He kept his hooded face turned toward Poppy and said calmly, "You will remember that you do not give the orders here, Lady Caroline. My partner has made a small nest for himself at the other end of the stables. He tells me it is only large enough for one man. When he leaves, I shall move there."

"And for tonight?" she said trying to control the waver in her voice.

"You can sleep with the child in the bed. I will move the cot where it can block the door. Now, you could try to go up the chimney or slide through the slats in the shutters. I would not put it past you to take that chance if you were alone. However, I doubt that you would be foolish enough to take the child out into the winter cold. It is not snowing, but worse, a cold sleet is falling, and I know that you would not jeopardize the child's health."

Of course, he was right and Caroline knew it. She had no idea of where she was or where to go if she *could* escape. "It would have served you right if you had to stay in here with Elroy for a week."

"I will make a bargain with you, my lady. I shall sleep outside in the stables tonight and you will have breakfast ready for my partner and me in the morning. Of course, you are to cook for yourself and the child every day regardless, but if I hear one more word of protest from you, I will move in here."

The words of rebuke which Caroline was ready to deliver died on her lips.

"Now if I remember correctly you had a great deal of practice once before with pleasing my men's palates. Your bread was far lighter than Mr. Peen's as I recall. I think you will find a good supply of meal and grains in the sacks along the wall and my partner will bring in what fruits we have. There are potatoes, too. Simple fare, I am afraid, but then we had not expected such distinguished company."

Caroline looked with dismay to where he pointed to the sacks and jars stacked against the walls and on the few shelves over the counter.

"Tomorrow morning before dawn I want you to have breakfast ready for the two of us. I will awaken you with a knock on the door."

"Peek-a-boo!" said Poppy, pulling a corner of the comforter over her head.

"I am glad to see that one of you approves," he said, bowing himself out the door.

Caroline did not sleep much that night. She got up twice to put more wood on the fire to keep the kettle of water hot, and was up before the crack in the shutters showed any light. The clothes had dried overnight. She took off her pretty red velvet surcoat and put on Elroy's shirt and trousers and pulled on his boots.

In the meantime, Caroline had discovered the chamber pot under the bed the night before and with great relief found that Poppy knew what it was for. That solved one problem, she hoped.

Poppy was sitting on the hearth stones in her warm wool dress and Caroline on a stool, feeding her from a bowl of porridge when there was a knock on the door.

"Come in," Caroline said, sweetly, and watched with amusement as the two men entered to see the table set and the aroma of hot coffee and porridge steaming in the iron pot over the fire.

Her host's manner was not as polite. "Give us two bowls of whatever you have made and fill the mugs with coffee. We will eat outside," he said, holding his hands out to the fire.

Poppy looked up at the tall figure in black hovering over her and reaching up pulled on his long coat. He ignored her.

Caroline's good humor disappeared and her eyes narrowed, but her tone remained as polite as if she were serving tea in the Green Salon at Cavendish House. "If you'll please sit down, I'll have your food ready as soon as I finish feeding the baby," she said, never taking her gaze off the spoon Poppy had just stuffed in her mouth.

The man in blue sat.

The Bandit King stayed where he was. "You will get our food now, Lady Caroline."

"Of course, my lord," she quipped. "I forgot that you must be served first." With that Caroline thrust the bowl of porridge into the bandit's outstretched hands, none too gently. "And I am sure you won't mind feeding a hungry child while I do so."

Poppy studied the hooded man looking down at her, then with great seriousness held up her spoon to him.

He didn't move.

The bandit in blue jumped up. "I'll feed the little girl," he said.

"There is no need," the Bandit King barked, putting the bowl on the table just as Caroline brought two trenchers of porridge and the mugs of coffee on a large wooden cutting board. He took it from her and handed it to his partner. "Take the food outside. My horse still needs to be saddled, and I want you finished with your breakfast before I leave."

As soon as the man in blue had departed, the Bandit King whirled on Caroline. She had the uneasy feeling that he was not too pleased with her.

"I'll be away for a day," he said.

"Good!" Caroline exclaimed.

"Ah, I think the lady protests too much."

Caroline looked at him quizzically. Before she could remark on his paraphrasing the Bard, he pulled her to him and reaching down inside her shirt, yanked out the black pearl pendant.

Caroline gasped. It had been out of sight when she wore the surcoat, but she'd forgotten that Elroy's shirt lay open at the neck. She looked at the pendant as if she'd never seen it before.

"Then why do you wear this, my lady?"

Caroline had asked herself that question many times. She only knew that the nearer he came to her now the faster her heart beat. "That is no business of yours."

"But I believe it is," he said tilting her head back. "I am going to kiss you, you know, and there is nothing you can do to stop me."

# Fourteen

Caroline closed her eyes. She knew she should be telling him not to, but since he was going to have his way regardless, she was helpless. Wasn't she?

"I want you," he said, raising his hood and capturing her lips so quickly she had no chance to see his face.

"Me, too!"

Either the thundering in his ears had affected his hearing, or else Lady Caroline's voice had risen several decibels. Besides, he was kissing her. She couldn't have said anything.

"Me, too!"

He felt the tug on his coat somewhere around his knees, too low for her ladyship's hands to reach.

"Hug Poppy, too!" piped the wee voice, louder.

He quickly pulled his hood over his face and looked down.

Poppy stood on tiptoe tugging more desperately now. "Hug Poppy!" she wailed, and held up her arms to be lifted.

"Good lord!" growled the Bandit King, quickly dropping his arms from around Caroline. The moppet was bouncing up and down and flapping her arms as if that was going to make her airborne.

Poppy grinned, her eyes showing her delight in finally being noticed.

The Bandit King reached down and picked the child up and handed her to Caroline. "Your virtue is safe, my lady. You have nothing more to fear from me."

"Well, I hope not," Caroline said, turning so that he would not see the disappointment in her eyes.

He opened the door to admit his cohort who was standing outside. The big man entered quietly and handed Caroline a basket of eggs and a slab of bacon.

"My partner will keep you company to make sure you behave while I am gone," the Bandit King said, shutting the door behind him.

With one fast swoop the masked man in blue picked up a wooden bench and placed it in front of the door. Then, seating himself squarely in the middle, leaned back completely blocking any chance of escape.

Caroline turned and vented her exasperation by pounding her fists into the bread dough on the counter. She would see if she remembered how Millicent Copley had taught her to make unleavened bread when they'd been kidnapped once before by the black-hooded rogue.

Poppy however was not the least intimidated by their captors. She stood with her finger in her mouth studying the man in blue. After a few minutes of close scrutiny, he fumbled inside his cape and came out with a white stick about six inches long and thrust out his arm toward the child.

"Don't you touch her," Caroline said, rushing forward with a wooden spoon raised above her head.

The big man pressed back against the door. " 'Tis only barley sugar I picked up for the wee lass, m'lady," he sputtered.

Caroline grabbed the stick out of his hand and after inspecting it, gave it to Poppy who promptly stuck it in her mouth. "All right," she said, "just don't you dare put so much as a finger on her."

"Yes'm," he replied timidly.

The Bandit King returned two nights later. He'd been away a day longer than he'd said he would be, and this caused some consternation on Caroline's part. She heard his horse come in and she waited, but he did not come to see her. How could she possibly be drawn to a man whose face she had never seen? He was dangerous. He was a rogue. He liked to tell people what to do and he expected to be obeyed. Worst of all, he was a thief and if he were caught he would be hanged. Yet, Poppy liked him. And worse still, Caroline had to admit that she was disturbingly attracted to him.

She was after all, Lady Caroline Cavendish, the daughter of an earl. The Incomparable. At least until this Holiday Season when she had fallen from grace with the *beau monde.* There again it was the fault of a man—Kendale. He was handsome and rich. If she closed her eyes she could hear the sweet melody of his voice, the lilt of his brogue, the broad shoulders, the sly grin and those green eyes. Poppy adored him. He made her laugh and yet, Caroline had sensed something deep inside, hurting him. Elroy had mentioned that Kendale could speak in twelve languages, so he had to be a learned man.

That made her think of another person who loved books. Someone who had become very dear to her. Someone who had the same green eyes. A man who was sweet and understanding and let her prattle on as if what she had to say was important. He had a title. He was an earl like her father, and even though he was up in years, he could dance so divinely that it took her breath away.

It was a long time before Caroline fell asleep and then it was to dream that she was a little girl and Miss Plunkett was helping her pull a half-drowned puppy out of the pond at Cavendish Manor. She named him Dipper.

Caroline awakened with a longing to go back to Gloucestershire—to Cavendish Manor—home. But homesickness could not break the resolve she'd made to Suzette—that she would not return until she was properly married to a proper husband.

That was unlikely now considering her present circumstances. Even if her father paid the ransom, it did not guarantee an early release by the Bandit King. He seemed a man who insisted on making his own timetable.

And speaking of time, her captor would surely be coming in at any moment demanding his breakfast.

Caroline jumped out of bed and lit the candle on the table. Then quickly pulled on Elroy's trousers and boots. Poppy rubbed her eyes and sat up. "Num-num?"

"Your breakfast will be ready in a thrice," Caroline said. Then pulling out the chamber pot from under the bed, she sat Poppy upon it, ran to put more wood on the fire, filled the kettle hanging on the hook in the fireplace with water from the barrel in the corner, ran over to get Poppy dressed and back to pour hot water over the oats and barley she'd set to soak the night before.

With some difficulty but with great determination, she lugged the monstrous iron pot to the fireplace and pushed it into the hot ashes. Into this she dropped large chunks of bacon, the three remaining eggs and the contents of the porridge pot. She took the long-handled wooden spoon and whacked the eggs to break their shells, then stirred the mixture well. Her first attempt to make bread had failed miserably and she hadn't tried again.

Poppy had already crawled up onto one of the benches at the table, picked up her spoon and now sat with an expression of great expectation written all over her face.

Never again, Caroline thought, would she sluff off as insignificant the duties of a nursery-maid, cook or even the lowly pot boy. A great deal of hard work went into the simplest of household duties. But in spite of trying to tell herself that her present situation was quite grim, she found herself chanting a nursery rhyme. Just as she finished making the coffee, she heard the sound of heavy footsteps outside the door.

There was a knock. The two men entered. The one boldly, the other hat in hand.

To her surprise, the Bandit King told her they would eat inside. "It is getting colder," he said, seating himself so that his back was toward her and only raised his hood enough to uncover his mouth.

Caroline proudly served up the steaming bowls of porridge. The big man in blue ate heartily, but whatever her expectations had been to please the Bandit King they were soon dashed.

First he had the ill-manners to pick the egg shells out of his bowl. Then after that he inspected each spoonful of food before putting it in his mouth. Although Caroline felt he was watching her as she refilled their bowls and brought their coffee, he said nothing more.

On the other hand, Poppy held no such reservations and bestowed her attentions equally. She would have been genuinely pleased to have one man to entertain, but two at once seemed beyond her wildest dreams. She greeted both with squeals of delight and to Caroline's horror began to play peek-a-boo over her bowl of porridge. When she tired of that, she flapped her arms and called, "quack-quack" across the table. Finally, she pulled out her precious scrap of fur and reverently showed it to both men.

Finally the Bandit King rose and with a nod of his head, motioned to the other man that it was time to go. At the door he paused. "My partner will be leaving tonight. We will be together for the next three days at least, my lady, so I advise you to try your best to rub along well with me as best you can," he said, as if he naturally expected her to comply.

Poppy climbed down from the bench and ran toward him. Disappointment showed in her face as he whirled and quickly escaped from the room.

If Caroline had not experienced the heat of his ill-humor and seen his boldness in manner toward those who dared to cross him, she would have said that the Bandit King was as terrified of the child as she first had been.

* * *

During the next few days, the Bandit King came and went as he pleased to eat or sit by the fire, silently observing Caroline and Poppy through the slits in his black hood. No matter how much Poppy tried to get him to play peek-a-boo with her, he made no move to show that he even heard her.

Caroline finally learned to ignore him and spent her time inventing games to play with Poppy. The child was quick to learn and picked up new words every day. So perhaps it was just as well that their abductor was silent most of the time. No telling what he would have taught her.

On the third day, the Bandit King sat brooding by the fire. He had not said a word to Lady Caroline since he'd come in an hour before. His partner had not yet returned with news of whether the amount of the ransom had been agreed upon.

Caroline put Poppy to bed and sang her a little song until she was asleep. She had just poured herself a cup of tea when the sound of hoofbeats was heard outside.

Instantly alert, gun in hand, the Bandit King rose and placed his ear to the door. They heard the creaking of hinges as the stable doors opened and closed. Shortly after there came a knock and a few words identified their caller.

The Bandit King pulled open the door and admitted the man in blue. The two stood in the doorway conversing in whispered monosyllables for a few minutes. The Bandit King guffawed and slapped the other on the shoulders. "Well done. Well done."

"Give me that hot cup of tea," he said authoritatively to Caroline and without a by-your-leave took it from her hand and gave it to the man in blue. He ignored the scowl she sent him. "Here, friend, this will warm your insides."

"Well, I never," Carolyn said, watching the large man tilt back his head and gulp down the hot drink in one swallow.

Carolyn turned her back to them, poured herself another cup of tea and sat down before the fire.

Her captor paid no heed to her snub and went on talking to the other man as if she weren't there. "Later after you have stabled your horse and have had something to eat, we will indulge in something stronger to celebrate our success."

"I had a hearty meal at a tavern on the way here," his partner said. "After three days on the road, I shall be glad to see my mattress."

"Then I shall come with you now and we will discuss what next we must do."

"The authorities are probably already looking for Poppy and me," Caroline interjected.

"I doubt it, my lady. I wrote your father that he is to tell no one in his household that he had been contacted."

"Hah! But my friends in London would have set off an alarm before he received your note," she said.

"I also ordered him to inform your staff that you had changed your mind about going to the ball and had planned all along to take the child and visit friends in the country. For once I was thankful for your impetuosity, my lady, because your servants and acquaintances are so used to your topsy-turvy, here-one-day-gone-the-next nature, that they will not think it out of character. Now I am sorry to say, I must leave you to consult with my partner."

"Good riddance," Caroline said as their voices faded away into the recesses of the large barn. Shivering, she scooted her stool nearer the fire. Then she shivered again. Turning around she sighed in exasperation to see the door wide open. "Just like a man!" she said, knowing full well neither of them could hear a word she was saying.

Caroline had just slammed the door shut when the Bandit King opened it again and entered, rubbing his hands.

"You could at least have closed the door behind you."

"Ah, my sweet Lady Caroline. Your barbs cannot hurt me," he said, pulling over the wooden bench nearer to her stool.

She kept standing. "You are despicable," she said, not quite hiding her curiosity in her voice. "How much did my father agree to pay you?"

"Everything that I asked," he said.

She glared at him. It did no good. He just sat there, a maddening chuckle coming from under his hood.

"Now pour me a drink."

Caroline placed her hands on her hips. "I am not your servant," she said heatedly.

He was towering over her before she even realized he had stood up. He did not touch her, but his voice was deep, husky and vibrant with meaning.

"You are mine, my fair Lady Caroline. Mine and mine forever. You have no voice in the matter, you know. Fate has decided for us. Understand that." She was spoiled, privileged, and very beautiful, but it was her spirit which enticed him. He knew full well that she was attracted to him for why else was she still wearing the black pearl? She would not surrender easily and that challenge alone sent his blood roiling. Only time would tell when she would come to him willingly.

Caroline was beginning to feel uncomfortable. "Oh, do sit down and I will get you your drink."

He threw back his head and laughed. "You are indeed becoming a very agreeable woman, Lady Caroline."

"Do be quiet. You will wake the baby." Caroline glanced toward the corner of the room. Usually the minute Poppy heard either of the men's voices she raised a fuss to be held. Frowning, Caroline tiptoed over to the bed. "She's gone!"

"Gone?" He was beside her in seconds.

Caroline looked under the bed. "She must have gotten out when you left the door open," she said accusingly.

The Bandit King was across the room and out the door in a second. "She cannot get out of the stables. The doors are closed. She probably is looking for my partner."

"He gives her sweets."

"You didn't bring your coat. It's cold out here."

Poppy had on only her shift," Caroline said, already beginning to shake.

"Here," he said, pulling off his surcoat and wrapping it around her. "Come, I am sure we will find her with him."

He brought her to the end of the corridor and pushed aside a small door. There was no response to his call.

"This is where he sleeps, but he is not here either. He must have gone to the village," the bandit said.

Caroline heard anxiety in his voice. "Wait I think I see a light inside."

They had to stoop to look in. It was a small arca, more a cupboard than a room. A straw mattress covered the dirt floor on one side. Opposite the mattress a board had been removed and the light came from the other side.

"It's a door. I didn't see this when I slept in here," the man said, pushing it wider. Steps led down into a passageway. A single candle set into a sconce on the wall only illuminated about eight feet of the corridor. The bandit took it. A strange frisson of doubt shot through him. All was not as it should be. "Wait here," he said.

"I am not staying alone," Caroline said, the same excitement she'd felt in her last adventure beginning to return. "I'd rather take my chances with a renegade like you. Who knows what's back there in the stables? Besides, it may take two of us to rescue Poppy."

"Then take the candle and get behind me," he growled, reaching for his gun. "The minute you hear or see anything, blow it out."

She was a woman like no other he'd ever known. He'd seen her fearlessly challenge thieves, scrub floors in her velvet gown so that her friends could eat and march through winter storms to find help. Now she was willing to face unknown dangers to save a child. Lady Caroline Cavendish was his kind of woman and he vowed he would never let her go.

They had traveled several hundred feet along the twisting and turning corridor chiseled from the earth when he stopped abruptly. "Hush!" he whispered, throwing her against the earthen wall with his free arm. "I see a light ahead."

Caroline immediately snuffed the candle and peered around his shoulder. "Voices," she whispered near his ear.

He turned and placed his hand on her shoulder and lowered his head. "Stay here."

"I'm coming too."

"You are a stubborn woman, Lady Caroline Cavendish."

His mouth was so near her face she could feel his breath through his mask. A tremor shot through her. "I know," she said.

"Then stay behind me. I have a gun. You do not."

"Well, I hope you know how to use it."

She couldn't tell if his response was a snort or a laugh. He was already moving toward the slit of light and she grabbed a fistful of the back of his shirt and followed.

With their backs pressed against the earthen wall, they inched toward the light. It proved to be coming through the crack left by a thick wooden door left ajar. Inside a man's voice—high and excited—was being answered by the low murmur of another.

The Bandit King and Caroline, peeking from under his shoulder, peered through the crack. Their narrow view of the cluttered room was oddly distorted by the flickering candlelight and the movements of a large man, his cape flying round him like giant wings, as he paced back and forth. Behind him they caught a glimpse of a stocky little mustachioed man, his bald pate shining in the candlelight, seated on a medieval throne set high on a dais.

Caroline gasped. On one of his knees he balanced a tray piled high with pastries. On the other sat Poppy wrapped in a blanket contentedly stuffing her mouth with a large biscuit, while her gaze flicked back and forth between the two men conversing in agitated tones.

At the same time Caroline heard the sharp intake of breath from her companion, and before she could stop him, he had thrown open the door and charged into the room, gun raised. Caroline rushed in after him. The brave fool would probably get himself killed.

The big shadow whirled round to face them. Caroline did not recognize the man's face, but the blue many-caped coat identified him. He was the Bandit King's partner.

To her surprise, the Bandit King dropped his gun to the floor and rushing to the dais, fell upon his knees, crying, "Oh, my lord! My dear Lord Blackmere!"

"Goodness gracious!" the odd pumpkin-shaped man said, clasping his hands to his chest. "My dear boy, please do get up. I feel most uncomfortable seeing you on your knees like that."

Poppy slid off Lord Blackmere's lap and trailing the blanket behind her, hurried as fast as her chubby legs could carry her over to the bandit. Putting her arms around his hunched shoulders, she said sympathetically, "Poppy hug Quack-quack."

The Bandit King pulled the hood off his head and Caroline saw his face. "I do declare!" she exclaimed, "Kendale! *You* are the kidnapper."

The startled little man, his bushy mustache quivering, squinted toward the sound of her voice. "Oh do come in. Please do, my Lady Caroline. Oh, yes, I know your name. Jon has told me who you are."

Caroline approached the dais cautiously.

Kendale's gaze did not leave the face of Lord Blackmere. "You are all right then, my lord?"

"Oh, my, yes," the earl said. "Never been better."

"Thank God for that!" Kendale then addressed his boyhood friend. "Jon, how did you find him?"

Jon shuffled his weight from one foot to the other and looked down at the floor.

"You knew all the time that he was here?" Kendale swung back to face Lord Blackmere. "It was a hoax?"

"I am afraid I never do get anything right," the earl said wistfully.

"It was you who ordered me to abduct young men for ransom?"

Lord Blackmere glanced nervously over at Caroline. "Oh, my," he said raising his hands to his blazing cheeks. "It was badly done, I am afraid."

Caroline could not believe what she was hearing. "Do you mean to say that you orchestrated these kidnappings?"

"I did not mean for him to be kidnapping ladies and babies."

Arms akimbo, Caroline stepped forward to confront him. "Well, that is exactly what he has done," she said indignantly, "and it is all your fault."

Lord Blackmere looked contrite. "I thought it was quite creative at the time . . . and it rather got the better of me, I'm afraid."

"You ought to be ashamed of yourself," she scolded, stamping her foot.

"But I particularly specified that he was only to abduct young peers," the earl complained. "They are so expendable, aren't they? Completely worthless until they come into their titles. And even then it is a gamble that their here-and-therian ways can be curtailed in their latter years. They can't think of what to do with themselves, you know; so they spend their time gaming and chasing light-skirts, excuse me my lady," he said, "but who should know better than I. I became so used to doing nothing, that by the time I became the Earl of Blackmere, I was totally useless."

"But you were good to me," Kendale said, his eyes pleading with him to make him understand. "You saved me from making thievery my career. You made me work hard at my studies and encouraged me to make something of myself. You gave me the only affection I'd known. You were the one who made me believe that when I went off to sea that if I worked hard, I would succeed. It was you who gave me the determination to do well."

"Ah, but you see," Lord Blackmere said, taking the time to carefully select a sweetbread from the tray on his knee, "I knew you had gumption and I was a total loss. I had no talent whatsoever in running the estate. Within three years after you left, I was penniless. My tenants began to move away and the lands went to ruins. Jon was the only one who stayed with me.

"Then I came up with this fine and dandy, brilliant idea to close the castle and pretend that no one lived here anymore. He followed my instructions and spread the word that I had departed the premises."

Lord Blackmere waved his hand encompassing the room. "I had the place boarded up and I moved into the cellar. Quite nice, don't you think? I have all my books, and Jon picks up more for me in London when he visits there. These pastries come from London too," he said, holding out the tray to Caroline. "Would you like to try one? Your little girl has been enjoying them."

Caroline shook her head in bewilderment, trying to take in all that he said. "You mean we are in the cellar of Blackmere Castle?"

"Yes indeed," he said proudly. "I never left, you see. If I did want to get out a bit, I would dress as a tinker and ride round with Jon in his donkey-cart. I probably saw more of England that way than I did all the first part of my life."

"But why didn't you let me know? I would have gladly given you the money to restore your lands and the castle," Kendale said, still not quite believing his beloved mentor was sitting in front of him safe and sound.

"Because I knew that was exactly what you would do," Lord

Blackmere said. "You would not have invested in building your business. You would not have been able to purchase all those ships. Jon tells me you are having another one built to your own specifications. Isn't that splendid?" he said to Caroline. "He wouldn't have been able to do that if he'd been spending it on this old mound of rubble. That is why I had to think of another way. I am sorry you gave away all your pearls. I didn't expect that."

Caroline's hand flew to the chain at her neck. What had the black pearls to do with this fiasco, she wondered?

"But," Lord Blackmere said, clasping his hands together, "no harm done, heh? The young lady will be able to be home in time for Christmas. A pity, though," he said, sighing, "that if Mr. Bennington is as plump in the pockets as Jon reported, I am sorry that we could not have had one more bountiful Holiday Season. Now I suppose I shall have to cut down on expenses this next year, unless . . ."

Lord Blackmere looked hopefully at Caroline and bit his lower lip. "I hear that your father, the Earl of Favor, is not as bad off as he once was—now that he has a rich wife. Perhaps . . ."

# Fifteen

"Don't even consider it," Kendale barked.

"I didn't think you would go for the idea," Lord Blackmere said, chewing the tip of his mustache. "In fact by the tone of your voice, I distinctly feel that you are put out with me."

Kendale tried to make some sense out of what he was witnessing. He was beginning to think he couldn't even trust his reasoning anymore. Lady Caroline stood there in his great coat, dressed in a man's shirt and trousers, her golden hair falling in disarray around her shoulders, and yet to him, she looked every bit a queen. He knew he dared not look into her eyes—afraid of the disgust or ridicule he would see there. So he kept his gaze on Lord Blackmere. "What I want to know is why you ever thought up such a story in the first place," he said.

"It all started when your letter came saying that you were going to be coming back to England. I had to do something. I couldn't let you see what I had become. That was when I decided I'd just pretend that I had gone away. My creditors were hounding me, and I had a row with my man of business in London. I told him I would take care of my own affairs."

Lord Blackmere's arm flew around in circles again. "You can see where it got me. Lost everything. I told Jon to hire some men from the village to board up the castle and have No Trespassing signs put up, and I moved into the cellar. At least, it kept my creditors from finding me. They knew in the village that any letters which were posted to me were to be picked up by Jon.

He told everyone that he had instructions to leave them in London, and then he brought them to me here."

Kendale began to pace up and down in front of the throne, stopping periodically to confront the earl. "I still cannot see how you could do this to me. For nearly five years I have thought of you being tormented and tortured and living in the worst of conditions. You have caused great grief to many families."

The earl pouted. "You have done well, have you not? Jon has kept me informed of your progress. That is why I specified that none of your own fortune was to be used for the ransom."

Kendale raked his fingers through his hair. "I came back from the Orient with seven black pearls. They were to be my insurance—my collateral to start my own fleet of merchant ships. Breaking the law went against everything you had taught me. You forbid me to spend any of my own blunt, so the only way that I could think of to make amends to the families of the young men I'd kidnapped was to send them a black pearl. Each pearl alone was worth four times as much as you demanded of them in coins. I now have only two left. After this Holiday Season, I would have had only one. I was already in a panic trying to think of what I should do if you were not released by next year."

"Oh dear, I do see that you are disappointed in me. I only meant it to be for a year or two, until I got my feet on the ground, so to speak. But it was nice to have all that money coming in, and Jon said you were doing so well . . ." his voice trailed off.

"How could you have written those dark and frightening letters—sending me lists of victims for me to choose from?"

"That little detail did show a certain flair, did they not?" Lord Blackmere said. He stopped talking for a moment to select another pastry from the plate. "I always wanted to be a writer you know, but Father forebade it. He told me to go to London and kick up my heels, sew my wild oats . . . and find a suitable wife. But when I did the former—there didn't seem to be time for the latter."

"You are a wastrel!" said Caroline.

"I am, aren't I?" he admitted. "But Kendale was the only good thing that came into my life, you see. And you too, Jon," he said, nodding to his servant "By the by, I think my wig should be dry by now, don't you? Would you please fetch it for me? My head is cold."

Jon dutifully ambled over to the fireplace and plucked the hairpiece from a rack in front of the fire.

"I even sent one of my last wigs to London with Jon for you to wear, my boy. See, I was thinking about him," Lord Blackmere said to Caroline. "By the by, how did he do with his impersonation, my lady? Did he make me a gallant fellow?"

"He made you out to be far more a paragon than you really are, your lordship. The Lord Blackmere I knew was sweet and considerate and understanding. He spent hours of his time trying to straighten out my father's library. And he can waltz divinely," she said with what sounded suspiciously like a giggle.

Kendale looked at Caroline in surprise. Was she praising—or only making fun of him? Surely she did not condone his charade.

"Can you waltz, my lord?" Caroline asked innocently, not acknowledging that she was even aware that Kendale was staring at her.

The earl looked bewildered. "Waltz? I don't even know what that is. Oh, thank you," he said, as Jon handed him his wig.

All conversation stopped as the cherub-faced man placed the pitiful mop upon his head, first this way, then that, until he had it where he wanted it. It looked deplorable.

However, the transformation was astounding. With his long-tailed coat and black knee breeches, worsted stockings and ruffled shirt, his great sweeping mustaches and now the atrocious wig, Caroline saw how well Kendale had imitated his lordship.

Until she looked fully in his face. "Why your eyes are brown not green."

"Always were," said Lord Blackmere. "My parents' eyes were brown too. Never had any green eyes in the family that I know of."

"But . . . Kendale's eyes are green."

"They are, aren't they," he said. "By Jove! I'd forgotten that."

In the meantime, Poppy was giving the newly wigged Lord Blackmere a great deal of solemn contemplation, and when she had decided to accept him, she held out her arms to be picked up. The earl lifted her onto his knee, rewrapped the blanket around her, gave her another pastry, and went right on talking.

"A man was never more blessed than I to have two such fine young men as Jon and Kendale in his life. You both exhibited all that I never could: loyalty and ambition. A wonderful combination."

That brought up another painful hurt from deep down inside Kendale, too much so for him to accept that feeble explanation. "I take it I am *ambition,*" he said, "and you Jon, do you consider yourself loyal? How then could you have betrayed me?"

The big man stood wringing his hands. "I told you that my first loyalty was to his lordship, Master Kendale."

He gave that some thought. "Aye, that you did."

"The master did say as how I was to look after you. You never saw me, but I was there, just like he told me to be. I knocked some heads together more than once when footpads and slip-gibbets stalked you down on the wharf at night."

Kendale's gaze softened. "I cannot fault you for placing your heart as you did, Jon, and it is I, then, who am indebted to you."

Lord Blackmere, now seeing that there was indeed some hope that he too might receive a reprieve for his mischievousness, cheerfully interjected, "When I saw how eager and determined you were to go to sea, did you know that I sold the last of the family jewels—except m'father's signet ring, of course. Couldn't very well let that go, could I?" he said, looking down sorrowfully at the large gold and ruby ring on his finger. "I did sell my mother's diamond and ruby tiara, though, to finance your maiden venture aboard that ship leaving for the Asian Seas."

Hearing this, all hatred left Kendale, and he could not find it in his heart to scold the old man anymore. "You did that for me? I did not know. I was so entranced with those two books of Reverend Pickworth's on his adventures in the Malay Archipelago that I could think of nothing else. I must have read them through a hundred times."

Caroline gasped and then addressed the man ensconced on the throne. "Why one of those was the red leather volume you found in my father's collection."

Lord Blackmere raised his eyebrows.

Caroline flushed. "I mean, Kendale did. When he was Lord Blackmere, that is. Oh, I am so confused."

"You don't know how excited I was when I discovered it," Kendale said. "It only fueled my doggedness to find you, my lord, the man who had shown me the only true kindness I had ever known."

"My dear boy," Lord Blackmere said, quite overcome with emotion. "You always did paint me a lot saintlier than I was. I couldn't live up to your expectations. I did not mean to cause you a heavy heart. I meant only that you should not squander your own blunt on my extravagances. Besides, knowing you had an adventurous spirit, I thought you might find some enjoyment in all this derring-do," he said with a hopeful chuckle.

His lordship was nearer the truth than he knew, and for a second, Kendale's eyes narrowed and flames of excitement ran through his veins as the memories of his years at sea returned: the intrigue of the Orient, the battle he'd fought with the pirates which won him his first ship, the Emperial Courts of China and Malaysian splendor, and the years of searching for those seven black pearls. All this ran through his mind, and no matter how the world would look upon the earl, to Kendale he would always be the symbol, the champion, of the little River Rat from the Thames.

Lord Blackmere sighed, for he only saw the intense green fire in the boy's eyes. Not a good sign, he thought. No reprieve from his rapscallion ways. "Now that you have found me out, I suppose you are going to turn me over to the authorities."

Kendale knew that to do so would only put the rope around his own neck, as well as Jon's. No, it would be best for him to mend his fences and let the Bandit King disappear. The rapscallion earl was what he was. It just had taken Kendale a long time to realize that no one could be as perfect as he had built Lord Blackmere in his mind. But it would not hurt, he thought, to let his lordship sweat a little for all his chicanery.

"Well, we just might have to do that," he said contemplatively. "We shall have to see. After all, you have been a knave of the worst proportions."

"True, true," Lord Blackmere said as he wiped away a tear running down his cheek. "I am a reprehensible hugger-mugger, a rascally trickster, totally worthless."

Poppy's little mouth turned down. "Poppy hug," she said, putting her arms around Lord Blackmere's ample belly.

"Well, I have never heard anything more pickle-headed," spouted Caroline to Kendale. "You cannot be thinking of turning Lord Blackmere over." She would have said more if Poppy hadn't chosen that moment to tug so hard on Lord Blackmere's mustache that he let out a yelp.

His lordship seemed quite bewildered as to how to go about unlocking her fingers, and looked frantically to his guests for help.

"Oh, Poppy, you mustn't," Caroline said stepping onto the dais.

Lord Blackmere's eyes began to bulge. But Poppy was determined not to let go, and she began to cry.

"What is it dear?" Caroline asked, prying the little fingers away from his lordship's mustache.

"Poppy's!" she screamed, pointing to Lord Blackmere's face.

Caroline picked her up, and as she did so, the blanket fell off onto the floor, leaving the little girl in her shift.

Poppy glanced down at her chest. There was the blue satin ribbon with the piece of fur still securely attached. The man had not taken it away from her after all. She giggled. "Poppy's," she said, showing it to the earl.

Then to Kendale's horror, the little minx held it out to him before rubbing it against her cheek. "Quack-quack," she said gleefully.

Caroline went into a fit of the whoops. "Poppy knew all along," she said, shooting a glance at Kendale. "You didn't fool her one bit. You are Quack-quack, and Poppy's amulet is your mustache. Or should I say toothache?"

Kendale felt his face burning. His humiliation could not be more complete. But standing as she was now, holding the baby in her arms, he was so mesmerized by her beauty, her wit, and her spirit that he could not turn away. What a fool he must look to her.

But that was not how he *looked* to Caroline at all. She was recalling the shadowed look he had given her in Hyde Park when he was Kendale, and how gallant he'd looked in the park when he rescued Poppy. She remembered the way he had looked at her in the library when he was Lord Blackmere, and she thought that he reminded her of Dipper. She remembered the Bandit King's kiss. She saw the way he was looking at her now, and she knew that what he was thinking was not like Dipper at all. It was then she knew that she loved him. All three of him. Handsome, rich, and exciting.

"Will you marry me?" she asked, for Lady Caroline would always be a plain speaker, no matter how many times she later regretted being so.

"What a splendid idea!" Lord Blackmere exclaimed. "Do say, *yes*, my boy."

There followed a few seconds of profound bewildered silence before Kendale managed to find his tongue. "After all that you have heard, are you certain that you would want to marry a rogue like me?"

"Especially now that I have found out about you. I told Suzette that I would not abide a dull-stick, a pennypincher, or a pattern-saint. You are decidedly none of those, Mr. Kendale."

For an instant a glimmer of hope shone in Kendale's eyes and the corners of his mouth slowly crept upwards. "Did you find nothing else to your liking, Lady Caroline?" he asked, looking at her lips.

"Well, yes," she answered, giving him a sideways glance, "you do waltz tolerably well."

The hope that had lighted his face one moment changed quickly to one of doubt. His eyes narrowed. "Your impulsiveness has landed you on hot coals before, my lady. Quizzing a man such as myself only invites danger. Marriage? That is not a subject to jest about, and I advise you to think of the consequences such a flirtation can cause—for I may force your hand."

Her declaration may have seemed a rash, crazy, madcap thing to say, but Caroline realized that she had meant every word of it. This was the man she wanted for her husband, and she thought it most unreasonable of him to question her line of thinking at this time. The exasperating man ignored her completely and spoke to Lord Blackmere as if she weren't even there.

"It is almost Christmas," Kendale said. "Lady Caroline has a family. She will want to be with them."

Caroline realized that was true. She wanted to be at Cavendish Manor. She wanted to see her father, and she began to wonder if Mary had had her baby yet. Suddenly homesickness threatened her determination. Then she remembered her vow to Suzette that she would never set foot in her father's house again until she had a husband, and her resolve returned.

"No, I have made up my mind, Mr. Kendale. You are going to marry me first before we go to Gloucestershire."

Kendale still did not look at her. "I shall be taking her and the child to Cavendish Manor."

"Well, I reckon that is that then," Lord Blackmere said sadly. "I suppose you will want to start for Gloucestershire tomorrow."

The rogue was not even listening to her. But Caroline was no simpering milksop. No, indeed. And she was not going to let Mr. Kendale off so easily. "You don't like me?"

Kendale knew she could not even contemplate how he felt about her. He turned around to face her and put his hands on her shoulders. If she hadn't been holding the child, he would have pulled her into his arms and kissed her. "I have worshiped you ever since I first laid eyes on you three years ago."

"Then what can the problem be with marrying me?"

"You have nothing to gain by such a union; I have much."

"Then you cannot possibly have any objection, so I shall proceed with my plans."

"Do tell us what they are," said Lord Blackmere jumping down from his throne. He was not nearly as short as Caroline had thought him to be. It had only been with two such tall men as Kendale and Jon hovering around that he had seemed so. "Please do have some of my pastries," he said, offering Caroline and Kendale the last two cakes on the plate.

Caroline looked down at Poppy who had seemed to be unusually quiet during the conversation. She was fast asleep. "No thank you," she said. "I need to get Poppy to bed. Tomorrow I shall tell you what I have in mind."

Of course, Caroline had no idea at all what she should do, but she was certain that by tomorrow a very clever solution would present itself.

"Do come for breakfast," said Lord Blackmere. "Jon will have his usual array of dishes. He is quite an excellent cook, you know. Yes, indeedy, I don't think that even the Regent's chefs could surpass him."

"Jon can cook?" Oh, how Caroline wanted to give Kendale a piece of her mind, but he was already holding the door for her to enter the passageway, and she got no more out than, "You knew all along that he could cook and you made me . . ."

Kendale stopped her with a finger over her lips. Then he lifted the sleeping child from her arms and motioned with his head for her to follow Jon back to the stables.

Caroline was too tired to try to say more. Besides, she had a lot of thinking to do before daybreak.

Back in the stable room, Caroline quickly lit a candle and rekindled the fire while Kendale carried Poppy to the bed. He waited for Caroline to turn back the comforter. Then together they tucked the child in and stood looking down at her, suddenly too shy to look at each other.

But for Caroline embarrassment did not last long, because weakness of heart was not a trait found in Cavendish bloodlines. In fact if she had felt any small twinge of shyness at all, it departed quickly.

It was Kendale who was startled to find that not only had Lady Caroline thrown her arms around his neck, but she was kissing him with more abandon than the Bandit King had kissed her.

"I shall not let you take me to my father's house until you marry me," she said, as she stopped to let him catch his breath.

Kendale held her away from him. "I don't believe this," he said. "You are really serious. If you do not want to go to your father's, I will take you back to London."

"No! That will never do," Caroline said, shaking her head. "You said that you told my father to write to my staff in London that I had taken Poppy to visit friends. They are expecting to see me at Cavendish Manor the day before Christmas."

"Then where pray tell do you expect to go? You cannot stay here."

"I declare, Mr. Kendale, you have no romance in your soul," said Caroline. "Lord Blackmere is far more clever than you at things of this sort. I shall write to my father telling him that I was rescued from the clutches of the Black Bandit by the bold and gallant Mr. Kendale of London, who sent the kidnapper running for his life. Mr. Kendale has taken me to Blackmere Castle near Wickett where I am presently under the protection of his guardian, the earl himself. I will tell him that when I am fully recovered from my ordeal, the Lord Blackmere will send me home in time for Christmas."

"People will still think you have been compromised, Lady Caroline."

"Not if I am already married."

"We do not have time to post banns, nor can we find a cleric to grant us a special license without going back to London."

"Then there is only one solution," she said. "How far are we from Gretna Green?"

"That is an impossibility. The Scottish border is nearly two hundred miles away, so put it out of your mind."

She threw her arms around his neck again and kissed him. "You sailed the world. You have been leading the lives of three separate men and alluding the law for nearly five years without being caught. Nothing is impossible to you."

"You are very beautiful, Lady Caroline, but I am beginning to fear for my sanity if I stay with you much longer this night."

Caroline kissed him once more. "Even if I have to kidnap you, we are going to Gretna Green."

This time it was Kendale who did the kissing. "You are very persuasive, my lady," he said huskily. "Gretna Green it will be. Now I will leave you before I do something you'll regret."

"I doubt that I would," she called after him as he went out the door.

When Lord Blackmere heard their plans in the morning, he was ecstatic. Jon had made a good breakfast and then taken Poppy up to the stables to pet the horses so that the other three could drink their coffee in peace.

"I do believe you are a match for me, my lady," Lord Blackmere said with admiration. "I am sorry that I did not meet someone like you years ago. Of course, Kendale is right. I have made such a rigmarole. I only hope that things turn out for you. Perhaps if I had some of your gumption I would not have lost my inheritance."

Kendale shook his head. "Mr. Chumbley tried to advise you as to what to do."

"He called me a nincompoop," Lord Blackmere said, pouting.

"You were worse than a nincompoop," Caroline said tartly. "You should be ashamed of yourself."

The earl looked about him forlornly. All I have is this place," he said. "It is a shambles, isn't it? Of course, if I had been bold enough to seek a wife mayhaps she would have kept the place tidy. But by the time I arrived at the point of thinking I needed one, I had convinced myself that no self-respecting woman would have me, don't you see?"

"I have the blunt, your lordship," said Kendale. "Let me make Blackmere Castle what it was when given to the First Earl of Blackmere. You should not be living like this. I shall pay off your creditors. I owe it to you."

Caroline snorted. "I think it is his lordship who should be

making it up to you for all that you have gone through these last few years."

Lord Blackmere raised his eyes to the scraggly little evergreen boughs hung with faded red ribbons about the room. "It was all Jon could find," he said, apologetically.

Then he picked up a tiny unidentifiable wooden creature from the table beside his throne and ran his finger down the irregular gouges on its back. "You carved this pony for me the first year you came to Blackmere Castle. Do you remember?" he asked Kendale.

Caroline could tell by the twitch in Kendale's jaw that he did.

Lord Blackmere didn't wait for an answer. "You had a good life here, didn't you?"

Kendale still didn't say anything. His gaze was directed toward the little animal, but his thoughts were where she couldn't follow them.

"The house was full of servants, then," the earl explained to Caroline. "We had roasted goose, and a yule log, and all the village children came and sang carols on Christmas Eve. I let Kendale hand out our gifts to them."

Lord Blackmere then sighed so deeply that his cup rattled in its saucer. "I suppose you will be off to Gretna Green now and then to all the happy festivities at your father's house?"

"I shall see that Lady Caroline and the child arrive safely at the Cavendish seat in Gloucestershire," Kendale said. "She will be with her family for the holidays."

"And I shall spend another Christmas all by myself," Lord Blackmere said, taking out his handkerchief and blowing his nose.

As Caroline caught the woeful expression on the sly old reprobate's face, pity rekindled itself in her heart, and she was sorry she had scolded him. She wondered if she had some strange malady, for she found herself feeling sadness if someone were unhappy, and she hurt when someone was in pain.

"Do you not think that we should ask Lord Blackmere to accompany us to Gretna Green?" she whispered in an aside to Kendale. "After all, I will need a chaperone to guard my reputation until I am married."

He looked at her with amusement. "And then what do we do with him? I hope you do not plan on having him chaperone us on our wedding night."

"Poppy needs two caretakers and then of course, he will come with us to Cavendish Manor. We cannot leave him alone on Christmas."

Kendale picked up her hand, and turning it over, kissed her palm. "You know, you are as kindhearted as you are beautiful, Lady Caroline."

Now she understood why, when the fake Lord Blackmere had kissed her hand in the library, chills had run down her spine. "Not that much, sir. I only began to think it might be expedient to have him where we can keep an eye on him—for it seems that his lordship has a great propensity for mischief when left alone."

He laughed. "I must add to my initial accolade," he said. "Not only is the lady beautiful and kindhearted, but wise as well."

Before dawn the next morning, the little party set off from Blackmere Castle for Gretna Green.

The black hackney with its pair of horses, Jon and Kendale in the driver's box, Lady Caroline, Lord Blackmere and Poppy inside. There was not enough wardrobe amongst the five of them to warrant more than two trunks and a portmanteau for Caroline's and Poppy's necessities. Jon had packed a hamper of food and drink.

They raced the wind, traveling sixteen hours the first day, stopping only to change horses and refresh themselves. The weather cooperated in that only a slight mizzle of rain fell.

"Isn't this splendid?" said Lord Blackmere, having as much fun as Poppy bouncing about the carriage. "I do believe I have not had such sport since my friends and I used to race our chariots down Ludgate Hill."

At first they traveled muddy, rutted country lanes until they hit the post-road to Manchester where they stayed the first night at an inn. The next day Lord Blackmere accompanied the ladies while they shopped for clothing. Caroline purchased two gowns for herself and three for Poppy. She vowed, she couldn't understand how one tiny girl got so dirty on a coach ride.

Never in her life had Lady Caroline owned a ready-made dress, but even she agreed that the dark blue bombazine made a practical traveling dress and she chose a rich green gown to be married in. Ready-mades may have been below her station, but they decidedly were an improvement over what she had been wearing for the last six days. Besides, she flatly refused to get married in Elroy's tired old shirt and trousers.

While the ladies shopped, Kendale and Jon bought two additional horses to tie to the rear of the coach, for they had no idea how few and far between would be their chances of switching their cattle on the roads they now had to take toward Gretna Green.

Near midnight of the second day, they pulled into an inn just outside Carlisle.

Their trip had been so hurried that Kendale and Caroline had little chance to speak during their mad dash north. He pulled her aside as Jon carried the sleeping Poppy up the stairs behind the serving maid.

"Tomorrow we will cross the border into Scotland," he said, enfolding one of her hands in his. "Gretna Green is only about ten miles away. If you wish to back out of this marriage, now is the time to do so."

If the promise in Kendale's eyes was any indication of what life would be like with him, Caroline was all for going on. "What? And miss out on the chance to marry three men at one time?" Laughing, she slapped him on the wrist to release her hand from his grip, and escaped up to her room before she disgraced herself by kissing him right then and there in front of all the other travelers.

# Sixteen

Early the next day, Mr. Kendale and Lady Caroline Cavendish were married in Gretna Green by the old soldier David Laing, one of the most famous, or infamous, blacksmiths of the little marriage-mill town.

Lord Blackmere witnessed the simple ceremony, dabbing his eyes with his handkerchief and even letting out a sob or two when he couldn't contain his happiness any longer.

From the safe haven of Jon's arms, Poppy played peek-a-boo with the man who officiated.

Kendale placed the Blackmere signet ring, which the earl had given him for the occasion, on his bride's finger. She had to close her fist to keep it from falling off, but that did not seem to bother her. She only giggled. Then he kissed her, wishing he could do more, but time was not on their side.

They were in the carriage and on the road heading back to England by noon. If his calculations were correct, Kendale reckoned they would be at Blackmere Castle in two and a half days, where they would switch to the Blackmere traveling coach.

The earl had assured Kendale that Jon had kept the coach in splendid order over the last several years. They would keep four horses for the remainder of their journey, always with two tied to the rear of the carriage. If all went as planned, they could be at Cavendish Manor by Christmas Eve.

Kendale could not yet get over his good fortune. He had not only won the heart of the most beautiful woman in all England, but she was now his wife. He had always thought that Lord

Blackmere was the philosopher and himself the practical one. But Kendale's years in the Orient had actually given him a certain mystical outlook— an acceptance that life handed man his destiny.

He was not of high birth, as far as he knew, yet through a strange twist of fate he had been fortunate enough to catch the eye of a young lord. From then on, it seemed that everything he had done was leading up to this point.

Kendale swore that he would let nothing—neither weather or time—stand in the way of his giving his lady a wedding night which she would never forget

Around six o'clock approximately thirty-five miles south of Carlisle, Kendale pulled the hackney into the courtyard of the Blue Swan Inn. He had noted it as an exceptionally clean and well-run establishment when they had stopped to change horses on their journey north. The food had been savory and he'd had the cook pack them a hamper to take along with them. He had particularly paid attention to the proprietor's large staff of serving maids, because he was determined that he would hire as many as it took to watch Poppy during the night. An army if necessary. He, himself, would not trust Jon or Lord Blackmere to keep her from running off, and he was not going to have his bride worrying about the child all night.

Expense was no concern to Kendale, comfort for his party was. But he found that although his presence and authoritative tone of voice drew him respectful attendance, it was the titles of earl and lady that had the proprietor jumping to do their bidding. In an hour's time they'd had a savory meal served in a private dining room, and were all now retired to large accommodating rooms. Even Jon had a small room attached to his master's.

Kendale's and Caroline's room had a large four-poster bed with a canopy, a dresser, two straight-backed chairs and a table with a washbowl and pitcher of water on it. There were several hooks on the walls for hanging clothes, and suddenly it occurred to Kendale that she only had two dresses to wear. There also were none of the luxuries that his bride was used to; no maid or private dressing room.

A coal brazier burned inside the fireplace, giving little warmth on the cold winter night, or much more light than the candle on the table.

He watched her now, as she gazed around the room. He decided he would rather face a whole band of pirates in the South China Sea than to see disappointment in her eyes.

"Well, my lady wife?"

Her eyes stopped at the bed. "We really didn't need such a big room, Kendale."

Inwardly he heaved a sigh of relief. Outwardly, he grinned. "I shall leave you for a few minutes," he said, starting toward the door.

"Whatever for?"

"So you can get ready for bed."

"Good heavens! I only have my dress to take off," she said, starting to unhook the buttons.

It was true. Caroline was undressed and in her nightgown and into bed before Kendale could close his mouth. She punched up two of the feather pillows, scooted back against them, and folded her hands in her lap.

Kendale blinked. He'd never seen a woman undress so quickly in his life. "Now what are you doing?"

"I'm watching you."

Kendale blew out the candle on the table and except for the soft glow from the brazier the room was thrown nearly into complete blackness.

Caroline listened with amusement to several grunts just before she heard the thunk of heavy leather boots falling on the hard plank floor. Then a few curses were emitted after a crash which sounded very much like a chair being knocked over, and finally, the sound of cloth ripping.

"Are you coming to bed?"

"I was thinking about it."

"Well, do not think too hard. It may tire you before you get here."

Caroline screeched as she felt the whole bed shake when he leaped beneath the covers.

"Come here," Kendale said, drawing her into his arms.

"Which are you going to be tonight?" she asked, finding his face with her hands and kissing him around his lips. "A lord, a sea captain or a bandit?"

"I planned on trying all three," he said, and you can tell me which you like best."

Caroline told him later that she couldn't make up her mind.

"Perhaps," he said, burying his face in her soft hair, "it is better that you don't try to come to a decision too quickly on so important a matter."

"No, I suppose not," she said, and with a smile on her lips, Caroline fell asleep.

Two days later, the Earl of Blackmere's coach and four drew up to the entrance of Cavendish Manor. As soon as the small party had been relieved of their outer garments by the liveried footmen, they proceeded down the Great Hall to the drawing room where it seemed a small army was waiting to greet them.

All heads turned in unison, all eyes eagerly watched them as they entered.

Lady Caroline swept into the room with such elegance and beauty that even her ready-made green wool appeared to be no less than the latest design of fashion.

At her side marched a tall gentleman, his lean frame, broad shoulders, black hair and riveting green eyes made him so overwhelmingly handsome, that no one—especially the ladies—could tell you later what he had worn.

Along with them came a shorter and stouter, but no less

courtly, pink-cheeked, mustachioed gentleman dressed all in black: long-tailed coat, knee breeches, and wooly white wig.

Behind him loomed a giant of a fellow, every bit a proud gentleman's gentleman, whose wide happy grin made it evident to everybody assembled that he felt what he had been entrusted to carry in his arms was a jewel beyond price. A blond, blue-eyed young lady of tender years, dressed in green, who waved to everybody. He set her on her feet and she took Lady Caroline's hand. The two looked like peas from the same pod: green dresses, blond hair and blue eyes. The one with a single pearl pendant on a silver chain and the other a dab of fur on a blue satin ribbon as their only ornaments.

Caroline's gaze encompassed everybody in the room. Most of them were familiar: servants, family and friends. She suddenly realized how near and dear they all were. Her father and Mary, the Benningtons, Suzette, dear Miss Plunkett and some of her staff who had accompanied them to Gloucestershire.

With tears in his eyes, her father was first to embrace her. He, of course, had been the only one to know that she had been kidnapped. He pumped Kendale's hand and bowed to the Earl of Blackmere in a stately manner, which made Caroline proud. He even kissed Poppy's hand and received a giggle in return.

Mary, more rotund and prettier than the last time Caroline had seen her, and who obviously had not given birth yet, was overwhelmed by the sight of the child.

Poppy stuck her finger in her mouth and began to study each person as they came forward to greet Lady Caroline and her guests.

"She is adorable!" Mary said with a sigh. "The doctor does not think I shall have my baby until after the first of the year. Now that I have seen Poppy, I think I may like to have a girl."

"I must warn you," Caroline said, laughing. "She is a little minx and has to be watched every minute."

"I don't believe you," Mary said. "Not an angel like that."

At which point Poppy squealed, and before anyone could grab her, headed as fast as her little legs could carry her toward the other side of the room.

Caroline looked up to see her footman George standing against the wall, resplendent in the Cavendish green and gold livery. At his side was a similarly clad page.

"Tom-tom! Tom-tom!"

The boy stepped away from the wall just in time to catch his sister in his outstretched arms. "Poppykins," he said, laughing, as she covered his face with wet kisses.

George grinned, his face turning a bright scarlet.

Then Caroline saw Miss Plunkett and Suzette coming toward her pushing a wheeled chair between them. In it was a frail, brown-haired, young woman, a lovely peacock-colored silk fringed shawl covering her shoulders.

Tommy could not contain Poppy once she saw the woman. "Mom-mom!" she cried, wiggling out of the boy's grasp and clambering up into the chair and onto the lap of the lady.

Then the story was told to all by George, who caught Tommy sneaking around the London house too many times. Tommy confessed that it was he who had put Poppy in the basket. George's cousin Mortimer Diggers paid a visit to Mrs. Beetle in the tenement house, and under threat of arrest, forced her to admit she'd had Momma removed to the poorhouse.

On hearing this, Miss Plunkett had immediately given orders that the unfortunate young woman be brought to Cavendish House in the Square where she was put to bed in a room near the nursery. Caroline's old nurse also declared that they would bring along Tommy and Momma to be reunited with Poppy at Lord Favor's Christmas gathering.

Caroline also found out from Miss Plunkett that when the London staff had received word from her father that instead of going to the Masquerade Ball, his impulsive daughter had decided to visit friends before coming to Gloucestershire for

Christmas, it did not overly concern them, because they were quite used to their mistress's helter-skelter, nit-natty changes of mind.

Elroy, however, was not as forgiving.

"Zounds Caro! I always knew you were a little loose in the upper story, but this caper was one of your wackiest. I don't care if you did run off, but to leave me abandoned at the ball without m'clothes was really a ramshackle affair."

"I am sorry, Elroy," Caroline apologized, "but Suzette said they brought you back with them to London when my hackney didn't arrive. No harm done. Nobody recognized you, did they?"

"I wished they had—spent the whole ball dodging the lechers and coxcombs. Don't know how you women stand it. Jamie Stessels tried to pull me behind a potted palm in the conservatory where I was trying to hide. Even m'own bosom beau, Poindexter, tried to buss m'cheek when I was off guard."

"Oh, no!" said Caroline, laughing. "Whatever did you do, Elroy?"

"Gave him a facer he won't ever forget, I tell you," Elroy said, indignantly.

"It is a pity I wasn't there. I am sure we would have won the Grand Prize."

"Well, don't ask me again to be part of one of your brickety-brackety schemes."

"I won't, Elroy, I promise," Caroline said.

Just before she went up to her apartment with Suzette to dress for dinner, Caroline watched Kendale go into the library with her father. She wished she could be there to see and hear his reaction to the news that they were married.

Now, while Suzette combed her mistress's hair, Lady Caroline sat at her dressing table, telling all about her adventures of the last two weeks, up to, but not including, the trip to Gretna Green. Of course, Caroline was giving Suzette her own romantic version of her kidnapping by the notorious Bandit King and her gallant rescue by the very brave Mr. Kendale. And not only how he saved her, but how he found the missing Lord Blackmere as well.

"Suzette knew," the little French woman said, "that something was amiss when you walked into the drawing room this evening and she saw that Lord Blackmere's eyes had suddenly changed to brown and Mr. Kendale's were still green. But I am sure that none of your staff will say anything about it, *mademoiselle,* because we were all so glad that we would be here with you for the holidays."

"That is not all of my story." Caroline twisted around to look at Suzette. "You are truly my friend, are you not?"

"*Oui,* mademoiselle. I always like to think so."

"Good! You must keep all that I tell you tonight a secret until I say you can tell."

"Suzette's lips are sealed," the French woman said.

"Mr. Kendale and I were married in Gretna Green two days ago."

"*Oh, mademoiselle!* Did he . . ."

Caroline laughed and clasp her hands together. "It was not like that, Suzette. He did not force himself upon me. I love him. I truly believe that he is everything I told you that I wished for in a husband: Handsome, wealthy, and daring."

"But he does not have a title, *mademoiselle.* You insisted on that."

Caroline settled back in front of the dressing table. "I have changed my mind. My father married a commoner and I have never seen him so happy. He even kissed me. I never remember him doing that before."

"That is because he loves you."

"Do you think so, Suzette?"

"Of course, *mademoiselle.* His new wife has taught him to show his affection."

Caroline again swiveled around so quickly that she nearly knocked the comb from her maid's hand. "Then I am glad that he married her. I think I was a little jealous, Suzette, and that is not a nice feeling."

"No, *mademoiselle.* We only make ourselves miserable if we dwell on things we cannot change. Now do sit still and allow me to finish dressing your hair."

"I am not jealous anymore," Caroline said with conviction, "because now I have a husband of my own to love. We talked about adopting Poppy, but now that we know that her mother is still alive, I think we will have to adopt all of them—at least take them into our family. George thinks that Tommy is a bright little fellow, and Kendale said that he will see that he gets an education like Lord Blackmere gave him."

The little French maid twisted a curl back into place on Caroline's head and stepped back to see the effect. "Miss Plunkett told Suzette that they can always use another pair of hands in the nursery to take care of Poppy, and who is better able to help but her own mamma?"

Lady Caroline, wondering what her husband was telling her father down in the library, observed herself in the mirror with little interest. "Everything has worked out well, has it not Suzette?"

Considering the lack of care it had been given for over two weeks, Suzette was pleased with the way that her mistress's coiffure looked. "*Oui, mademoiselle.* Mr. Kendale is very nice and you are still the Incomparable—but if you do not sit still you will not be much longer. Your hair will look as bad as Lord Blackmere's wig."

At dinner, Lord Favor announced the marriage of his dearest daughter to Mr. Kendale, the ward of Lord Blackmere. Caroline was relieved to find that her father seemed quite pleased with her choice, and he was the first to propose a toast to the newly-wedded couple. He even said it was the best Christmas present he could have gotten from her.

That evening as Kendale and Caroline ascended the steps to go to bed, Lord Blackmere came up behind them and asked timidly, "May I speak to you both for a moment before you retire?"

"Of course," Kendale said, ushering the earl into the sitting room of their apartment. "Come over by the fire where it is more comfortable."

"My dear boy," Lord Blackmere said, perching on the edge of his chair, "Lady Caroline was right about me. I am a scoundrel, and I have thought hard and long about what I could do to make it up to you for how naughty I have been. I cannot give you back your black pearls, but I may be able to give you something else that you have always wanted."

"What is that, my lord?"

"Blackmere Castle."

The earl held up his hand to stop Kendale from saying anything. "Let me finish, then you can give me your answer. Now I don't know what you want with that old pile, but there is also a stipulation—or a catch you may say—to my offer."

"And that is?" Kendale asked suspiciously.

"You have to agree to being the next Lord Blackmere. The castle and title go together, you see. That means you will have to give me permission to adopt you and make you Viscount of Wickett until I hop the twig." Lord Blackmere sat back and raised his brows hopefully.

When the earl got nothing but an open-mouthed reaction from both Kendale and Lady Caroline, he added, "As soon as the holiday season is over, I promise I shall even swallow my pride and go see that crotchety old rumstick Josiah Chumbley about drawing up the papers."

Kendale turned to Caroline and took her hand. "He is offering me the one thing that I could not give you," he said.

Both men waited for her answer.

Caroline looked only at her husband and saw in those deep green eyes what he wanted her reply to be.

"I married you without a title, but I do think it a wise idea," she said with a sideways glance at Lord Blackmere, "because if we are often at the castle we will then have a legitimate excuse to keep close tabs on his lordship."

Kendale laughed and reached out his hand to his guardian. "I am honored, my lord."

Lord Blackmere could hardly contain himself. He patted his mustache, made a few coughing sounds, and finally pulled out his handkerchief to dab at his eyes. "Well, son, what say you that we tell everybody first thing tomorrow morning? After all, it will be Christmas Day."

When the earl had gone, Kendale turned to Caroline. "Did my decision please you?"

Caroline raised her hand to the black pearl at her throat. "To tell the truth, I thought that calling myself the mate of the Bandit King would be far more exciting. I hope that being the wife of an ordinary peer of the realm will not prove dull."

Kendale pulled her into his arms. "Tonight, my Lady Caroline, I promise to show you that you will not be disappointed."

"Yes, my Lord Wickett," she said, tilting her face up to his to be kissed.

Dear Reader,

Thank you for your many letters telling me that you enjoy my books so much that you read them over and over again. Because of this response I was delighted to hear that my publishers decided to re-release two of my favorites, *A Father for Christmas* and *A Husband for Christmas,* into this one volume.

I always like to hear from readers. Your letters make it all worthwhile. If you wish to write to me, I may be reached at P.O. Box 941982, Maitland, FL 32794-1982.

Cheers,
Paula Tanner Girard

## JAM TARTS

Young Rupert Copley in *A Father for Christmas* loved his jam tarts. Multiply the basic recipe for larger amounts.

1 cup flour
2 tbsp. margarine or butter
1 tbsp. sugar
water
6 tbsp. jam

Combine flour and margarine in large bowl and pinch together with fingertips until mixture resembles breadcrumbs. Stir in sugar and add enough water to form firm dough. Roll out on lightly floured board and line an 8-inch flan dish. Spread the jam over the base and decorate with thin strips of pastry in a lattice design. Bake at 400 degrees F. for 30 minutes until pastry is golden brown.

To make individual tarts, cut out equal amounts of shapes. Spread jam on one and top with another same-size piece of dough. Pinch edges to seal. Make slit in top and sprinkle with a little sugar and spice.

## CUCUMBER SANDWICHES

Although the custom of placing meat or cheese between slices of bread has been around for a long time, it was John Montagu, 4th earl of Sandwich, who lent his name to this popular mode of consumption in the 18th century. Tiny sandwiches, such as the following, became tea-time favorites in the finer homes.

Start with thinly sliced brown or white bread, preferably a day old. Remove crusts after the sandwiches have been filled.

cucumber    thinly sliced bread
vinegar    butter    salt

After you have peeled and thinly sliced some cucumbers, place the slices in a colander sitting in a deep dish or bowl. Sprinkle a little vinegar and some salt all over the cucumber and leave for 30–40 minutes. Shake the colander to remove excess liquid and pat the cucumber slices dry with a paper towel.

Butter the bread, arrange overlapping layers of cucumbers on top, and cover with another slice of bread. Press the two together firmly. Trim off crust and cut in four triangles.